GREAT MISCHIEF

GREAT MISCHIEF

THOMAS DORDRECHT IN 1759

By Jonathan Carriel

iUniverse, Inc.
New York   Bloomington

iUniverse books may be ordered through booksellers or by contacting:

iUniverse
1663 Liberty Drive
Bloomington, IN 47403
www.iuniverse.com
1-800-Authors (1-800-288-4677)

ISBN: 978-1-4401-1523-3 (pbk)
ISBN: 978-1-4401-1524-0 (ebk)

Printed in the United States of America

iUniverse rev. date: 1/26/2009

Cover art and design by David T. Jones

"A little neglect will breed great mischief."

– Benjamin Franklin, **Poor Richard's Almanac**

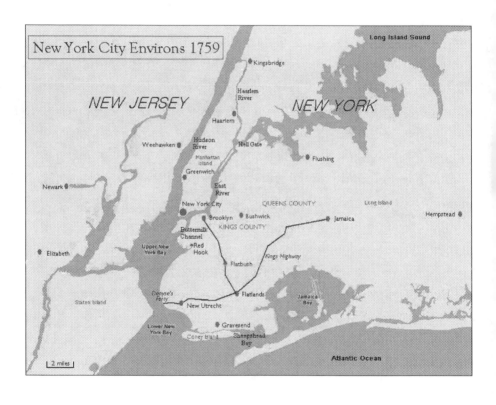

New York City Environs 1759

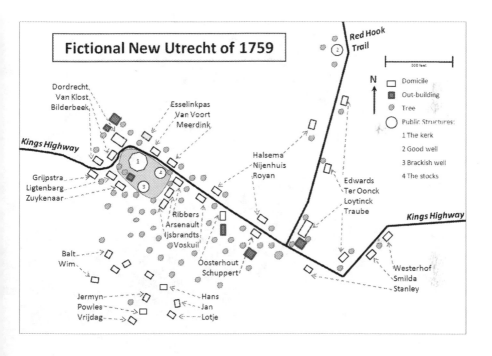

Fictional New Utrecht of 1759

Red Hook Trail

500 feet

N

Domicile
Out-building
Tree
Public Structures:
1 The kerk
2 Good well
3 Brackish well
4 The stocks

Dordrecht
Van Klost
Bilderbeek

Esselinkpas
Van Voort
Meerdink

Halsema
Nijenhuis
Royan

Edwards
Ter Oonck
Loytinck
Traube

Kings Highway

Kings Highway

Grijpstra
Ligtenbarg
Zuykenaar

Ribbers
Arsenault
Ijsbrandts
Voskuil

Balt
Wim

Oosterhout
Schuppert

Westerhof
Smilda
Stanley

Jermyn
Powles
Vrijdag

Hans
Jan
Lotje

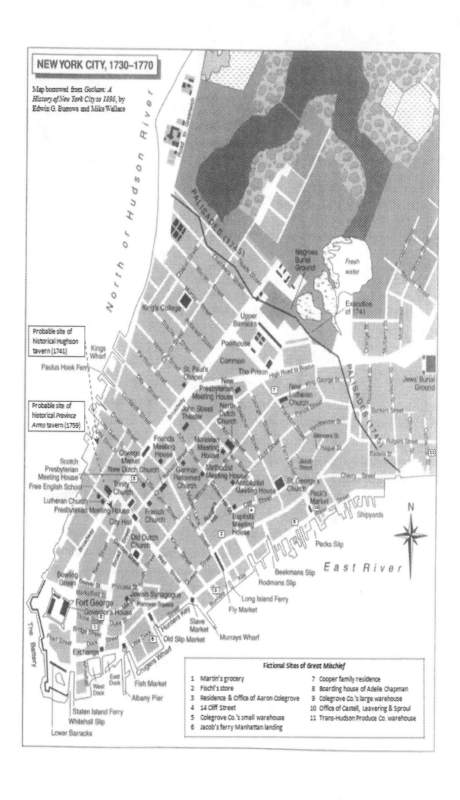

NEW YORK CITY, 1730–1770

Map borrowed from *Gotham: A History of New York City to 1898*, by Edwin G. Burrows and Mike Wallace

North or Hudson River

PALISADES (1745)

Negroes Burial Ground

Fresh water

Execution of 1741

King's College

Upper Barracks

Probable site of historical Hughson tavern (1741)

Kings Wharf

Poorhouse

Common

Paulus Hook Ferry

St. Paul's Chapel

The Prison

High Road to Boston

Jews' Burial Ground

Probable site of historical Province Arms tavern (1759)

New Presbyterian Meeting House

New Lutheran Church

John Street Theater

North Dutch Church

Friends Meeting House

Moravian Meeting House

Scotch Presbyterian Meeting House

Oswego Market

New Dutch Church

German Reformed Church

Methodist Meeting House

Anabaptist Meeting House

St. George's Church

Free English School

Trinity Church

Peck's Market

Shipyards

Lutheran Church

French Church

Baptist Meeting House

Presbyterian Meeting House

City Hall

Old Dutch Church

Pecks Slip

N

East River

Beekmans Slip

Rodmans Slip

Bowling Green

Princess St.

Jewish Synagogue

Long Island Ferry

Fort George

Fly Market

Governor's House

Slave Market

Hunters Key

Staten Island Ferry

Old Slip Market

Murrays Wharf

Whitehall Slip

Exchange

Crugers Wharf

Fish Market

Lower Barracks

West Dock

East Dock

Albany Pier

Fictional Sites of Great Mischief

1 Martin's grocery
2 Fischl's store
3 Residence & Office of Aaron Colegrove
4 14 Cliff Street
5 Colegrove Co.'s small warehouse
6 Jacob's ferry Manhattan landing
7 Cooper family residence
8 Boarding house of Adelie Chapman
9 Colegrove Co.'s large warehouse
10 Office of Castell, Leavering & Sproul
11 Trans-Hudson Produce Co. warehouse

Principal Characters

- Wouter Van Voort—Selectman and Dominie of the Dutch Reformed Church
  - Reuben—The kerk's slave, a resident of Gravesend
- Gosselick ter Oonck—Selectman (a widower, father of Anneke ter Oonck Dordrecht)
- Lodewyk and Katryne Nijenhuis—Close friends of the Dordrechts
- Karel and Machtel Schuppert—The town's ailing blacksmith and his wife
  - Bette—Their slave (granddaughter to Jan and Anne, half-sister to Roosje)
- The Arsenault, Edwards, Esselinkpas, Grijpstra, Halsema, Ijsbrandts, Ligtenbarg, Meerdink, Oosterhout, Ribbers, Royan, Smilda, Traube, Voskuil, Westerhof, and Zuykenaar families
- Other slaves named: Saal (owned by Ijsbrandts); Nonna and her son (Edwards); Dael (Westerhof)
-
- Robert Scoffield—Traveling commercial factor, staying at the Dordrecht inn
  - Justus Bates—His indentured servant
  - Yvette Bates—The latter's wife

IN FLATLANDS:
- Claes and Betje Dordrecht Hampers—She the eldest daughter of Emke and Cornelis
  - Willemina—Their daughter (elder sister of Engelbertus)

IN FLATBUSH:
- Berend and Geertruid Dordrecht Kloppen—She the eldest daughter of Rykert and Chastity
  - Their children—Derk and Betje
- Armand LeChaudel—Captain of militia
  - Nanette—His daughter
- Elijah Ellison—Militiaman
- James Polden—Militiaman

IN HAARLEM:
- Brevoort and Mary Constant Dordrecht—Second son of Rykert and Chastity and his wife
  - Aalbert—Their son
  - Martin Constant—Her father, a candle maker

<u>IN BROOKLYN</u>:
- Joe Wicklow—Constable
- Darius Gerrison—A solicitor

<u>IN NEW YORK CITY</u>:
- Aaron Colegrove—Merchant
  - John Glasby—His chief clerk (and uncle to the late Sgt. James Hannamore)
  - Joachim Bauern—German immigrant, indentured to Colegrove
- Gershom Ingraham—An itinerant impresario
  - Régine—His doxy
  - Simon, Katherine—Volunteers in support of his theatrical enterprise
- William and Janna Dordrecht Cooper—She the second daughter of Emke and Cornelis
  - Charles Cooper—Their second son
- Adelie Chapman—An *artiste* of many talents, living independently
- Nicholls and Jack—Two sailors, previously known to Thomas Dordrecht
- Zecharias Jameson—Captain of the *Hasty*, of Newport, R.I.
- Benjamin Leavering—Merchant, lately of Philadelphia

On the **_JonathanCarriel.com_** website can be found fictional genealogical charts of the Dordrecht family, the related Loytinck and Van Klost families, and Zwarte Jan's family. Also to be found there are expanded color maps of the New York City area, lower Manhattan, and the fictionalized New Utrecht, in 1759; diagrams of the Dordrecht family's town property; capsule biographies of the real historical characters mentioned in the story; discussions of historical problems and anomalies; and an attempt to explain the pronunciation of Dutch words and names.

CHAPTER 1

November 1758

The nightmares began the very night I returned to my family. At three o'clock in the morning, my shrieks woke not only every last one of the ten Dordrechts in the house, but two paying guests, and even Meneer Van Klost next door. Musket in hand, my eldest brother Harmanus burst into my attic room, sure there was an intruder. He actually dressed and walked around the yard, searching for boot prints in the snow, as Van Klost sternly watched from his window. Grootmoeder became hysterical, probably convinced I'd seen a ghost, and had to be soothed by Anneke while Mother and my sister Elisabeth struggled to bring me to my senses.

It was Will Ferris, a mate from my corps in the war. A French regular was bayoneting him, over and over, in the neck. Hogsheads of bright red gore were spewing from his throat. And there was nothing I could do! Because a corpse—whose ant-covered face had been blasted to shreds—was lying across my chest, pinning me to the ground. Then Ferris was somehow still pleading for mercy as a blue-painted savage industriously scalped him … and there was nothing I could do!

Panting, sweating, and shivering in the dark, frigid room, I held tight to my mother as Elisabeth managed to light the candle. It took me more than a minute to shake off the phantasm and regain full lucidity. All the while I was whimpering incontinently about Ferris and Frogs and Hurons. I was greatly embarrassed as I came fully awake.

Anneke came in, bringing a cup of warmed milk laced with rum. She looked back to the door on hearing my brother's—her husband's—footsteps. "Nothing?"

"No," he said quietly, his bulk filling the doorway. "Come back to bed."

For a panicked second, I clung to my mother all the tighter; then, shamed, I almost thrust her away as I fell back.

"You should change your nightshirt, Thomas," my sister said softly, handing me another one from the chest.

"I'm sorry," I managed to croak as they all nodded good night.

"That's not like him, Harmanus," I heard Mother say as she closed the door. "He hasn't screamed like that since he was Willem's age."

"Thank the lord Willem isn't as loud!" was the gruff reply.

I drank the milk, changed the shirt, and blew out the candle, sunk in mortification. I was a war veteran, soon to be nineteen years old.

My nephew was only five.

*   *   *

In the morning we all seemed to be trying to pretend nothing had happened. Perhaps because my homecoming had been so unexpectedly fraught even before the nightmare, our forced conversation concentrated entirely on antics of the youngsters, invariably a handy topic for nervous adults.

But Harmanus, as always, brooked no delay in setting about work. "You ready, Thomas?"

Eager to retrieve any sort of normality, I was uncharacteristically glad I'd promised to assist with the year's last wheat harvest. I gobbled up my remaining porridge and followed him out the door.

The morning was blessedly bright and clear, and portended warmth that would make short work of the frost and the dusting of snow. With leaves of red and gold still shining on the trees, my native town never looked more inviting as we crossed the churchyard on our way to the east field. New Utrecht had been chartered over a century ago, before the English conquest, but it was still just a tiny country village lost in rural Kings County. There were probably no more than ten score people in total, almost all of them descended from the founders of the New Netherlands and primarily conversant with their ancestors' language. My family was unusual because my mother hailed from old England; so my siblings and I were half-and-half by blood, and not just by assimilation.

There were the slaves too, of course. There were probably half as many Africans in New Utrecht as there were Dutchmen. They mostly had huts off to the south side of the square, nearest the sea, separated from their masters by a few trees. New Utrecht is barely two miles north of the Atlantic and two miles east of Lower New York Bay. To our east stretch a hundred miles of flat, sandy Long Island farmlands, among the most useful of North America.

And five miles north of us is the great metropolis of New York City, which I understand now numbers some eighteen thousand souls!

"We repainted the doors while you were gone," Harmanus observed casually, pointing at the octagonal kerk, the pride of our town and its only public structure.

I nodded with perfunctory approval, then looked again, astonished. "Mother recommend the color?" I asked.

Harmanus frowned. "Aye, she and Vrouw Nijenhuis. But Dominie Van Voort said it was all right."

Well, well, well. It was surely rather *bold* to paint a Dutch Reformed church's doors a dark blue!

You could count the Dordrecht family home as a public structure too, I suppose, given that my grandfather had deliberately built it big enough to double as a respectable tavern and a hostelry. Under my mother's management, it was now much called upon by commercial travelers using the difficult roads to maintain their contacts on the south shore.

Waiting for us by the stocks on the far side of the square were Karel Schuppert and Meneer Loytinck's slave Wim. Harmanus had contracted both of their services for the two days the harvest would take us. Schuppert, the town's gaunt, sickly blacksmith, was paying off his debt to our tavern; Wim was paying off his master's account. Both nodded and fell into line.

Schuppert tentatively inquired after my health, between deep puffs on his pipe and hacking coughs that indicated his own had further deteriorated. Insisting I was fine, I realized with sinking heart that the commotion I'd caused overnight was already common knowledge across the town. Yesterday afternoon, I was a sturdy returning war hero; this morning, naught but a grown man terrified of his own shadow. I quickly inquired after his wife and his adopted girls, and he obliged me by bragging of the latter pair's accomplishments all the way to the plot.

Harmanus pulled off the canvas with which he'd covered the four biggest scythes he'd been able to borrow, shook off the snow, and set us each out in a different quarter. He gave Wim the largest field and Schuppert the smallest—evidently not expecting the feeble gray-hair to accomplish much. Though I was prepared to work on the next-largest section, Harmanus as usual indicated the smaller of the two, and trudged off to the larger himself. I felt a little absurd to realize I'd have been irked no matter which decision he'd made. The plain fact of the matter is that I don't really care for any aspect of farming, and my relationship with my brother—who is ten years my senior and who believes farming is God's command to all mankind—has always been troublesome. But it is high time I started behaving in a more adult manner and put such juvenile peevishness aside.

I commenced slicing away at the ripe crop, and was bored within twenty minutes. Wim presently gathered a huge armful and with a gesture inquired where we should consolidate the gleanings. I said to put it by the path, and was met with incomprehension. I'd spoken in Dutch. Like their masters, most slaves in Kings County were bilingual, many spoke only Dutch, and a few—such as Wim—only English. Inadvertently I smiled as I restated the order, but he frowned and quickly turned his head away. He'd acquired an awful scar on his forehead while I'd been gone, I noticed, still livid enough to show against his dark skin. One isn't supposed to pay attention to the slaves at all, but I could never help the fact that I felt far more comfortable around some of them than others. Wim, a big, strapping brute with a particularly grim set to his face, always made me wonder exactly where I'd left my musket. I sensed that few of his fellow slaves liked him any better than I did. He did do his work without protest, but always sullenly, reproachfully. I turned back to the job to free my mind of him.

But concentrating on the harvest.… Harmanus can do it; I can't. Certainly I swung away to garner my full quota, but my thoughts wandered.

The big question outstanding was what Thomas Dordrecht was to make of himself. I had had a grand—if often terrifying—adventure in the far North, courtesy of the colonial war effort, and I had come back home unexpectedly rich, thanks to our regiment's great luck with prize money. But now I was facing yet another dreary winter in my sweet but tiresome hometown with my sometimes sweet and frequently tiresome family. *Ah!* Suddenly I flushed with shame over the ingratitude of my own thoughts, but the hard truth was, I couldn't thrust them entirely away. I long for wider vistas, for excitement, for new challenges. Nothing ever happens in this simple, simple-minded place! Could I ever afford to seek my fortune independently in the big city?

And how, exactly, would I contemplate going about that anyhow? It would be the height of folly to squander my earnings in indolence, yet I admit I feel no urgent call to a vocation. Unless you count music, that is! But I know that music is but a hobby in our provincial lives, nothing that could ever reliably put even a lone man's food on the table. What I love to do is to practice on the kerk's harpsichord … and also to study. I do wish to be learned. I hate being pulled away from my books to perform the myriad chores of a working family farm and tavern. The chores never cease, however, so the only real escape would be to get myself away from them. But I'm unprepared for that step just yet. I need time. Just a fortnight ago, after all, I was living in a tent on the frontier of civilization, wild Indians for my neighbors!

Further ruminations were halted when Schuppert fetched his cart, its wheel promptly fell off, and we spent over an hour repairing it.

I had another nightmare the next night. I was in my canoe, which was overloaded with goods that were somehow illicit, paddling frantically to escape the booming cannonballs that were pursuing me, shattering boulders not twenty feet away. In desperation, I made for the rapids, rather than portage, and....

At least I managed not to scream. But once again my shirt was soaked through. Exhausted, I fell back without even changing it. I hadn't had but a single nightmare when I was actually up on the frontier, right in the midst of mayhem and horror and even murder. Why was I suffering them now?

The next morn was unusually warm, but overcast, calm and humid. Schuppert and Harmanus agreed that bad weather was coming, and so we worked like Dutchmen at the dike to complete the task. The sun came out at midday and it was suddenly so hot I doffed my shirt as well as my jacket. We completed the cutting in mid-afternoon and, as black clouds marched toward us from the northeast, hustled to secure the wheat in the barn. In our haste we never noticed that the temperature had dropped fifteen degrees. We were gratefully stowed as dusk and the storm hit simultaneously, and I hunted around in the rain to find my clothes. My brother and I were both drenched by the time we reached the house. As Harmanus fervently intoned a thankful grace for our harvest ... I fainted at the table.

That night I became violently ill.

*   *   *

Much of what has happened in the ensuing weeks I have pieced together only from the reports of others, as I evidently spent over a month in a state of near-delirium. That very night, Mother was so deeply alarmed that she prevailed upon Harmanus to saddle up and fetch the doctor all the way from Brooklyn town. This expensive worthy came up with a diagnosis of latent camp fever, and prescribed regular bleeding and infusions of Peruvian bark. The thought that it was camp fever, which had done in my friend Sergeant James Hannamore and scores of our fellows, certainly gave no peace to my mind.

At one point shortly after *Sinterklaas* Day early in December, I had recovered lucidity, but my bodily weakness was so severe they anticipated losing me nonetheless, and sent for Dominie Van Voort, who administered last rites and solemnly announced that my survival was in the hands of God. An hour later, Mother was having difficulty spoon-feeding hot soup into me, and I was more than usually passive. "You have to eat, Thomas!" she insisted.

Suddenly I was horrified that I might be remembered only as an ingrate who'd run off to the army without his parents' knowledge or permission. "Will you forgive me, Mother?" I begged, startling her with what was apparently my first grammatically coherent statement in weeks. Stubbornly, she merely pressed the spoon against my lips, which I kept as stubbornly shut.

She set the spoon down with a flourish of exasperation. "I'll forgive you, boy," she said in an angry tone, "if you pull yourself together and live! If you die on me, I'll be furious!"

I fell back and turned away, staggered by the cruelty and injustice of the statement. My own mother! I writhed on the bed for half a minute before I could even look at her again. She was staring me hard in the face, but there was just the slightest arch to her eyebrow. Again she filled the spoon and put it to my lips. "Well?"

I swallowed it. And again. And again. And she smiled—the most beautiful smile a man can ever hope to behold! I took another spoonful ... and suddenly began to laugh, for no reason I could imagine. She held the spoon up for some time before having to set it down as she too began to laugh.

It wasn't long before my laughter was interrupted by a coughing fit—just long enough to notice she was weeping and laughing at the same time—and she called for my sister to finish the job. Elisabeth rushed in, white-faced, fearful of the worst. "See that he eats all of this, lass," Mother commanded. "Thomas has decided to bide with us a while yet, and I must attend to supper downstairs!"

*   *   *

My convalescence still required a matter of weeks. Taking two steps to the chamber pot exhausted me for the longest time. The kindness of my relatives and the people of the town I had so often disdained was manifested in their constant visits, solicitude, and favors. My throat was sore for days, and so I merely listened as ladies filled me in with eight months of local gossip, men brought me to date with weather and business and political reports, and children shared exploits of the schoolroom and playing field. Finally the agony was mitigated and I was at least able to hold up my end of conversations, and even regale my nephews with eagerly sought tales of the wildness of Ticonderoga and Oswego.

One visitor of unexpected regularity was Dominie Van Voort, who offered repeated thanks that the Lord had spared me. Each time, I had to squelch the glib retort that perhaps He didn't relish having me under foot in paradise. The dominie first arrived one afternoon while my sister was spooning gruel into me—I'd progressed from broth to gruel—and he bade her stay as we talked. That he chose to include her in our discussions was pleasing as, in addition to being the most beautiful girl in town, Elisabeth is extraordinarily bright and enjoys serious talk. The dominie inquired after the spiritual life of such of the Indians as I had met, which prompted the relation of my brief friendship with an Onondaga scout, a lad my own age who'd been educated by Jesuits! The dominie grimaced involuntarily, as it was common knowledge that Jesuits were the most abominable of all Romanists, but he was bemused that the savage had been perplexed by their explanation of the doctrine of the Trinity. Then I had to confess that the scout had begged for *my* explanation, and that I had been equally inadequate to the task. I looked at him hoping for *his* clarification, but he shook his head and said, "Oh dear, oh dear!" and changed the subject.

He was extraordinarily attentive to me, surely one of the least of his flock, always arriving at the same time of day and kindly urging Elisabeth to join our discussions. He brought me the latest book he'd read, sermons of a Massachusetts minister named Jonathan Mayhew whom, to my surprise, he deemed sound. "It's not about doctrine, Thomas, so much as about society, and it's really quite startlingly modern!" I was relieved that it wasn't about theology, as the previous day he'd expatiated on the chief controversy within our own church, whether clergymen might be ordained by their congregations here in North America, or whether it was essential that they return to the old country for examination and approval by the *Classis* of Amsterdam. Though himself ordained in the Netherlands, he was undecided on the issue, and bewildered me by querying my opinion. Somewhat irked that this issue was foremost on the mind of a man who'd failed to elucidate basic Christian doctrine for me, I was spluttering out something noncommittal when my brother arrived to invite him to join his family for their bible-study, prior to supper. We were all somewhat astounded that, while he accepted the invitation to dine, he protested that he had to complete his discussion with me, rather than join Harmanus in bible-study. I do believe Meneer Harmanus Dordrecht was unsettled!

A few days later, after another visit which he'd inexplicably cut short, I was feeling so much improved that I was almost cocky, and I said to Mother that I thought Harmanus was jealous of the dominie's preference for my company over his own. Mother rolled her eyes and muttered, "You flatter yourself, boy!" I was flummoxed. "Am I the only one in this house with eyes in her head? Honestly!" Now my mystification was total, but I had to persist to get an explanation. "Not a word of this to anyone! Promise?" I crossed my heart. "It's not your company that interests him, silly, it's your sister's!"

"*Elisabeth's?* But…. Where is she, by the way?"

"I sent her next door, to inquire after her dear friend Vrouw Hampers." The hint of sarcasm indicated that the suggestion had not been timed accidentally.

The clergyman had only stayed ten minutes. "But she's—"

"She's less than half his age, and it's just preposterous, and I won't have it!" Mother was suddenly quite worked up. "Why the man doesn't marry your cousin Willemina I can't imagine. She's still a fine young woman and they'd make a splendid pair. It's not as if Betje hasn't been trying to push them together for years!"

"But—"

"I've said enough!" She stormed out of the room, leaving me quite flabbergasted. Reflecting back on it some minutes later, I mused that it was good to be dragged back into the mundane problems of the world, the real world that did not revolve around me!

After the first fortnight of my illness, my sister-in-law had ushered Grootmoeder and her knitting into my room during the daytimes, as she'd often done when her own children were sick. Grootmoeder had gone dotty four years before, and did nothing much more now than knit an everlasting nine-inch column of wool, but she did have enough presence of mind to set up a wail if an incapacitated person needed help. Only one person, my elder sister Geertruid, could truly communicate with Grootmoeder, though Father and Harmanus were usually able to decipher what the matter was if she cried. Mother dutifully saw to her feeding, but they'd never been close, so it was Anneke who kindly took it upon herself to attend to the old lady's comforts. She was the first to perceive how important the knitting was to her. When the column had gotten over thirty feet in length, Anneke had boldly separated it as the old woman slept, finished it into useful apparel, and begun varying the colors of the yarns, so that even in her dotage Grootmoeder was contributing to the household. Her unobtrusive presence was actually helpful, especially the time I took a fall and she set up a howl that brought young Hendrik running to my rescue.

Two people of whom I did not see much were my father and my lamentable cousin and erstwhile best friend Bertie Hampers, each of whom had little excuse for his failure to pay sick calls. Elisabeth had waited until I was well mended before telling me that Pa's drinking had gotten worse, and that he'd once last summer gotten so abusive that he and Mother began throwing crockery at each other. Harmanus, to her great relief, had finally overcome his Fifth Commandment reservations and shoved Pa into a chair. Neither of us had any idea how to resolve this horrible situation.

*　　　*　　　*

When I happened to inquire about the forthcoming Christmas feast, Mother surprised me by announcing that the dominie would not be joining us after the service, as he had for three years past. "Katryne has insisted that it's her turn for the honor!" A significant glance passed back and forth between us, and I was startled to realize that my mother had engineered a social fraud, and was blithely content that I should be aware of it. Obviously, she didn't *want* the dominie's presence, and she'd twisted her best friend's arm until he'd been invited elsewhere! I was barely recovering my breath when she added, "The Van Klosts are coming over instead. Poor Constantija is simply exhausted from looking after Jenneken and they are, after all now, our family!"

Another raised eyebrow invited further conspiracy. Poor Constantija indeed! Vrouw Van Klost is one of the dreariest women I've ever met, a malingerer who relies on her slaves for every last effort while complaining that she does all the work. The idea that she might be fatigued from attending her daughter's last weeks of pregnancy was ludicrous.

The Van Klosts have been our neighbors since our house was built, two years before I was born, but we'd never before invited them to share a festival dinner. I've grown up feeling disdainful of them, particularly the patriarch, a strutting windbag whose rule-bound leadership of the New Utrecht militia I've been forced to endure for four years now. He *had* been unduly thoughtful during my illness, I have to concede—and that's more than I can say for my own father. Yet his persistence in treating me as a great war hero is at least as embarrassing as endearing.

Their daughter, Jenneken, though only Elisabeth's age, is now a married woman imminently to be a mother, so I must reconcile myself to ceasing to regard her as the insufferable brat next door. When they arrived, she was leaning heavily on the arm of her husband, my excessively charming cousin Bertie, the great weight she'd always borne now much amplified by her familial state. It was this unexpected marriage that had suddenly made one family out of two often-quarrelsome neighbors.

A simple change in seating arrangements gave me an unanticipated jolt of adolescent pride. Though Elisabeth and I understood that we were chiefly responsible for conveying food to and from the table, we were for the first time permitted to sit with the adults. My clever niece Berendina would now be charged with keeping her squabbling younger brothers from making spectacles of themselves. On all previous holidays, Lisa and I had sat with the children, banished to the side, desperately minding our manners. Was it because I was now a war veteran of somewhat independent means? That wouldn't explain my sister's elevation. In addition to friends from the town, we usually also had a few paying guests of the inn who had to be seated with my parents. But perhaps due to unusually mild weather, there were none this year. Just as we sat, I tumbled to the obvious explanation: Jenneken. No matter what her age or personal level of maturity, an expectant mother could hardly be asked to sit with five-year-olds. Elisabeth, her coeval, had to be placed opposite, and I, two years her senior, was added as a matter of form. Though somewhat deflated as I straightened all this out, I was nevertheless glad to be counted at last among the grown-ups.

It had only been in the past few days that I had managed to dress and sit with the family for dinner at all, and my father had absented himself from all but one of those occasions. Harmanus had presided from the side of the table, and I was surprised to realize that everyone was habituated to that arrangement. This afternoon, however, Father had made himself presentable, and was officiating … with, I noticed, alarmingly tremulous hands. It had been years since Father has mustered the spiritual wherewithal to say grace. He normally passes that job to Harmanus, who will generally accomplish it in an earnestly pious minute or so. Today Pa had a gleam of mischief in his eye, however, and begged Meneer Van Klost to do the honor.

My heart sank as my lugubrious expectations were realized. Van Klost prayed in a soft monotone for a full quarter of an hour. He called down blessings on every last citizen of New Utrecht; their homes, their farms, their livestock, and their businesses; their neighbors in the county, the province, the continent, the empire, the globe; the spirits of the dear departed.… He only came to his senses and concluded when Petrus, the youngest, began audibly to weep. Pa shot Mother a triumphant smirk as he passed Harmanus the knives to carve the mutton, and she involuntarily scowled back before turning solicitously to Jenneken to inquire after her health.

Food, as always, restored us all, and the meal then progressed in a more civil fashion. Mother attempted to discuss local personalities, a topic that was invariably entertaining when Katryne Nijenhuis was around, but which Constantija Van Klost rendered dull within two minutes. Talk passed to the men.

Harmanus and Meneer Van Klost were deep into everybody's harvest yields and sales successes in the city—apparently extraordinary this year for all concerned—when my father suddenly blurted out, "What's that old bastard Loytinck ever going to do about selling his land?"

Everyone froze for a second. Near tears, my Mother expostulated, *"Rykert!"*

"Oh. Sorry!" Pa said perfunctorily. "You think he really means to sell any of it?" he proceeded.

Van Klost, red-faced, coughed and fidgeted before replying, "My understanding is that Meneer Loytinck does mean to divest himself of some of his holdings, as he considers it improper to leave anything but cash in the hands of his granddaughter, who is as yet unmarried."

Teunis Loytinck, by far the largest landholder in the town, was also by far its oldest denizen. And he was furthermore one of the least-loved personages of the locality, a codger with an eternal grudge against the world who particularly enjoyed cutting down anyone who assumed that his advanced years had made him infirm.

"Nothing has actually changed hands, then?"

"As far as I know, nothing has even been formally put on the market."

Harmanus dutifully looked to see whether Pa would respond. Seeing him quiet, he said, "Why is it so generally assumed that he *is* trying to sell the land, then?"

"Well, the man is past eighty years of age! Even he must know he should make some disposition of his worldly effects before time takes its toll."

"I heard he tried to sell off some of the slaves," Harmanus asserted. "He wouldn't be doing that unless he planned to sell the land too."

Van Klost shifted about uncomfortably. "Yes, I heard he tried to sell Lotje and her grandchildren to an Englishman from Gravesend, but he wasn't interested." He cleared his throat. "Word got around," he added ominously, bringing seconds of grim silence to the table. Nothing upsets the burghers of New Utrecht more than the thought of open discontent among the local slaves. And the most disruptive incident in memory had in fact revolved around the Van Klost family. "I do believe Meneer Nijenhuis attempted to remonstrate with him, but I doubt he listened. He never does."

"It would make sense to sell the land first, and to sell the slaves with the land," Harmanus observed reasonably. "That way, they aren't separated from their … fellows." Oh, my brother is such a prig! He's talking about the slaves' *families,* of course. "It'd be better for all of us if he'd proceed that way."

"Well, pardon me," Mother interrupted, "but why can he not simply leave his entire estate to his granddaughter? Everyone knows Juffrouw Marijke Katelaar has been running all his concerns for nearly a decade!"

"I do believe she assumes that she'll inherit it," Anneke added in an alarmed tone.

Both Harmanus and Meneer Van Klost reddened at the suggestion. "Well, but you simply can't do that, my dear Vrouw Dordrecht," the latter spluttered. "It simply wouldn't be proper. Not feasible. How would she ever manage without his … authority backing her up?"

"She seems to love that farm, too," Anneke added wistfully. Their sympathy surprised me, as I'd never before heard either express the slightest interest in the reclusive Katelaar spinster.

"That's neither here nor there, Anneke," Harmanus argued. "Unlike our farms, where Meneer Van Klost and Bertie, or Father and I and Thomas can be on the spot, the owner of that one must rely completely upon servants for every lick of labor to be accomplished. Given that, a young girl—"

"She's thirty-two," Anneke asserted.

"Oh very well, a young woman, alone, will never be able to handle free men or indenturees, much less slaves, by herself!" Not even Mother was ready to contest him on that point. "If you ask me, Meneer Loytinck has been plain irresponsible in not finding that maid a proper husband! On the other—"

"Well, he likes having her around to take care of himself, the selfish old brute!" Mother said.

"I'll admit, she seems to have done amazingly well with her corn, this past year particularly, but—"

"Well, we *all* did well this past year!" Van Klost said smugly.

"Thank the Lord for that!" Harmanus agreed.

"Amen!" we all dutifully mumbled.

"Thank the Lord, or the Army," Pa concurred, absently changing the subject. The British military, having brought thousands of redcoats into North America through New York, had driven the prices of local produce to record levels. "Heaven help us if they ever win this war. They'll all move to Québec and bring supplies up the St. Lawrence!" A sobering thought indeed.

"What do you think, Tom," Bertie sang out jauntily, "are they going to win anytime soon?"

Not having expected to be asked to say a word during this meal, I was startled to have all eyes suddenly fixed upon me as if I were the local military expert. "*Um*, not that I can see, Bertie," I stammered out. "My observations were very mixed, last summer."

They all looked at me in confusion. "None of you has told him?" Mother demanded.

"I thought you had," Harmanus protested.

"Oh. Well, there's been some good news, Thomas. General Forbes's campaign in the far west has been victorious, and that fort, *uh*...."

"Duquesne, in Virginia."

"Pennsylvania, I believe?" Van Klost suggested.

"In the Ohio country. They've just taken it! A few weeks ago. Since you've been home."

"*Uh huh*," I mumbled, annoyed that I'd stupidly assumed the war had come to an end with my safe return from it. "Well … that's grand! I remember the officers saying that Duquesne was even more important than Fort Frontenac." As my elders evaluated rumors of continued army requisitions, I fear I rather rudely permitted my mind to drift back into the vast, dark green northern forests. Britain had had four engagements in America this past year, and I'd participated in two: the disaster, Ticonderoga, and a spectacular success, Frontenac. The government must be happy, now, to add Fort Duquesne to its earlier victories in Nova Scotia and Upper Canada. I wondered if the poor sods who'd built a highway across the mountains to get at it had found a warehouse full of beaver furs, as my mates and I had, to compensate their trouble.

"But surely he doesn't mean to disinherit his granddaughter," Anneke was protesting. "After all, she'll be his only surviving relative!"

"Except for father, of course!" Jenneken blurted out.

"Jenneken!" Constantija reproved. "Don't—"

"Well, he could leave the lands—"

Floris Van Klost was shaking his jowly head. "Child, we don't even think of that! Meneer Loytinck will do as he pleases, irrespective of any of our expectations."

Oh yes. It was all coming back now, having to be recalled from memory because no one had ever observed the remotest hint of family affection between Loytinck and the Van Klosts. Floris' late mother, Aeltje—an impossible woman who'd unfortunately been a great crony of Grootmoeder's—was the daughter of Loytinck's elder brother, long dead. Loytinck had managed to have three sons, all of whom had died without issue, and one daughter who had been killed with her husband in a ferry accident, orphaning Marijke Katelaar at the age of three. The girl had been shuttled to various aunts around the county, but landed back on her grandfather's doorstep at fifteen. To universal amazement, she'd quietly taken over his widower household, and eventually his farm.

"Well, what do *you* think he's going to do, Uncle Rykert?" Bertie piped up to ask. Bertie seems to get along more easily with Pa than any of his own children do. "You talk to him more than anyone else!"

Bertie was skating on thin ice, not that that would ever slow him down. Loytinck and Pa frequently *drink* together, after which carouses one will walk home … and the other will pass out under the table. "Damned if I know, boy," Pa blared, his profanity again causing us all to jump. "If I know Teunis Loytinck, he plans never to die, that's all!"

Everyone sighed. Van Klost looked at my father hesitantly. "Maybe you're the person to try to reason with him, after all, Dordrecht," he said—a startling opening from a man who'd quarreled with Pa for decades. "He certainly won't listen to me. Nijenhuis tried but didn't get anywhere. And he won't give the time of day to anyone under fifty, not even Dominie Van Voort."

Pa was as surprised and wary as the rest of us. "What would you have me say to him, Van Klost?"

"Well.… I doubt there's anyone in town who could afford to buy all of those lands intact," Van Klost began. "Certainly I couldn't. Not that he'd ever.…" His voice dropped off as he grimaced and suppressed his thought.

"I couldn't, either," Pa asserted breezily—prompting raised eyebrows from both Harmanus and Mother. I knew enough about our family finances to realize that, while Pa was absolutely correct, he hadn't done the homework to prove it, and Mother was the only one with any real grasp of the subject.

"If he broke up his plots, however, I might be able to buy one. You might be able to buy one. Nijenhuis might be able to buy one, and so forth. If he were to do that, we'd keep ownership of the lands here in town."

"And the slaves, too," Harmanus added. And I suddenly realized that was the point of all this. Were outsiders to buy the lands, particularly as a single unit, the fate not only of Loytinck's slaves, but of all the slaves in New Utrecht—because they were interrelated with each other quite irrespective of their ownership—would be thrown into a cauldron.

Pa frowned dubiously. "More work for him. Why should he care?"

"Well, it's the only way he'll sell out to people from the county!" Van Klost exploded, his ire directed, for once, more at his great-uncle than my father.

"If he means to do the right thing by his granddaughter, Rykert," Mother said, "he really should face facts and try to sell properties he can no longer manage!"

"And he should get it accomplished before the Almighty calls him to his reward!" Harmanus added stiffly.

"I'll think about it," Pa conceded.

Conversation turned to more relaxed matters—weather, Jacob's ferry service at Red Hook, the possibility that the Van Klosts' other son-in-law, Substance Coldcastle, would run a horse in the Hempstead races next spring— as Lisa, Berendina, and I cleared plates and brought out three wondrous-looking apple pies that Aunt Betje, the most renowned baker on the south shore, had sent us by Bertie.

Like their creator—Betje was the only one of Grootmoeder's children who was universally loved—the pies elevated everyone's good humor. Even Meneer Van Klost was disposed to make idle conversation. "What have you and the dominie been discussing all this time, young Thomas?"

"Mostly about the books we've been reading, sir."

"Ah! Wish I had time for such things!" I feared a recitation of his schedule, but a scowl from his wife blessedly throttled it. "So tell us what you have been reading," he commanded.

"Well, the book that's most interested me," I said, my enthusiasm mounting as I gathered he was serious, "was the text on astronomy that I borrowed from Mr. Colegrove in the city, actually, not from the dominie."

"Astronomy?" Van Klost said, dumbfounded.

The others—Lisa excepted—looked at me with a mixture of awe, contempt, and sheer disbelief, but I waxed warm to the topic. "The most amazing thing is actually going to happen in the next few months, sir! There was a scholar at Oxford, you see, a Mr. Halley, and he made a prediction, years ago now, long before he died, that we shall be seeing a great comet in the sky this very winter."

"How on earth would he presume to know that?"

"Comets are miracles, Thomas," Mother protested mildly. "They're acts of God."

"Perhaps some comets are, to be sure, Mother, but Mr. Halley took it upon himself to compare the historical reports of the sightings of comets, and found that one in particular occurred in exactly the same fashion, in the same part of the sky with the same intensity, for the same length of time, every seventy-six years or so!"

"Come come, Thomas," Harmanus snorted. "We know that God has ordained the celestial bodies to move regularly, but the scriptures would surely have explained such a thing if it were true!"

"And would this not appear to deny God His prerogative to create miracles at will?" Anneke added supportively.

Oh dear. The tome had amply detailed Signor Galileo's difficulties with scriptural literalists. "All Halley was saying, Harmanus, is that he personally saw a bright comet in 1682 that completely matched the description of one seen in 1607, and that both resembled another described in 1531. Which suggests, therefore, that we'll be seeing it *again* at any moment!"

"That's the most preposterous thing I've ever heard!" Constantija Van Klost exclaimed, and the whole table burst into laughter.

I must admit that my first impulse was to take offense but, with Mother staring hard at me, I'd mastered it by the time they'd gotten over their amusement. "We shall see, ma'am!" I asserted, smiling cheerfully. And they laughed again.

*   *   *

"So ... Bertie!"

"So ... Meneer Thomas!" We touched our mugs of spiced hot cider and rum together, enjoying a private moment by the front window after everyone had risen to stretch their legs.

"You're to be a papa soon!"

"Any day now, lad. Your mother says it's any day!" Mother not only ran the tavern and the inn, she was ever more frequently the midwife of choice for half the county.

"I stand amazed!" And it suddenly struck me that the whole town, having applied itself to arithmetic, must be joining me in amazement that a couple wed only in early July should be anticipating familial consummation before the New Year. Such a prodigy, my cousin! "You're looking forward to it?"

"Should I not be? We all have to grow up sometime, Tom!"

Not you, Bertie, I thought, with very mixed feelings. Engelbertus Hampers was a comely and amiable-looking lad two years older than me. He had grown up a few miles away in Flatlands, but we'd been…. Suffice it that I'd felt far closer to Bertie than to either of my brothers, or anyone, really, save Lisa. And yet his betrothal had been a perfect thunderclap. Worse, a betrayal. The reason for its underhandedness and precipitate timing was of course now as apparent as could possibly be in the huge belly of his child-bride, and so it was about time I swallowed my annoyance and made my peace with him.

"How are you getting along with the Van Klosts? Are you planning to continue living there for good?"

"Don't see why not, Tom. We're staying in Jenneken's old room. Plenty of space there with her sister gone." He looked over at her, talking to Anneke, with real fondness. Anneke was herself heavy with child—but it was to be her fifth and she had some months to go. "And it's so far, so good, with the old man. Her mother…. Well, we'll see what happens when the baby comes."

"You're working with him on the farm?"

"Aye. He's all right. Never pushes me around like your brother tries to do with you!" It had been Bertie who'd persuaded me three years ago to put up a fight against Harmanus' abuse; I'd always have to thank him for that.

"He's just boring beyond endurance!"

"Oh be serious. Your family's prejudiced against the man for no good reason." Bertie was sounding earnest like me, and I was sounding frivolous like Bertie! The two of us suddenly burst out laughing at each other.

I changed the subject. "You, Engelbertus, might stand someday to inherit, through your wife, the largest property in New Utrecht!"

"Heaven forbid, Tom," he said airily. "If I had all that land, I'd *really* have to work!" He contentedly sipped his potion. "Actually I had an even better shot at it last winter, when both our mothers were pushing me in Juffrouw Katelaar's direction!" My jaw dropped. My entire family were full of surprises! "Oh yes. That woman's a decade older than me, but…. Well, you heard how desperate they all are to keep the holdings intact! They'll be after *you* to marry her!"

"Oh no! Oh no you don't." I had nothing against Juffrouw Katelaar. Other than being too old, bossy, plain, hidebound, and fat, she was perfectly fine. Looking at Jenneken, it was obviously not the latter objection that had bothered Bertie!

"Trust me, mothers are always conspiring matrimony. Of course, they'd failed before in that endeavor."

"Eh?"

"The lad they really wanted to marry her was *Harmanus*. Ten years ago they were laying it on him with a trowel. He only escaped when old man ter Oonck brought his daughter to the rescue!"

"I never heard this! How'd you find all this out?"

"I asked, of course, Tom. Asked Harmanus himself, when they were dropping hints to me right and left. I think they tried with Brevoort too, notwithstanding she's so much taller!"

Amazing. "Why *didn't* Harmanus marry her? You'd think he—"

"—could have reconciled himself to all that land? Yeah, well, I gathered that the woman's insufficiently pious for your brother!"

"Oh that."

"And can you imagine any woman trying to tell *him* what to do?"

"Besides Mother? There's trouble!"

It suddenly passed across the room that the young *vrouw* of Engelbertus Hampers was genuinely exhausted, and our party broke up with fervent wishes for her successful delivery.

CHAPTER 2

"Thomas, you must take over, here!" Mother demanded, three afternoons later. "I've already cleaned the rooms and restocked the larder. All you have to do is take charge."

"But—"

"No 'buts!' Jenneken's time has come, and I must get next door directly. Elisabeth is already there. Time she learned! Harmanus is out in the fields, but Anneke and Berendina may be able to give you a little help."

"Pa?"

"I don't know. Up to you." She grabbed a satchel she kept for her midwifery, and headed to the door. "Don't let the stew scorch!"

So. Convalescent or no, I was in sole charge of the family hostelry until further notice. I stirred the stew, poked the fire, and ran to bring Dr. Mayhew down from my room.

Though I might have been more comfortable in my bed, the afternoon passed quietly enough, with no customers, until Jenneken's screams pierced the neighborhood air and froze my blood. For one reason or another, I'd not been present at any of my sister-in-law's deliveries, and the howls I heard terrifyingly reminded me of those I'd heard from men on the battlefield.

Bertie came in, looking very pale, and asked for a glass of gin. He drank it in silent, morose gulps, shuddering deeply each time a new cry resounded. His father-in-law came in an hour later and also asked for gin. Each took his long-stemmed clay pipe off the rack we kept for our patrons and sucked deeply upon it between swallows. Their tension was so great it affected me, and I was much relieved when Hendrik, Harmanus' oldest boy, beckoned me to the door, saying he wanted to show me something. The two men first looked at him suspiciously, afraid he'd been sent to relay bad news, but the lad's gap-toothed grin reassured them. They followed, eager for any diversion. Hendrik pulled me out to an open spot in our yard, and pointed into the black, clear sky in the general direction of Flatbush, except up. "What's that, Uncle Thomas?" he asked. "Is that the star of Bethlehem? Or that thing you were talking about at Christmas dinner?"

To my astonishment, there was a sort of smear of light, low in the sky to the northeast, different from any star or planet. What else could it be but a comet? "Well, aren't you the eagle-eye!" I exulted, mussing my nephew's hair. "Will you look at that!"

"Is it an omen?" Bertie asked breathlessly, hopefully.

"Well, Bertie, it's a natural phenom—"

"You're a prophet, Sergeant Dordrecht," Van Klost exploded, using the military title I had repeatedly tried to discourage. "You said it would come, and there it is!"

"Oh but sir, it was the scientist Halley who—"

"A prophet!" Van Klost insisted.

"It's a *good* omen, isn't it?" Bertie asked me, tightly gripping my upper arm. There was another shriek from the Van Klost home. "Isn't it?"

"I'm sure it's a good omen, Bertie," I affirmed, deciding this was not the moment to contend against superstition. Jenneken screamed again, louder than ever. Shouting her name, Bertie tore off in a panic around the corner of the house … where he collided full on with Harmanus, who is at least a stone heavier. Both men fell, winded, to the ground, and Van Klost, Hendrik, and I had some difficulty getting them back into the house, beside the fire.

Mother walked in an hour later, looking tired but content. The filthiness of her apron, however, which had many dark red stains, instantly alarmed us all … until she said, "Congratulations, Bertie! You're a papa! You've a good-looking baby boy!" Bertie collapsed to his knees and raised his hands together, so that I thought he was going to join Harmanus in rapturous thanksgiving, but it was only to bury his face and burst into fervent sobs. We all pounded him on the back. Van Klost, however, still looked at Mother anxiously. "She's fine, Floris, perfectly fine. It would be a good time to visit. She'll need sleep soon."

"Thank you so much, Chastity," he said, taking my blubbering cousin's arm over his shoulder. "Your son's a prophet! Did you know that?" They shuffled out.

Mother silently removed her apron and poured herself a gin, and then joined her sons and grandson by the fire. *"What?"* she said.

Hendrik explained how he'd discovered the comet, and his father related the accident in the yard with rather more humor than I expected of him. "Good thing I wasn't carrying my pitchfork!" he added.

"Men!" Mother exclaimed, shaking her head.

Bertie's dictum that mothers are forever conspiring matrimony was demonstrated anew as we made our traditional visits to celebrate the new year of seventeen fifty-nine the following Monday. We of course stopped next door to view baby Maurits and his proud progenitors. Mother and Constantija professed to perceive Bertie's eyes and Jenneken's mouth in the infant; all I could see was a noisy, red-faced, squashed-looking lump.

But given the propitious weather—the warm respite was over and it had snowed, but it was wonderfully clear and sunny—we hitched up the sleigh for a visit to my sister Geertruid's family in Flatbush. I'd always liked Geertruid and my brother-in-law, Berend Kloppen—though she tends to be awfully demanding—and I certainly looked forward to my first excursion out of town. A neighboring family, the LeChaudels, had also been invited to dine. They had a girl my age named Nanette, who was comely and pleasant, but sadly dull—at least when compared to Lisa or my friend Nogert's wife. Her parents, however, were so exclusively fascinated by my war stories that they were positively rude to everyone else, even their hosts, none of whom appeared to object to my monopolization of the conversation.

Lisa and I sat together on the back edge of the sleigh for the trip home, holding onto our nephew Petrus, who promptly fell asleep across our laps. "What was all that about?" I wondered aloud.

"You can't guess, Thomas?" she said. "They were examining you, lad! That's why they were there! They have thirty-seven acres and only one child, and they aren't about to see her married to just anyone."

"They were looking at *me*, as a prospective spouse for Nanette?"

"Of course they were, silly."

"But I didn't even—"

"What's liking her got to do with it?"

Was she jesting? She was. Thank heaven!

*   *   *

In the next few days, it became apparent that my health was largely restored, and that the only real want of my corpus was for exercise. When Mother asked if I was ready to resume the shopping trips into New York City that had for years been among my duties, I positively leapt at the chance. Mother was much relieved, as she'd taken over in my absence and found the excursions a great disruption.

It was not merely the thought of exercise and family duty that excited me, of course. I had returned from the North with a pocket full of gold, and—Hollander prudence be cursed—it was bursting to get out. Restoring the tavern's inventory of comestibles would take barely an hour, and surely

I wanted to acquire some presents for my family—I'd been empty-handed as gifts were given on Sinterklaas Day—and I particularly wanted to make some exchanges at a draper's. But most of all I yearned to acquire for myself a musical instrument! Should it be a lute, a mandolin, or a guitar? Or could I conceivably afford a harpsichord with my lucky pelf?

As Zwarte Jan—Van Klost's ancient slave, our regular factotum for these expeditions—and I started walking up the path to Red Hook on a particularly fine winter morning, I had a substantial list of duties to perform, but no other *thought* than my eagerness to visit Mr. Fischl's establishment on Pearl Street, where I'd often seen musical instruments for sale, in addition to books, stationery, sewing notions, and hardware.

Jacob's ferryboat is no more than an open sloop whose passengers are ordered from side to side as he tacks. Exposed to wind and spray, our carcasses were half-frozen by the time he deposited us on New York's island, spurring the vigorous expedition of chores as a matter of restoring circulation. To the grocery first, to purchase many gills and tuns of staples for the family and our customers, and to renew my acquaintance but forestall demands for stories from its worthy proprietor, Mr. Martin. Then I visited a furrier who, I was relieved to learn, was now able to redeem the promissory note he'd given me with gleaming, newly minted gold and silver specie. Off to a draper's, where I was pleased to exchange my eight yards of elegant yellow French silk for the same quantity of plain dark green satin for Mother plus five yards of pink linen for Elisabeth! I found hats for Pa and Harmanus, purple wool for Grootmoeder and blue for Anneke, a book of poetry for my niece and an ingenious tavern puzzle hammered out of nails for my nephews.

With these goods I dispatched Jan, with tuppence to warm himself in a tavern near the ferry that served slaves, while I proceeded to my last errands unencumbered.

I rapped the knocker of Mr. Aaron Colegrove's mansion on the Broadway, and was flustered when the master himself abruptly pulled it open. "Yes?" he demanded.

Ah. He didn't recognize me at all. But then why should he? Though I regarded him as my patron, he'd only seen me twice before in his life, the last time eight months ago. "Thomas Dordrecht, sir. Is Mr. Glasby in?" John Glasby serves as Mr. Colegrove's secretary.

Colegrove, a vigorous man in his fifties, of most imposing stature and mien, examined me coldly for a second before nodding me inside and shutting the door against the elements. "Glasby's not here at the moment," he said flatly. "What is your business with him, pray?"

I explained that I was returning two books Glasby had lent me from Colegrove's library. "Will he be back this afternoon, sir?"

"No. You may leave the books on the table there, Master Thomas, that's fine." He was about the reopen the door as I moved to comply, fighting my perhaps over-sensitive resentment of his form of address—after all, he'd called me *Mister Dordrecht* last spring! But I was yet hoping for an opportunity to borrow more books, and took inordinate seconds tugging the volumes out of my haversack. Examining my Indian coat with evident disdain, Colegrove rather suspiciously asked, "How is it that you came to be among my borrowers, lad?"

"The pastor of my church is among your acquaintances, sir—Dominie Wouter Van Voort, of the town of New Utrecht?"

His hand on the doorknob, Colegrove appeared completely stumped for five interminable seconds. "Oh…. New Utrecht," he finally said. He remained frozen for another heartbeat, until recognition finally struck home. "Oh! You were the boy last spring who went off to join my cousin DeLancey's regiment along with Glasby's dolt of a nephew!"

I gulped, stunned by the harshness of Colegrove's assessment and fairly shocked by his readiness to speak ill of the dead. "I served with Sergeant James Hannamore, yes sir."

He made no move to open the door. "New Utrecht," he murmured inscrutably.

"When Sergeant Hannamore passed away, our platoon elected me to replace him," I observed uneasily, unsure what might be appropriate to say.

"Indeed! Well, then, *uh*, Sergeant…. Glasby will be in tomorrow. He's on an errand today. He's usually in."

"Thank you, sir. I should very much like to borrow again, if I may."

He worked up a smile. "Of course. Good day to you!" The door was opened, and I hied myself out.

How very peculiar! I mused. But I forgot all about it as soon as I reached Mr. Fischl's. There I spent a full hour wrestling my better judgment to the ground and emerging six pounds four shillings poorer, a happy lad with the dearest and most beautiful Spanish guitar that had been on offer.

*   *   *

"*Six pounds!*" they all howled at once. They'd been happy enough with the presents I'd bought for each of them, but when I proudly brandished the guitar my family were unanimously horrified. "Do you think you're *made* of money, Thomas?" Pa had demanded as Mother and Harmanus shook their heads and even Lisa hung hers down in speechlessness. They weren't a bit impressed that you could see your face reflected in the varnish! It might've helped, I suppose, if I'd had the slightest idea how to play a tune with the thing.

I fear I shammed a recurrence of my illness for the next two days, and spent the entire time in my attic room, testing scales and chords and progressions as Mr. Fischl had suggested, until my fingers ached. Grootmoeder seemed to enjoy it, although it was hard to tell. Hendrik was delegated to bring up my meal the first night, and stayed long enough for me to show him how the pitch is conformed by tightening or loosening the pegheads. On Wednesday evening, just prior to supper, I was strumming away when Harmanus, red-faced, clomped into the room and bellowed, "We are *attempting* to read the Lord's book, downstairs!" Scowling, he added through clenched teeth, "It would be *helpful* if we could enjoy God's peace while we did so!"

What, I fumed, gave this man the unbearable gall to presume that he had more rights in this household than his brother did? Was I not equally entitled to my own pursuits, barring my parents' objections? I was drawing myself up to give battle when I realized that doing so would inevitably give rise to issues with which I was not prepared to deal. Did I actually enjoy equal entitlement here, I who was avoiding the labor of the place, and who obviously wanted never to take it up again? "Very well, brother," I conceded, irritably backing down. "I shall resume after supper, at your pleasure."

"My *pleasure* would be never, Thomas!"

The gall! "In that case, I shall resume after supper, Harmanus!"

Clearly, he was as furious as I. He turned on his heel and stomped out, slamming the door. I tried to calm myself with deep breaths, and looked about the room. Grootmoeder, whose presence both of us had ignored, had dropped her knitting.

The poor old lady was weeping.

Mother brought some food up to me two hours later. "Harmanus tells me you're much improved, Thomas!" she said brightly. Before I could overcome my shock and protest, she added, "I wonder if you'll be ready to make another journey to the city tomorrow?"

"I thought you only made one trip a week during the winter," I observed warily, stalling for time.

"There were some items I forgot," Mother asserted—with the same frank stare with which she'd announced Vrouw Nijenhuis' unexpected need to host the dominie at her Christmas table. It didn't take me long to translate it as, "They want you out of the house, lad!" But I had my own reasons for wanting to be out of the house, so I quickly consented.

Lamp oil, rum, tobacco, a half-gross of candles, more sugar—that was all. The list was too short to be credible. When she recited it the next morning, I briefly grew indignant at her eagerness to get me away, and challenged that I knew we had enough of all but the oil to last through to the regular shopping day. "We fear the river may freeze, Thomas," Mother blithely returned. "You may have to go all the way to Brooklyn to get a boat as it is. Harmanus said you and Jan could take the gray and the trap."

"How kind of him." Mother scowled at my sarcasm, making me regret it. "I don't really need Jan. It's so little, I can handle it by myself."

"Very well, dear." She gave me a kiss. It seemed as warm as ever. "Do be careful!"

A gravelly voice made me jump: "Put a blanket over that horse, Thomas. It's damned cold out!" I hadn't even realized Pa was in the room.

*   *   *

Three hours were needed to reach the city, hours that were tedious and bitter. As my formal business would be quick and I really had no private errands in mind beside brief visits to Fischl's and Mr. Colegrove's library, my idle mind dwelt on the sorry apprehension that my family wanted me out of the house, wanted me out in this indeed cold, cruel world.

Mr. Martin, with whom today I'd have been glad to pass time in conversation, was away attending to his own marketing when I arrived at his emporium on Stone Street. His polite but taciturn assistant expedited my purchases before I'd even thawed through.

Mr. Fischl's establishment bore a note on the door announcing that, due to an inability to locate firewood, he would be unable to open today, and deeply regretted the inconvenience to his customers, etc., etc.

Trinity Church's bells were tolling the noon hour as I sounded Mr. Colegrove's doorknocker. Mr. John Glasby, a man of some forty years, dressed in plain but neat dark gray business clothes, presently responded, and his mien changed from politeness to welcome as he recognized me. "Mr. Dordrecht! Do come in. Mr. Colegrove told me we'd be expecting you."

"Thank you sir, it's very good just to be indoors!"

"Let me take your coat."

"Thank you, but.... Would it be impolite to keep it on? I am well and truly frozen."

He smiled generously. "As you wish, but come into the library. We keep it pleasantly toasty."

And indeed the library, though devoid of people, had a blazing fire, and the room was warmer than the public room of our inn. It struck me as most prodigal, however gratifying. I stared at the fire briefly, warming my hands and wondering how the extravagance was managed when poor Fischl couldn't even open his shop. "When Mr. Colegrove's ships take supplies up to Albany," Glasby explained, having noted my wonderment, "they bring back lumber from his estates for the shipwrights. This is merely filler wood that completes the ballast." I nodded, impressed with the logic of it. "But I have happy news for you, my lad," Glasby exclaimed. "We have an assortment of pamphlets by Dr. Franklin just available! I believe you've already read his description of the kite experiment, but there's much here—some proposals for education, *Advice to a Young Tradesman, Observations on the Increase of Mankind....*"

He set them on a table in front of my eager eyes. How kind of him to recall my enthusiasm for our American sage! "*Rules for Making Oneself a Disagreeable Companion?*" I exclaimed, amused but unsure the title had been printed correctly.

"Franklin is often disposed to write with his tongue in his cheek, I believe," Glasby observed, smiling. "You may take the lot, plus a book this time, Mr. Colegrove said."

"That's very kind, sir," I exclaimed, rather amazed that Colegrove had concerned himself, and feeling my spirits warmed as much as my body by such generosity.

"I'll leave you for the moment, then, Mr. Dordrecht," Glasby said. "I've ledgers to attend to."

My thanks were profuse as Glasby left me alone in the library. How wonderful to be trusted among the beautiful and valuable possessions of a wealthy businessman! It was not a room of great size, but there were substantial shelves on each wall, filled with books. The candles in the wall sconces were of course not lit—that would be a folly not even Colegrove could afford, but their polished brass shone handsomely against the pale pink of the wall and the elegant white moldings of the ceiling. I sat at the table, idly disposed to estimate a count of the tomes ... and guessed near a thousand by multiplying the twenty shelves by the fifty volumes I'd found on one.

But I was becoming no wiser by admiring the decor of the place. I took off my coat—a garment I'd not anticipated removing before April— and commenced perusing the shelves next to the windows on the street side. It was the "M" section, I deduced. I got caught up for a few minutes each with Macchiavelli and Marcus Aurelius. Aha, there was the dominie's friend, Jonathan Mayhew! I kept looking until I lighted upon the Baron de Montesquieu, whom newspaper essayists had hailed as the most important theoretician of our time, barring Mr. Locke. I pulled out *L'Esprit des Loix* ... and it was of course in French. Difficult French. I toyed with challenging myself with it nonetheless, thinking I could make lists of new words for Dominie Van Voort to translate for me; then I noticed that Montesquieu's history of the Romans looked altogether simpler, and would be more appropriate to my still-intermediate level vocabulary.

Glasby returned and peered over my shoulder. "Ah yes, I've heard that's very worthwhile!"

"Indeed? Have you read most of these yourself, sir?"

"Ah! Not half of them, my friend. A man of affairs is hard-pressed for time, as perhaps you'll someday discover!"

"Mr. Colegrove must be extremely learned, I suppose? There are many books here not only in Latin or French, but in Italian, in German, and in Greek!"

Glasby avoided my eyes for a second, then responded softly, "I fear Mr. Colegrove is even more pressed by his business, sir. All these books are, I believe, being accumulated as much in the pious hope of attending to them in the future as in the actual exercise in the present." Though taken somewhat aback, I tried to nod sagely. "But I came in to inquire whether you have dined, Mr. Dordrecht? I am about to take my dinner, and would be pleased of your company."

"Why, I'd be delighted, Mr. Glasby," I spluttered, overwhelmed by the cordial friendliness of a man twice my own years. "But I cannot permit you to buy my meal again, sir. That would be unworthy." It had been one thing to let him do so last November, when he was clearly desperate for my news of the last months of his nephew's life; this would be quite another matter.

Glasby shrugged and grinned. "Oh, it would be my pleasure, and no matter, but if you prefer, we shall … I believe the expression is, we shall 'go Dutch.'"

He had cocked his head to the side and said this with a wry smile and a complete absence of rancor, so I attempted to respond in kind by saying, *"Ja, natuurlijk,* Meneer Glasby!"

He entered my borrowings in his log, and we repaired to a nearby public house.

During the meal we shared I took, for the first time, a personal interest in the man I had only thought of as Mr. Colegrove's subordinate or Sergeant Hannamore's uncle. Mr. Glasby's plain face, average height, slight frame, and modest, precise demeanor all belied an active intelligence and a sense of humor that far surpassed those of his late nephew. As the waiter served me a hot toddy—the brief walk had chilled me again—I tried to elicit his history, and learned only that he hailed from Westchester County, was barely more traveled than I'd been before last summer, was a widower who hoped to marry again, and had been in Mr. Colegrove's employ for four years. He grew enthusiastic when I enquired the nature of the business projects he worked upon, and even remarked that he was concerned that the great increase in military supply orders the firm had received over the past two or three years might eventually make it difficult to adjust back to the primary purpose of supplying the continent.

We spent much time talking of books as we ate—Glasby is an admirer of Franklin and Montesquieu, and acknowledged some respect for Mayhew.

He's an Anglican, of course, as Hannamore was, but he hastened to state that he understood the "Presbyterian" point of view disapproving clerical establishment. I rather jocularly avowed that though my own roots were in the denomination with the *largest* plurality of New Yorkers, I too concurred with the "Presbyterian" contention.

Enjoying the company and in no rush to face the cold trip back home, I perhaps foolishly ordered another hot rum. Glasby—who also seemed to be in no hurry—inquired after my family and home and plans in such detail that I was charmed into ignoring the oddity of it. Our conversation drifted back to my military experiences, and he surprised me by asking, "Did James ever mention a hope that he might one day be employed by Mr. Colegrove?"

"Indeed he did, Mr. Glasby. I rather think he was eagerly anticipating it."

"Ah me. Well, we did have a position ready for him, in fact."

"Really?" Blind to what was coming, I was suddenly on the verge of boredom.

"Mr. Colegrove and I have speculated whether *you* might be interested in it!" Disconcerted in the act of swallowing a large draft of rum, I gagged. "My good fellow! Are you all right?"

Mopping myself up with some embarrassment, I assured him I was. But my attempts to elicit precisely what sort of employment was contemplated were gently rebuffed with, "I believe Mr. Colegrove would prefer to tell you himself."

"Now?"

"He is in his office this afternoon," Glasby observed with an encouraging smile. "When would be better?"

Astounded but instantly in agreement, I downed the remaining rum for fortitude. As I rose, a trifle unsteadily, it briefly occurred to me that it might have been wiser, for the selfsame reason, to leave the tankard unfinished.

*   *   *

Glasby knocked on his superior's office door and announced my presence. "Oh?" I heard Colegrove respond. "Well, have him wait outside. I'll be with him in just a moment."

"Shall I remain as well?"

"No need." Glasby closed the door, shook my hand and wished me good fortune, and then disappeared into his own office.

Twenty minutes passed. I could easily tell, because I was looking directly at the handsome hall clock, and could hear every second tick away. After thirty-five minutes, my mental faculties even less prepared for the meeting than when I'd re-entered the house, I was regarding the closed door with positive dread, as if I thought battalions of shrieking Hurons were momentarily to issue forth from it. But I was looking away at the instant the door opened, and jumped as Colegrove said, "Dordrecht! Do come in."

Recovering, I walked into a handsome room and remembered just in time to remain standing until invited to sit. Settled at his instance at last, I was hoping for a modest word of apology for my protracted detention, but perhaps what he next said was meant to stand in for it: "I was about to have a glass of whiskey, my lad. Would you care to join me?"

Nothing in my experience suggested that any response other than grateful acquiescence might be appropriate. "Thank you very kindly, sir." I had a moment to admire his handsome light grey suit and perfectly styled periwig as he poured from a gleaming crystal decanter into two clear glass goblets. Each of these items was incomparably finer in manufacture than anything in the Dordrecht household, and *nobody* in New Utrecht wore a wig!

He poured at least two fingers' worth into each glass, and handed me the one with a slightly bigger portion. "Your good health!" he toasted.

"And yours, sir," I agreed, taking a swallow. I was well befuddled, but not so much that I, the son of tavernkeepers, did not recognize the liquid to be excellent Scots' whiskey.

"Well, then, to business. Did Glasby explain what might be required of you?"

"No sir. He said you might prefer to do that yourself."

"As he should. I need a reliable clerk in my warehouse on Front Street, Dordrecht. He will have to manage the stevedores, care for livestock and produce, and keep precise records. He will be needed twelve hours a day but only eight on Saturdays, and I believe I can find a room for his lodgment."

"Here?" I blurted out, dreaming of a warm nook in a brick mansion.

"Oh no, in a house I own closer to the wharves." Ashamed of my interruption, I merely nodded. "We can only afford three shillings a week— and some of that might not be in specie. That might not be much, but it's a start in the business world, and one that does not involve the commitment of apprenticeship."

Dumbfounded and stupefied, I fear it made a terrible impression that I merely stared back at him. He seemed to think I should be thrilled—as perhaps I should have been were I not a lad with a capital account that dwarfed the annual wage under discussion. I was struggling to think whether the training I'd receive might make it nonetheless worthwhile.

Mr. Colegrove, however, seemed only mildly irked by this apparent ingratitude. "You need some time to think about it?" I am not normally brought easily to a loss for words, but this unanticipated dilemma raised issues that could dictate the course of years of my life! "Well. Perhaps you can tell me something of your qualifications, Dordrecht? You come, I recollect, from Long Island? Your family?"

"Yes sir," I finally managed. "My family has a farm and a respectable tavern in the town of New Utrecht. I should need their permission before I could accept employment in the city." This was mere stalling, as my family was making it eminently clear that my presence at home was superfluous. "I … have done my parents' shopping, and their bookkeeping, for some years, sir," I stammered. "And I also served as Sergeant Hannamore's adjutant, last summer."

"Indeed." He looked askance, and I feared he now was finding me tiresome. "What crops does your family produce?"

This query would have stumped me for its sheer irrelevance, had I not eagerly greeted a line of discussion that posed no difficulty in responding. "Wheat and corn, for the most part, sir. They're the staple crops of the locality."

"Indeed!" Colegrove exclaimed with inscrutably great satisfaction.

"My family is unusual in that we have more livestock than most, and dedicate more acreage to vegetables and orchards, to supply our hostelry.…"

"Yes? How many acres does your father own?"

"Twenty-seven, sir."

"Aha. Is that a medium-sized plot?"

"The two plots together are slightly larger than most, sir." Colegrove nodded and looked thoughtful. Uncomfortably, I dismissed my perplexity over his lack of curiosity regarding his prospective employee, and pondered ways of keeping his interest at all cost. "Actually, the land belongs to my grandmother, sir, my father's mother."

"Oh? How is that?"

"Under Dutch law, you see, she inherited it directly when my grandfather died."

"I beg your pardon? Under *Dutch* law?"

"Dutch property law, yes sir. It was part of the agreement, at the time of the, *uh*, conquest … that there'd be no change in existing property arrangements in Kings County."

Colegrove's jaw dropped—but he seemed as amused as indignant. "I hadn't realized that any *agreement* was involved in the matter. Are you sure?"

"I've always been told so, sir."

"Very curious."

"It's no issue, as far as my family are concerned, as my grandmother has gone dotty, and practically speaking my father controls the land anyway." I certainly didn't intend to explain that, *practically* speaking, it was my mother and my brother who managed the family properties.

"You mean that legal title is actually in the hands of an old woman who's daft?"

The situation had never before struck me as remotely peculiar. "Well, yes."

"Ha! What are the other townsmen like? Are they all Dutch?"

Doesn't he want to inquire after my mathematical capabilities? "There are two families of British, and my own is actually half-English; the rest are Dutch or Huguenot. But of course it's not that many all told, sir. New Utrecht's the merest hamlet—just two dozen households."

"I see. How big is the plot of the leading citizen?"

"Old Meneer Loytinck? He has several plots, sir. I believe they add up to about eighty acres." Relaxing slightly, I took another swallow of the scotch.

"*Uh huh....* Would you remain liable for militia service there if you removed to the city?"

"I trust not, sir," I said, brightening at *that* thought. "I imagine I'd be required to join a city unit." Eventually. I certainly wouldn't hasten to volunteer.

"What do you *do* in the New Utrecht militia?"

I shrugged. "Just parade around, honestly. Not much threatening us there. I'm still shy of nineteen, but I'm the only man who's ever seen any military service."

"Small fry, to you, then?"

I smiled at the implied flattery. "Well, it does seem particularly silly to strut about the common hollering imprecations at the King's enemies, when you've seen what artillery can do."

"Indeed."

"And our captain"—Van Klost had relentlessly hauled us all out in the snow on Saturday—"is so bound by the rules he learned thirty years ago that he wouldn't know a bayonet if it poked him in the arse!" Mr. Colegrove affected to find this uproarious, which only encouraged me all the further. "He's a preposterous martinet, worse than anything the army had to offer." I blush to say I was inspired to mimic our militia captain's eyes-bulging, jowl-shaking *right-face* and *left-face*, not neglecting to parody his Dutch-accented English commands.

"Oh very funny, Mr. Dordrecht!" Colegrove laughed. "The man must be a perfect fool!"

I sobered briefly, wondering if Van Klost was really so much more intolerable than McPhail, the redcoat who'd mercilessly drilled me for hours in the June sun. "Well...."

"A perfect fool!"

Colegrove suddenly recollected a pending appointment and terminated our interview, encouraging me to return and speak to Mr. Glasby again next week.

With much to ponder—and an excessively well-oiled brain to ponder it with—I arrived home after dark, frozen solid. Rather pointedly, no one questioned my tardiness or inquired after the events of my excursion. But mother had made us oyster chowder, and that went far toward restoring my spirits.

*   *   *

For three days, my family and I generally avoided each other. I spent most of the time in my room, bundled up against the cold, playing on the guitar with numb fingers, telling myself that I was debating the idea of working for Mr. Colegrove at three shillings a week when in fact I was just practicing my instrument. My brother's scowls became ever more ferocious, and his wife and children found excuses to cut conversations short.

Throughout Sunday dinner, the tension grew. Harmanus, I noticed, was casting repeated imploring glances in Pa's direction, and Pa was studiously ignoring him. We were about to rise and leave when Harmanus put both fists on the table and said, "We *must* talk about Thomas' future!"

Anneke bustled the children to their studies. Although Elisabeth looked as if she'd be willing to stay and be my ally, Mother ordered her to attend to the kitchen. Pa stared down at his empty plate. I straightened my back. "What about my future, Harmanus?"

"You are not contributing to this household as you should, Thomas!" He looked again to Pa for support.

"We're not rich, boy!" Pa asserted morosely.

"We can't afford to keep anyone in idleness, Thomas," Mother added, her eyes glancing nervously about the room.

Feeling myself under attack, I'm afraid my heated replies ventured into realms of illogic that would've had my instructor, the Reverend Isaac Watts, rolling in his grave. Matters rapidly descended into a family squabble. My brother insisted that I'd not done a single thing to justify my existence since my recovery, that I'd spent all my time practicing "that ungodly instrument"— which I supposed to mean any instrument not used in a church service—and that he'd seen me "smirking" during Dominie Van Voort's sermon that morning. I denied everything with a vehemence that belied the basic fact: the primary business of the Dordrecht family of New Utrecht was farming, and I did not want to be a farmer. As matters reached the highest pitch of vituperation, I revealed that I'd been invited to join a commercial firm in the city ... and that I intended to do so. Directly.

"Good!" said my brother stonily. He marched out of the room, head erect as always. My father poured himself another glass of ale and walked over to sit by the fire.

Ashen, my mother sighed and said, "This is not the outcome he wanted, Thomas. He doesn't want you to leave, he wants you to stay and help out. Your brother needs you to run this place."

He needs Pa! is what I thought. But that was one subject I never dared raise with my mother. "I'm sorry," I said aloud.

The next day was our regular marketing day and, the feared ice not having materialized, I executed the family commission for, I supposed, the last time, in order to see Mr. Glasby and settle my own plans. I hastily returned home to arrange my effects. I cleared the attic room, left the bulk of my cash and some old clothes in a trunk which I stowed in the barn's hayloft, and put all else save the guitar into a satchel.

Only Mother was about the following morning before dawn, as I prepared to set out and seek my fortune in the big city. She insisted I stay long enough to eat some hot food. "I'm not happy to see you leaving, Thomas," she said wistfully as I obediently ate her eggs and bacon. "I'd hoped you'd want to stay until you married and began tilling your own farm, someplace nearby." Sullenly, I made no response, and she sighed again. "But this is better than running away, at least, Thomas!" I cringed. "You promise you'll never do that again?" On that point I could and did meet her eye. "Then go on with my blessing, lad!"

It was not like my mother to weep in front of her children, but her face was struggling against it as I kissed her goodbye and she saw me to the door.

CHAPTER 3

With dismay I beheld the slouching clapboard structure of number Fourteen Cliff Street, Mr. Colegrove's house near the wharves. Though substantial buildings were in sight at the corners, number Fourteen and the adjoining abodes seemed ready to collapse of their own weight. Girding my resolve, I entered and presented myself, as Mr. Glasby had instructed, to the widow Brown, proprietress of the tavern that occupied the ground floor. A blowsy, genial, but evidently rather dim woman, Mrs. Brown presently recollected that her landlord's runner had informed her to expect me, and summoned her son to show me my room upstairs. The son, Eddie by name, some years my senior, did not appear genial at all, and I was relieved to see he was six inches shorter than myself, his surliness having inspired instant distrust.

The room itself was even tinier than I'd expected, smaller than my attic room at home. There was a thin pallet on the floor, a stool, and a rickety table. The one amenity was a little hearth. Great care would obviously have to be taken with its use, however, and the required sand bucket was only half-filled. I set my guitar and my satchel down in the corner furthest from the unsmiling Eddie, untied the canvas cover of the window, and pushed open the creaking shutters. I was rewarded with a magnificent view of the East River quays ... and an arctic blast that froze the room.

"Hey!" Eddie protested.

I pulled the shutters back, re-tied the canvas, and noted that plenty of cold air was still coursing in. "Where's the privy?" I asked.

"Out the back, three doors up to the north," he replied indifferently. Further from my room than at home! He held his hand out for a gratuity.

"Thank you, Eddie," I said, deciding that nothing he'd done merited one. His scowl deepened, but he closed his palm and left without shutting the door behind him.

I shook away my irritation and my rising distaste for my surroundings, and concentrated on what I had to do before starting work at six o'clock on the morrow. Though resolved to learn to live on my income, I had decided to bring five pounds out of my reserve, thinking it might afford a few luxuries and entertainments that would not be covered by my earnings. But I now observed that I had a pallet, but no blankets. A hearth, but no firewood. No cooking pan. Candle holders, but no candles. And the several extra chamber pots we had at home were of no avail to me here. All of this had to be rectified without delay, before the markets closed.

Making a mental list, I departed to effect these purchases in the cheapest way I could manage. I was well into the process when it occurred to me to wonder whether Eddie might help himself to the guitar in my absence. I rushed back and saw that that fear was unfound—though neither Eddie nor his mother deigned even to nod as I returned—so I breathed a little more easily. Nineteen shillings I was down, and I'd not even started work!

On the other hand, no one was demanding I should curry the horses or muck their stalls, either. I elected to read Dr. Franklin for the rest of the afternoon, and reveled in the luxury of privacy. Taking care to hide the guitar under a pile of clothes, I went out for supper. On my way back I treated myself to two apples for a farthing from a black woman selling them on the curb. I suddenly recalled it was my birthday, and felt very grown up, though I was yet two years shy of twenty-one.

Determined to make a good showing at my job, and mindful of the continuing frigid weather, I burned one of my candles to study Montesquieu rather than parade about town. But my reading was presently disrupted by the unmistakable rhythm of fornication in the next room. Assuming it would presently be concluded, I spent some minutes mending my jacket. But no sooner had I resumed the studies than the amorous grunting commenced all over again. The woman's moans were the same as before. The man's were entirely different. Exasperated, I tried practicing the guitar ... only to be rewarded with hammering on the wall and the woman shouting, "Hey, cut out that racket!"

I continued nonetheless. When I blew out my candle, she was starting with a third customer.

*   *   *

Mr. Glasby met me in front of the warehouse, which was on Burnet's Key, a part of Front Street, directly facing the river a block above Wall Street.

It seemed a reasonably solid wooden building, quite vast inside, three stories in height, with a hoist at the top. Glasby assured me it was unheated as much from concern about a conflagration as from parsimony. It was at least a relief to be out of the wind.

When we lit the lantern, we both passed our fingers over the candle to restore some feeling. Through the gloom I noted impressive stacks of cut lumber and partially finished tree trunks. I also observed a dark stain on the bottom edges of the walls and a pervasive musty odor.

"We were flooded, early last month. That awful nor'easter!" Glasby said, following my gaze.

A storm? Oh—while I'd been delirious. "Doesn't look as though there was any permanent damage."

Glasby frowned. "Well, there wouldn't have been, if your predecessor had had any common sense. The drunken fool simply locked up as usual, though anyone could see the water was far higher than normal. We had livestock in here at the time, and he just left them. Nothing he could've done about the cattle, but we lost six sheep and a slave thanks to his negligence."

Horror doubled the shivering to which I was already subject. "They drowned?"

"No. That would've been a mercy. Water was never over a foot in here. The cold got 'em." He stood up. "Let me show you around, it'll warm us up to move." I followed him about, trying to memorize the locations of the various stores. The second floor had vast racks of dry goods … plus a flock of sheep and one of turkeys. "They'll need to be fed and mucked directly," Glasby instructed.

"Aye," I assented, wondering if I'd ever escape barns.

"We've a little hearth on the third floor. We can brew some tea." I eagerly followed Mr. Glasby up the broad plank stairs. There was more cloth, plus innumerable bags of grain and seed there, and a feeble light was beginning to show through the canvas windows, so we were easily able to make them out. Glasby showed me where he kept flints, kindling, and small logs, and how to crack the hole in the roof above.

At long last we had mugs of hot tea in our hands. "Does Mr. Colegrove deal much in slaves?" I asked, to make conversation.

"Very seldom, actually. We had two in from Charleston when the storm hit. We were only transporting them for a client in Fishkill; but of course we had to pay the indemnity for the loss of the one. Mr. Colegrove was very annoyed."

"*Uh huh*," I nodded, relieved that all I'd have to manage would be resentful sheep and turkeys. "So the bulk of the traffic is in lumber?"

"Lumber, dry goods, some livestock. Mr. Colegrove wants to deal more in cloth and food staples, given the huge demands of the army in the last three years." I nodded, cherishing the warmth of the mug. "There'd be better profits in armaments, of course, but others have got most of that market locked up."

We'd finished our tea, and Glasby methodically began listing my duties. As he'd often managed the warehouse himself when junior clerks could not be found, he understood exactly how to explain the requirements. As opposed to my brother—or his own late nephew, for that matter—Mr. Glasby was unfailingly patient, methodical, and clear. And genial! I was to receive and store supplies, supervise the one stevedore, and to remit goods to customers presenting receipts from Mr. Colegrove or Glasby himself. "When will this stevedore get here?"

"Joachim? He lives here, but he's at the big warehouse today, eight blocks up. Colegrove just bought his indenture a year ago last summer. Five years to go. Seems all right. Strong. Honest. Huge. You don't speak any German, by any chance?" I shook my head, and Glasby shrugged. "I trust you'll manage."

Glasby remained with me the whole day, and I had the opportunity to observe him servicing both suppliers and customers, and updating accounts. I was to bring the accounts to the house at the end of each day, but otherwise I'd be on my own. "Is that room satisfactory?" he inquired as we were locking up.

I'd been wondering how to voice my concerns all day long. "Well ... I don't really trust Mrs. Brown's son, Mr. Glasby. And I have a few property items that are fairly valuable...."

"You could keep them safe here, if you don't need them daily."

"Oh? Grand." That hadn't occurred to me. "And, *uh*, my immediate neighbor is apparently a, *uh*, harlot."

Glasby sighed. "Ah. I hadn't known that, lad, but I'm afraid it's not that unusual. No escaping it in the big city. Maybe you'll be able to afford better by the time next winter rolls around."

I'd been hoping he'd have an instant solution to that too. I gulped manfully as we shook hands and parted.

*   *   *

Relief and exhaustion briefly immobilized me as I watched Mr. Glasby hurry west toward Colegrove's house: I had apparently passed my first test. But the frigid wind cut my reverie short, and I set off to the north in search of supper. I'd conceived the notion of trying a different establishment every night—So many possibilities!—and my spirits rose excitedly as I realized that the next few hours were truly at my own disposal. I was free! Grown up! Free to explore the big city and its wonders, the high and the low, the magnificent and the squalid, the brilliant and the preposterous, the mighty and the pathetic. All of it I wanted. My curiosity was ravenous.

But then, so was my appetite. It was pitch dark and bitter cold, and a tavern that looked acceptable and affordable was in front of me. I'd walked six blocks I'd not seen before, so I shelved further peregrinations and had myself a meal—which I noted down as acceptable, nothing spectacular. When I emerged, the streets were as deserted as New York City ever gets—it *was* January—and I trudged back to my room.

Brown's was so jammed, so raucous, and so befouled with pipe smoke that I passed unnoticed up to my room, where the clamor was still so great that my neighbor's exertions were barely audible. I chose to practice my guitar. Presently the walls were hammered in protest, notwithstanding the overwhelming din from below. I ignored both. Twenty minutes later, as I was deciding to retire, there was commotion in the hall and a husky female voice was bellowing, "I thought I asked you to keep—"

My door flew open and crashed against the wall. A large, disheveled, red-faced woman of indeterminate age froze in the act of barging inside. Her furious demeanor instantly turned conciliatory. "Ooh, what have we here?" she gushed. "A pretty boy just off the farm, I'll wager!" Unbidden, she sat next to me on the floor and availed herself of my hearth. "You don't mind, do you, dearie? I'm fresh out of wood."

Stunned speechless, I gaped at her. On closer look, she must be nearing thirty—quite old for the oldest profession. Heavily rouged, the features she'd been born with were not unattractive, yet I found her presence disquieting, and it was a good minute before my curiosity surmounted my repulsion. As she nonchalantly warmed her roughened hands—had she been wearing more clothes, she'd not be suffering so from the cold—I suddenly nearly laughed, wondering how my eldest brother would've managed this intrusion.

Harmanus would've chucked her bodily down the stairs, piously quoting *Leviticus* as he did so. Of course, Harmanus would never in a hundred years have become a resident of Fourteen Cliff Street.

Though still wary, I calmed down. She seemed perfectly at ease, and devoid of overt malice. She began asking about me and I was still too thrown to do more than reply. After a couple of minutes, we were interrupted by Eddie, who appeared in my doorway, grunted, and nodded his head toward her room. My neighbor—whose name I'd still not learned—patted my knee, rose, and departed, blowing me a kiss from the door.

The whole encounter must have lasted less than five minutes. I resolved to take my valuables to the warehouse in the morning. *Welcome to the great metropolis!*

The next days swam by. The weather moderated—that is, the wind dropped and it didn't snow. The gigantic Joachim's painful shyness proved a greater obstacle to our communication than our lack of a shared language. Mr. Glasby seemed content when I reported to him each evening. I walked a few new blocks and tried a new eatery daily, before returning through a packed tavern to my solitary, anonymous room. I plowed through a chapter of Roman history in French before retiring. I heard, but did not again see, my neighbor.

On Saturday, I was on my own resources by two-thirty o'clock, and it was still light! For recreation, I ambled through the finer streets of the town, reacquainting myself with what was now—at least for the nonce—my city. The better thoroughfares put my tawdry block of Cliff Street to shame. They had solid frame homes with neat yards and fences, and many boasted their very own private outhouses! Many lanes had so much traffic that it would clearly soon be necessary to cobblestone them. Toward dusk, in a haze of urban excitement, I was walking east by the common, when I spotted a shockingly improbable couple peering into a store window. I ducked behind a delivery wagon to observe them.

The woman was the beautiful and renowned Miss Adelie Chapman, whom I'd seen singing in several public venues, not only taverns but in front of the City Hall on the King's birthday. She had, I'd heard, even once performed in the Anglican cathedral in a regular church service! Though I can only imagine that some of our more devoutly Protestant folk might not look upon her in an admiring light, I'd loved her voice and I think any woman allowed to sing in church must have something to recommend her. While I couldn't see the pattern of her gown, buried as it was under overcoats against the cold, I smiled to note that it was of the very same pink material that I'd selected as a present for my younger sister.

However, she was leaning on the arm of a man with whom I was personally acquainted and not at all fond: one of my first cousins, in fact, Charles Cooper, younger son to my Aunt Janna. I'd not seen him since Geertruid's wedding nearly five years ago—he had made himself despised by the whole of Kings County on that otherwise-joyous occasion—but there was no mistaking the supercilious, back-tilted head, the greatly exaggerated gestures, or the piercing, high-pitched voice. Charles—if I recall, he's eight years older than I am—managed to combine a normal physical form and perfect fashionability of dress ... with being unbearable to behold. At least *I* couldn't bear him. He was even wearing one of those absurd white *macaroni* wigs, teased upwards in three front-to-back rows....

And yet there he was *with her.* They were chatting away as if she were not among the most beautiful and he the most repellent of creatures. They passed without seeing me, and I was again amazed to observe that no one else stopped to gawk at them as I had. How curious these city people are! Or are they rather incurious?

Zounds! I made out an exchange of their conversation. Each addresses the other as *Darling!*

Disconcerted, I made my way back to my lodgings. Unable to read, I practiced my guitar, and resolved to begin weekly lessons with Mr. Fischl on Tuesday. I paid my duty call to my dreary uncle Frederik on Sunday, postponing Aunt Janna for the moment.

It was extraordinary how completely this chance encounter threw me. Many strange sights in the city had stunned and dazzled me, but the juxtaposition of Adelie Chapman and Charles Cooper I simply couldn't reconcile.

*　　　*　　　*

Returning to the warehouse was therefore a relief, and I avidly committed myself to my work. I was most pleased on Wednesday, when Mr. Glasby, having trudged through heavy snowfall to verify my progress, proposed that we have supper together as Joachim locked up behind us.

There was one tavern, dearer than my usual, which I'd mentally reserved for just such a function. When I suggested it, Glasby enthusiastically agreed, saying he'd always wanted to try it, and we were comfortably settled twenty minutes later. Eager to impress him with my interest and devotion, I asked many questions about the goods we were handling, their origins, destinations, and eventual purposes. Mr. Glasby seemed pleased to humor me.

"The lumber? Most of those tree trunks are headed east to New England shipyards, Mr. Dordrecht, although a goodly number of the finest might get all the way to Portsmouth. The island of Britain has been virtually stripped of tall trees, I understand, with the Navy's incessant demand for them."

"They come to New York for trees?"

"Backwoods New Hampshire and New York are the favored sources of white pine, yes. Most of the cut lumber we'll sell to the builders hereabouts."

"What about all the grain? And the livestock?"

"Ah. The larger parcels are headed to the Indies or way down south—Maryland, Virginia. We sell them foodstuffs and they sell us smoke. Whatever tobacco we don't need here we repackage and ship off to Europe."

"But why don't the Virginians just grow their own food?"

"Land's too valuable, lad! You always have to consider the value of the land. Why grow food when you can grow tobacco and make enough money to import all your food and more?"

"That actually works, Mr. Glasby?"

"If it didn't, they wouldn't keep it up for long, now would they?"

"Extraordinary. Why don't we grow tobacco, then?"

"You can trust it's been tried, Dordrecht. Doesn't work as well in our soils, our cooler climate. More's the pity." He must have seen me pondering this as I swallowed a deep draught. "This is the kind of question you need to think about, if you've any notion of becoming a man of affairs, Dordrecht. The issue is, where will goods be *most* needed, *most* prized. The factor who best understands that will be the likeliest to succeed in public business."

I had the sense that I was being offered invaluable advice, but it slipped right by as another question struck me. "Those great bags of rice. Where did they come from? Where are they going?"

"All from South Carolina. Most of it's going to the troops."

"Really? I never saw any rice on the front. We ate beans forever, and prayed for a nibble of pork."

"It's mostly consigned to the redcoats, I believe, though … I do recall our sending at least one shipment to the DeLancey regiment last summer…?"

"I never saw it—and I did most of our corps' cooking."

Mr. Glasby seemed baffled. "Perhaps I'm mistaken."

"It only comes from Carolina?" I asked.

"From *South* Carolina, yes."

"Not North Carolina? I assumed they were just the same, like East Jersey and West Jersey."

Glasby laughed. "Not my understanding, Dordrecht. I've heard they're completely different."

"What, as different as New York and Connecticut?" I asked, somewhat surprised. I've never *been* to our neighboring province, but everyone says one might as well venture to Scotland, or Hanover, or Sweden!

"All I know is that the rice comes from the south colony, and that the biggest problem of getting it here is traversing the capes of North Carolina in safety. Mr. Colegrove lost a ship there, not two years ago."

We were interrupted by the arrival of our meals. "How is your Shepherd's Pie?" he asked, after we'd both tucked in.

I paused to consider. "Good … but not as good as my mother's."

"Loyal!" he observed, smiling.

"No, really," I demurred, "it just isn't." Mr. Glasby obliged me with a recitation of his business career, about which I'd expressed curiosity. Like me, he came from a nearby farmstead, didn't care for the endless repetition of agricultural life, and enjoyed the vibrancy of the city. Apparently, he'd had even fewer resources at the start. He had first worked for a Mr. Yeaman, a Quaker merchant who had taken him under his wing and trained him in the factoring of wholesale commodities for over a decade. He had been describing the nature of his training when, with some reluctance, he explained that he had married the Yeamans' only child and had been looking forward to the fulfillment of his dreams ten years ago ... when his wife had expired in childbirth. The infant had survived for six agonizing weeks before she too had died, leaving both Mr. Glasby and his in-laws devastated. When Yeaman died four years ago, his widow sold the business to Mr. Colegrove, and Glasby had stayed on to manage the accounts with which he was the most familiar.

Now I cast about for any other subject, eager to drop one that was noticeably causing Mr. Glasby distress despite the passage of time. "So you first came to the city in 'forty-one? That was the year of the smallpox epidemic, was it not?"

Glasby relaxed. "No, lad, that had been two years earlier." Looking me appraisingly in the eye, he took a long pull on his ale and set the tankard down with satisfaction. "Seventeen forty-one was the year of the Great Negro Conspiracy!"

I was dumbfounded. "What Great Negro Conspiracy?" I asked, genuinely at a loss.

Glasby had introduced the topic with a certain sharp edge to his voice—a manner of speaking I'd never heard in New Utrecht, but had occasionally heard in the city, as if he were testing each statement as he pronounced it. He had, too, a peculiar expression on his face, more animated than before, breaking through his characteristic modest, earnest demeanor. "*Hmm*," he murmured, "that might've been a good question to ask at the time, but.... You've never heard of the Great Negro Conspiracy, Dordrecht?"

"Never, sir. I can tell you all about the siege of Leyden or the St. Bartholomew's Day Massacre, but—"

"Aha. Your family has cared to protect its innocent children, I take it?" I could only shrug. "Well, it made a great impression on me, I can assure you, because I'd not been here two months when it got underway, and it preoccupied everybody in New York for a whole summer. I was just your age at the time. You're twenty-one? Twenty-two?"

"I've just turned nineteen, Mr. Glasby." I have to admit I was a trifle flattered by how surprised he looked.

"Ah. Well, I was twenty-two, and I'd taken the cheapest room I could find, which was in an inn on the Hudson side that made the widow Brown's look as respectable as the *Province Arms*." I whistled softly, impressed. "And although my patron had advised me—*instructed* me, rather—to avoid fraternization with anyone in that establishment, I was lonely and homesick enough that I was at least civil with the publican, a Mr. Hughson, despite the fact that his regular clientele was decidedly unsavory—vagabonds and sailors and blacks both free and slave."

"*Free* blacks?" I interrupted.

"Well, yes," he replied, shaking his head. "City has quite a few of them. Always has." As Mr. Glasby proceeded, I did recollect that while all the Africans of my home town were bound, there was a tanner in Flatbush who'd bought his own liberty—and two in Gravesend for that matter. "Hughson and his wife had a girl indentured to them, Mary by name, a comely Irish lass who worked the tables, and—"

He interrupted himself to look me in the eye. "I hadn't meant to preach to you, Dordrecht, but—"

I trust I appeared duly appreciative of his intentions.

"—but I can tell you that I thank my stars to this day that I did not heed certain impulses that that poisonous little baggage was doing her best to encourage in me!"

"Indeed, Mr. Glasby?" The admonition caused me some alarm, and I now hoped for the full story—although how a Negro conspiracy could figure into it perplexed me.

"Ah! Well, let me back up. The town, you know, was not as prosperous then as it is at the moment. We'd been through an awful winter—even worse than this one, if I recall—and there were a number of serious shortages— wheat particularly. I doubt anyone was starving to death, but many were going hungry for extended periods that spring. Then there were fires, many suspicious fires, and you know how scared we all are of that. Rumors abounded that slaves had been seen *enjoying* the fires.

"A merchant's house was robbed of coins and small valuables, and who should step forward to denounce her own employers as a party to the crime but this girl, Mary—Mary Burton. A constable came in and questioned Mr. Hughson, who denounced Mary for an ungrateful hussy, and.... Nothing happened right away, except that my patron Mr. Yeaman demanded that I vacate that house immediately, which I did. And I think it was the very next night that there was a big fire inside the fort itself. Damaged the old chapel pretty badly. A black man was seen running away from it—"

"One would hardly expect him to run *into* it," I observed impetuously.

"Well, yes. But everyone's nerves were raw and his running from it was instantly taken as evidence of arson. And this girl, Mary, came forward yet again, to suggest that there was a vast conspiracy of arson, and that it was all directed out of Hughson's tavern, and that Hughson and his wife were inciting the slaves to rebellion, and—"

"Good heavens!"

"—and planned to burn down the entire city, murder all white males, and commandeer all the women into brothels!" I gaped. "Then she said Hughson would make himself into the king of all the slaves!"

"Sweet lord! Whatever would make him think he could get away with such a thing?"

"Well.… Dordrecht, I for one don't believe that any of it ever happened."

"You mean—"

"Exactly. The wench was lying through her teeth. She made all of it up."

"All of it? Why would she—"

Glasby shook his head. "Beyond me, lad. One … despairs of making sense of such things at times."

"But surely the magistrates would never.…"

"I fear you're mistaken. The magistrates fell for Mary Burton just as I nearly had—only the consequences were far more severe. The Hughsons were both hauled off to jail, they were tried with amazing expediency—it didn't help that both were illiterate and they couldn't afford an advocate—and they were hanged not a week later."

I could barely breathe.

"And that was just the beginning. Mary presently began naming some of the slaves who'd come into the tavern for a drink, and each of them in turn was jailed, tried without defense, and hanged. Each time one was on the gallows, hints of clemency were offered if they'd implicate others, but most went silently to their doom. Then the authorities began to burn them at the stake. Have you … ever watched a person burnt, Dordrecht?" I vigorously shook my head. "The screaming only continues for a moment, before they choke, but the writhing goes.… Dear lord, I forget myself. We're eating."

I'd stopped some time before.

"I beg your pardon!"

"Nay sir, I … am curious about the story." For better or worse, I'm possessed of a strong stomach, and I presently resumed my meal.

"Well, the first two to be burnt stayed silent until they were tied to the post and staring at the torch … and then they commenced shouting out names. The magistrates took careful notes but, in retrospect, one can only imagine that the slaves were just hollering out every name they could think of." He paused and smiled wryly. "The officials were about to remand them back to jail … but the public wouldn't have it!"

"They'd been promised clemency.…"

Glasby shrugged. "Blood was up. They were executed. Ghastly to watch."

"How do people get so carried off, Mr. Glasby?"

"Ah! Well, I don't really know, lad. Perhaps it was some excuse that there'd been a big slave revolt down in the rice country—"

"*South* Carolina."

"Aye. Two years before, if memory serves. And one in Barbados or Jamaica. And ... well, people who own slaves never sleep as easy as people who just own cows and horses, Dordrecht. It's the way of the world for them to be prey to evil imaginings."

I interrupted him to mention that I'd been reading Montesquieu's relation of the Spartacist slave revolt, which had terrorized the city of Rome for three full years. He nodded noncommittally. "What happened next, Mr. Glasby?"

He sighed. "Well, it went on and on, all summer long. Completely disrupted all normal commerce. Half the slaves in town were locked away. All the whites became suspicious of each other, because any hint of doubt or desire for leniency was regarded as tantamount to complicity. No one from abroad came into the city if they could help it." He paused. "A customer of Yeaman's told us—he was whispering in Yeaman's shop, I remember, because everyone was so nervous—that he had testified under oath that his slave, one of those who'd been named, had been right at home when the fires began, but the slave had been condemned anyway. I think there were about forty executions before it was all done, mostly slaves, of course. But they also sent dozens off to the sugar islands and, you know, being hanged might've been preferable to that."

"Whatever made it stop?"

Glasby paused to think. "The Hughsons had been the only whites executed, though many whites and blacks had been banished from the province, and after months of fury, some citizens were finally speaking up in objection to the costs they were incurring—as great as if plague had infested the city, they said. It was also objected that it was inconceivable that slaves were capable of organizing a conspiracy of such a magnitude—"

"The same was said about Spartacus!" I blurted out enthusiastically.

Mr. Glasby merely raised his brows and continued. "And the girl Mary—whom the authorities still appeared to credit—began accusing some of the whites of the town, including some fairly prominent individuals. One was a man named John Ury, a schoolteacher I'd once met at church. She accused him of being a papist, and plotting to deliver the city to the Spaniards—Britain was at war with Spain right then—and it was all because he taught Latin! That was the whole evidence of his Romanism!

"Hoping that something, somehow might avert further tragedy, I made the error of attending Ury's trial, and as I walked in, damned if the little wench didn't lock eyes with me, extend her arm, and shout, '*Him!*'"

I had to grip the table to keep from fainting.

"I was struck dumb, but the next thing I knew, two redcoats were hauling me bodily out of the courtroom and down to the cells in the basement, where I was kept for four days in an agony of terror—and unspeakable squalor— before Mr. Yeaman managed to redeem me."

With some difficulty I resumed breathing. *Glasby* accused of inciting slaves, plotting arson!

"During those four days, poor Ury had been condemned and hanged, and it seems that it was that injustice that finally brought the town to its senses ... which is the only reason I'm still here today."

"Merciful heavens, Mr. Glasby!"

"A close-run thing, Mr. Dordrecht. Makes one wonder how easily we mortals are led astray. In the years since, I've conducted perfectly straightforward business with people whom I watched cheering the execution of some of the wretched blacks...."

I shook my head in disbelief, my outrage mounting—to Glasby's apparent amusement. "But this is appalling, Mr. Glasby! This is the foulest of crimes. Did no one bring this horror to the attention of the King?"

Glasby laughed aloud and stretched. "The *King,* my good fellow! Oh my, you can rest assured His Majesty doesn't greatly concern himself with such minutiae as the peril of his falsely accused subjects in the colonies!"

"But—"

"A thin reed to cling on to, that one!"

"But—"

"It was the honest Yeaman to whom I owe my life, Mr. Dordrecht. He it was who saved me, and not without risk to himself, I may add. Thank the good lord such people exist!"

"Amen, sir."

We sat in silent contemplation for some time. Church bells sounded the ninth hour. "I've kept you too long, young fellow," Glasby asserted. "We'll need you sharp in the morning. I hope these relations will cause no distress to your sleep?"

"No no, sir!" I avowed, wondering the same myself.

"I've been most selfish, I fear. It relieves me to recite this tale, and since my father-in-law died there have been few I've trusted with it."

"Surely it's a very long time ago, now, sir, and—"

He chortled as we divided the bill for our fare. "Ha! A long time ago for *you,* laddie. Believe me that you can find many about to this day who would've told you this tale in a very different light!"

Again I was briefly speechless. "Well, at least you'd have the support of Mr. Colegrove today, as you once—"

"Colegrove! Oh no, lad, Mr. Colegrove knows nought of this sorry adventure. I trust I can rely on you not to disabuse him?"

"I.... I.... Of course you may, Mr. Glasby."

"As a man of affairs, Dordrecht, one learns to be chary of trusting all men equally. One concentrates on performing one's own tasks honestly, and takes each individual for the worth one sees—or fails to see—in him."

* * *

I did suffer a nightmare that night. I can't remember what it was, though I recall being deeply terrified. Either I've learned to stifle my yells, however, or the denizens of New York City can't be roused to care.

Mercifully, few customers or suppliers appeared at the warehouse the next morning, which afforded me some hours to shake the extraordinary sympathetic horror Mr. Glasby's tale had elicited in me. Many times, as I sleepily counted boxes of nails and bags of rolled oats, I reflected on the frightening adventure, and on the ingenuous character of Mr. Glasby, and how remarkable was his trust in myself. I found myself musing, too, on his assertion that my family must have endeavored to protect its children from knowledge of the Great Conspiracy that had happened when I was but an infant. Was that it, I wondered? Had my parents themselves known much about it? Though a scant five miles away, New Utrecht seems another world from New York City.

Did people not discuss such things because they wished to preserve the innocence of children, or because they had come to feel ashamed of their own behavior?

The demands of my employment intervened that afternoon and these speculations were set on the shelf. My mood lightened as my travail grew heavier, and Mr. Glasby's story became just one of many others in my internal library. By Friday evening, I was so tired, I resolved to try an extremely convenient tavern I'd thus far avoided: Brown's.

As always, it was loud, rank, smoke-filled, and populated with braggarts and toughs who seemed almost eager to pick quarrels with each other. I betook myself to a relatively quiet corner and ordered an ale. As I was served, I noted my nearest neighbor, a substantial, florid, oddly dressed individual with untied gray hair flowing copiously over his shoulders. "*Thank* you, master of the house," he was declaiming, "it is indeed a privilege to partake at such a noble establishment!" He grandly hoisted his tankard to the barkeeper, and then to his neighbors on either side. Bewildered, I nodded back at him, and he immediately turned to join me.

The barman caught his wrist. "That *will* be two pence, friend," he said emphatically.

"Oh! Of course, of *course!*" the man blithely agreed, producing the coins. "How could I be so neglectful?" he asked me in a smiling undertone. As he'd no doubt guessed, my impulse to flee was checked by my thirst for my own full glass. Unbidden, he introduced himself at great length. Gershom Ingraham was his name. He was lately from London, visiting all of North America—Boston most recently—in the hope of business. He was, to my great astonishment, a theatrical impresario who even now was preparing a presentation of *Hamlet* for a few weeks hence. I confessed myself thrilled and desirous of viewing this prodigy, and he immediately began expounding on the glories and travails of his peripatetic life.

"Who is playing your lead, Mr. Ingraham?" I inquired in all sincerity. I had actually read the play in a compendium of Shakespeare that had been one of the first books I'd borrowed from Mr. Colegrove.

"Why, I am, of course, my lad."

"Oh," I blurted out directly, "but I thought Hamlet was supposed to be a young fellow?"

Instantly I knew I'd misspoke, but the plastic facial metamorphosis whereby Mr. Ingraham conveyed first that he was tragically hurt, then forbearing, then forgiving, then again enthusiastic … was all rather magical to behold. "Ah, the miracles of the theatrical arts will presently have me looking like no more than your own elder brother, my young sir!"

Not that! I nearly exclaimed aloud. I quickly inquired after the other members of his company. Few traveled along with him, it seemed. In every city, for every production, he started virtually afresh, acquiring patrons, a house, subordinate casts, and supporting assistants. In America, even more than in Europe, it appeared the very idea of public theatrical performance throws many of the gentry into paroxysms of righteous horror—until the moment of the performance, which they insist upon seeing—and this creates even more difficulty for him.

I had intended to quaff my beer and repair immediately to my room, but I now found my energies strangely revived, and I called the barman for another round. Mr. Ingraham, without uttering a word, managed by looks and gestures to call attention to the fact that his glass too was empty, and to suggest that, were he not so sadly low on funds at the present, he would be delighted to imbibe another and continue our acquaintance. Amazed, I found myself inspired, for the first time in my life, to offer him a drink … which he gratefully accepted.

"Thank you, Mister…."

"Thomas Dordrecht, sir. Your servant!"

"A Dutchman, upon my word! I once had the pleasure of a visit to your city of Amsterdam." I would've protested that the only "Dutchman" I knew who'd ever set foot in the Netherlands was Dominie Van Voort … but he was busy regaling me at length with the production of *Julius Caesar* that he'd brought off in the capital of the United Provinces. As I was completing my second glass, I interrupted his narrative to assert that I would be extremely curious to observe his work in progress.

"Aha! But why be content to observe, good Mr. Dordrecht, when you could so easily participate? There is, after all, a great deal of work to be done in bringing such efforts to fruition!"

"I'm sorry, Mr. Ingraham, my employer requires me twelve hours a day as it is…."

"Oh, no matter," he exclaimed, waving dismissively. "So do those of all in my company. 'Tis the cross we must bear!"

Against my better judgment, his appeal was seducing me. "*Um*, may I ask, would there be any pay for this work?"

"*Pay!*" Ingraham exploded, mock horror suffusing his face. He then turned away and exclaimed directly into the back of the man beside him, "Oh *surely* the lad doth jest!" I felt a great compulsion to crane my neck to verify there was no dwarf there to hear, as if I didn't know perfectly well…. He turned back to me and declaimed, "The pay, my fine lad, comes not in the form of filthy lucre, but in *glory*, the great and splendid glory of bringing the restorative poetry of the Bard of Avon to this desperately"—he vigorously shook his head from side to side, causing his wattles to shake in a manner that would have made me perish with laughter were I not so awed by the entire delivery—"*benighted* province!"

"Benighted, sir?" I asked, knowing full well he desired me to question the judgment.

"Ex*act*ly, lad, benighted!" he thundered. "Though not perhaps so devoid of all true civilization as"—the tremulous horrors only increased—"the pious preserves of Massa-*choooo*-setts!"

Exhaustion now truly overtook me, and I passed on buying myself—and him—a third glass, and begged my leave … which he magnanimously granted only after I'd consented to appear at his *studio* at three on the morrow.

Too tired to seek out any supper, I collapsed on my pallet and essayed a scale or two on the guitar before giving out completely. As I nodded off, I heard my neighbor giggling, and her customer roaring, "Exactly, darling. Ah! That's it, ex*act*ly!"

*   *   *

Mr. Ingraham's *studio* was no more or less than the reeking public fish market, the business of which is concluded by noon every day. Though I learned it had just received its weekly swabbing, its sole advantage lay in being a large, flat room minimally protected from the elements. It was sunny, if arctic, outside, and I blinked for some time to adjust to a panorama of chaos indoors: some three dozen people, men and women, most in the garb of common laborers, conversing easily with a few dressed in great, if antique, finery; all huddling as close to the feeble hearth as they could manage. I located Mr. Ingraham, expostulating broadly to a pair of sullen-looking lads in green and purple hose that rose well above the knee, and made bold to tap him on the shoulder.

"What the—" Ingraham said, wheeling to face me. "Ohhh...."

"Thomas Dordrecht."

A glowing smile transformed his face. "Yes! Yes. Simon!" he yelled. A dusty, defeated-looking workman of middle years shuffled into our purview. "Simon, this *dear* boy has come to *help!* Put him to use, will you? There's a good fellow." Ingraham immediately turned back to the two lads and snarled, "That's not how you say it at all, you fools!"

Simon moved away to a far corner, apparently indifferent whether I followed him or not. It occurred to me that, however cold, it really was a fine day for a walk ... but curiosity got the better of me and I strode after him. He put a saw into my hands and pointed to a board with a charcoal mark across it, and nothing more needed to be said.

Over three hours later, neither my activity nor anyone else's having abated for a minute, Mr. Ingraham shouted, "Right! Court scene! Are we.... *Where* is our royal Gertrude? Has that bitch even showed her—"

"I am right *here*, of course, Ingraham," bellowed a strangely familiar woman's voice. And to my total stupefaction, my disreputable fellow boarder progressed out from a side room in a flowing purple gown much bedecked with jewels, a crown askew on her head. "I can't get this damn thing to stay on straight!" she was exclaiming to no one in particular as she came abreast of Simon and myself. Halting with apparently reciprocal surprise as she saw me, she recovered first and exclaimed, "Ha! My adorable young neighbor!" Leaning on Simon's head—Simon had rendered me even more speechless by kneeling and making a sarcastic obeisance to the "queen"—she carefully straightened and smoothed the collar of my jacket. I was still too befuddled to protest. "There! Well! The appearance of our court has certainly been enhanced today!"

"Don't scare the boy, missus," Simon protested, rising. "He's actually of some use, backstage."

"Is that so, peasant?" she cackled as they exchanged histrionic regards of one another. "Ingraham!" she shouted.

"What?" he shouted.

"Ingraham, do you know this darling child is possessed of a fine guitar, and is a veritable *virtuoso* upon it?"

Mr. Ingraham ceased berating his actors in mid-sentence and joined us. "He what?"

She repeated her assertion, imperiously forestalling me from protesting the imputation of virtuosity. "If we had a guitar, *maestro,*" she observed meaningfully, "would we have any need to rent a clavichord for that one *bloody* song?"

"Your majesty is a genius!"

"My majesty knows"—she looked me up and down with quite shocking, open indecency—"a good thing when she sees it!"

"Ex*act*ly!" they exclaimed together. Roaring with mirth, they joined the other performers arm-in-arm, leaving Simon chuckling and me shaking my head.

Two hours later, though the rehearsal was still proceeding, Simon and I, along with several others among the company's artisanal class, stowed our work and tools. "Come along, lad," Simon said, tugging my jacket's elbow. We repaired to a vile-looking dive I'd not previously dared to explore, right on the river edge. Quite sober as we entered, I took a care to move my money purse inside my belt. By the time I left, I was no longer sober, I was fast friends with Simon and the half-dozen others, and I'd promised to attend all the remaining rehearsals, play the guitar in performance, build and operate the "ghost scene" apparatus, and carry a spear in the court scenes. "Should be a halberd, of course," Simon explained between hiccups, "but we ain't got any halberds, so it'll have to be a spear."

As I passed my neighbor's door—business was under way as usual—I recalled Katherine, one of the seamstresses, leering and saying, *"Allegedly,* her name's *Régine."*

For a moment I felt a strange conviction that New York City was as wild and unpredictable as the savage borders of Lake Ontario. I was moved to close the feeble bolt on my door. Then I felt foolish and undid it. Then I locked it back again.

*   *   *

The next day, I effected my duty call upon my Aunt Janna Cooper. Mercifully, no one was at home, so a brief note sufficed. I'd been perplexed to learn in the tavern that rehearsals would continue on Sunday in the fish market. The artisans were prohibited, however, as likely to cause sufficient noise to attract the constables, who'd be only too glad to protect the holiness of the Sabbath at the expense of itinerant thespians. Unfortunately, yet another snowstorm began in mid-afternoon, driving me back to my lair, where I practiced my guitar with renewed concentration.

I was pleased to discover how much interest I found in my employment. Being in charge of the warehouse made me feel important and respectable, in a way that being held responsible for the upkeep of our barn at home never had. Unbidden, I had pondered how to improve our access to stores and our ability to manage the animals, and I'd found the exercise somehow rewarding for its own sake. Joachim remained morose but cooperative; I finally realized that he was unhappy because he hated the city and missed … farming!

I'd not presumed to hope that Mr. Glasby, on making his weekly inspection, would again care to ask me join him for supper—but he did. After business topics had been discussed at some length, I made bold to confess my excitement about the theatrical venture. Mr. Glasby appeared to find my ardor amusing and cheerfully agreed to attend the performance, but he blanched when I hinted that I would like to construct the scenic effect in an empty section of the warehouse. Mr. Colegrove, he asserted gravely, would regard that as unacceptable.

We were bundling ourselves into our coats when a nagging curiosity occurred to me. "Mr. Glasby, that girl, the barmaid who accused you?" His face darkened. "Whatever happened to her?"

He sighed heavily as we passed outside. "Mary Burton? The authorities gave her a hundred pounds reward!"

"Reward! After all the havoc she'd—"

"For helping 'to preserve the city,' it was!" I shook my head, amazed at the folly of it all. "No one's ever heard from her since. Rumor says she left the province."

I was standing stock still, snowflakes accumulating on my coat collar. Glasby indicated my need to turn it up and bade me good night. "Mustn't be overwhelmed by such things, young Mr. Dordrecht! I brooded over it far too long myself. One has to keep going!"

"Aye. Good night to you then, sir!"

We began to trudge through the drifts in our separate directions, but he turned back, a curious, sardonic smile on his face. "She was only sixteen, you know!"

CHAPTER 4

Despite ever-worsening weather, life in the big city continued to enthrall me. The clangor excited and invigorated me. My disreputable habitation I romanticized into an amusing tale to be told to some far-off future grandchildren. My employment made me feel connected to a wide world of trade and commerce, a tiny cog in a great wheel of useful, productive endeavor. Merely contemplating the array of choices in food, clothing, and entertainments made me feel urbane and sophisticated, notwithstanding the stark fact that I couldn't afford any of them. And I looked forward to Saturday afternoon with huge anticipation.

My second foray among the Shakespearians was almost as entertaining as the first. My next-door neighbor not being called, I was spared any more embarrassing caresses. "She does that to all the lads, you know," Simon explained. "You'd think she was a whore, they way she behaves!"

To this amazingly oblivious statement I could formulate no coherent response. Simon, a real adult, didn't *understand* about "Régine?" Should I tell him? *No*, I quickly decided.

One revelation came out later at supper, as the artisans were discussing—with considerable malevolent glee—the capabilities of the various members of the performing cast. There was only one whose art met their rarefied approbation: the woman who was to play Hamlet's fiancée, Ophelia, whose plaintive song I was to accompany. It was to be the celebrated local beauty, Miss Adelie Chapman.

Though Sunday's weather was calm with sporadic peeks of sun, I took only a couple hours of exercise. Practicing my guitar seemed suddenly critical and pressing. It had long been dark before my stomach demanded I leave my room.

I had by now observed that, although no vicissitude of the climate would excuse my absence from work, our clients and suppliers were far fewer in number on days of foul weather. When I woke to a blizzard on Monday morning, I therefore pocketed my volume of Montesquieu, anticipating that there would be little for me to do once the paperwork and the animals—pigs at the moment—had been attended to.

At one in the afternoon, then, Joachim was asleep and I was engrossed in the horrors of the reign of Nero. Suddenly the entry bell was ringing. I tapped Joachim awake and dashed downstairs. Someone was now slamming his fist against the door. We had one window on the side, and I noted that the drifts had reached the sill as I hurried to the threshold. Blinking as I pulled it open, I was startled to find a covered *chaise* sitting on the ground. Three of the four black bearers were stoically standing at their posts, an inch of snow on every hat. The fourth, a tall but slight fellow, hunching his back against the wind, rasped, "It's Mister. Open the main bay!" When I hesitated for a second, pondering who he meant and whether the contraption couldn't be brought through the door, he impatiently reiterated, "Open the ... bay!" and I detected an urgency that had trouble eschewing expletives—which were not, of course, permitted to his station.

Hastily, I shut the door and unlocked the main wagon entry. The slaves rushed inside, set the litter down, and stood to shivering attention while I re-secured the entry. The leading bearer pushed the snow off the roof with his naked hands. Presently, the *chaise's* door was opened and my employer casually stepped out, wearing a splendid—and perfectly dry—greatcoat over his elegant blue business suit. Ordinary shoes, not boots! I was astonished to feel warmth: there were heated bricks in a metal tray on the *chaise's* floor! He looked as if he'd simply walked from one room of his house to another! "Mr. Colegrove," I exclaimed, "what an unexpected honor!"

"Good afternoon, Dordrecht. Have you seen much...." He crinkled his nose. "What is that? Oh, the swine, of course. Have you mucked them today?"

With infinite relief that I'd subdued my strong impulse to postpone the job in the hope of fairer weather on the morrow, I replied in the affirmative.

"*Hmm.* Let's move upstairs, then. You may light the hearth." As we reached the second level, the relief of the four bearers at being at last able to shake the snow from their clothes was mirrored by my own dismay that the hearth had long since been burning up Mr. Colegrove's wood. But Colegrove affected not to notice as we arrived in the small third floor office. Joachim jumped up, bowed deeply, and touched his knuckles to his forehead. His master barely acknowledged his existence, and seated himself in the one solid chair. "Is the indenturee attending to his duties?"

"Joachim's efforts have been exemplary, sir."

Colegrove looked over at him—quivering with cold, fear, or both—and his nose turned up yet again. He grunted dismissively and turned back to me. "Yes. Well, I stopped by, Dordrecht, to see how you were doing … and because Glasby is working at the big warehouse today and I needed to tell you we have a timely order to be fulfilled—"

"What's that, sir?" I chirped, pushing whatever brightness I could into my voice.

"Four pigs, to the barracks. The officers are having a feast on tonight."

"Indeed, sir." Instantly, I began calculating. On a fair day, one could walk to the barracks, just north of the common, in a quarter-hour. However, it would take all afternoon to transport four live animals there in a blizzard. "We shall set about it immediately, sir," I avowed, rising hopefully.

He gestured me back down. "Peace, boy, there are other matters."

I sat again, but he seemed in no hurry to proceed. "May I get Joachim started on the job, sir? Wouldn't want the officers to be disappointed at having to wait!" Colegrove's annoyance seemed overcome by this appeal, and I hurriedly used gestures and pidgin Deutsch to convey: *four pigs into pens.* Joachim fled, thundering downstairs two steps at a time.

"At least you're getting use out of the brute," Colegrove sneered. "Good. My own opinion is that you get better value out of the blacks than these Germans."

For once, rather than offering a mild "Is that so?" I managed to hold my tongue altogether.

"I see the warehouse is in good order." It was a declarative sentence, but it sounded like a question.

"I hope so, sir. I have rearranged some of the stores, to make them more accessible and easier to count."

"*Hmm.*"

"Actually, there was a discrepancy that I brought to Mr. Glasby's attention, that greatly concerned me. He showed me his log of our lumber deliveries, and one indicated half-a-dozen wagonloads fewer than I know we sent, sir!"

"Ah yes, Glasby told me. You needn't worry."

"It must be worth a great deal of money, sir?"

"I have that in hand, Dordrecht. You manage here, that's fine."

It was inexplicable that he really didn't seem to care that the accounts should be corrected, but I had no business being impatient with my employer. I was thinking I should also have told Joachim to hitch the horse to the sleigh wagon, and that simply getting the pigs into it would take an inordinate amount of time. "Are you comfortable at Cliff Street, Dordrecht?"

It was the last question I'd expected. Mr. Colegrove's indifference to his slaves and to Joachim hardly portended great concern for myself. "I'm fine, thank you, sir."

"Do you miss your town?"

"You mean New Utrecht, sir?"

"Yes. That's where you're from, isn't it?"

"I've not thought much about it, sir. I've been very busy."

"Ah. No thought of returning soon?"

This personal line of inquiry, however flattering, made me uncomfortable. "I expect so, sir. It happens that both my sister-in-law and my sister are expecting, and soon to be delivered...."

"*Hmm.* Does your family not grow any barley, Dordrecht?"

Barley? I gaped for two seconds before replying. "We have in the past, sir, but my brother has concentrated on wheat and corn for the past four or five years. Varies as crops are rotated, of course."

"Do others grow barley?"

"I believe Mr. Loytinck tills several large fields of it. And I know there are extensive plots nearer to Flatlands."

"Is that so? That's the elderly gentleman, Loytinck?" I nodded, mystified. "Have you heard whether any disposition of his properties has been made yet?"

Meneer Loytinck and his properties were quite remote from any thought I'd had in the past weeks. "No, sir. I ... could inquire, if you'd like!"

"No no. Not necessary at all. Just curious. Do the people there speak only Dutch?"

"On the contrary, sir, most are bilingual. Even the bulk of the slaves. Dutch is the preferred language, however."

"How quaint. Do they harbor dreams that the Netherlands republic will return in force to the New World?"

"Oh I doubt that, sir. It's been a century, after all."

"So. Well, I've taken enough of your time, Dordrecht. I must be off to see Mr. Glasby at the big warehouse."

"I'm sorry we have no provision for your refreshment here, sir."

His face turned rather severe. "It's quite right that you should not, Mr. Dordrecht!" As we marched down the stairs, I thought to ask whether the bearers might be imposed upon for a minute, to help hoist the pigs into the wagon.

"I suppose so ... if it won't soil their uniforms."

Concentrating on the task at hand, I shrugged off the statement's absurdity. Joachim and I alone would have suffered mightily, hoisting the pens into the wagon, but six men together managed with speed and ease. I reckon we saved half an hour in three minutes. Mr. Colegrove, however, seemed riled, with me particularly, tapping his foot and leaving without another word. After Joachim and I had hitched the wagon and I was struggling up William Street, it occurred to me that he objected to the fact that I'd lent my arm to assist the slaves. I should have stood aside, I suppose: more in keeping with my enormous dignity!

The churches were tolling seven p.m. before I got back to the warehouse. What an awful day!

*   *   *

Mr. Glasby had another engagement following his weekly inspection tour that Wednesday, so I'd no occasion to express my bewilderment over our employer's oddities. Perhaps it's just as well!

By Saturday frantic rehearsals were on-going inside my own skull, not of Shakespearean small parts, but of how I should behave when introduced to Miss Adelie Chapman. Should I bow as Simon had? Should I attempt to kiss her hand? Should I offer to shake hands? What should I *say?*

All for nought: she wasn't there, and I was presently immersed in construction of the ghost scene, every detail of which Simon told me how to build. I was a bit annoyed by his interference until he explained that *he* was playing the murdered king's ghost. We had built the free-standing framework, stretched a black gauze over it, and were attaching shelves for the candles when, above the cacophony that normally obtained there in the fish market, a piercing male voice shrilled, "Why it's Tommy Dordrecht, my charming young cousin from the *loooong* island!"

There was no avoiding him. "Good day to you, Mr. Cooper," I said, mustering such dignity as I could—now much bespattered with paint and sawdust. He ignored my rather soiled hand, but continued to beam at me. I looked at the lace trimmings on his coat, unable to bear the horrid wig. Simon rolled his eyes and turned back to our project.

"Whatever brings you here, dear laddie? I'd no idea you were in town, or I'd have sooner sought out your company!"

Hoping to conduct this mortifying but inescapable conversation more privately, I moved apart from the others and replied softly, "I'm working for Mr. Aaron Colegrove's business firm, managing the—"

"Oh him!"

Him? "I'm managing his warehouse on Front Street, and I hope to gain—"

"No Tommy, whatever brings you *here,*" he hollered, "working with your bare *hands* in this execrable fish market, as the merest dogsbody in this lamentable excuse for thespian endeavor?"

"I—"

"*Don't* tell me Mr. Ingraham persuaded you to slave away for nothing more than the glory of the Bard!"

"Well—"

"Oh Ingraham, you're *such* a fraud!" Cooper expostulated. Ingraham was mercifully out of hearing, but a dozen others were not. "Taking advantage of this innocent country lad! Shocking, shocking!"

I imagine my face was scarlet by this time, but some of the seamstresses near us were howling with laughter—whether at Cooper's or Ingraham's or my expense I couldn't guess. "Do tell, Mr. Cooper!" Katherine exclaimed.

Thinking to extricate myself before I should be motivated to violence, I said, "If you'll excuse me, Mr. Cooper, I am needed—"

"Oh it's 'Charlie' to *you*, Tommy!"

I was about to growl, *And it's 'Mr. Dordrecht' to* you, *god damn it*—when Adelie Chapman appeared, smiling, out of nowhere, and took his arm.

"Adelie! *Darling!*" Cooper gushed in full voice. They kissed each other's cheeks, twice, in what I gather is the French fashion.

"Good afternoon, Charles," she said simply, her voice warm and clear. The sweet produce of beehives did come to mind.

"Adelie, my own, you must meet one of the few presentable members of the Dutch side of my family. This is Tommy Dordrecht, my mother's—"

This was *not* how I'd imagined it. I drew myself tall. "Thomas Dordrecht, ma'am," I interjected hastily. "Your servant."

She offered her hand and I … shook it. She seemed gratified, and I exhaled a tiny sigh of relief. "Pleased, Mr. Dordrecht!" she said, regarding me directly.

"Tommy is my mother's brother's son, they're from way out in the country where they still haven't figured out who George the Second is, and—"

"You're the lad who plays the guitar!" she exclaimed.

"I've only recently taken it up, ma'am."

"He has an older brother who scares *my* older brother, if you can believe that!" Cooper babbled.

"We shall have to arrange a rehearsal, Mr. Dordrecht," she said, ignoring him.

"I am at your disposal, ma'am. That is, at any time when I'm not at my employer's disposal, ma'am!"

"But of course, Mr. Dordrecht," she said, smiling.

"Miss Chapman, darling!" Ingraham was suddenly bellowing. He joined us, took her by the elbow, and deftly turned her toward the central hearth. "We must work over the scene with Laertes."

Cooper followed after them without another word. Miss Chapman turned back briefly, smiled, and nodded.

I was completely dazzled.

*   *   *

When Mr. Glasby next did me the honor of inviting me to join him for supper, I fear I imposed on his patience with endless effusions of praise for Miss Adelie Chapman. He seemed quite content to endure descriptions of her pretty, oval face, splendidly proportioned stature, and fair, wavy brown hair. He exhibited little impatience with the details of her cornflower blue eyes, her straight nose—which I conceded might be considered "slightly aggressive," and her full, cherry lips.

But when I began itemizing the cut and decoration of her elegant though simple pink linen gown, he broke in with, "How old is this woman, Mr. Dordrecht?"

How ... *old?* The question had, of course, occurred to me, but aside from noting the obvious fact that she was senior to myself, I'd not given it much thought—or perhaps I'd *avoided*.... "I suppose she may be all of twenty-five, Mr. Glasby, although—"

"She lives with her parents then, I presume? Who are they?"

He'd stopped me cold in the instant of raising a chunk of mutton to my lips. These were, of course, the very first questions asked about any unmarried woman—and they'd not even occurred to me before this moment. I set my knife down and stammered, "I recall one of the women artisans saying she'd come over alone, some five years ago, to serve as a governess to the children of Reverend Thwaite."

But Thwaite, as everyone knew, had found colonial life intolerable and long ago returned to England. "And since?" Glasby persisted. I could only shrug. "Remarkable for an unattached woman to manage on her own resources," he observed, perfectly straightforwardly. Now thinking of it, I knew that most people would be rushing to make undignified assumptions about Miss Chapman at this point. Perhaps it had not struck me so odd because I knew my own mother had arrived in America unchaperoned—a curious history the reasons for which she'd never really disclosed to any of us. "Remarkable," Mr. Glasby repeated.

We immediately began discussing when the rivers might thaw so that local commerce might resume in earnest.

It was disappointing that I received no summons to rehearse with Miss Chapman. The next sighting I had of her was a full week after the last, amid even more frantic preparations for the performance, now but seven days away. Mr. Ingraham announced that, to his great regret and chagrin, the site he'd planned for the performance had proven unavailable and therefore the play would take place ... right there in the fish market. A large quantity of new lumber had been delivered, and he hoped his loyal artisans could construct a stage—one that could be dismantled during the hours of business and quickly reconstructed as needed.

"Bloody hell!" Simon muttered.

Despite the ferocious clatter of the crewmen, including myself wielding hammer and saw until my arm ached, the rehearsal proceeded apace, the director shouting his commands—and the actors their lines—over the din. Everyone stayed at work until near ten p.m. I sought out Miss Chapman at that time, and said that I hoped we might have a chance to rehearse— particularly since I'd no idea what the song was.

"Oh of course, Mr. Dordrecht, of course!" she exclaimed, looking distracted and harried ... and beautiful. "I'm sorry, I'm afraid I'm preoccupied at this moment by the fact that Mr. Ingraham has asked me to paint the scenery drops, which I'd planned to do here tomorrow, but which is now impossible." She looked questioningly at Simon, who'd joined us.

"Afraid so, Miss. Me and three other lads will be working here all day tomorrow. Need the whole floor."

"I just need clear space for about six hours, Simon!"

"I know that, ma'am. And I've no idea what's to be done."

"The constables?" I interjected.

He snorted. "Been taken care of, lad. But we mustn't have more than four at work, even still."

Miss Chapman sighed deeply ... and it occurred to me that the floor of the warehouse was at the moment clear and free of livestock. And that painting was a quiet occupation. And that Joachim, whom I felt sure would not betray me, had told me no one ever stopped by on Sundays....

Suffice it that my idea had no sooner been conceived than it was carved in stone. The arrangement was made that I was to bring the sleigh to the fish market at ten o'clock, take the scenery cloths and paints to the warehouse, where I'd assist Miss Chapman in the painting, so that it could all be returned before dark.

It was only as I fell onto my pallet an hour later that I realized I'd not eaten all day.

*   *   *

Miss Chapman painted with a speed that was quite staggering to me. I'd imagined that canvases of the size contemplated would take weeks, at least, to accomplish. From paper sketches, she outlined each "backdrop" in charcoal in a matter of minutes. One was to represent the dark stone exterior of Castle Elsinore, the other a festive court reception room. She kept me busy mixing paints, making measurements, and drawing straight lines for many hours—during which I felt rather deliriously elated. Joachim stood aside, awed.

We had completed the exterior and were making great strides on the reception hall when the entry bell rang. Our concentration was so great that all three of us squawked in alarm. A constable I feared, rather than my employer. I pulled myself together and strode over to answer it. It was ... *the wig*.

"Tommy!" my cousin yowled. Not wanting any passing stevedores to see him, I hurried him inside. "And there's my darling Adelie!" I slammed the door shut. "How are you both today? My, what a dreary establishment!"

Joachim was staring, open-mouthed in shock. "This is Joachim, Mr. Cooper," I said.

"Indeed. Good heavens, you actually *work* here, Tommy?"

"Oh do let the lad alone, Charles," Miss Chapman said with formidable equanimity. "Do you think I have the right shade of blue in the sky, there?"

She pointed to the exterior drop, and Cooper unexpectedly turned stock still and contemplated her question for a full minute. "Yes," he finally said, "but the gray of the stones is too light."

She stood up and moved over beside him. "You're right, it wants more shading."

"It might be nice to make the red roof tiles a little brighter?"

"It's supposed to be gloomy," she protested.

"Even so."

Miss Chapman contemplated her work for another minute, then mixed a bit more vermillion into the red pot and, in just another moment, had—to my amazement and speechless admiration—lightened the roof tiles and altered the mood of the composition. "Much better," Cooper said.

It then occurred to me to wonder how Cooper had discovered us. "How did you find out—"

"I make it my business to know *everything* that goes on in New York City, Tommy!"

"I beg your pardon?"

"Your cousin is what is known as a scandal-monger, Mr. Dordrecht," Miss Chapman said forthrightly.

"Heavens, Adelie, how you talk!"

"Rumor has it that the scribblings of '*Sejanus*' are attributable to his pen."

This suggestion caused me some consternation. Letters from *Sejanus* had much upset the town's aldermen the previous fall, when he'd forecast a sweep of the press by the Navy. If he was truly that writer, it could be as dangerous to know him as it would've been for an ancient Roman to know his namesake, the evil spy and henchman of the emperor Tiberius. "Is that the case, Mr. Cooper?" I asked.

"Surely you can't imagine such a thing, cousin," he said blandly.

"Charles, you do understand that it's imperative that Mr. Dordrecht's employers never learn of our presence here this afternoon?"

"Adelie, whatever do you take me for?" She rolled her eyes sardonically and dipped her brush carefully in the blue bucket. "I would never put our Tommy at—"

"Charles, for heaven's sake!"

"Our *Thomas*, yes. He needn't concern himself on my account."

She is amazing! How did she know he was infuriating me with every address? How did she get him to stop with four words? We both watched her paint in a pair of heraldic banners, which looked exactly as if they were hanging from wooden rafters.

"As a matter of fact," Cooper announced, "I came here not merely to observe the glorious progress of high culture in our province, but to convey Mother's invitation to supper this evening."

"That's extremely kind, Charles, but we're hardly dressed!"

"Oh, I explained that to her, and for this event she waives the formalities, so eager is she to have her beloved war hero of a nephew to the house!" My recollection of my aunt's proclivities made this sound quite dubious. She'd always struck me as one for whom formalities were invariably to be honored … and the rest was preposterous.

"I've been a guest at your aunt's before, Mr. Dordrecht," Miss Chapman said, "and I do declare she sets a good table. So I'd be pleased—We'd never make it before seven, Charles!—but only if you care to consent?"

Both turned to me, and I froze in a quandary, suspended between fascination with her, distrust of him, and feeling duty-bound to my aunt. "I was rather hoping you might also favor us with a rehearsal of your song," Cooper added smoothly.

"Yes of course," I said.

He managed to pat my cheek before I realized what he was doing. "We'll see you around seven, then."

After I'd closed the door behind him, Miss Chapman shook her head and said, "He put his mother up to it, of course. He's incorrigible!"

*   *   *

My cousin Charles virtually monopolized conversation during an excellent, much needed meal. His mother appeared to regard his every word as brilliant. His father, a furniture dealer—well-to-do though not in Mr. Colegrove's class—struck me as combining sourness and resignation in equal measure. He scowled at the liberal quantities of red wine his son poured, but said almost nothing. The elder brother, my cousin Henry, was absent. He was recently ordained a Presbyterian divine and now resided in a manse on the edge of town. He was apparently an even less loved sibling to Charles Cooper than Harmanus was to me. Their younger sister, Mary Cooper Fitzweiler, the only member of the household I remember truly liking, lived nearby with her husband's family, and was presently expecting her fourth child.

My aunt and uncle retired immediately after the meal—quite to my regret, as we'd barely come respectably to date with our mutual family. Charles—at length I'd been coaxed into using given names—took Adelie and myself into the drawing room, where the servant had set a fire, and insisted we rehearse our song. Adelie was very patient with my effort to read and play the accompaniment, and Charles was suddenly considerate, encouraging, even helpful. Much to my relief he took off the hideous wig, and the only problem with him was that his hair had gone thin. On my third try, I managed to get through the song nearly *a tempo*, so Adelie tried singing it through with me—which was enchanting. We essayed it once again, and she pronounced us ready to face Mr. Ingraham.

Charles produced three glasses of Madeira—which I'd never before even heard of, and which I quite liked. Adelie and I were sitting together on the settee, and Charles balanced himself on the arm of it, next to me. Presently, the three of us were crammed together, facing the fire and savoring the cordial. I was rather awed to listen to them as they gossiped and bantered across me, talking with equal ease about the fashions of Paris and the "most recent absurdity" to emanate from the city council. They seemed so sophisticated, so wise to the ways of the world; their conversation ranged to topics undreamt of in New Utrecht, and I eagerly absorbed it all, daring only occasionally to put in a word.

I admit that however much they excited me, they also made me rather nervous as they leant against me to refill their glasses.

A nearby church's bells struck ten o'clock. "It's snowing again," Charles sighed. "You must both stay the night! Adelie can have the guest room and Thomas can—"

"No," said Adelie simply. "Thank you, Charles, but I'll see myself home."

"It's *snowing*, darling!" he wailed.

"It does that, most winters."

I finally roused myself to the emergency. "Of course I'll be honored to escort Miss Chapman," I announced, weaving upright.

"Oh very well," Charles pouted.

As Adelie and I reached her residence—a boarding house directly across from Mr. Martin's grocery on Stone Street—I was rather hoping she might favor me with a kiss…. "Thank you so much, Thomas," she said, shaking my hand with the candid directness I now regarded as characteristic. "It's been a pleasure working with you today!"

With a smile and a nod, she closed the door. Nonetheless, I felt no heavier than a snowflake as I trudged my way home.

*   *   *

The lingering reek of the swine, I was relieved to observe, overwhelmed that of the scenery paint—substantial in its own right—and my illicit escapade went undetected. I cemented Joachim's silence with a pork pasty the next day, which apparently firmly established me as his friend for life.

The week passed swiftly, events merging into a blur as surely as Adelie's colors had smoothed from blue to gray to black. I must have played that blessed song a hundred times. The weather broke on Friday, and was well above freezing on the day of the performance, which gratified the members of the company, who considered that weather had much to do with the willingness of paying customers to attend.

And attend they did, and applaud they did, although it was often difficult to follow the play given their constant talking, eating, smoking, and spitting. A great many derisive whistles greeted the ghost effect in Act One, but Ophelia's song was met with demands for an *encore*, which we duly provided. The bloodbath at the end—which I for one had found quite difficult to credit—touched off great moans of horror and shock, and led to a tumultuous ovation for the entire company.

The entire house swooped backstage after the curtain, and I saw my cousin knowing and greeting everybody. My aunt and her neighbor were kind enough to praise my guitar-playing. And Mr. Glasby seemed pleased and even flattered to be introduced to Miss Chapman. However, the celebration was not scheduled until the following Thursday, when the profits, however modest, were to be divided—according to a schedule of contributions that guaranteed me at least tuppence. Given that I was likely to squander a whole shilling on meat and drink … oh, no matter!

Tuesday's *Intelligencer*, however, contained a letter from "Sejanus," that affected to analyze the recent performance of *Hamlet* … and thoroughly savaged it, with the "luminous exception" of Miss Chapman's performance as Ophelia. Mr. Ingraham was instructed in the harshest terms to ponder his own character's advice to his players before he ever again set foot on a stage. "Notwithstanding the lamentable quality of the production," "Sejanus" wrote on, "we can only deplore those interfering citizens such as the pompous Rev.

Henry Cooper, who would petition the city to proscribe all thespian activities in the future, a move that would indubitably ensure that New York's status as a provincial backwater remains permanent."

His willingness to offend absolutely everyone took my breath away. It was amazing he hadn't complained about the chords I fumbled.

Even more surprising was his presence at the party. I heard his inimitable voice the instant I walked into the tavern, and saw him talking with Simon—who was evidently as ignorant of my cousin's double life as of my neighbor's. But I'd just taken my first swallow of ale when Simon squawked, "He *what?*" at the top of his lungs.

All conversation ceased. Simon was deeply flushed and clearly suffering a press of emotion.

"You were expecting him?" Charles said with suspicious equanimity. "But I saw Régine and Mr. Ingraham boarding the packet for Philadelphia that left on the four o'clock tide."

Simon swore loudly and bitterly. "Forget the shilling in profit," he exploded. "The bastard owes me thirteen and eight for my out-of-pocket!"

Others clamored in, protesting with equal vehemence and indignation, not least Adelie Chapman. "I suppose I can at least claim the paints and the brushes," she moaned. "They'll be somewhat useful for my sign-painting work."

As speechless as all the others, I could offer no condolences or suggestions. Presently, however, the tavern-keeper rang a bell and announced that Mr. Ingraham had, as a parting gesture, contributed four kegs of ale toward the evening's festivities, the first of which had just been tapped.... This token did not succeed in restoring Mr. Ingraham to any high level of estimation, but it unquestionably eased the bitterness among his former colleagues. Many a jape was declaimed at his expense, but the overall mood soon lightened. My cousin I spied at a table, by himself with pen and paper, scratching away in a frantic ecstasy of concentration. Some twenty minutes later—I was on my fourth tankard, having neglected to partake of any food—Miss Chapman rang the barman's bell and climbed onto a chair, flourishing the very same papers. After a brave show of vocalizing, she began, *a capella*:

> *Mr. Ingraham was protector of the Bard's pure light*
> *When he boffed our Régine on one fine night.*
> *This fornication bore, you see,*
> *A production of* Hamlet, *ex-act-lee!*
> *Oh ho ho, the wind blows free,*
> *And we open next month in Philadelph-i-ee!*

There were two more verses, and she had to repeat the lot, and then the entire assemblage had to sing it all twice. Then Simon came up with a verse, and it had to be repeated four times, and what's-his-name, Polonius, had another. Like all the merry crew, I was laughing so hard I'd no chance to consider how shocking it was, how rude, or how particularly appalling it should be that Mish Chapman, who'd seemed so respectable, was shinging such scurrilous shongs, such scurrilousness, such scurrility, scurvy-ous scurrtionality!

I remember a gleeful snowball fight in front of the fort, as Trinity's bells were chiming eleven, and that a faintly familiar *chaise* passed by and got hit by one such missile just as I ... upchucked.

How I got home ... I've no recollection.

*   *   *

"Dordrecht! Are you all right?"

It was Mr. Glasby. It was my room at Brown's. It was light out. "What...?"

"It's nearly nine o'clock, lad!"

"Oh my ... heavens, Mr. Glasby," I moaned, rising to a sitting position and instantly feeling the worse for it. "I'm so dreadfully sorry. I shall be at the warehouse in twenty minutes, I assure—"

"I'm afraid that will not be necessary, Dordrecht." I struggled to focus my eyes and speak coherently; regaining dignity was not in the cards. "Mr. Colegrove, I'm sorry to tell you, has seen fit to terminate your employment, effective immediately."

This was staggering to me. "Because I am tardy this morning? Sir, I promise I shall make it up to him, and—"

"No, Dordrecht, because he chanced to observe you in public last night. 'In the company of uncouth ruffians,' was how he put it."

"But—"

"I greatly regret his decision, Dordrecht, and I'm confoundedly sorry he's not more forgiving, but.... Yeaman endured far worse behavior from me, I assure you, but...." It took a solid minute for the full realization to sink home. "I'm afraid he insists that you also directly vacate your room here." That too? *What a deprivation!* Glasby indicated the volume of Montesquieu on the chair. "Oh, and is this one of his books?"

"I'm only up to Diocletian!" I protested. Then shame overtook me. "I beg your pardon, Mr. Glasby."

"There is the Society Library, you know," he said. "If you've any of your prize money left, you could afford a subscription." But he took the Montesquieu. "Are you ... in need of ready funds, Dordrecht?"

It took five frantic seconds to locate my purse. But only four pence were inside it. Just enough to get me ... *home.* "I'm quite all right, thank you kindly, sir," I said with relief.

"Sure?"

"Aye sir. I didn't bring all my money here."

"Most prudent. I shall leave your remaining wages in Joachim's care next Wednesday." He stood up, and I scrambled awkwardly to join him. "If there's anything you do need, Mr. Dordrecht, rest assured that you still have a friend in John Glasby!"

I was nearly overcome. "I thank you most humbly, sir, and I vow the same to you."

"Good day then, lad." We shook hands.

And when he was gone, I was overcome.

CHAPTER 5

Perhaps there might've been some way I could have avoided throwing myself on the mercies of my family, but my fixed idea of the day was to retrieve a portion of my resources from the barn ... and then decide my next move. My dismissal had stunned me so severely that perhaps I was not thinking sensibly. Among other things, I wasted a considerable part of my energies angrily contemplating the injustice of it.

It should not have been a surprise—but it was—that my homecoming from New York City was not met with the rejoicing that had greeted my safe return from the army four months before. I walked into the middle of what appeared to be a very glum, uncomfortable family repast. My father was slouched in his chair at the head of the table, and everyone was glowering at him. Fortunately, there were no guests present. "Oh look," he roared, "the prodigal son has returned! Where the hell have you been?"

Only my sister Elisabeth rose to embrace me, and her glance beseeched me not to voice the offense I felt. Universal irritation with Pa was apparently overwhelming any pleasure—I was not positive I detected any—at seeing me. "I'll get you a bowl of stew," she said kindly.

Silence prevailed. Berendina and Hendrik only moved aside when Elisabeth set my bowl between them. "To what do we owe this honor, Thomas?" my father inquired ominously as I sat.

Preoccupied as I'd been with fury at Mr. Colegrove, I'd rehearsed my reply to this question only once. I'd not imagined the entire family facing me. Pushing my chin high, I said, "I've been sacked."

The only reaction was that every shoulder appeared to droop a little lower. "What's 'sacked'?" Petrus asked.

"Time for bed!" Anneke replied, rising with difficulty. Her huge belly reminded me that her time was obviously close. The moment of clatter allowed me to ingest a few morsels. I was expecting pots of sarcasm from my brother, but he merely stood up, looking completely exhausted, and escorted his wife up the stairs. He has wisps of gray on his temples, I noticed. I felt a cad for having written only once while I was away.

"Your room's made up," Mother said quietly. "We'll talk in the morning. I'll help you clear, Elisabeth."

Suddenly I was alone in our main hall with my father, whose interest—and venom—seemed to have evaporated. Now I was both upset and curious. "What on earth was going on when I walked in here, Pa?"

"Don't take that tone with me, boy!"

"Pa!"

"None of your damn business!" He rose and stomped out of the room, leaving me shaken by this reminder that my problems were not the only ones in the world. I've seldom felt so lonely or chastened or bereft as I did when I blew out my candle that night.

My discomfiture was only increased when I again overslept in the morning. It was nearly eight o'clock when I sheepishly asked Mother if there was any porridge left. "Your father," she explained as she handed me a bowl, "quarreled with Juffrouw Katelaar yesterday afternoon. In public. Just outside the kerk."

It was totally incomprehensible. "With Juffrouw Katelaar?" The Loytinck lands did not abut ours. I couldn't conceive any occasion for disagreement—much less a public scene.

"He was telling her she ought to tell her grandfather to sell off some of their properties, and she politely but firmly told him to mind his own business."

"Oh," I groaned. "But isn't that what Meneer Van Klost was hoping Pa would do?"

"Meneer Van Klost asked him to talk to Loytinck himself, and privately!" Mother sighed with exasperation. "He really should have known better than to ask Rykert to intervene, he's just not—"

"Mother, come quickly!" Elisabeth was calling. Mother rushed upstairs. "It's Anneke's time, Thomas," Elisabeth explained to me excitedly a moment later. "Can you … manage here? We need you. Mother wants me to assist her with the deliveries!"

I suddenly saw a new maturity in my sister. "And you want to do this, Lisa?"

"Oh yes, Thomas! Very—"

"Water, Elisabeth!"

"Coming, Mother!" She turned back to me. "We'll need a lot today. Can you make a couple trips to the well? Oh, and get word out to Harmanus—the north field this morning—and try to keep the children out of the house. And can you put a full kettle on the fire right now? Thanks." She took a small pail and hurried up to Anneke and Harmanus' bedroom.

By late afternoon, the household began to realize that something was horribly wrong. My sister-in-law's screams seemed, if anything, more intense than those of Jenneken. Anneke, Lisa reported in nervous haste, was suffering unusually. Berendina had taken her brothers to visit friends on the far side of the square. Harmanus, back early from the fields, came down after an hour with the women, pale and trembling, and asked for *genever*—Dutch gin. From him, that was a ringing indication of distress. "This isn't normal, Thomas," he whispered hoarsely. "She didn't have this much trouble with the first one. I—"

"What does Mother say?"

"She won't say. First she told me to go to kerk and pray.... Then she ordered me to have a drink!"

Oh. Anneke wailed again, and Harmanus took a big gulp. I thought of pouring one for myself, but decided liquor had gotten me in enough trouble for one week.

"I.... We could ... *lose* her, Thomas," Harmanus moaned, his lips quivering. "I can't imagine how—" The front door slammed, and Grootmoeder pattered obliviously to her rocker by the fire. Perhaps she's gone deaf? Harmanus seemed to pull himself together by sheer willpower. He imbibed the remaining half of his glass with one swallow, coughed, and said, "I must go back and be confident and cheerful, Mother said."

I am seldom moved to pious expressions, but "God be with you!" seemed right for the moment, and Harmanus appeared to rally a little. "Thank you, brother," he said. "God save us all."

Twenty minutes later, Bertie Hampers walked in. "Thomas!" he exclaimed, stopping to give Grootmoeder her due kiss, "I didn't know you were home. When did you get here?" My explanations were interrupted by shrieks from upstairs. "Whew!" he breathed. "But ... Jenneken and the baby came through all right." I poured him the requested ale. "Uncle Rykert, I'm sorry to tell you, Thomas, has been ... stranger than ever."

"Drunk all the time now?"

"Aye. And quarrelsome. A farmer from Flatlands told me he's traveling directly to New Jersey, to avoid staying here."

"He picked some quarrel with Juffrouw Katelaar yesterday, outside the kerk?"

"He did. Drew a crowd, and people got really upset. And ... you know, she's not that easy a woman to sympathize with, Thomas, but there was no doubt who was causing the bother."

I grimaced, wondering what had gone so terribly wrong with my father's better nature. "Have you seen him today? Any minute, we hope to have a grandchild for him, and he's hiding in a barn somewhere?"

"Saw him on the square, an hour ago."

"He's not—"

Screams from upstairs came simultaneously with a commotion of angry bellowing outside. The door flew open and my father, a crazed, gleeful look on his face, dashed in, shouting, "They're after me!" He looked frantically about the room, like a child playing a hiding game. "They're after me! Where can I—"

Another scream from my sister-in-law drew his attention upwards, and he dashed for the stairs as Meneer Schuppert, wheezing, barged furiously into the room. *"No, Pa!"* I shouted, rushing to the foot of the stairs. Two more men ran into the house. "Bertie, don't let them up!" I heard Schuppert yelling at Bertie as I reached the top ... and heard Harmanus, Mother, and Elisabeth yelling at Pa. He'd run into the very birthing chamber! I got to the bedroom's door in time to see Harmanus chasing Pa out from under the bed—where he was still yelling "They're after me!"—and into my clutches at the door. As angry as I'd ever seen him, Harmanus put his hands on Pa's neck and began to squeeze. From struggling to control Pa, I now struggled with Elisabeth to keep my brother from literally strangling him. We were only successful when Bertie joined us, having talked decency into the men below.

"Out!" Elisabeth ordered. All four males obediently shuffled into the hall. "Not you," she said, tugging Harmanus by his sleeve.

Harmanus, panting, looked urgently between his father and his wife and the angry men below. "I'll manage this," I asserted. He looked at me, wide-eyed and desperate. Again Anneke screamed.

"Let me handle it, Harmanus!" I persisted. Dazed, he allowed Lisa to pull him back inside, and she shut the door.

Pa took the moment of our distraction to flee up to the attic. Bertie and I, followed by two of the younger men of the town, dashed after him. But before we'd even made it to the top, I heard a familiar, unmistakable *clunk* followed by a *thud*. We found him flat on his back, blood dripping from a gash on his forehead. He'd hit the rafter. Still panting heavily, he leant to one side ... and vomited. The smell, heavy with alcohol, was—

"Oh my *god!*" Bertie groaned.

Three others joined us, the last being Dominie Van Voort. "Bring him downstairs, lads," he ordered us authoritatively, holding his handkerchief to his nose. "He must answer for this."

For what? I wondered anxiously, as the four of us younger men took my barely conscious sire by his extremities and negotiated him down our narrow staircases.

Over a dozen people were angrily milling in our main room, and their ire grew vociferous as we propped Pa on the floor with his back to the wall. He fell over to the side. "Quiet *please!*" I begged as another howl from above pierced even this din. The clamor abated. "Will somebody please tell me what's going on?"

Many began talking at once, but Meneer Loytinck strode forth and announced, "Rykert Dordrecht is under arrest!"

Loytinck, I recalled, had the authority to say this by virtue of being the town's *schout*—the office the English call a sheriff. Election to the thankless post was curiously more likely an expression of public disdain than an honor; nonetheless, its few distasteful duties had to be faithfully executed—and arresting those who disturbed the peace was one of them.

"On what charge, Meneer Loytinck?" I demanded.

"Drunkenness and ... public indecency!" Loytinck hissed, his worn face scarlet. People growled and shook their fists at my immobile father.

"Oh no!" Bertie moaned.

"Exactly how did this come about?"

"He accosted my own granddaughter, an honest woman, on the square, and he dared to call her—"

"Wait!" Dominie Van Voort strode to the front door and opened it. "Children, out!" he commanded. The three youngsters, knowing better than ever to challenge an order from the dominie, vacated the house in seconds. The adults seemed appreciative of a nicety they hadn't themselves conceived. The dominie nodded to the schout.

"He dared to call her a 'fat bitch!'" Loytinck said, furiously.

The townsfolk looked horrified, and I confess I'd not imagined their affront to be so dire. "But—"

"Well she is fat and she *is* a bitch!" my father yowled, unexpectedly revived.

Uproar. There were many demands that he should be flogged, though all knew that would involve the authorities in the county seat. Vrouw Schuppert was shaking her finger in Pa's face, which provoked a snarling, "And *you're* a skinny old—"

Bertie clamped his hand over Pa's mouth just in time to prevent his digging his hole any deeper. Loytinck, Van Klost, and Van Voort closed into a conference, and the room finally became subdued as all awaited the result.

The wait was at least three minutes. Finally Loytinck drew his aged frame upright and announced, "Twenty-four hours in the stocks!"

Though I'd feared worse, my head reeled with concern over the management of this sentence as my heart sank with the sheer familial humiliation of it, which would make it difficult for any Dordrecht to hold his or her head high for months to come. "Let's go!" one of the younger men roared, grabbing my father under one arm.

"Not now," Loytinck protested.

"Tomorrow noon, then?"

"Sabbath!" Van Voort said indignantly.

"Monday noon?" Van Klost asked.

Van Voort was about to nod. "Gentlemen," I managed to protest, "may I beg, on behalf of my family, a mercy?" My sister-in-law fortuitously shrieked on cue. "Can you give us a week to prepare for this? Please remember that, though my father has forgotten himself on this day, the rest of us are hoping for a blessed event at any hour...." And fearing the worst, I didn't need to add.

The three went back into conference. I wished Anneke's father, the eminently sensible Meneer ter Oonck, were not away visiting his sons. Van Voort delivered the verdict. "We will consider your request on the morrow, but your father must be constrained until he is stocked. And the usual place...." Is in our cellar, the only one in town with full standing room. We had once kept a runaway indenturee there overnight, but I couldn't recall any other use of it.

Van Klost stated what had been obvious to everyone else: "You will have to swear to maintain your father in chains, Sergeant Dordrecht."

Another howl from above kept me from fainting, and rallied my wits. "May I ask.... If others will be so good as to *put* him down there ... I will vouch to *keep* him down there. Please don't ask me to—"

"Reasonable," the dominie judged, forestalling an objection from Loytinck. He nodded to the two younger men, who lifted my father to his feet and dragged him to the cellar door, where Bertie showed them the way.

*   *   *

Anneke's anguish—and that of the Dordrecht family—was not relieved the instant they all vacated the house. Lisa said it was unusual for women to be given spirits to ease their pain, but Mother had allowed Anneke two tots of gin. Word having gotten round of our several miseries, no one popped into the tavern to offer encouragement or even to partake of an afternoon tipple, so I jumped when mother's friend Katryne Nijenhuis suddenly appeared at my side shortly after dark, having come in through the kitchen. "Oh, sorry to startle you, Thomas dear!" she exclaimed, setting baskets down. I was moved to embrace her as heartily as I did when I was twelve. Vrouw Nijenhuis is Mother's age, but plump and blonde and ebullient rather than slim and dark and thoughtful. But it was her invariable good nature that relieved me now. "Any word, upstairs?"

I shook my head. Anneke hadn't broken the peace for some time, I realized, an absence that was as alarming as consoling.

"It takes time, Thomas," she said, looking me in the eye. "Don't despair!" As always, she was very comforting. "I brought some food. All of them have to eat, whether they want it or not. Even your father."

She knew, of course. But neither of us were eager to talk about him.

"Berendina is staying overnight with the Schuppert girls, and the boys are staying with Lodewyk and me."

It shamed me that I'd not given them a single thought. "Oh. Thank you!"

We heard a scream while Vrouw Nijenhuis was showing me how to prepare the food she'd brought in the kitchen. Both of us started. "You know, Thomas," she babbled as we chopped turnips and carrots, "bringing *you* into the world caused your mother a good deal of anguish. You took a long time!" I stared at her, dumbfounded. "I remember very well. Your poor brother, the invincible Harmanus, was frightened out of his wits, sure she would die."

"Because of me?"

"Aye."

"*Hmm!* And … what was Pa doing?"

Vrouw Nijenhuis shook her thick graying-blonde tresses. "I don't know what's happened to your father in the last few years, Thomas. We were all horrified when little Aalbert died, but…." Following her nods, I lifted another log into the stove. She changed the subject. "It was when your mother was so impressed by Vrouw Zuykenaar's help with your birth that she decided to take up midwifery." Now I was speechless. "You were a *big* baby! She told me she believed Vrouw Zuykenaar had saved both your lives, and she more or less apprenticed herself to the woman until she died, four or five years ago. And now, look, your mother is in demand and makes real money for the family!"

"Do you think it's right that she should be pulling Elisabeth into this too?" This question had been nagging at me all day.

"Of course, Thomas, if the girl's willing. Me, I earn an extra penny or two taking in mending, so we can afford our fancy little cakes for Pinkster, but I could never work up the nerve to be a midwife!" She checked the fire. "Good: no more than half an hour! Chastity will judge whether Anneke should eat anything, but *I* say you're to stand over the other three until they've each downed a full bowl, you understand?" She gave me another hug as she bustled out, murmuring, "What a good thing you came home, Thomas!"

Mother set the example, half an hour later, by forcing herself to eat the stew. Neither Harmanus nor Lisa wanted any, and Vrouw Nijenhuis had been right that I practically had to force them to eat it.

Then I forced myself to eat a bowl.

Then I had to deal with Pa.

*   *   *

"Where have you been, Thomas? Get me out of this!" my father commanded. I placed the candle on a storage box.

"Here's a roll, Pa. I'll bring you some stew in a minute."

"The key's under the cutlery bin in the bar."

A two-foot chain held his wrist to the floor. He could lie down but not stand up. "Do you need a bucket?" On closer inspection, I could see it was already somewhat late for that. I found one and placed it near him.

"I *need* to get out of here!"

"Anneke's still fighting it out. Mother's not saying what she thinks, and Harmanus is at his wits' end."

Pa shocked me by sneering, "Harmanus! Goddam crybaby!"

Many's the time I've cursed my eldest brother, but *that* had never occurred to me. "I'll get the stew," I announced, turning back.

The roll hit me in the back of the head. "Get the damn *key*, Thomas!"

Making no rush, I returned with a bowl of stew and a jug of water three minutes later. "Vrouw Nijenhuis was good enough to—"

"Did you bring the key, boy?"

"No sir."

"I told you to fetch the key."

We'd never before come to a direct impasse. "I'm not going to fetch the key, Pa."

"What do you mean! I told you to—"

"If I let you go, Pa, Meneer Loytinck will arrest me, and we'll *both* end up in the stocks!"

"Why should he ever know? Now come on, boy!"

"No, Pa." I realized he'd nag and wheedle as long as I stayed there, so I set the food down, and turned to leave.

"I'm not going to forgive this, Thomas! This is—"

"Well, begging your pardon, Father, but it'll be a sweet long time before I or any of your family or your neighbors forgive *you* for your antics this afternoon!"

"Come on, boy, you can't leave me like this!"

Oh yes I can. "Do you want me to leave the candle?"

"God damn it!" I picked up the candle and started up. "Leave the candle," he called morosely.

I stepped back down and replaced it on the box. Then I left him.

There was one great roar of rage and frustration from the cellar, as shattering as any of Anneke's screams from her childbed, but then I heard no more.

*   *   *

Anneke's labor continued through the night. I took a shift watching at the bedside around dawn. I'd sooner keep watch for tomahawk-wielding savages.

When Mother finally reappeared, she detained me until she'd first reappraised her sleeping patient. "Thomas, you do realize it's essential that you escort Grootmoeder and the children to kerk this morning?" It was Sunday, and the last thing I'd been thinking of was going to church. "Elisabeth, Harmanus, and I simply cannot leave, and … given what happened yesterday.…"

"Pa?"

She nodded uncomfortably. "Please, Thomas. I know you don't want to—"

She astounded me, as she so often had before. How the heck did she know that? I barely knew it myself, and was only at that instant inspired to realize that I'd never attended once in New York.

"—but if we've ever meant anything to you, I beg you to—"

"Ma, Ma! Of course I'll go."

"One family member must hold his head up and candidly greet our neighbors."

"Yes ma'am."

"And remind the dominie to pray for Anneke."

"Yes."

She exhaled, apparently more relieved than I'd have thought necessary. She smiled. "You'd best shave before you go, Mr. Dordrecht!"

Instantly my hand went to my chin. She was quite right, it had been days. Anneke stirred as her travails began again, and I took my leave.

Had she ever called me *Mister* before? I don't think she had.

I felt more self-conscious in my role as Representative of the Dordrecht Clan than I had as Spear-Carrier to King Claudius, but I think I managed to bring it off. The children—rushed home to don their Sunday best, get reassured by Aunt Lisa, and get lectured by their father—behaved with unexpected perfection. If Grootmoeder noticed that she was holding onto a different grandson's arm, she gave no indication. Meneer and Vrouw Nijenhuis greeted us warmly, but I had to make a deliberate point of wishing everyone else a good day.

Two who apparently left by a different aisle to avoid us were Meneer Loytinck and his granddaughter, Marijke Katelaar. Several people greeted them ... and cast dubious, suspicious glances in our direction. Though I began to feel stifled—and suddenly intensely homesick for the reeking streets of the city—it drove home how necessary my attendance had been. Unless faced down immediately, everyone in the family was going to suffer terribly for Pa's misbehavior.

Taking care to avoid any impertinence, I studied the outraged Juffrouw Katelaar, whom I'd not seen in over a year, wondering if she had a vindictive streak. She seemed too decent for that; perhaps her grandfather might. Marijke Katelaar was an unusually large woman, both tall and inclined to stoutness, plain of face and figure and style, and very reserved. Except, I recalled, when discussing crops or livestock, when her visage would suddenly become enlivened with interest and intelligence, if not beauty. Over the dominie's head I could now see them both intently making polite conversation with him and another elder. One had to grant the woman's fortitude some respect.

Katryne Nijenhuis caught me looking at her and observed curiously that it had been some months since she and her grandfather had themselves appeared in kerk. Perhaps she too had felt it necessary to confront her neighbors with her head erect. Wearied, I led our family group into the fresh air outside.

*   *   *

"The blessed event has at length occurred?"

"Yes, Dominie, two hours since. Mother and daughter have both survived thus far." After thirty-two horrific hours, I thought it a miracle anyone had survived. I'd nearly swooned looking at the babe's hideously malformed head, but Mother had insisted it was all right, perfectly normal.

"Heaven be praised!"

"Amen, sir."

The aged schout of New Utrecht perfunctorily seconded me. Both men were standing awkwardly in the tavern's main room in their black Sunday garb, where I was still presiding over an unpatronized establishment.

Dominie Van Voort delicately cleared his throat. "We actually came to talk about your father, Sergeant Dordrecht."

"We came to *see* your father, Dordrecht," Loytinck insisted pugnaciously. "It's my unpleasant duty to—"

To check up on me, I thought, unreasonably irritated. "Of course. Let me get a candle."

Mercifully asleep, Pa was a most unwholesome sight, as I'd noted when I'd brought him food and news an hour before, and the cellar now smelled as foul as the stable. They stayed only long enough to verify, from his reddened wrist, that he'd remained chained. "We believe the sentence should commence tomorrow at noon, Thomas," Van Voort said, relaxing his formality back upstairs.

The implication, as I thought it through, was appalling. The stocks … is no light or casual sentence. Aside from excruciating discomfort that sometimes leads to permanent deformity, people take it upon themselves to torture the helpless prisoner. If the prisoner has any family or friends, it's incumbent on them to stand guard and protect him or her from the worst abuse, as the authorities are not to be relied upon in this regard. But all of my family were asleep, and probably wouldn't wake up before noon tomorrow!

"Gentlemen … pray, Wednesday?" They looked upset. "We've just been through two ordeals at once, so—"

"No!" Loytinck said.

Van Voort took him by the arm and they both faced away from me for half a minute. "Tuesday, Thomas," he said finally. "Tuesday noon. He has committed a very grave offense!" he added.

"Thank you, sirs," I said miserably.

Once they were out of sight, I ran over to the Van Klosts' to seek out my cousin, hoping for his assistance in our predicament. Bertie shrugged and avowed that he'd long promised his father a few days of work back in Flatlands, and that he was committed to go there on the morrow. It seemed suspiciously convenient timing, but I was in no position to protest.

There was no help for it, Mother and Harmanus agreed the next morning. I would have to fetch our brother Brevoort all the way from Haarlem.

Though the weather was still horribly cold and wet, the ice in the waterways had broken up. There was just enough of it left to be a real danger to my Indian canoe, which I paddled nervously to my brother's town, new to me, eight long miles north of the city. I was somewhat stumped, given the place's name, that no one spoke Dutch, but I was more perplexed that no one in the tiny hamlet seemed ever to have heard of Brevoort Dordrecht. Finally, the fourth person I accosted said, "You mean Breff, Brother Constant's son-in-law?"

Dimly recollecting his wife's maiden name, I concurred, and presently found my brother in a reeking candle-making shed. Bent over, stirring a huge vat of bubbling wax with a paddle, he didn't even notice me for half a minute, and I held my tongue to get over the agitation I felt at the change in him. Brevoort is only five years older than I am, but he seems twice his years. Always shorter and stouter than the rest of us, he'd gained yet more weight in the fifteen months since I'd last seen him, and his hair was thinning and turning gray too—which most unpleasantly suggested that I might follow suit earlier than I'd imagined!

When I called out, Brevoort was so startled he dropped the stirrer, and had to spend a full minute retrieving it. He seemed even more amazed by my appearance than I did by his, but he managed a smile and called his son over to shake my hand. I was sorry to find my nephew Aalbert a glum, slow little fellow who bore no resemblance to our late brother, his namesake, who'd brightened every room he ever entered. He was sent off to fetch his heavily pregnant mother, Mary, who barely managed to break her apparently habitual torpor to extend me a dutiful greeting. She in turn had to be argued into waking her father, the proprietor of this establishment, from his midday nap; and my brother and I were finally able to walk out into the woods when the old fellow grumpily took over.

Brevoort, I was confounded to realize, was less in touch, and less concerned with our family than I'd ever been. "I have a new life here now, Thomas," he explained somewhat defensively. As a new life was precisely what I too was seeking, his explanation prompted very mixed feelings. I was sure I didn't want anything that resembled *his* new life.

And when I explained the purpose of my visit, he was furious. At everybody, but particularly Pa and Harmanus. "Harmanus actually expects me to drop everything and go back home for two days? How am I to explain to my father-in-law that I have to rescue Pa from a stoning for public indecency, Thomas? What's *your* suggestion, eh?" He seemed as mad at me as anyone else. Though eager to get under way—the fierce currents of Hell Gate and the East River would soon turn against us—I suffered him to sermonize at length on the same injustice that I'd felt and ridden out two days before. Finally depleted, he asked whether I'd told anyone else why I'd come. I shook my head. Still looking exasperated, Brevoort contemplated the situation for another minute before fixing me with what I realized was a bargaining stance for his filial duties. "Thomas, Mary's due in less than a month, and we can't afford a midwife. If Mother would be willing, and if you'd ferry her up here...."

How many more days of my life would this idiocy cost me? "All right," I agreed—committing Mother no less than myself.

"And I'm going to tell them Pa's *ill,* Thomas. I doubt anyone from Haarlem will ever be the wiser."

Ugh. Suppose he's wrong? "All right, if you insist."

Brevoort gave me a look that was far from fraternal affection. "You say we don't even have time for dinner?"

Not really, no. "Perhaps. If we hurry."

But Brevoort and his family dawdled over the meal and then he put up an enormous fuss about boarding the canoe. One would think he'd expected a frigate! He seemed inordinately slow to grasp the basics of paddling and weight distribution. Shortly after we were finally under way, he nearly capsized us by jerking around in alarm when, in response to his question, I was telling him about my unexpected war bounty. "Forty-five *pounds!*" he shrieked.

"Watch out!"

"You actually came home with—"

"Brevoort, it was pure luck, it really was."

"Forty—"

"Four of the thirteen men in my corps didn't come home at all, Brevoort."

"But you came back rich!"

I related my own brush with death in the woods and how, thanks to camp fever, I'd received last rites only in December, but it didn't seem to be making any impression. My brother was desperate to escape his father-in-law and buy himself a farm, of all things … but he had no money.

"You thinking of joining up again?"

"No. Never."

For twenty minutes we concentrated on negotiating the maelstrom at the confluence of the East and Haarlem Rivers.

"You know the province is offering a special fifteen pound bounty for this season?"

"I heard. But it's not worth it, Brevoort. Nothing would be."

We arrived home long after dark, exhausted, Brevoort exclaiming he'd hated every minute he'd spent in the canoe. Mother and Harmanus had retired, but Lisa had forced herself to wait up for us. Anneke and the babe— Gesina was to be her name—were still alive, she assured us, but still under close watch. Bertie had been prevailed upon to take the four older children to stay with their great-aunt Betje in Flatlands. Pa was howling—raving—in the cellar, which upset all of us. We ate hungrily but without much pleasure, and Brevoort availed himself of one of the empty guest beds rather than again share with me.

CHAPTER 6

Mother permitted us to sleep late—and soggy snowfall discouraged any attempt to rise—but her three sons and younger daughter were marshaled in conference by mid-morning. "I know this town," she said grimly. "It's a good place, but if we don't pull together today, it will take us years to regain our standing here. Harmanus, you must wear your blue suit. We needn't wear Sunday finest to get pelted with snowballs, but shoddy work clothes would imply—"

"Mother," Harmanus protested in alarm, "you're not suggesting you and Elisabeth are going to present yourselves by the stocks?" Brevoort and I both shook our heads in horror. "That simply wouldn't be respectable!"

"We shall stay through the formalities, Harmanus."

"Oh no," he moaned.

"I've already arranged for Katryne and Jenneken to watch over Anneke and Gesina. Once the formalities are over, I think you three should stay there together for a few hours—for the worst of it—then you can arrange turns overnight. What you must do now is to get your father presentable. Here are clean clothes for him. You're going to have to barber him somehow. Loytinck will be here well before noon."

"But—"

"Come, Elisabeth," Mother said, rising.

As they climbed the stairs, I heard Mother giving Lisa precise instructions for her dress and decorum, and it suddenly dawned on me…. "My god, Harmanus, what's this all going to mean for Lisa's chances at marriage?"

He didn't even answer, he just leered bitterly as if to say, *What do you think?*

"What do you think it'll mean for *your* chances at a good marriage, laddie?" Brevoort smirked.

Pa was quiescent for the first half-hour we worked over him, allowing us to strip and bathe him, brush and tie his hair and pick him over for lice. We got him into his clean togs but, when I came to shave him, he screamed and jerked about every time the razor came within a yard of him.

"Mad?" Brevoort breathed uncomfortably.

"Is it worth it?" I asked.

We three looked him over for a minute, then Harmanus wearily said, "He'll have to do, as is," and we left to get ourselves ready.

Rather than suffer Loytinck's henchmen to drag Pa to the stocks, Harmanus and I performed that office. Mother and Lisa, piously carrying psalters and leaning on Brevoort, followed directly behind in order to keep the schout and his armed deputies at a distance. Upon reaching the common, the deputies—Halsema and Oosterhout, the newest householders in town— roughly grabbed Pa and pushed him onto the stump, not even brushing off the accumulated snow, and then clamped his ankles into the stocks. Harmanus and I stepped back by our siblings and attempted to mimic Mother's erect, stony-faced bearing as Loytinck inspected the evil device and hammered the locking pegs in place. Pa looked both terrified and uncomprehending, but there was nothing to be done for him at this point.

The fact that it had ceased snowing was no reason for the Dordrechts to rejoice. Virtually the entire town, free and slave, were milling about, hoping this brief respite from labor might be an opportunity for merriment despite the gloomy day. Oosterhout's repulsive eight-year-old brat had already racked up a pyramid of snowballs. Dominie Van Voort came out of the kerk and made a stately progress through the crowd to Loytinck's side. "Let us pray," he began.

Everyone bowed his head as he prayed, but I kept my eyes up and alert for trouble. A three-year-old, prompted by the Oosterhout boy, gleefully trundled forward with a handful of snow. Balancing on Lisa, I stuck one leg out and forestalled him. When the dominie finished, Loytinck, struggling with the English words and his weak eyesight, sonorously read out his commission from the county and the text of the public disturbances ordinance. "In compliance with the terms of this edict," he concluded, "and by the judgment of the Selectmen of the town, Rykert Dordrecht will remain here for his sins until noon tomorrow. Let no one release him, under peril of equal punishment!" He closed his law book with a snap and turned to go, evidently content that we would do his protective duty for him. Before I'd even shifted my stance, a snowball had flown through my legs and hit Pa on the neck.

"If I may add a few words, Schout?" Van Voort said hastily.

"Of course, Dominie," Loytinck agreed, off-guard and clearly much irritated.

Dominie Van Voort, whose brevity in the pulpit—relative to his predecessor—has made him much beloved by the townsfolk, commenced an unexpected homily on sin, defamation, retribution, justice, good works, education…. After twenty minutes, I was positive I was hearing the same lecture on the *Five Main Points of Doctrine*—or was it the *Three Forms of Unity*?—that I'd heard on Sunday. Though deeply eager to fidget, Mother's unflinching, stiff-backed attentiveness brought me to the realization that Dominie Van Voort was extending himself for the express purpose of preserving my father's health. Furious as I was with Pa, the possibility that permanent injury might compound his moral lapse was too grim to contemplate, and I imitated her somber example for the duration.

One by one, people began drifting away, called by their postponed routine chores. When, thank heaven, it began to snow again after half an hour, they fled in droves. Only a few of the hardiest were still waiting when Van Voort folded his note pages ten minutes later, intoned "Amen," and majestically returned to the kerk with only the briefest glance backward—directed at my sister, I noticed, not Mother or Harmanus.

The instant Mother, Lisa, and Loytinck were twenty yards away, the frozen missiles flew in earnest. My brothers and I huddled together, facing Pa, and got clobbered. Pa got some of his just deserts too, as various urchins took advantage of his unprotected back. One had even carried out a chamber pot and got a little on Pa's coat before Harmanus shoved him.

But thanks to the snow and the long wait, the worst was over in half an hour. We finally turned outward to behold an empty square full of swirling snow. "Get yourself some dinner, Thomas," Harmanus ordered, "but get back as fast—"

"I can wait, Harmanus. You don't have to coddle me."

He grimaced with disdain and impatience. "Go! The sooner you get back, the sooner Brevoort…." He looked contemptuously at Pa, slumped wretchedly in the snow, and disgustedly shook his head. "Bring the old horse blanket from the stable. We'll put it under him so he doesn't literally freeze his butt off."

*   *   *

It happened that I took the Midnight shift that night. Not a soul was to be expected abroad, given the cold, clear weather, but we were still afraid to leave Pa alone. As Brevoort piled blankets onto my shoulders, I observed that if we wanted to catch the afternoon flood, we'd have to set off immediately after Pa's release. It stung me when he growled, "I'm never getting back in your blasted redskin canoe, Thomas! I'll take the ferry across and walk home."

Fine. "As you wish."

He suddenly turned on me. "Did you *have* to tell Mother about attending my wife's lying-in right in front of *Harmanus?*"

"I had to tell her, and he happened to be there, Brevoort."

"Well that's just grand, isn't it? Now he's complaining of my 'extortion,' and he'll never let it go as long as I live!"

"Well that's not fair!"

"Thanks a *lot,* Thomas!"

"Well … that's not fair either, Brevoort!" But he'd stalked off, leaving me doubly dispirited.

The slow rise and fall of the mound of blankets under which Pa was buried was the sole clue that our sire was still alive. I took a good look around and resolved to try to nap.

Curious. I'd never realized it before: Brevoort finds Harmanus even more insufferable than I do!

I woke with a start some time—hours?—later. Pa had shaken off the blanket covering his head and was also looking about. "What the hell was that?" he rasped.

At least he's coherent, I thought. I stood up and scanned the square and its surrounding houses. Finally I noticed a diminutive figure leaning into the old well, thirty yards away on the south edge of the common. I stretched, picked up my musket, and went over to investigate. The figure took no notice of my approaching footsteps until I was ten feet away, then it—she—turned with a jerk and, brandishing a stone, frantically whispered, *"Hekserij! Hekserij!"*

Should one cry or laugh? Both relieved and dismayed, I set the musket against the well and placed one of my blankets over my trembling grandmother's frail shoulders. In the middle of the night, wearing no more than her nightdress, she was carrying on about witchcraft. She threw the stone into the well and made the sign of the cross. *"Hekserij!"* she breathed again.

I took her by the arm, and she seemed amenable to being led back to the house. "It's Grootmoeder, Pa," I called. There was a grunt. "I'll be back in ten minutes."

Though I tried to communicate with her, there was no telling what on earth had impelled her out here. At least she had no awareness that her first-born was but a few feet away, enduring punishment for public indecency. We'd have to ask my elder sister to decipher this mystery. All I could do was tuck her back into her bed next to the kitchen.

Pa eyed me suspiciously when I returned and proffered him the roll and cheese I'd found. I had to hold them so he could gnaw away. "She's gone daft," he observed trenchantly, once finished.

I was speechless. On the one hand, she'd been daft for years: was he just noticing? And was he any marvel of sanity himself? On the other, it was a true and rational statement—the first I'd heard from him since I'd returned. "Has she ever gone walking outside in the night before, Pa?"

"A few times, maybe."

"Where to?"

"Don't know. Zwarte Jan brought her home once."

"Jan! What was she doing in the slave quarter?"

"No idea. Jan thought she'd been down to the ocean. Looking for Gerrit, my guess."

Good lord, does this never end? I'd only learned of my uncle Gerrit's existence two years ago. The family's black sheep, he'd simply disappeared after a quarrel with Pa and Grootvader. He'd shipped out to sea, they learned, but in thirty years nothing more has been heard of him. I stared at my father. Was he masticating the last of the cheese or ghoulishly contemplating his brother's probable fate as lobster fodder? What was wrong with *him?*

I was about to pursue this question, when he said, "What's the matter with you, Thomas? You've got to pull yourself together, boy!" Now I was breathless. "It's high time you settled down. It's beyond me that you haven't used that loot to buy a farm and get married. Your mother will find you a girl. They said that LeChaudel lass was pretty enough, but you don't have to take the first one she comes up with. Harmanus didn't, why should you?"

All right: it appears we're having a rational father-son discussion, notwithstanding that it's the middle of a winter's night and he's sitting disgraced in the stocks! "I don't want a farm, Pa. I want to live in the city."

"What, live there? Like Frederik? Like Janna and that sourpuss husband of hers? Make your home *there?* Why?"

"Because I find it exciting, Pa."

"Oh that's absurd, boy, that's ridiculous! I can't stand New York City, it's filthy, it's dangerous. The people are all loud, all rude, all pushy, and.... They're *obnoxious*. And the merchants there will cheat you at the drop of a hat!"

But at least it's not boring! I thought, withholding any response.

"You're crazed, boy, you're mad!"

And I was seriously wondering if that quality ran in the blood.

"Thomas," he persisted, "you don't want to help with the farm, right? You don't want to buy your own farm, you don't want to help with the tavern, you don't want to rejoin the army, you don't want to study for the clergy in Leyden, and you don't want to get married! So what *do* you want to do?"

It is very disconcerting to have the town drunk put you on the defensive with a perfectly rational question. I hesitated before owning up the truth. "I don't know, Pa. I haven't decided."

"We're not rich, Thomas. Your name's Dordrecht, not Van Renssalaer!"

"I know that."

"Being a 'gentleman of leisure' is not a possibility, Thomas."

"Yes, Pa."

He shook his head disapprovingly. "My son, the guitar-player!"

"Pa!"

But he'd run out of fight, and so had I. We both nodded off again.

*   *   *

A snowball in the kisser brought me around shortly after sun-up. Stiff, I couldn't rise as fast as I thought I could, so he escaped before I could wallop him: one of the slave children, grabbing a rare opportunity to get back at the Dutch. I stretched, touched my toes, looked over at Pa, and groaned. Too late. They'd ripped the blanket off his head and dumped a whole bucket of snow onto it.

Somehow we got through it, though the last hours were among the worst. Loytinck arrived ten minutes late, followed us as we carried Pa home, and then had the gall to demand that I serve him a drink. Brevoort left with the most perfunctory grace, not neglecting to explain how he planned to send word when Mary's time came. Both Pa and Grootmoeder developed fevers. I nursed a cold. Anneke and the baby were still not out of danger. Harmanus put in hours in the fields before dressing to attend his vestry meeting—he'd been elected a deacon of the church before our current embarrassment—after supper.

Thus we mended, slowly and feebly, until Friday afternoon, when Bertie brought the children back, and Aunt Betje along with them, for a deeply relieved family reunion. After supper, as we downed the superb pear pies she'd brought, my aunt said, "I heard you playing your instrument as we arrived, Thomas."

"Yes ma'am?"

"Well, why don't you bring it down here, lad, where we can all listen?"

Startled, Mother looked to Harmanus, as if expecting him to disapprove such *ungodly* entertainment, but my brother—for the first time wearing the traditional paternity cap Vrouw Nijenhuis had given him—seemed suffused with joy at finding all members of his increased family still alive, and merely shrugged. I fetched the guitar, and played some simple popular tunes— "Greensleeves," "Early One Morning," and "The Little Turtle Dove." All I could manage was the chords, but Aunt Betje gamely joined in, and then the children joined in, then all the rest. I essayed accompanying myself on Ophelia's song; though applauded, my singing did not garner the *encores* Miss Chapman had. The Van Klosts all stopped by—to pay their respects to my aunt—and stayed for over an hour, ordering freely from the bar. Further, not only the Bilderbeeks, but a traveler returning to Staten Island stopped in for a quaff. After lingering over his food and drink, the latter announced he'd stay the night rather than continue on to Denyse's Ferry. Mother and Harmanus looked at each other in disbelief, then at me in wonderment. I concentrated on playing and didn't dare meet their eyes.

Slowly, despite continuing awful weather, the Dordrecht family returned to normal, or rather assumed a new balance. Anneke, the baby, Grootmoeder, Pa, and I all slowly mended. Harmanus toiled from dawn to dusk, and occasionally cast irritated glances in my direction that suggested he was irked by my apparent indolence, but he refrained from baiting me. I tried to forestall resentment by offering my mother threepence a week for my room and board. She bargained me into committing to bi-weekly shopping trips, plus handling "emergencies," but sweetened matters a hair by reducing my outlay to a shilling a month. Somewhat hesitantly, worrying that "emergencies" might easily multiply, I accepted. Harmanus still seemed disapproving ... but then he'd uncharacteristically suppress whatever complaint might have been on his mind. Rather peculiar, as one thing my brother is *not*, is mysterious.

Mother announced one evening that she'd brought Pa to an agreement to restrict his liquor intake, and she enjoined us all to help enforce it. Pa presently began to appear at table and, though he seemed increasingly cynical and bitter, he was very quiet and never disruptive. He did not volunteer to assist Harmanus with the farming chores, however.

The first "emergency" arrived a fortnight later, in the form of Mother's summons to Haarlem, which had been swiftly relayed by the kindness of four distinct travelers none of whom owed the Dordrecht family the least favor. I spent hours whittling a third paddle, as Mother insisted Lisa was also to attend our sister-in-law.

Spring had officially arrived, according to *Poor Richard*, but you could've fooled us as we toiled through the busy waterways of New York harbor amid sleet and fog. It was all the more astounding, on our arrival, that my female relatives avowed they'd found the trip—their first, and a far more demanding one than Brevoort's—to be exhilarating. If some wise man can explain what I really should expect of people, I'd appreciate it!

My brother's welcome was far more polite than his departure, and even involved a respectable repast. Many neighbors stopped to pay their respects—all of whom called my sister-in-law *Sister Mary*, which confused us until a perfect stranger called my brother *Brother Breff*; I finally understood this to be the odd way that Baptists address each other. Even more unsettling was asking little Aalbert in Dutch if he wanted to play catch ... and being met with total puzzlement.

Mother and Lisa examined Mary after our meal, and Mother asserted confidently that she'd soon be delivered. I begged leave overnight to visit the city. Mother looked a trifle provoked, but granted me permission.

Honestly, I had no urgent business in town. I'd already collected my remaining wages and joined the Society Library on a shopping excursion, and I was as yet reluctant to look up my friends. I simply wanted to visit the city itself. I'd been away only three weeks, yet it seemed an eternity. I'd changed so much and it.... *Ha!* The restaurant where Mr. Glasby and I had dined had been converted into a haberdashery!

I did visit Mr. Fischl's, and he invited me to join him for supper and a wonderful harpsichord concert that evening, the net effect of which was to make me yearn to return as soon as.... As soon as I could figure myself out. It would be foolishness to squander my capital as I was doing that evening. I determined to spend the minimum on my own comforts that night, and domiciled myself at Brown's.

The next morning I paid my second visit to the Library, which was as well-stocked if not as elegant as Mr. Colegrove's. Determined to finish the Montesquieu Roman history, I procured a copy in English translation, then snatched up an advice book as I rushed to catch the flood current. In Haarlem I found happiness all round, Mary having produced a young lass—to be christened Susan Dordrecht—in a "relatively painless" span of eight hours. Mother and Lisa had gotten a good night's rest and were ready to leave. Brevoort and his father-in-law, perhaps somewhat shamefaced over the manner in which we'd been summoned, tripped over themselves to escort us back to the jetty.

*   *   *

While Grootmoeder had resumed her usual chirpy absent-mindedness, Pa had relapsed into pneumonia, and became the family's new invalid just as Anneke was now and then managing to rise from her bed. The babe—whose head had, to my relief, somehow reshaped itself—seemed stronger, and louder, day by day. By stoutly holding their chins high, the family members stared down the occasional snubs of their neighbors. I completed the history and then read the tome purporting to advise young gentlemen in search of careers ... but it merely annoyed me with its pious cheerfulness. My eldest brother continued to behave in a manner I found so singular, I asked my sister for her thoughts. She'd not observed anything odd at all.

On the first Sunday in April, which was also the very first day that hinted the bitter winter might at last be over, we enjoyed a fine lamb dinner after services, topped by yet another dessert from our aunt. After a closing grace, we were about to rise and attend our separate pursuits, when Harmanus cleared his throat and said, "The Lord has provided us such a beautiful day, I should like to take a walk. Thomas, would you care to join me?"

What now? was my first thought. This was doubly unprecedented, in that Harmanus had never undertaken anything so feckless as a *walk* in his life, and would surely never choose to share it with me if he did. The children were instantly clamoring to come too—an eventuality he'd obviously not anticipated. He flushed and sternly insisted they attend to their devotions first … and said perhaps he'd go out with them later.

Astounded, I looked from his face to Mother's to Anneke's, and none of their eyes quite met mine. Lisa shrugged in mystification. I hesitated a second too long before replying, and Harmanus stood up and said, "We'll go over to the Bay, you always like that!"

Mother vanished to the kitchen, and Anneke was corralling the children to their rooms. Mother called Lisa to assist with clean-up. Harmanus was at the door, evidently assuming I'd follow. Given an intensity of curiosity on my part … he was correct. "Shall I bring a bucket? We could dig for clams."

This seemed to distract him. "If you wish. I doubt I can stay that long."

The heck with that, then!

Harmanus set out at a fast clip westerly along the Kings Highway toward the Narrows, which took us up a long, slow rise. Thinking to put us both out of our misery, I made bold to ask what this was all about, but he ignored me and strode on. He made evasive small talk, and I did the same. I managed to learn that Grootmoeder's nighttime wanderings were more frequent than I'd imagined, that he hoped Pa had learned his lesson but despaired of his ever again contributing to the family's welfare, that he thought Mother's interest in midwifery was hurting her ability to maximize the value of the tavern and the inn, and that he too worried that her training Lisa in that profession might be detrimental to her ability to attract a husband.

By this time, I was positive I was in for an arduous lecture on my failures as a brother, family-member, citizen, and Christian, and I was girding myself to give back as good as I might get. We reached the top of the rise where, the land being fallow, there was a fine view of the lower bay, Staten Island, and the Atlantic highlands of New Jersey. Harmanus abruptly turned off the road over to an oak that had been left standing, where he slumped onto the ground and leant back against the trunk. "Pretty impressive mountains over there, eh?" he said as I joined him.

It struck me as forcefully inane, because I'd made the same foolish remark a year ago, only to see hills that dwarfed those little dunes all through the Hudson Valley, and true mountains that dwarfed them in the Adirondacks—and been told that they in turn were dwarfed by the Alps. Ten years my senior, Harmanus had seen even less of the world than I had. For a quarter-hour I related some of the marvels of my excursions, and he seemed content to listen. His children had long since heard these stories; their father had never before sat still for them. Finally, I simply stopped, hoping that would at last bring us to the point.

Nervously, Harmanus coughed and swallowed. "I was wondering, Thomas.... Does it happen that you still have any of your prize money left?"

I nearly blacked out with rage. The implication that he thought me capable of squandering forty-five pounds in two months was infuriating. I heaved myself upright shouting, "Of course I have! What on earth do you take me for? And what the hell business is it of yours anyway, Harmanus?"

He seemed shocked by my reaction, and greatly apologetic—and that presently calmed me. "Thomas, Thomas! I'm ... sorry, really! I didn't mean—"

"*What?*" I demanded crossly.

"Please don't swear, Thomas!"

I clenched my fists in irritation. He practically calls his own brother a worthless lout, and then he gets upset by a cuss word! After twenty seconds, I sat back down. "What is it that's on your mind, Harmanus?"

Again he cleared his throat. "You know, we made a great success on our wheat and corn last fall. We actually managed to net a significant pot of capital."

"Yes?"

"But ... we've had some expenses this spring—with the cow dying, and the south fence falling down—and—"

"Yes?"

"And so we can't go ahead with ... something I'd wanted to go ahead with, even though we still have a substantial amount...."

I almost had to laugh. My parents each had some capability of being devious; I fear I can be devious, and possibly even Lisa can too. But Harmanus? Risible. "And?"

He gulped. "I was wondering if we might be able to arrange a loan, Thomas?"

A *loan*. I shook myself in an effort at reorientation. I was not going to be sermonized; weeks of bizarre behavior were in one word explained; and here was Harmanus the deacon pleading with his nineteen-year-old sibling for a loan! I just restrained myself from guffawing aloud when I saw, from his grim, far-off look, how much that one sentence had cost his pride.

But I had my own considerations to calculate. I'd never thought of lending or investing the cash in any way. Like everyone else, I had squirreled my nest egg away in a hiding place. But I rather liked the thought that the money might be used, and certainly having it used for some productive purpose by my family would forcibly prevent me from slowly frittering it down, which I allowed was unfortunately not beyond possibility. And though I might find my brother maddening from time to time, I felt absolutely no question of his probity, and was positive he'd keep any bargain he made to the last jot and tittle. "What did you have in mind, Harmanus?" I asked levelly.

He took a deep breath. "Well, as I say, we have some capital built up, but we need just a bit more to—"

"Yes?"

"We could pay interest, I think, Thomas! Mother said we could possibly pay two percent per annum, and—"

That cat's loose from the bag! "Mother knows about this?"

He turned bright red. "Yes," he murmured.

Two percent, eh? Not bad, from my readings of such things in the newspapers. "How … much is it you were thinking to borrow, Harmanus?"

Again he had to push himself. "If we had thirty pounds more, Thomas, it would set us right."

Thirty pounds. I had thirty-four left. Twelve shillings interest on money that, at best, would otherwise sit still in the barn for a year. And at worst…. "I believe I can do that for you, Harmanus."

"We may not need all thirty!" he exclaimed eagerly.

"Indeed?"

"But we do need to have it available."

"*Uh huh.*"

"I'd be—we'd all be … very grateful, Thomas."

I shrugged. "It's not as if I too won't profit of it, Harmanus."

"Nonetheless…."

We both stared at a merchant ship struggling to beat up into the harbor. "May I ask what brings this about? I'm just curious." And I have some right to be asking, of course! "Thirty pounds is a lot of—"

"It's two hundred eighty pounds we're trying to bring together, Thomas."

"*What?*" I'd no inkling. "You plan to buy a patroonship, Harmanus?"

He smiled wanly. "No."

"Another barn? Race horses? A distillery?"

"No."

A thought distracted me. "You made two hundred fifty pounds on the farm and the inn last year?"

"No no, over the past several years. Mother saves very carefully."

Whew! "Well, what are you thinking to buy with all that money?"

Again he swallowed, looked askance, and actually bit his lip before facing me.

"I.... We need to buy a Negro, Thomas."

CHAPTER 7

For ten seconds I couldn't move or breathe. "A slave?"

"A male. Prime. A seasoned field-hand. They're very expensive."

I gaped. My mind was swimming. On the one hand, it was the most common thing in the world. My family was one of very few in New Utrecht that had no slaves. Every third pair of legs in town had a black face above it. But aside from Aunt Janna's ancient housekeeper—inherited by her husband—no Dordrecht had ever owned one. "But we've never—"

"Things change, Thomas."

"We always had indenturees. Sven? Ulrich?"

"I've looked, Thomas. Can't find any."

"They're cheaper than slaves!"

"No, I don't think so. Depends, really. One black who can last fifteen years in the fields will leave you better off than two indentured servants for seven years each, is my understanding."

"That's *very* chancy!"

"Aye. So's all life."

I felt preposterous, because I'd been around slaveholding all my life and never thought much about it; yet, confronted with the prospect that our family might actually acquire one, the mere idea violently repelled me. "What about Grootmoeder?" I spluttered. "I thought we never had any slaves because she couldn't bear the sight of blacks, and—"

"Oh that was just a ruse, Thomas," Harmanus said deprecatingly. "It was Grootvader who couldn't deal with them. People twitted him about it and he put up a fuss that it was all out of concern for his wife! I wish Grootmoeder—"

"It was Grootvader?"

"Aye, and Pa too. But frankly, Thomas, given Grootmoeder's inability to speak up for herself, it wouldn't really matter if she did object, because—"

"Couldn't you just hire people as you need them? There's nobody in this whole county who's looking for work?"

"We can't deal with this moment by moment, Thomas. Be serious. Right now we can sell everything we can grow, at very good prices. We have to work every square inch we've got, every day ... and save for our bad times."

"So you're thinking of putting years of savings into one slave, one Negro who could get an ague and die within three weeks?"

Harmanus shuddered violently, then steeled himself. "I fear that's the risk we have to take."

"Dear heaven!"

"Don't—"

"That's not swearing!" The merchant ship had finally bested the Narrows, but the tide was now against it too. Perhaps it would reach the city by midnight. "Harmanus, why is this so suddenly necessary? Why—"

"Not sudden, Thomas."

"It's the first I've heard of it!"

"Aye. And whose fault would that be?"

Oh all right. "Well, why do we need one right now? In another year or two, things could be very different."

Harmanus sighed. "Hendrik is only seven, Thomas. He should stay in school for at least eight more years; Willem, for nine; and Petrus, for eleven. What am I to do in the meantime?" As he well knew, I'd no answer to that. Certainly I was not going to make an obscene joke by suggesting he could work harder. "I'd been hoping, of course," he continued, "that *you* would see fit to help the family out until you married and started out on your own."

This was so common an assumption about a younger son's progress through life that I almost felt churlish to protest. Almost. "So it's *my* fault that we need a slave, is that it? *Criminy!*"

"No one's fault, Thomas," Harmanus said, more tolerantly than one might've expected.

"Well, it's simply not fair, Harmanus! Look, lots of people in this world are not cut out to be farmers, and I'm one of them, all right? I have a perfect right to determine my own profession without everybody in the family breathing down my neck!" The ship tacked—and I desperately wished I were aboard her.

"I can ... allow that, Thomas—"

Oh! Magnanimous!

"I don't understand it, but I can allow it. But the long and short is, I'm one man, and I've now got eleven mouths to feed, not counting yours." A cloud cleared overhead, and I suddenly looked at the tired, craggy face of Harmanus Dordrecht in an entirely new light. He wasn't even thirty, but his face was deeply lined. "Mother's an enormous help, of course, but—"

"You buy a useless slave, and you'll have twelve!"

"Well, we mustn't buy a useless—"

"It's Pa who's really let us all down, isn't it?"

Harmanus looked away, refusing to say a word that could dishonor one of our parents. "In practical terms," he admitted reluctantly, "Berendina has been more help over the last year, than Pa has. Maybe he'll turn over a new—"

"You're sure there's no possibility of an indenturee?"

"I asked Uncle Frederik to look for one in the city."

Frederik! Oh lord. Uncle Frederik makes Brevoort look like a sparking Leyden jar. "Perhaps … I could make some investigation, Harmanus. I don't know much about this, but—"

"I was hoping we could ask you to *acquire* the slave, Thomas. I hate giving up a day here just to go hunting for one."

"Oh no, Harmanus, don't ask me to do that, please. I suppose I can *look* for you, but—"

"Whatever you can do, it's very much appreciated, Thomas."

Bertie and I had often walked this road with our arms over each other's shoulders. I was briefly inspired to put mine on Harmanus' as we returned … but I didn't.

*   *   *

With deep misgivings, I trudged along the rutted trail to Red Hook the next morning, wondering where one would go to locate indentured servants. I had high hopes that Mr. Glasby would be able to provide key information in this regard, and was at least looking forward to seeing him again. Lost in my own thoughts, I paid no attention as a horse-drawn cart pulled up behind me.

"Dordrecht!"

"Good morrow, Meneer Loytinck!"

"Well don't just stand there like an idiot, hop up."

"Thank you very kindly, sir," I said, climbing onto the plank beside him. Glancing into the cart, I was startled to behold no produce, but one of his slaves, lying on his back. "Good morrow, Vrijdag," I said, disconcerted. I'd known the fellow all my life, he was just a little older, and I'd always—I *thought* I'd always gotten along with him. But there was no response.

"How the devil's your Pa?" Loytinck blared. "Lord knows he made me mad, talking as he did about Marijke, but there's no one like him for a good time in a tavern!"

"He seems to be on the mend now, sir," I said, casting glances backward. Vrijdag's face was frozen in a taut grimace. My blood ran cold when I noticed his right wrist was manacled to the cart. The bondsmen of New Utrecht are never literally chained: the constraints of bounty hunters, the militia, and the improbability of escaping from a flat island are more than sufficient ... as a rule. "Is he ill?" I asked Loytinck.

"Eh?" the old man shouted. I recalled he's almost deaf and repeated the question. "Vrijdag? Nah. Gotta get rid of him. Need the money." Vrijdag slowly pounded the floor of the cart with his free fist. I looked back in alarm, but he wasn't struggling or threatening. If Loytinck heard it, he took no notice. "They all tell me I'm about to die!" Loytinck cackled. "Need some cash to bribe my way into heaven!" This is not the way Dutch Reformed congregants usually talk, and a questioning look from me brought a sardonic grin in reply. "It was your old goat of a Pa that told me I've got to start selling off, so my granddaughter will have an inheritance she can handle."

Oh no. Pa had completely botched the commission his neighbor had assigned him. For several minutes, I endeavored to salvage the suggestion that Loytinck could sell small plots of land—and slaves with them—to other farmers in the locality. Harmanus might be advised to use all the money in the heavy purse he'd foisted on me for that.

Loytinck seemed to be listening to me thoughtfully—or he might have just been concentrating on the reins. "Not the dumbest idea that ever came from your family," he roared at length. "You're the only one in that house with any sense, you know!" I was gagging, having overcome the flattery in a flash. "Your brother's an ass and your Pa's just an old souse!"

Much irritated, I demurred on defending either of them and protested, "My mother's a very sensible woman, Meneer Loytinck!"

"Eh? Women don't count, boy! Haven't you—" He badly negotiated a sharp twist in the road, nearly spilling us over a ten-foot escarpment. "Anyway, my mind's made up. Mustn't dither about! This one will fetch a good price, so off he goes!"

I looked back again. Every muscle in Vrijdag's body was rigid. "Don't you ... need him for your field work?"

"I've got Wim, Hans, Powles, and Balt, that's enough for the heavy work. This one would rather spend time with his harem anyway," he chortled. "He's got another one in his wench's oven, but I won't get anything out of it because she belongs to Van Klost! That stupid Van Klost woman complains everlastingly about having to take care of slave children, as if trading them off hasn't pulled her husband out of bankruptcy at least twice that I know of!"

Vrijdag's fist again hammered the cart, and I felt a panic rising in me. When we were ... when I was a boy, he and I had often played together.

Happily. A Dutch translation of Defoe's ever-popular *Robinson Crusoe* had been one of the first books I'd ever read, but it only now struck me that Loytinck must have imposed the name *Vrijdag* on his orphaned young slave in the hope of replicating the famously faithful service of Crusoe's companion in isolation. As I grew older, though, I didn't see him for months at a time. Then he got in trouble by running off—it was the same month my younger brother died. They'd apprehended him in the city trying to join the crew of a smuggler, and it took him a year to recover from the whipping. Whether it had been time or Christ or Roosje—the gal who did all the real work in the Van Klost house and was mother to his two kids—who'd pulled him through, Vrijdag had for the past three years been esteemed New Utrecht's model slave.

"Didn't you hear the ruckus those women made? I thought it would reach New Jersey, not just your side of town! I knew he wouldn't go willingly, so I took no chances and had Wim knock him out from behind to get him on the buggy!"

And the whole slave quarter's undoubtedly in an uproar, you old fool! I tried to think calmly—particularly difficult when you knew there was no way to keep the shouted conversation out of the ears of the desperately affected man. This was exactly what the respectable burghers had *not* wanted to happen. "You'll never get a good price when they see his back, you know," I said in English. "They'll see he was a runaway."

"Nah! He's over that, he knows better. He's settled!"

Except you're taking away everything he's settled *for!*

"Why are we talking in English?" Loytinck roared. I nodded backward to indicate my discomfort. He looked back and made a face. "Well he knows English as well as you do, Dordrecht. Are you witless?"

Of course—and I guess I must be. I reverted to Dutch. "Is he really such a ladies' man? Is he no count in the field? Is that why you're selling him?"

"No no no!" Loytinck shouted, annoyed. "He's strong as an ox! I just don't need him and I want the cash, that's all."

"Why'd you rent him to Schuppert all that time?"

"Because Schuppert needed him in the smithy and he could pay!"

"Oh, I'm sorry, I don't think you're going to get very much for this fellow, Meneer Loytinck!"

"I'm not taking a farthing less than three hundred!"

Bluffing wildly, I affected to find this outrageously funny. "I'll bet you haven't a prayer of two hundred! You're taking him to the Wall Street market?"

"Exactly so. And we'll see this afternoon, won't we, oh clever one!" We crested a ridge and the shore came into view. "Maybe I did price him a little high when I told your brother he was three-fifty," Loytinck said a trifle more modestly.

It took a great effort to show no reaction. Harmanus *knew* this slave was on offer? Why on earth didn't he bargain for him? "Well of course," I said, struggling to take breath in without whistling. "What did he say?"

"Just that he cost too much. As if Harmanus had anywhere near that kind of money!" he added with a sneer.

Why hadn't he told me this? Harmanus *is* a fool, I swear! I looked back once again and saw that sweat had broken out all over Vrijdag's face, despite the coolness of the April morning. I'd never entered the foul-smelling slave market and had never even tried to follow the pricing, as I had for grains and sugar and lumber. But Harmanus had thought two-fifty wouldn't be enough, and Loytinck conceded three-fifty too much. "Meneer," I said, putting a hand over his wrist to get him to halt the horse. "It happens that my errand this morning is a commission from my family to acquire an indenturee—"

"Can't find them anymore," Loytinck piped up. "They all go to Pennsylvania these days."

"I'm not so certain. I think my friend Mr. ... Colegrove knows someone among his DeLancey contacts up-river—"

Teunis Loytinck did not become the wealthiest man in New Utrecht by allowing striplings to pull the wool over his eyes. "I'd be very surprised if that proved out, Dordrecht."

"It's a long shot, I suppose," I conceded blandly. "Still, given that Vrijdag is at least familiar with the farming done in New Utrecht—"

"He's strong as an ox, Dordrecht!"

"I don't think I'd be violating my commission if I offered one hundred fifty for him."

Loytinck flicked the reins and drove on to the jetty in silence. The ferry was in sight in Buttermilk Channel, a smart breeze on its quarter. Vrijdag thrashed back and forth in the cart, his eyes wide with alarm. And I wondered how long I could keep this up. The ferry turned to beat up to its dock. "If I were to bring the price down," Loytinck ventured, "I can see it'd save me a few shillings in commissions...."

I nodded as if I'd never thought of it. "And taxes, too, I dare say?" He frowned. "And two ferry fares. The horse and cart would be a great deal extra—if Jacob can manage them at all. Or perhaps you're thinking of leaving them here and bribing a constable to drag him from the dock to the market?" He was toting it all up, I could tell. "Not that that's really a consideration. Of course, there's the sheer waste of your valuable time, too. And mine as well. And they might not be ready to auction him today, they might require you to board him for a week—"

"Two hundred fifty," Loytinck said.

I searched the heavens for guidance. "I don't know, they really didn't want a black servant under foot. Grootmoeder's very sensitive, you know. Little things set her off." He set his jaw and folded his arms across his bony chest. "Two hundred?"

"That's an insult, Dordrecht! This man's a valuable young field slave!"

"Two-twenty?"

He paused. "Two-forty. Do you even *have* that kind of money?"

I loudly rattled the coin purse inside my jacket. "Two-thirty?"

He sighed, then we both grinned. "Done!"

It took the two of us to turn the cart around on the jetty's landing, me calling directions from behind. One of the blessings—or curses—of my life is that I can always see, or think I see, the emotions in the faces of others, the old, the young, men, women, even dumb animals. And slaves. Much thought and emotion was now playing over the face of an enslaved man with whom I'd once innocently raced hoops: relief, amazement, hatred, longing. But part of it, very clearly, was: *how dare you?*

We pulled into our yard an hour later, and the news was all over a very jittery town within ten minutes. Ignoring Constantija's furious cries, Roosje rushed out of the Van Klost house the instant Loytinck unlocked the manacle so Vrijdag could stand. Unable to bear the flooding tears, I assisted Loytinck in backing out the gate.

I turned around and saw the two slaves in a shuddering embrace. Roosje broke away and came to stand in front of me. She *was* with child, I'd not noticed before. I had no idea what she might do next.

"No, Roosje!" Vrijdag called.

Roosje knelt on one knee, took my hand in hers and pressed the back of it against her wet cheek, then fled to the service of her squalling mistress.

*   *   *

Now what? Where was everybody? Vrijdag looked at me expectantly if hardly eagerly. I had just purchased him, and it was therefore my place to give him some command or other. I'd felt no special awkwardness giving directions to Joachim—but in the final analysis, however debased Joachim's standing was, he'd voluntarily submitted to it. Though I knew sooner or later I'd have to organize orders for the family's slave, at the moment I couldn't even muster the courage to say, "Stay here." I simply left him by the fence and went searching inside the house for my mother.

She wasn't there. Grootmoeder was absorbed in her perpetual knitting, the children were of course in school, and I didn't want to wake Anneke from her nap. Walking out the back way I found Pa unconscious on Grootmoeder's bed, reeking of spirits. Where had he found them? We'd have to do better at locking them away. I moved back outside. Vrijdag stood mute and immobile by the fencepost.

Harmanus was scowling at Vrijdag, his face flushed. He threw down the rake he'd evidently carried all the way from the plot. "So it's *true?*" he howled, turning the force of his ire on myself.

"I bought him," I acknowledged.

Harmanus came rushing at me, as he'd done years before when angered. Knowing better than to attempt a strike, he grabbed me by the forearm and tried to tug me into the stable. Furious, I wrenched my wrist free and stood my ground. "Come inside," Harmanus ordered.

I refused. He repeated it. Finally, after deciding this situation had to be dealt with, I moved inside of my own volition, and he slammed the stable door closed after us.

"How could you?" he screamed, shaking both fists in my face.

"This is my thanks, Harmanus?" I yelled, bitter irony contending with my own anger. "I got him for two hundred thirty, you know. I saved you fifty pounds—and any necessity of a loan!"

"And that doesn't matter a fig when he's obviously *the wrong slave*, Thomas! How could you be such a fool?"

"What is wrong with him, Harmanus? I don't see anything wrong with him!"

"He's not a field hand!"

"Well of course he is, he's done field work for years."

"He's Schuppert's boy, he's got airs because he worked in the forge."

"Don't be ridiculous, he's a muscular, capable male and…. Whatever happened to your grand desire to keep the slaves from getting all upset? Loytinck told me the women were in a fury in his end of town."

"Did he put you up to this? Did that conniving old—"

"Loytinck even told me he'd made an offer to you. Now why didn't *you* tell me that? I assumed his price was too high, but I had no trouble bargaining him way down."

"It wasn't the price. He's obviously all wrong."

"What's all wrong? He's steady, he's lived here all his life, he's got a woman and children now, he'll never run off again, he speaks both Dutch and English—"

"That's it, you dolt, don't you see?"

"See what?"

"I don't *want* a slave who speaks Dutch! I don't want one under foot who understands everything we say, that's why I said he should be *seasoned*. They season the Africans in Barbados or Jamaica. In English, Thomas, English alone."

"Well it's a fine time to be telling me now, Harmanus!"

"Anyone with any sense would have seen that as a priority, Thomas. And besides, you said you were just going to town to look, you didn't—"

"*You* said you wanted me to acquire a hand, and that anything I did would be appreciated!"

With alarm I saw over his shoulder that his youngest boy had wandered in through the small door and was standing agape at the spectacle of his father and uncle in a shouting match. Harmanus was too carried away to notice. "But I never expected this! Why on earth couldn't it have waited until you checked with me?"

"Because he was about to board the ferry, of course. We'd never have gotten him so cheap—"

"Is that all you can say?" he shrieked. "Cheap? Now we're stuck, don't you understand, *stuck!* We're stuck with him in our family for the rest of our god-damned lives!"

Well that was emphasis, all right! That must have been the first time Harmanus Dordrecht had blasphemed in his entire life. Petrus, who was just old enough to know what swearing was and how dire it was supposed to be, burst into tears and ran howling from the stable.

"Oh no," Harmanus wailed, shocked, pounding his fist against the structure's frame. "Oh no oh no oh no! Do you see what you've caused?"

I managed to suppress my indignation at this pathetically ludicrous charge. "I don't think you really want to be a slaveholder, Harmanus. You've no more idea what to do with him than I do, and—"

"Well I really don't have much choice about it now, do I, brother?" he said furiously, storming out after the child.

*   *   *

Once again the Dordrecht household slowly underwent a readjustment. The slave continued to live in the slave quarter, as he had when under the command of Meneer Loytinck, but he was frequently found on the family premises, assisting his new masters with the innumerable chores that our communal enterprises entailed. His attitude toward us all was perfectly correct—or perhaps perfectly chilling—but there was no behavior of which anyone could complain. I'd fretted that Harmanus might take his frustrations out on the slave but he too acted with restraint, as a model country squire should. If the boys attempted to tease Vrijdag, he sharply slapped them down. To me, however, he remained very cool.

One afternoon I was disturbed to overhear Willem referring to the attic as "Sir Thomas' castle." Where'd he get that phrase, I wonder?

Controls over the spirits locker were tightened, and Pa was sober more often than not. His demeanor was sour enough, but by avoidance, he caused no scenes among the neighbors.

Other than suffering a persistent nightmare—in which the worm-ridden ship that had transported me to Albany last summer was raided by corsairs, and its entire human cargo sold into Algerine bondage—I remained in good health. I executed the biweekly shopping trips, practiced my guitar—on which I fancied I was becoming proficient—and enjoyed reading and contemplating one of the several lengthy volumes of *Cato's Letters* that Mr. Glasby had praised. When Mother and Lisa were called over to Gravesend to assist in another childbirth, I managed the tavern and inn, to which a few patrons once again returned.

A few mornings after Easter, Anneke went up to the attic to put some blankets away for the season, and discovered puddles on the floor and a two-inch hole in the roof. I was embarrassed I'd not noticed; I tend to go straight to my private eyrie and shut the door. Then we found stains in the ceiling of the boys' room below. That afternoon, all the adults gathered in the attic to consider the scale of the problem. Vrijdag stood by to help move the trunks and furniture around. The roof had not been touched since the house had been built over twenty years earlier. Pa put his hand through the hole and easily chipped off additional soggy, rotted cedar shingles. "The rafters are all right," Pa concluded—it was refreshing to us all to have a moment when his judgment seemed both authoritative and reasonable—"but all the shingles have to go, and the sooner the better."

Mother and Harmanus looked at each other in dismay as we trekked outside for another view. The twenty pounds saved on the slave had immediately been reincorporated in the jealously guarded family treasury—and I was positive my brother would sooner face hellfire than again ask me for a loan. But the job was a huge one, given the size of the house and the relative steepness of its roof—Grootvader's conceit having been not just to slough off snow, but to imitate the grand houses of Amsterdam—or at least Albany. It was at minimum a month's work for two men.

As I considered the job at hand, I was impetuously moved to offer a proposition. I'd been feeling a lack of exercise, feeling somewhat useless, given my continuing uninspiration toward any particular profession, and I was also eager to smooth over the raw edges of my connection to my family and to undo the mutually irksome cash arrangement. "I could do it," I said. "If you'll let me stay through the year, I'll do it."

"That's a professional's job, Thomas," Harmanus snorted.

"Well, hell, let him do it, if he thinks he can," Pa said. "He'll need a man helping him, though."

"You think you can actually get up there on that roof?" Harmanus challenged. He had a farmer's loathing of heights, I recalled.

"Of course," I said, smugly glad to best him in any way.

"Well we'd still have to find him a mate, and I don't think—"

"I help Meneer Schuppert shingle smithy roof," Vrijdag announced, startling us all.

"I need you in the fields!" Harmanus retorted instantly. Mother and Pa looked hesitantly at each other.

"How long did that job take?" I asked Vrijdag.

"I need him in the fields!"

"Three weeks, about. But could be done more fast."

"It's a lot of money, Harmanus," Mother warned.

"I'll still need to spend two days a week marketing, Harmanus. You can have him back then." Vrijdag's face fell slightly and I sensed that, now safely back in New Utrecht, the slave's wish, same as mine, was to spend as little time as possible at the beck of Harmanus Dordrecht.

It began to rain, driving us all indoors. After another hour's wrangling, the decision was that Vrijdag and I should start work as soon as possible.

And that we did, three days later, after I'd bought two cartloads of supplies in the city. Our work proceeded well enough, but I was chagrined to realize I'd made myself a terrible bargain: the project would require weeks of physically draining labor worth a great deal more than the few shillings I'd exchanged for it. But there was no more hope of going back on the contract than there was of selling Vrijdag back to Loytinck. An unexpectedly intriguing aspect of the project, for me, was the development of my relation to the slave. Knowing myself committed to dozens of hours alone with an intelligent slave who could make life really unpleasant without ever committing the error of overt defiance, I'd been anticipating some awkwardness. For his part, Vrijdag seemed equally wary of me, doubtless wondering how aggressively I might lord it over him. The peculiarity was, that the instant the two of us were on the roof all this was forgotten. The requirements of the job took precedence over all else, and we were temporarily as at ease with each other as we'd once been playing catch. We could freely debate how many inches of flashing should surround the chimney. He could use the imperative, "Pass me the hammer," without a whiff of offense. But when we again returned to the ground, the status of master and slave froze such simple rapport.

We'd been at it a week when I came close to killing myself. I had climbed the sharply pitched roof to the apex to relax for a minute. Vrijdag was working just below me, right at the edge. Pa, who occasionally roused himself to give assistance with tools and supplies, was napping under the apple tree. I had often checked whether the ocean could be seen from our house and decided it could not. So I was startled—thrilled, honestly—suddenly to perceive the topgallant sails, though not the hull, of a great ship approaching the harbor. Petrus walked into the yard, returning from school, and I excitedly told the lad about it. He didn't understand, so I began to use my hands to name and indicate the various sails, and—

My feet slipped from under me and in two seconds, shrieking, I was dangling over the eaves. We'd nailed horizontal cleats and suspended working ropes to support ourselves, but the momentum of my careless fall had been too great, and I was staring at twenty-five feet of air between me and the gravel below. Why wasn't I already broken or dead there? Because Vrijdag had grabbed my wrist at the last instant and managed to hold me! He was holding me with one hand and the end of his rope with the other—groaning with the great stress to his back. It must've taken seconds for me to overcome my shock and terror enough to realize I was looking at the eave's support beam and could use my bleeding free hand to put weight on it. When I did this, I saw it was also impossible to pull myself back onto the roof. "Pa! The ladder!" I screamed. Petrus ran to Pa but couldn't budge him.

"Can you get your other hand onto it?" Vrijdag asked.

I made a frantic, desperate choice. "Yes. Let go." And in a terrifying second, I had two bleeding hands holding my full weight.

"Meneer, Meneer!" Vrijdag called to Pa. But despite the huge strain he'd just endured, Vrijdag moved a lot faster than Pa did. He was down the ladder, lifting it, and carrying it before Pa joined him. They positioned it beside me and Vrijdag instantly dashed up to lift my feet onto a rung before my strength gave out. Flat on *terra firma* a moment later, I vomited from sheer fright.

Mother rushed out and, ignoring the blood and splinters, examined both me and Vrijdag for broken bones. "God be praised!" she exclaimed. "It's a miracle neither of them has so much as dislocated his shoulder." In intense pain, nothing seemed miraculous to me at all.

It was only in thinking about it much later, that I realized I owed Vrijdag my life.

CHAPTER 8

It took three days to overcome my lacerations, muscle strains, and newfound wariness of the roof, but I finally forced myself up the ladder to resume the job. As I watched Vrijdag cautiously climbing up after me, I suspected he may not have found field work so objectionable in the interim. But our resumed efforts progressed well in weather that was at long last fine.

Early the following week, I noticed that the strap of the weathervane, a proud iron rooster attached to the south chimney so as to be visible from the road, was rusted through. In fact, the merest test of its strength served to collapse it. "Schuppert make new brace," Vrijdag observed. "Easy. Should double strength. Last longer." When we finished for the day, I took Vrijdag with me, to make sure Schuppert understood what didn't seem clear to me. The forge, however, was shut down.

We found the smith sitting in the yard behind his modest house, wrapped in blankets. He apologized for not rising to greet me. "Bad cough," he groaned. "Seem to be losing my strength."

"Nonsense!" exclaimed his wife, bursting out the door carrying a basket with which she proceeded to collect laundry from the line. "Losing your faith is more like it!"

Schuppert grimaced and coughed. "Machtel's right, of course. What can I do for you, young Thomas?"

I explained the problem and motioned Vrijdag to show him the broken piece. Schuppert took it from him and, though he'd offered the slave no greeting at all, discussed repair possibilities with him for a full minute.

"Bette!" Vrouw Schuppert called. "Some cider for Meneer Dordrecht!" Their slave girl presently appeared bearing a welcome glass, which she handed to me. She also brought a crude clay mug, which she set down where Vrijdag could reach it. He did, and his wink reminded me they were somehow related. The mistress heaved an irritated sigh, as if she was insufficiently irked to make a public fuss, and gave the girl the full laundry basket to take inside.

Schuppert handed the vane back to Vrijdag, airily waved him away, and beckoned me close in order to whisper. "Look, I've been down two days already, and I don't think I can go back tomorrow. But this boy could do it himself. Ordinarily I wouldn't want, you know, to let him, but.… I've also got two customers waiting on two other little jobs. I'll let him do your vane for cost, if you'll get him to do those jobs too. Shouldn't take more than a couple hours all told."

This sounded like a great deal to me, but … how should I convey it to the slave? I repeated the whole proposition aloud, to Schuppert's chagrin. Vrijdag listened stonily and shrugged. "We'll throw in a chicken at Pinkster," I added grandly. He smiled for a second.

"That's not how you deal with slaves, boy!" Schuppert wheezed.

Nonetheless it got the job done.

✳   ✳   ✳

Visiting the city twice a week for supplies, I was painfully reminded how much I missed living there, and I girded myself to overcome the humiliation I felt and attempt a resumption of my friendship with Mr. Glasby. He was congeniality itself—a response I never should have doubted. We met at a public house for a pleasant midday dinner. As opposed to everyone at home, he never berated me for failing to occupy myself with more than reading and guitar-playing. "Soon enough," he shrugged.

I did elicit the opinion that Mr. Colegrove would never take me back— and that Glasby remained baffled by his sharp reaction. A replacement had long since been found for me at the warehouse, who Glasby uncomfortably intimated was not much to his liking. "I looked up your friend Miss Chapman!" he declared, changing the subject. "We needed a sign for the big warehouse, and I remembered you said she did that sort of thing. The result is quite splendid, I think, although"—he chuckled—"she complained it was rather boring."

"Boring?" What an outlandish thing to say!

"All we wanted was 'Colegrove Co.,' in capitals, in black on white. She begged me quite prettily to put the name in blue, with a red and purple border, but I knew my employer would never countenance the extra expense."

I laughed. "She's … most unpredictable!"

"Indeed. Still, she needed the work, so there it is."

And I rushed to examine it, directly we parted. It was the handsomest sign of the locality.

At home the following evening, Mother and I worked late to reconcile our accounts. When done, we took a glass of genever together. "You realize Lisa and I shall be called away again, Thomas, before May is out?"

"For Geertruid? Is she well?"

"Yes. I anticipate no problems, but I'd like to stay an extra day or two...."

"Of course." Another emergency. But how could I deny her time with her daughter and grandchildren?

"I'd hoped," she began cautiously, "that you might take over the management of this enterprise altogether, Thomas. You seem to do well at it, and—"

"I believe my fortune lies elsewhere, Mother."

"Let me finish, lad! The inn needs work, Thomas. We used to make more money from it than we do now."

We both knew the primary reason for our declining patronage. "Perhaps, if Pa—"

"I'll attend to your father, Thomas," she said conclusively. "But we need someone to take full charge here, and—"

"That's always been you, Mother."

"True, but ... I'm being called upon more and more, and it's distracting me from problems close to home, and...." She sped up, perhaps eager to forestall any objections. "You seem to have some sense of money, Thomas—although you often misplace it—but the sorry truth is that you and I are the only ones in this family who do!" The definitive harshness of this judgment shocked me, and I must have looked skeptical. "I don't know how Cornelis Dordrecht, who never let a farthing slip his fingers," she railed, "sired such a horde of financial incompetents! Rykert has no sense, his brother has no sense, his sisters have no sense. Harmanus struggles with economy but *I'm* the one who figures out what's most profitable to plant. Brevoort has no common sense at all, and it's a mercy that Geertruid married some, as she's none of her own!"

"For heaven's sake, Mother!"

"It's true! It's not a matter of being foolish or slothful, you understand," she added more gently. "It's having money sense, Thomas, the realization that irrespective of habit or inclination, some efforts bring better returns than others."

I did have an inkling of what she meant. I was amazed and honored by her confidence in me—and unsure that I shared it. But although innkeeping struck me far more interesting than farming, that was no high recommendation. "Mother, I'm sorry, I.... Can we just leave our agreement as it is for the time-being?" She sighed, and I tumbled to her predicament—never before having quite tumbled to the fact that parents *have* predicaments. She wanted to be free of the inn almost as much as I wanted to be free of the farm and the town. But she at least had a goal, a specific purpose to follow. "Perhaps Berendina or Hendrik will take an interest one of these days."

If Mother was disappointed, she refused to show it. "Perhaps," she said bravely. "I hope you're not offended, Thomas, it seemed a reasonable thing to suggest."

I loved her wholeheartedly. "No, no, of course not!" She rose and hung up her apron. "I did have an idea for the inn, however."

She wheeled back around, startled and again hopeful. "Truly?"

Perhaps inspired by Dr. Franklin, I'd almost involuntarily begun to contemplate how the appearance and services of the tavern and the inn might be improved. "We need to make ourselves more conspicuous, Mother. The only reason we gain custom at all is that our neighbors direct travelers to the Dordrechts' house."

"Aye. So they always have. What would you suggest?"

"That we give the place a name, a public presence like the taverns and inns in the city."

"Is that important?" Her eyes flashed about as she answered her own question. "I suppose you have a suggestion? The Huron's Long-House? The Brown Bess and Betty? The Purple Dolphin?"

"No," I said, laughing. "My idea was a name in both Dutch and English, because the family's both, and our customers are both."

She ceased teasing, curious. "Yes?"

"So I thought we could name it for the royal house that united both, 'The Arms of Orange'—'*Het Wapen van Oranje*.' We could use King William's coat of arms!"

She looked perplexed. "I ... just find it hard to get used to the idea, son."

"We'd need a sign out front, Dutch on one side, English on the other. And I have an artist friend in the city who could paint it!"

*　　　*　　　*

Miss Chapman and I exchanged pleasantries in the sitting room of her domicile. It appeared that she hadn't actually noticed that I'd gone missing for over two months. But her warm, friendly manner was instantly reassuring. "What may I do for you, Mr. Dordrecht?"

"My family would like to create a sign to call attention to our hostelry in New Utrecht, and Mr. Glasby recommended your services in that regard."

"Mr. Glasby? How good of him! A tavern sign, then?" We discussed my notion of a bilingual sign. I was charmed by her growing enthusiasm, and we negotiated a perfectly reasonable price. She even knew of a lumberyard that had a suitable board. "You know what, Mr. Dordrecht? The weather is quite lovely, and I should be happy to escape the city for a few days. Why don't we pack up my paints, and I'll return with you this very afternoon?"

This had not been part of my plan. "I … thought you'd like to paint the sign here, in the city, Miss Chapman?"

"Alas, I've no studio, Mr. Dordrecht. I must always travel to the client's business. Would that be inconvenient?"

That it might, indeed, be somehow not convenient escaped my apprehension as I spent the afternoon delighting in Miss Chapman's company. We found a blank sign superior to the one she'd recalled, being already coated with white. At her direction, I purchased turpentine, varnish, and brushes. We had a pleasant ferry passage, which particularly entranced her after three unbroken years on New York City's island. When we debarked at Red Hook she spontaneously assisted me with the groceries and roofing supplies as well as her paints and baggage.

Not only did conversation cease when we arrived home in the middle of supper, all motion ceased as well. The entire family—and three customers as well—froze in addled stupefaction when Miss Chapman and I walked in. Their reaction disconcerted me, and it was left to Miss Chapman's amazing presence of mind to walk over to mother, proffer her hand and say, "You must be Mrs. Dordrecht! How do you do, I'm Adelie Chapman."

It took Mother five seconds to rise and shake hands. "Yes?"

"Your son has contracted with me to paint the sign for this fine establishment."

"You're … *you're* the 'artist'?"

"Yes, ma'am, that's right!" Miss Chapman's smiling confidence began to break through the universal assumptions that 'artists' were male—and exotic creatures deathly allergic to Long Island.

Again it took seconds, but Mother recovered herself before anyone else. "You … must be famished. Elisabeth, get Miss Chapman a bowl of the stew!" She gestured that room should be made at the table, and I noticed that Harmanus and Anneke automatically removed all their fascinated young to the farthest end. I procured my own bowl of stew. Harmanus loudly and insistently resumed a conversation with the customers, in Dutch, despite *their* obvious curiosity about the newcomer. "*Um,* what will you be painting for us, Miss Chapman?" Mother asked, still flustered.

"Now that's a question, ma'am! Mr. Dordrecht, how exactly *am* I to illustrate the tavern's name?"

Confusion. I'd planned to research that issue at leisure after having secured the original arrangements. "We do have the tile in the kitchen," I said lamely.

"That's just the Lion of Nassau, Thomas!"

"Perhaps the dominie might—"

"Grootmoeder's necklace!" Lisa exclaimed.

"Yes! Go fetch it, dear." Grootmoeder was dozing in her rocker.

"Her wedding present," I explained to Miss Chapman. "It has a silver coin from the decade she was born, in King William's time."

We waited impatiently until Lisa produced the necklace for Mother. "You're not going to use *his* picture?" Lisa demanded irreverently.

"No no, the other side, silly," Mother said. She turned it over to show the royal arms, which had the usual British four quarters, plus the Orange-Nassau escutcheon in the middle.

"Oh yes!" Miss Chapman said. "This will be very colorful. Reds, blues, golds—marvelous. And we'll put the name at the top in orange! On a gray scroll, I think? You'll have to spell out the Dutch for me, Thomas"—Mother's eyebrows shot up and Adelie immediately corrected herself—"*uh, Mr. Dordrecht.* I think it will be hugely attractive!"

*　　*　　*

Before we resumed our efforts on the roof the next morning, Vrijdag and I helped Miss Chapman set up her easel. From the window of the upstairs guest room where she'd been lodged, she'd chosen to work by the kitchen garden just outside the stable, in case of rain. "Thomas, have you considered where and how this is to be mounted? That should be decided before I start."

We walked around to the front of the house, which is set back only about fifteen feet from the turn of the Kings Highway. "I'd just imagined it suspended from two posts in the ground," I said. "That's what *The Mohican,* in Brooklyn town, looks like."

Miss Chapman looked thoughtful, and then tugged my arm and walked well out into the street, then twenty yards on towards the kerk. Vrijdag dutifully followed behind. "Ah!" she exclaimed, looking back. "Needs to be high up, Thomas. Usually on their own pole, aren't they?"

I had seen such. She was quite right. "Not much room for that."

"Oh yes, you are right on the road. But it needs to be mounted high—on the wall of the house perhaps—if you want it to be seen."

I sighed, adjusting to the need for further expense. She was perfectly right, of course. "Would Meneer Schuppert be able to build us a support for it?" I asked Vrijdag.

"Oh yes."

"The local smith," I explained. "Can you sketch out what we need?"

She was already doing just that on a pad. "There!"

Looking over my shoulder, Vrijdag shook his head. "Too small," he said to me in Dutch.

"He says it's not sturdy enough," I explained.

"Ah!" she said, apparently startled—not offended, just surprised—to have been evaluated by a slave. She shrugged. "Well, the board *is* very heavy. You're on your own, Mr. Dordrecht. Not my area of expertise!"

I impatiently thrust the drawing pad at Vrijdag as I followed her back to the stable. "You're right about where it should go!"

"Ideally, you should attempt to set your lanterns so they illuminate it in the evenings!"

Mother had grumbled over the amount I'd already spent. "Perhaps ... we can add that in the future."

Vrijdag rejoined us a moment later—I was dawdling, postponing my climb to the roof—and set the drawing pad down in front of Miss Chapman. He'd greatly expanded her sketch.

"Ah, I see!" she said. "Yes, that does look much stronger. Braced against the wind. And I love the curlicue, and the finial!" She hesitantly attempted to meet the slave's eye. "Very nice," she murmured.

*   *   *

Mother's comportment toward Miss Chapman, last night and this morning, had been businesslike to the point of frostiness. My sister had followed her example. I was all the more perplexed, therefore, to find this aloofness mysteriously vanished when I climbed down from the roof that afternoon. None of the three seemed inclined to explain their sudden rapport, however. And though Harmanus and Anneke remained cool, their four older children had clearly made Miss Chapman a favorite. I was completely befuddled to learn that Mother had promised several neighbors a concert that evening. Though bone weary, I excitedly hastened to prepare myself. It was all I could do to make my aching hands answer my command. Given that Miss Chapman was also fatigued, we managed to retire after but a half-dozen songs. I'd spoken up to discourage "Rule Britannia," as locally unpopular, despite it's being her signature song. Ophelia's song took its place, and had to be encored. She sang "The Eddystone Light" with the original words, which were quite challenging enough for local sensibilities. Dominie Van Voort, undoubtedly invited by my mother only to certify the propriety of the evening, reddened once or twice, but applauded heartily when all was done. I, meanwhile, was embarrassed to see him gazing more often in my sister's direction than Miss Chapman's. Pa appeared, spruced up by his wife, but he morosely sat near the fire drinking nought but sweet cider, trying to pretend that Grootmoeder provided him company.

The next morning Vrijdag and I again visited Schuppert—only to find him now confined to bed. Over his wife's objections, we were received anyway. Again he proposed that his former assistant should forge our tavern sign holder without charge, provided he would also execute other customers' jobs on his behalf. But these would take three or four days in total. Eager as I now was to see the inn sign finished and mounted, I demurred, knowing my brother would have a fit. Perhaps Schuppert would presently recover and obviate the necessity.

"I heard the rioting continued until nigh eight o'clock last night," Vrouw Schuppert observed unpleasantly as we were departing. "Next thing you know, there'll be dancing parties there!"

"Nay, ma'am, it was a quiet little concert, no more," I huffed, hastening to defend the tavern's reputation, however infuriated I might have been by her insinuations. "The dominie himself attended, and—"

"Well, we all know about *him,* don't we?"

It was enough to make me happy to climb to the roof.

When I climbed down ten hours later, Mother, Lisa, and Miss Chapman were "out for a walk," my father said. "Conspiring!" he added ominously.

Harmanus arrived, and I took the moment to mention Schuppert's proposal. "Oh no," he moaned. "You're almost done with the roof, and now you want more of his time?"

"We've already invested a good deal of money in the sign, Harmanus. We need to have it affixed to the house!"

My brother shook his head in uncomprehending disbelief. "Do what you have to, Thomas. But I don't know how we'll put food on the table next winter!" He stomped on toward the stairs. "I don't suppose it would speed matters if *you* were to lend Schuppert a hand as well? In order to get the slave back on the fields a day earlier?"

I groaned. That had not been any part of my idea. But on the other hand, it might be interesting....

Mother, Miss Chapman, and Lisa walked into the yard arm-in-arm, their happy faces as far from conspiracy as might be possible. "It's done, Thom— Mr. Dordrecht!" Miss Chapman exclaimed, running toward me. "Come and see!" And before I could elicit any explanation of the sudden female comradeship, she'd pulled me to the stable, garnered my genuine admiration, and instructed me to varnish and sand the sign four times before installing it.

She returned to the city with me the next day on my regular Thursday shopping trip, with thanks and good wishes from all my relatives, whose sudden enthusiasm I found puzzling. On Jacob's ferry, enjoying another beautiful sail in perfect weather, we were occasionally thrust against each other by the buffeting of the waves, which was … not unpleasant. "You soon became popular with my family!"

"It's a lovely family, Thomas! And I adore that house! The hearth tiles, the corbelled facade, the Dutch doors—charming! Not often seen anymore."

"I … always thought it was just odd."

"Don't be silly, it's delightful!"

"I never thought of my family as particularly lovely, either—except for Lisa, of course."

"Ah, your sister is a beautiful lass. Takes after her mother. But your brother is quite splendid too, I must say."

What? "You must have confused him with my cousin Bertie?"

"No no. Bertie's a comely lad, to be sure, like you, but I meant Anneke's husband. The woman is much to be envied!"

Would I ever figure an "artist" out? Everyone knows Harmanus Dordrecht is as homely as a potato! Next thing you know, she'll be admiring the looks of Charles Cooper!

I saw her back to the boarding house and helped stow her paints away. She arranged to join with me again after my marketing, and presented me with a packet for my mother and sister that aroused my curiosity so intensely that *all* my fortitude was required to keep me from peeking into it.

*   *   *

Once home—circumstances made it dusk before I arrived—the packet was swept away without explanation thanks to everyone's eagerness to inform me of the latest news, which had been received by the Dordrecht clan with some consternation. It seems that at the annual meeting of the townsmen, Meneer Loytinck had testily reminded them all that his term as schout was lawfully complete, and demanded relief. The worthy burghers, casting about for a new victim, had hit upon the name of Rykert Dordrecht, who'd not shuffled himself to attend. Amid great hilarity, and over the protestations of his eldest son, Pa had been confirmed *in absentia*.

"They just want him to buy his way out of it!" I objected. "And he should do that, of course!" I added sternly, as glum faces looked evasively around the tavern room.

"The fine's five pounds, Thomas," Mother sighed.

"He *earns* five a year if he keeps it," Bertie added.

"Pa wants to keep it, I think," Lisa observed.

"You never know. It might rally him," Bertie said.

"Well, but is it completely beyond possibility that the schout of New Utrecht might someday actually have to *do* something?"

Everyone shrugged, but the decision stood.

My curiosity about Miss Chapman's present so tortured me, I resolved to inveigle the truth out of my sister, by and from whom few secrets were withheld. It was a week later on Saturday afternoon, before the opportunity presented itself, thanks to a new disruption. Vrijdag and I had finally hammered the very last of the new cedar shingles into place and gratefully departed the roof. However, I'd no sooner announced the tidings than a commercial traveler brought Geertruid's summons to Flatbush. I followed Lisa about as she packed her clothes into a canvas bag. "Excited?"

"Of course. Things don't get more exciting—for women, at least."

"Miss Chapman seems to find many things exciting."

"I liked your Miss Chapman, Thomas," she said a trifle guardedly. "I'm glad you brought her out here."

"What, *uh*...."

"The package? She didn't tell you what it was? It wasn't a present; Mother paid her for it."

"Oh?"

"You remind me. This is the moment to first employ it!" She turned toward her dressing cabinet and hesitated. "We don't want the children to know about this, Thomas. Berendina was rather frightened when she brought Miss Chapman's water ewer and chanced to see hers." She pulled a narrow object from the back of a drawer: a dirk, some eight inches long, its leather sheath sewn tightly into a canvas bag with plain ribbons at the top and bottom. "It fits on thus," she explained, immodestly pulling her petticoats up to her knee. She tied the garters to her lower leg, pulled the skirts down, and looked me in the eye. "One for me, and one for Mother. And she showed us how to handle them."

This wasn't supposed to be needful in our civilized county. But it was hard to argue against the sense of it. "So Miss Chapman herself carries one of these? I don't suppose she's ever used it?"

"As a matter of fact, she said she had! She'd worn it for years, and was almost beginning to think herself silly, when a man she'd considered a friend pressed himself on her. Just last fall."

"She stabbed him?"

"Aye, in the upper leg. If he hadn't pulled away, she said she'd have gladly killed him."

I exhaled slowly, taking this in. How could one argue against this with women with a penchant for traveling abroad at odd hours? I normally carried my militia musket whenever out of town, day or night. "Miss Chapman is replete with surprises," I murmured admiringly.

"Thomas, I don't know that it's my place to say this, but.... You're supposed to be running around saving *me* from excesses of passion, you know!" We both laughed nervously. "You haven't any notion of proposing to Miss Chapman, Thomas?"

She'd caught me off guard. "I—"

"Thomas, Miss Chapman is a wonderful individual, but she'd be an absurd choice for—"

"*Why?*" I demanded indignantly.

"My dear, have you any notion of what her age may be?"

Oh that. "There are many marriages in which the wife is older than the husband. Aunt Betje's older than Uncle Claes!"

"Thomas, the woman has got to be at least thirty-four years old. Fifteen years your senior! She will soon be past childbearing age, if she's not already, and—"

"No!"

Lisa looked me pityingly in the eye, which was quite intolerable.

"How do you figure this?" I demanded. "You asked her?"

"Of course not. But it's easy to deduce … if one's ready to put one's mind to it. She became the Thwaites' governess in London when she was my age, she said, and—"

"Elisabeth, are you ready?" Mother called.

"Coming!" We shared a few silent, uncomfortable seconds. "Could you take the bag down for me? I need to gather my books and a few more things."

I shook myself. "Of course." I grabbed the bag and sullenly made for the stairs.

"Thomas? Wish us luck?"

"Of course."

*   *   *

My mother's departure meant that I was once again confined to the tavern. Shopping trips would have to wait, as would any arrangement with Meneer Schuppert. Harmanus was delighted. After I gave the sign another coat, I set it out in front of the house, rather than leave it in the stable. Even as I was doing this, the man from Gravesend appeared. "A handsome sign, there, lad. What does it mean, though?"

The Dutch side had been facing up. "Ah, it's 'The Arms of Orange,' Mr. MacDonald," I said, turning the sign over before proceeding inside to fetch him a drink.

His face became somber. "Those are King Billy's arms?"

"Aye, the king of the Glorious Revolution, you see!" He grunted, took a long pull on his whiskey and sighed. "Is something wrong?"

"Not with the whiskey, lad, but … oh, it's a long time ago. It was his minions who sat down as guests of members of my clan at Glencoe, you see, and then murdered them by the dozens as they slept!"

"As they *slept?* Surely not, sir, that's too horrible to imagine!"

"So I've been told, Mr. Dordrecht." He finished the whiskey and paid. "My granddad escaped by a hair, I understand. Perhaps the Dutch folk hereabouts will be pleased with the name?"

"We appreciate your custom, Mr. MacDonald!" I called … to his back.

As if in a conspiracy to make me feel abashed, Meneer Nijenhuis and Dominie Van Voort presently came in for an ale to finish their discussion of kerk business. Nijenhuis presently excused himself home for supper, but the dominie was pleased to pass some moments with me. After we'd reviewed the local minutiae, I mentioned the dismay I'd felt over MacDonald's revelation. "*Stadhouder* Willem was not beloved by all the Dutch, either, Thomas," he said.

"Oh? But I thought…. He was a Dutchman who became King of England!"

"Yes, but back in the disaster year of sixteen seventy-two, most authorities agree he was complicit in the murder of the Grand Pensionary Johan de Witt and his brother. He was about your age, then—before he married the Princess Mary Stuart. The English revere him because he saved them from rule by the papists, but the Netherlanders had already done that for themselves." Now well confounded, I was uncharacteristically glad to see Harmanus come in and start an entirely different conversation with the clergyman.

And all the more glad, two afternoons later, when Hendrik, studying by the window, suddenly looked disbelievingly at the scene outside. I heard a cart pulling into the yard. "Strangers?"

"Aye," he said softly. "Peculiar strangers."

But there was nothing odd about the tall, vital man of middle years who presently appeared in the door, looked confidently about and bellowed, "The 'Arms of Orange,' is it? What an *excellent* name for a public house!"

CHAPTER 9

———— ⟐ ————

It was very heartening. He looked all about the room, taking in myself, Hendrik, and Grootmoeder, and said, "Yes, this should be fine! You have rooms to let, lad?" Hendrik went out to attend to the horse and cart.

Rooms *to let!* "Aye, sir. That is, our inn has four rooms available, two on this—"

"May I inspect them, please?"

"Certainly. If you'll follow me, please?" I led him to the back of the house, around the stairwell and past the kitchen. "This is our best room, sir. It faces south and opens into the adjacent alcove, which has a circular table and is available for private dining or conferences. The bedroom opposite is almost of equal size." The man nodded and grunted appreciatively. "And we have convenient access to the privy, just ten yards away through the back door."

"The room's right next to the kitchen...."

"I'm afraid so, sir. But the local hours are very early, here. We stop serving supper at eight o'clock, even in high summer."

"*Uh huh.* And this little room? It's a closet?"

"No sir, that's my grandmother's room. She can't handle the stairs very well." He looked disappointed. "She's very quiet, sir, she's gone a bit daft." Thoughtfully, he seemed to be considering the entirety of the premises. "Would you care to see the two rooms above, sir?"

"The family also lives there?"

"Yes."

"No, thank you—I value my privacy, you see."

"Of course, sir."

"It's fine. I'll stay here. Need it for about a fortnight."

Good lord! When was the last time anyone had stayed two nights in a row? Without even asking the rate! "Would you prefer the south room or the north?" I stammered out.

"Oh, I'll take both, if you please. Need a bed for my manservant and his wife." The man astonished me into dropping my jaw, but Mother had taught me never to gainsay the domestic arrangements of one's customers—and that was certainly the gist of Franklin's commercial admonitions as well. "In a moment of weakness, you see, I permitted my servant to marry."

I searched for words. "Indeed?"

"And now I'm saddled with 'em both! Live and learn, Mr. Dordrecht!" Again, I was startled. "You are Dordrecht, are you not?" I nodded. "Ah. That's what I was told ... down the road."

"Oh yes? May we offer you some refreshment, Mr. ...?"

"Scoffield. Robert Scoffield." He thrust his hand forward, and I eagerly shook it. "Perhaps in a moment—and back here in this alcove, I think. But ... are *you* the proprietor?"

"No no, sir: my parents. My mother normally manages here, but she's been called away. She's also a midwife, you see, and she's over in Flatbush—attending my own elder sister, in fact. We hope for glad tidings by the hour!"

"And so do we all, my good lad!"

"Thank you kindly, sir!" The gentleman was most effusive! "This will be the third of her own grandchildren she'll have delivered in as many months!"

"My word! And your father?"

"He's ... attending to our livestock at the moment, I believe."

"Uh huh. Well, can you fetch some ale, please?"

"Surely. *Uh,* but you should understand, sir ... the rate is seven pence a night for the suite, and four for the north room, payable each morning. This includes—"

"Nonsense, we'll pay a week in advance. We can compute that as we imbibe, perhaps?"

"It'd be ... six shillings and five pence, sir."

"Oh yes? Right, well, I'll pick through my coins while you fetch the beer, lad. Bring four, please—one for yourself!"

Dazed, I left him in the little room and hurried to effect the service. Hendrik walked back in, looking out of sorts. "Can you manage here a while, boy? They're planning to stay for some time, and he wishes to talk with me for a moment!"

"Those people? Uncle Thomas, they're really—"

"Hendrik, all you have to do is holler for me if somebody comes in, all right?" I carefully picked up the loaded tray.

"But they're—"

"Good lad!"

It took earnest concentration to manage the tray onto the alcove table without a spill. When I looked up, I beheld a pair of individuals more incongruous than any I'd found in the diciest grog shops of the waterfront.

*   *   *

"Please do sit and join us, Mr. Dordrecht," Scoffield said, smiling expansively—as if he could imagine nothing in his bizarre associates that might give me pause. "Here's for our first week, by the by," he added, pushing coins in my direction.

In some agitation, I focused on counting the change—exact—as Scoffield commenced introductions. "This is my man, Justus Bates, and his wife Yvette. This is Mr. Dordrecht, son of the proprietor."

"Thomas Dordrecht, at your service," I announced mechanically, rising and shaking the limp outstretched hands.

Looking more directly, I was still dumbfounded that a gentleman of Scoffield's stature would own an association with the Bates pair. Mr. Scoffield was wearing a dark blue woolen business suit of a conservative fashion that I fancy my aunt's husband, Mr. Cooper, would find eminently respectable. Bates was a tall, slight man of advanced years, unshaven for days, with several missing teeth. He was wearing patched and dirty clothes that my mother wouldn't have let me wear on the roof. He had oddly evasive mannerisms, too—nervous hands and eyes that never quite settled anywhere.

But the wife was even more shocking. Half her husband's age, Mrs. Bates was dressed in the sort of cheap linen gown that my Cliff Street neighbor had worn when I'd first met her: dark red trimmed with light blue, low on petticoats, very low in the bosom. Though I'd seen such attire often enough in the city, the like had never been known in New Utrecht. Her hennaed hair was a profusion of unbound curls spilling over her shoulders. Her face was whitened and rouged to a degree Régine had not affected even when pretending she was royalty. There was a strange brown dot on her cheek that Miss Chapman had once explained as a deliberate "beauty mark." Although comely of figure, I found her face quite plain, despite the paint, and her demeanor offensively bold. She took a long pull on her beer, slammed the mug down, and said, "Christ, I really needed that!"

Mr. Bates appeared to find this not only indicative of his own sentiment, but funny. Grinning, he belched as aggressively as had any of my mates in the regiment.

Affecting to ignore—or actually ignoring—these antics, Mr. Scoffield smiled benignly and complimented the ale, which was from a particularly fine batch my brother-in-law had produced over the winter. "As you must have deduced, Mr. Dordrecht, I have some interest in the business of the locality."

Talking business would be a relief. "Is that so, sir?"

"Yes. I am a factor representing certain interests in the city—New York, that is, not Philadelphia or London—and we are looking to secure a great store of grains and other produce." I nodded, impressed and curious. "So we shall need to talk to all the farmers in the south of the county."

"That's a great many people, sir."

"We realize that. Perhaps you can assist me with some information?"

"I'll do my best, sir, of course."

It was not the usual local directions he was seeking, but extensive details on every farming enterprise of the town. Bates searched out pen, ink, and paper from their luggage so his superior could make notes. Mrs. Bates, after first falling asleep on the table, retired to the north bedchamber. After half an hour, I excused myself to check on my nephew. Scoffield tossed a silver sixpence to me and urged my quick return. Certainly did sweeten my disposition to comply!

*   *   *

Hendrik—reciprocally sweetened by a penny from me—continued to preside out front while I entertained Mr. Scoffield's huge curiosity about our home town. Bates had retired also, which certainly made me feel more relaxed. In the process, I found out a little about our visitor. He hailed originally from Barbados—which is why I couldn't place his accent. Like me, he was a younger son with no chance of inheriting his family's estate, which apparently was large. He'd spent some years in Philadelphia before coming to New York last fall. Bates' indenture was all that remained of his inheritance. He asked if I'd serve as his translator. As a courtesy, I agreed, though I explained that it would seldom be necessary.

"I fear I must apologize for the appearance of Bates and his wife, Dordrecht," he said an hour later as I delivered another round. "I imagine they're a trifle odd for this locality."

A trifle? "I fear Mrs. Bates, particularly, may not find herself welcome here, sir."

He grimaced. "Yes. Well, I'll … try to keep her out of public view as much as possible. Perhaps if we take our meals back here?"

"Ah, that might be—"

The front door slammed. "Twins!" Harmanus roared joyfully. "Geertruid had twins!"

Immediately there was commotion in the tavern room. "Would you be so good as to excuse me, sir?"

"But of course, lad," Scoffield said suavely. "My congratulations!"

"A boy and a girl, just this morning. All fine!" Harmanus was telling Anneke. "Berend's brother rode over to tell me."

"And their names?" my sister-in-law demanded, as Hendrik and I poured celebratory libations. Neighbors began to arrive.

Harmanus had to think. "Arjan! Arjan and Maria Kloppen!" After much discussion, the thankful consensus was that the names were eminently acceptable. "Where is Pa?" Harmanus asked me presently. I shrugged. "He has to be told. You or me?"

Awkward. "If either of us tells him," I said confidentially, "he'll insist on a tipple."

We both looked at my nephew. "Hendrik, go find your grandfather and let him know of God's beneficence in providing you with cousins!"

As Hendrik obediently ran out, Mr. Scoffield appeared from the back, startling the company. His disarming smile reassured them, however, and I effected introductions. Scoffield possesses that turn of personality always praised as "easy condescension," and quickly ingratiated himself with my brother and the neighbors. Under constraint of detailed questioning, I had explained that it was in fact Harmanus who ran our own farming operation, rather than our father, and Scoffield was eagerly pumping him for details of his soils and plantings as I presently excused myself to assist Anneke and Berendina, who were managing the kitchen in mother's stead.

"Thomas," my sister-in-law, paler than usual, demanded in an urgent whisper, "who are those people?" She vigorously shook her head at the closed door of the alcove. "That *woman!*"

She was attempting to exclude the child, who was plucking a chicken over the sink, but it was no use. "How come she's wearing her nightdress, Uncle Thomas, when it's not even dark yet?"

Anneke was dissatisfied with my explanation, and wasn't remotely mollified by the paw-full of coins I exhibited by way of justification. "Harmanus won't like her being here, mark my words!"

For twenty minutes, we worked hard at supper preparations. As I was stoking the fire, my brother—who never as a rule sets foot in the kitchen—came in, a dazed look on his face. All four of us began talking at once:

"Husband, have you seen—"

"Papa, who's that lady in the—"

"Harmanus, I have to explain to you—"

"Thomas, Scoffield has just—" Harmanus held his hand up, and indicated that *he* would speak first. "Thomas, Mr. Scoffield has just made us the most remarkable proposition!"

"He has? Harmanus, I have to explain—"

"Harmanus, have you *seen* the man and the woman he brought—"

"Wait, Anneke, this is business!" Ignoring his distraught wife, Harmanus pulled me out into the hall. "He's trying to secure great stores of wheat for next winter."

"Yes yes, so he told me."

"So he's offered to pay for it *in advance!*"

"In advance? What on earth?"

"He'll pay now for wheat to be delivered to him in November!"

"But that's absurd, Harmanus. The price of wheat goes up and down all the time!"

"Yes. That's just it. You fix a price in advance, you see. That guarantees both buyer and seller a reliable price."

"And one of them is disappointed, come November!"

"Perhaps. But at least they've got something to protect them against a drastic change in either direction."

Mr. Glasby had once told me businessmen were experimenting with such modern arrangements, but said he didn't understand how they worked in practice. "I see," I said dubiously. "Both sides take a risk, both sides forego their maximum possible benefit, in order to insure against their worst disaster."

"I knew you'd understand!" Harmanus exulted. "I knew you'd agree!"

My blood ran cold. "Agree to what, Harmanus?"

"We made a deal for one hundred bushels!"

"That's practically your whole crop, Harmanus! What…. Dare I ask what price you struck?"

"Twenty-seven pence. That's not as much as we made last year, but it's a penny better than we netted in 'fifty-seven!"

"That's eleven pounds, five shillings for your whole year, Harmanus!"

He looked startled but undismayed. "Yes? I thought it was almost nineteen."

"You divide by two hundred forty, not a hundred forty-four."

"Oh right. Well still…. Better than every other year before last!"

It was my turn to be angry with him. "Dutchmen are supposed to be able to *bargain*, Harmanus! You never just accept the first offer, no matter what it is! You wait on it overnight, and think—"

"Well, Pa liked it!"

My heart sank. "Pa's in there?"

"Aye. He and Mr. Scoffield hit it right off."

That concluded the matter, and there was no point in belaboring it. My brother and I stood back to let Willem and Berendina pass between us. It was clearly a busy evening for the tavern, and Anneke had the children hustling to set the tables and take out the bread and cheese. "Harmanus!" she called. "The children can't handle the soup tureen. You take it in!"

He had just grasped the heavy pot when Scoffield came back and greeted us cheerfully. "An excellent day, gentlemen! And I look forward to that fine-smelling supper, Mrs. Dordrecht!" He put his hand on the doorknob. "Oh, can we have three more ales, if you please?"

As he pushed it open, I somehow thought to put my hands beneath my brother's. Harmanus gasped and flushed beet red as, for two seconds, he directly beheld Mrs. Justus Bates. She favored us with a leering smile and wiggled her fingers at him as the door closed again. "I'll take the soup in," I announced. Harmanus offered no resistance.

*　　　*　　　*

But everything seemed much more reasonable the following morning. All of the family were out and about their business before Mr. Scoffield and his party rose, had their breakfast, and hitched up their wagon with the avowed intention of paying a call on Meneer ter Oonck, my brother's father-in-law, who keeps himself neatly in a small house with a small farm and one aged slave. I had no sanguine expectations for his success, given that gentleman's quiet conservatism … and Mrs. Bates' only slightly less outrageous appearance. However, I later learned that they'd chanced across the Smildas' youngest girl in the throes of one of her seizures, and Scoffield had leapt from the cart, carried the writhing child two hundred feet to her frantic mother, doffed his hat modestly, and left. The Smildas' oldest lad had shown up at ter Oonck's threshold an hour later to report her recovery and thank Scoffield, just as Meneer ter Oonck was about to dismiss him.

Mrs. Bates, however, had not fared so well. They had passed Vrouw Ligtenbarg on the highway, and her much-feared scowl had, it appeared, unnerved them. They'd persevered, however, until three slave women had frozen in shock while they passed.

All of this I learned from Hendrik, that afternoon. Back from school, he'd been on duty when she'd come in alone, proclaiming her sudden prostration, and asked him to bring an ale back to her bedroom, where she'd detained the lad for ten minutes to recount these episodes.

"What's that on your cheek, Hendrik?" I'd asked.

"Nothing," he said. "Something wrong?"

"All red." I turned his face to the side, and the boy blushed deeply.

"She made to kiss me," he said.

"*Uh oh.*"

"Wouldn't be so bad if she didn't smell like all those flowers I clear out of the kerk every Saturday."

I passed him my handkerchief. He rubbed it off and made a face.

But they'd stayed to themselves over supper, and the following morning had provided Mr. Scoffield with another opportunity for heroism, when he'd passed Vrouw Nijenhuis attempting to cajole her cat down from a tree, and instantly volunteered his assistance. "Why thank you, sir," she'd said, "but it's really not necessary. He'll come down of his own—" But Scoffield had insisted, Bates had fetched their ladder, and the beast had been promptly restored to Mother's friend's gratified bosom.

They returned late that afternoon from their first explorations in Flatlands. Mr. Scoffield exchanged pleasantries, requested a whiskey, and ensconced himself by the window in the front room to read the newspaper. Anneke and I were busy in the kitchen—she was telling me of her amazement that such a fine, polite gentleman would suffer the disreputable Mrs. Bates—when we heard Mr. Bates' voice all the way from the stable. Rushing out to see what the matter was, I made out a belligerent stream of profanity and abuse and scorn directed at—I entered the stable—Vrijdag. Vrijdag had his back to the wall, his arms crossed against Bates' verbal onslaught and physical proximity, his teeth bared in hatred. He was clearly having difficulty restraining himself from shoving Bates away—an act that would bring him no end of grief.

Although my brother's idea had been that the slave's strength would be conserved for the heavy duties of farm work, the other projects of the family—not to mention the slave's manifest preference—had inevitably encroached on his time. Particularly while my mother and sister were away, he'd been deferred late in the afternoons to assisting with the scullery and routine kitchen chores. "Well, Mr. Dordrecht," Bates fumed, red-faced, "perhaps you can teach this lazy black some manners!"

"What seems to be the problem, Mr. Bates?"

"All I want is for your stable boy to curry down the horse, for crying out loud, and he's giving me rank insolence—"

"He's not a stable hand, Mr. Bates. My sister-in-law sent him out here to fetch some firewood."

"Well don't you think he owes it to your customers to bear a hand here? It'd only take ten minutes, and—"

"Mistress Anneke say she want oven directly," Vrijdag said in Dutch, his chest heaving.

"What's he saying? What's that shiftless bastard saying?"

It wasn't easy to control my own temper. "I think you may be about your business, Vrijdag," I said at length, in English.

"You're going to let that ape get away with—" Vrijdag gathered an armload and started out, glaring at Scoffield's repulsive servant. Detecting a lunge at him, I interposed myself just in time, nearly getting toppled off balance. Vrijdag left the stable making a hissing sound I'd often heard on the roof when he was irked. "Well, I think that's bloody poor, Mr. Dordrecht, to treat your patron so shabby. I'll certainly inform Mr. Scoffield how you let—"

"My nephew will be along any minute, Mr. Bates. He's very good with horses, and I'm sure you'll be—"

Bates whacked the horse's rump, bellowed "Damn it!" and stormed out. Standing behind the animal, I barely escaped injury as it kicked its hind leg in protest.

When Mother returned the following afternoon, she waxed deeply furious with all three of her menfolk. With Pa, for reneging on his avowals of temperance. With Harmanus, for rushing unthinkingly into a binding commercial arrangement. And with me, for having allowed Yvette Bates ever to set foot inside *The Arms of Orange*. "For heaven's sake, boy, can't you tell the difference between a coquette and a hussy? We have enough trouble maintaining a respectable reputation as a tavern in Kings County without entertaining ... *whores!*"

"Mother, she's not.... She's Bates' wife!"

She snorted derisively. *"Phoo!* They're both frauds! First you convince me to spend a mint improving our image, and then you let that harlot parade about the premises half naked!"

This fulmination continued for some time. Finally I asked, "Well, what would you suggest we do now? Throw all three of them out? We've earned more cash from Mr. Scoffield in one week than from all our other customers this year, and no one in town has had a single bad thing to say about him. Even Vrouw Schuppert praised his good manners! If we evict them, he could legitimately decry our hospitality over the whole of Long Island!"

She sat down, exhausted. "Well, I don't like it, Thomas, but I suppose we must endure it. But if she makes one wrong move, they're out, do you hear me? Meanwhile, Elisabeth and Berendina, the boys —and even Anneke—are not to go near them. *You* are to attend to all their service requests."

Another *emergency*. "What about—"

"I don't trust them, Thomas."

She was being absurd—and obstinate. *"Ma!"*

"No!"

*   *   *

The next morning, Mr. Scoffield offered me a shilling to attend him as translator while he paid his respects to Meneer Loytinck. Bemused, I demurred that, though I'd be pleased to earn the money, it was hardly necessary, as Loytinck was perfectly capable in English. "Ah, yes thank you, but I understand both he and his granddaughter prefer to converse in Dutch."

"Indeed?" Although Loytinck had protested my use of English on our trip to Red Hook, I doubted he held any serious prejudice in that regard, or that Marijke Katelaar would, either. But it was not a point worth arguing—particularly when I stood to make a few ready coins.

"We'll start in just over an hour, if you please," he said. "Mr. Bates is taking his wife to visit a friend today, and we'll leave when he returns."

"It's … only a ten minute walk to their house, sir."

"I like to arrive in some style, Mr. Dordrecht."

Good lord. "As you wish, sir."

When Bates returned, I couldn't help watching for the direction of his arrival: from the west. There are but two further miles of the Kings Highway to the west. It terminates at the Narrows that separates New York's upper and lower bays. And there aren't many houses for any friend of Mrs. Bates' to receive her. Very curious.

We set off in such "style" as Mr. Scoffield's cart afforded. I sat in the wagon, there being room for only two on the bench. Mr. Bates was driving, and Mr. Scoffield twisted himself around to talk with me the whole way. "Could Mr. Loytinck's abode be called the 'manor house' of the vicinity, do you think?"

"I suppose so, Mr. Scoffield, though I've never heard such."

"A fine mansion, though?"

"Oh certainly." It wants a whitewash, however; he's let it go too long. "I believe it was built near half a century ago, when Meneer Loytinck was a young man and had a family."

"Really? I didn't know he'd ever had one."

"Oh yes. Three sons and a daughter, all of whom inadvertently died quite young, I understand—long before I was around. Very sad."

"Good heavens. And Miss Katelaar is…?"

"The daughter's daughter. Her parents died in a terrible ferry accident when she was a toddler, and she was raised, first, by her grandmother, Vrouw Loytinck, until she died, and then by various aunts around the county."

Mr. Scoffield appeared to be committing this tragic history to memory. "And now *she* has general charge of the farms?"

"Ah. Well, frankly, that depends on whom you ask, Mr. Scoffield. If you ask the white subordinates, or the slaves, yes—"

"But if you ask the old boy himself?"

"Meneer Loytinck, you'll find, is quite jealous of his control over his properties."

We arrived. Bates pulled into the yard and stopped in front of the stable, where Scoffield was content to leave him. He and I stepped onto the porch—the only house in town to possess such an extravagance—and were greeted by Jermyn, Loytinck's rather austere, elderly servant. Jermyn brought us indoors and was about to "inquire whether the master is available," when Loytinck—who'd clearly been listening—lumbered into the room. "So," he bellowed in Dutch, "the popinjay has finally presented himself on my doorstep! What the devil are you doing here, Dordrecht?"

Taken aback, I wavered an instant before deciding *not* to translate. "May I present Mr. Robert Scoffield, Meneer Loytinck," I said, stoutly in English. "He asked me to join him on this call in case you preferred having a translator."

"He did? What a jackass!" This was said more gently, as he surely realized Scoffield could decipher meaning from his tone. Loytinck switched to English. "Well, I've been expecting you," he said more civilly, offering his hand. "Have a seat." Turning toward the kitchen, he roared for lemon-water. "What can I do for you, Mr. Scoffield?"

Scoffield cheerfully, unflappably launched into what I realized was a standardized presentation of his business proposition—although I was surprised to hear him casually hint that, in addition to commodities, his backer might be interested in buying lands outright. Loytinck, I sensed, was somewhat intrigued, and was making a greater show of indifference than he truly felt. He allowed Scoffield to talk for over half an hour—during which no hard figures were mentioned.

"Well, thank you for your time, sir," he said at length, rising, as if no proposal his guest could possibly offer would interest him.

Scoffield looked briefly dismayed, but instantly recovered his aplomb. "By the by, is Miss Katelaar around? I should be honored to—"

"My granddaughter is not here at present," Loytinck said coldly.

"Ah, that's too—"

"If he thinks he can get *my* wheat for twenty-seven, he's crazy!" Loytinck suddenly snarled in Dutch.

For a second I was tempted to translate it exactly. But my annoyance at Loytinck's belittlement of my brother's ineptitude checked me. "Meneer Loytinck has kindly worried that I might've been bored, Mr. Scoffield," I said blandly in reply to his raised eyebrow.

"Aha! And have you?"

Furious shouts—from the direction of the stable—forestalled an answer. "A fight!" Loytinck exclaimed gleefully. He charged out the door without a further word. Scoffield and I duly followed.

Justus Bates was pummeling Loytinck's foreman, Eben Stanley, who was attempting to flee into the stable to escape him, but had been stopped at the door. Wim, Loytinck's evil-looking slave, was roaring with laughter until he saw us and then restrained himself to a grin. Loytinck and Scoffield each immediately began cheering for their own. "Give him one, Bates!" Scoffield called.

"Come on, Stanley, show some spunk!" Loytinck yelled. He shared a sporting glance with his visitor.

Stanley escaped Bates for a second, dashed inside, and tried to slam the door against him. But Bates caught his foot in it, faked him back and then managed to shove it forward so forcefully that Stanley was thrown back inside. The four of us and Powles, another slave, followed them. Bates now had Stanley by the shirt, backed against a post. Stanley, who was short but far younger, could easily have punched his face, but he settled for thrusting Bates backward a few feet. It was only a fortuitous clump of hay that toppled Bates over. "Better than nothing, Stanley!" Loytinck yowled derisively. "Never knew you had it in you!"

Bates sprang right back up and kneed Stanley in the groin, which felled him to the ground, where Bates continued striking him about the head and neck.

My own reaction, I'm afraid, was impatience with Stanley's unwillingness to defend himself. But....

Stanley and his wife were the newest residents in town, having moved here less than two years ago from Gravesend, when Juffrouw Katelaar had hired him as an overseer. Though hard-working and never objectionable, they were former indenturees who rented their tiny hut, spoke no Dutch, and kept to themselves. They'd arrived with both their mothers and six children, and the family was therefore the object of everyone's charity. Some of the slaves lived more comfortably. Worst of all, like the original founders of Gravesend, they were Anabaptists. That preposterous sect takes Christ's injunction to turn the other cheek *literally*. This earned them the disdain of our dominie and the great ire of our militia chief, who thought a healthy man in his thirties should be marching back and forth with the rest of us, not citing scripture as a rationale to avoid it. Van Klost had haled Stanley into court and—to Pa's huge amusement—been turned down.

Stanley's head was bleeding and he was moaning in pain. I looked to Loytinck to object, but he avoided my eyes and yelled, "Oh come on, Stanley, you little milksop!"

"Mr. Scoffield, this can't go on."

"Eh?"

"The man's religion won't let him strike back. He's an Anabaptist." Loytinck scowled at me as deeply as Wim did.

For a second, I thought Scoffield would leer and say, "Well, serves him right!" But his face became abruptly solemn. "Bates! Enough of this. Get off him, you damned fool!" Panting and grinning obscenely, Bates stood up. "Get out!" Scoffield screamed, nodding toward the cart. Bates nodded insolently, but turned and kicked Stanley one last time. Scoffield showed him the back of his hand, and he ambled outside. "I do beg your pardon, Loytinck," Scoffield said, as breezily as if lemon-water had been spilt rather than blood.

Loytinck simply grunted and turned outside.

Scoffield took his elbow. "Bates gets unfortunately carried off from time to time. I shall chastise him, of—"

"Time for my nap," Loytinck announced, pulling his arm away.

"Certainly, sir. May I call upon you again? I have other—"

"Suit yourself." Loytinck left us without another glance.

"Good day to you—" But the old man had disappeared. Scoffield rubbed his hands together and climbed into the cart. "Well, that went well enough! Come along, Dordrecht." Bates climbed back into the driver's seat and calmly took the reins.

Climbing into the back of a wagon for a half-mile journey made me feel a perfect fool. "Begging your pardon, sir, I'd prefer to walk."

"Ah. As you wish. We'll reckon up for your services later, then."

They pulled away, and if Scoffield was about to reprimand Bates for fighting, it was certainly not apparent. I turned back to the stable. Leaning heavily on Powles, Stanley was limping through its back door. I rushed over and held it open.

Stanley looked up, his round face full of blood, pain, and miserable emotion. "I thank thee, Mr. Dordrecht," he said hoarsely.

"What on earth began this, Mr. Stanley?"

He flushed with revulsion and loathing, and winced at his own reaction. "I can't repeat it, Mr. Dordrecht," he said, and turned away.

*   *   *

Later that afternoon, Mr. Scoffield paid a visit to our neighbor Vrouw Esselinkpas, and apparently made a very favorable impression. But we were all becoming too busy with holiday preparations to take much notice of him and his odd servant. On Saturday, Mrs. Bates was again taken to visit her mysterious "friend." I was tempted to follow out of ignorant curiosity—but it was time to report for militia practice and too absurd besides. Meanwhile, *The Arms of Orange* was blessed with yet another paying boarder, a genial horse trader from Staten Island. It was the first time in months that we'd actually rented an upstairs room, so it was fortunate we'd already removed the accumulated clutter to accommodate Miss Chapman.

For the crucial Reformed holiday of *Pinkster*—the Anglicans call it "Pentecost"—was upon us. After a lengthy sermon by the dominie, the Dordrecht clan stayed in the kerk to witness little Gesina's baptism. Despite all my quarrels with her sire, I was nominated the child's godfather!

Afterward, a huge, noisy, happy feast was laid on at the tavern. The Scoffield party had fortunately professed themselves Anglican and traveled up to Brooklyn to mark the day, so the sole unfamiliar guest was the horse trader—Rockinham, his name was. As the dinner was breaking up, Pa— who'd managed to drink at least his share—was becoming quarrelsome with Meneer Van Klost—with whom all the adult males were currently irked for a particularly tiresome militia drill in the rain the previous morning.

Van Klost was holding forth on the perpetual lament that the true religious significance of Pinkster was being lost amid frivolous seasonal festivities. I fear he was right as far as I was concerned: I couldn't begin to explain the holiday's liturgical basis. But Van Klost—thumpingly seconded by my brother—proceeded inexorably to decry the widely alleged "fact" that the Africans had made it into "little more than a pagan free for all."

"Oh nonsense!" grumbled my father.

"And furthermore," Van Klost declared, "I think the province should ban these three-day holidays. It's dangerous to let the blacks congregate and mock their betters and—"

"The dancing they do is outrageous!" Harmanus avowed.

"And how am I supposed to manage my household with no support at all?" Constantija Van Klost moaned. "Jenneken is busy with the baby and—"

"Oh, you're all being preposterous!" Pa exploded. "You think you'll get the Anglicans and Presbyterians to go along with a ban? You won't even get all the Reformed to agree!"

I'd have liked to think my father the Voice of Reason ... but I fear he was simply being contrary. Having heard all of it before anyway, I thought it best to excuse myself to attend some customers who just arrived.

The three-day Pinkster tradition of course applied to the Dutch as well as the Africans but, aside from the Sabbath, there was no proscription of labor by them on the following days, just *usual* labor. Assuming that shops in the city would remain shuttered, I'd spent Monday all by myself, contentedly playing my guitar on the ocean shore of Coney Island. We were wondering where Mr. Scoffield was—he'd paid ahead for another week—when his servant and his wife appeared without him, and asked for supper in the alcove. We shook our heads over Mr. Scoffield's apparent profligacy, but the pleasant mood was sustained by demolishing the previous day's leftovers. On Tuesday morning, I was amazed to watch Mrs. Bates stalk off toward the west alone, but resolved to try to ignore them both. Harmanus—probably as surfeited by Bible reading as his wife and children undoubtedly were—helped by insisting we should attack a huge tree stump that had long bedeviled him in the east field.

He conscripted Bertie, me, and his second son for this project, but it still took us over six hours to hack and saw and lever the monster out of the soil. We were walking back into town, gratified by the success of our labor, when a cart rumbled toward us over the rise, filled with people laughing and making music—Africans, of course. Normally, slaves driving a wagon would pull to the side of the road and stop as Dutchmen would pass, but we noted a fantastically elaborate colored headdress on the familiar driver. The Van Klosts' Zwarte Jan, we instantly deduced, had been elected the Pinkster king. Bertie tugged Harmanus and me over to the verge, where he elaborately gestured that he was yielding the right-of-way. "What're you *doing?*" Harmanus growled.

"Oh come on, cousin, it's just once a year!" The cart rumbled along, a slave woman who belonged to the Arsenaults sitting next to Jan throwing flower petals about as if they were Maundy coins, and half a dozen black children gamboling in the back. "Long live the king!" Bertie hollered in Dutch.

I feigned a fussy obeisance, twirling my hat several times as I shouted, *"Vive le roi!"*

"Huzzah!" Willem squeaked enthusiastically.

Harmanus stood erect, scowling, until Bertie literally kicked his butt. "Come on, Harmanus, unbend a little, man, it's the king!"

"Harmanus wouldn't bend over if it *were* the king!" I asserted drily.

Under duress, Harmanus did manage to tilt his towering torso a few degrees. Zwarte Jan drove past us, looking vaguely pleased but not quite looking us in the eye—as I suppose any monarch would do, whether king for life or for a day. Willem skipped along after the entourage for a few seconds as his elders stared, and I realized Bertie had picked out one youngster in particular: Bette, the Schupperts' girl, wearing a new white dress. "Well, *she's* grown up, hasn't she!" he exclaimed, grinning. "Comely little wench, if you like 'em black!" Harmanus' mouth dropped open, and I admit Bertie's insouciance tried my patience as well. He was not a year married, after all, and only five months a father. "Oh come along Thomas," he chided. "No harm in looking! You'll be as dour as the deacon here, if you don't watch out!"

What do you say to an incorrigible? We changed the subject and continued about our way. Once in town, Bertie and I, joined by Jenneken and the baby, chose to view the offerings of the fair, while Harmanus and Willem wearily collected the tools and returned home. There were at least two dozen lively concessions on the common—booths, tables, or plain blankets on the ground.

The black folk had arranged themselves on the south side, the Dutch folk on the west side near the kerk. None of this had ever been organized, it was merely spontaneous or traditional. Also not pre-arranged was the curious spectacle of startled Dutchmen dealing with enslaved Africans as independent buyers and sellers on their own accounts. I found it wryly amusing to observe a slave woman *deciding* whether to spend her hard-won ha-penny on Vrouw Ijsbrandts' pot-holder, while the latter fumed in silence because she *wanted* the ha-penny.

Meandering back and forth, gabbing convivially with everyone, we bought corn bread from Loytinck's woman Lotje, a curious egg-and-mushroom pie from Madame Royan, oysters from Lotje's brother Powles, and cider from Mrs. Edwards. As I was tipping back the last of my cider, I spotted … *them.* Mr. and Mrs. Justus Bates, their chaperone nowhere apparent, were raising eyebrows from one end of the square to the other. Vrouw Ijsbrandts and Vrouw Schuppert were mutually shaking their heads in disbelief at Mrs. Bates' naked neck and breastbone.

Personally, I wanted nothing to do with the repulsive couple … but the entire town knew where they were staying. I debated whether chatting them up would appear to be an attempt to endorse them or to steer them out of trouble. Deciding to hazard the latter, I made my excuses to my friends, and approached. "How are you this fine day, Mrs.—"

It was too late. She was quarreling with Lotje. "Now look here, you, I gave you a tuppence. I should get a penny and a half in change!"

"No, Missus," Lotje whispered, her head hung down over her heavy, stolid torso.

"Trying to cheat, are you?" Bates snarled. "We'll see!" He spotted Van Klost, flouncing about in his militia captain's regalia, and ran off toward him.

"No, Missus, you give me penny," Lotje moaned, shaking her lowered head. All commerce came to a halt, and several of the slaves cautiously approached—concern and trepidation on every face.

"Lotje, you must of course give the lady her due change," Van Klost asserted, arriving.

"She said the muffin was a ha-penny, but she's only—"

"You give me this, Missus," Lotje said, setting a copper penny on the blanket.

"Oh, she's hidden the tuppence!" Bates asserted angrily.

"No!" Lotje said, raising her voice and head for the first time, startling Van Klost, who was about to reiterate his demand. "Penny!"

"Well I never!" Mrs. Bates fussed.

"I doubt she'd ever dare to cheat you, madam," Van Klost had the sense to assert.

"But she gave her a tuppence!" Bates growled.

"No. This."

Van Klost looked flustered by the stand-off. Having made my own purchase only minutes before, I took an approach I thought might work. "Lotje, can you show us all the money you've taken in today?"

Lotje first shook her head in irritation, but then shrugged, picked up a bag that was in plain sight next to her, and up-ended it in front of us all. As I suspected, there was a great deal of wampum, but no copper larger than a penny. Van Klost sighed in relief.

Yvette Bates abruptly turned, straightened up, and flashed him an inane smile. "Oh! I must have been mistaken," she said. Without the slightest nod back to anyone else, she set her hand on my forearm. "Tell me, Sergeant Dordrecht, do you have these little fairs often?"

Nettled, but eager to preserve the restored traffic behind us, I led her away toward the well, then freed myself by casually clasping my hands behind my back. "People often set up temporary stalls on the common, ma'am, but there's no other scheduled fair."

"This fair is pretty small beer, lady!" Bates said disparagingly.

Lady? Curious way to refer to your wife. I was about to dumbshow my cousin signaling me to join him, when I did see the horse trader waving, and fled. Delighted to have sold both his horses, the man wished to know if he could offer his customer a drink.

We were all about to leave the square when old Jan's cart came tootling back, burdened with yet another half dozen rollicking Africans, who were met with great hilarity. The dry goods sellers began to fold up, and makeshift musical instruments appeared among the party as if by magic. The Dutch looked on, their expressions varying from righteous disapproval to indifference to cheerful enjoyment. My cousin, his wife, and I were among the latter—as were the horse trader and his customer. The younger slaves began to dance, and Bertie elbowed me behind his wife's back, his eyebrows twitching as he nodded at the girl Bette, who was writhing about in the manner that I supposed had so provoked my brother. I've always enjoyed dancing, whether watching others or attempting to do it myself.... What was so horribly sinful about it?

Not a few of the local burghers, I noticed, were attempting to savor young Bette's dancing without their wives' observation. Justus Bates, however, was staring at the girl with an intense frown of concentration, and coldly slapped his wife's hand when she tried to pull him away.

CHAPTER 10

Scoffield, I was sorry to discover, had still not returned. He seemed to be something of a restraining influence upon Bates and his wife, so he was at least missed for that. I hoped he'd not been detained.

The horse trader regaled both me and his purchaser with tales of his trips to the various colonies. He'd been everywhere, from as far away as Delaware way up to Massachusetts, and had curious stories to tell about each. But the new horse-owner excused himself after one drink, lest he impair his ability to control his unfamiliar beast on his journey back to Bushwick. Rockinham insisted that I celebrate his success with another brew and, tired from the travails of stump-removal, I complied. He nattered on entertainingly about Puritans and Quakers and Mennonites, and Delawares and Iroquois and wampum, and.... He lowered his voice. "By the way, I thought you did rather well with those people at the fair this afternoon."

"Oh? Thank you."

"How'd you know the slave woman wouldn't have a tuppence in her purse, though?"

"Two-penny coins are very rare here in Kings County, sir."

"Indeed? Bit risky, lad!" I'm sure I flushed as the truth of his remark hit home. "Now, there's a curious pair, to be sure!" I could only nod. "They're in the room on the right, as you go out to the privy?"

"Aye sir, the north room."

Rockinham grunted. "Curious. As I was tiptoeing out to the jakes on Saturday night, I heard the unmistakable sounds of conjugal congress."

"Hardly unusual, Mr. Rockinham," I said awkwardly, taken somewhat unawares.

"*Hmm.* Yes, except that the racket was coming from the other room."

Surely he was confused, I thought. The man does like his tipple. Mercifully, he changed the subject.

*   *   *

It became an effort to keep a dispassionate face while serving drink and dinner to the alcove. And I no longer had the comfort of thinking Mr. Scoffield's return would automatically improve matters. But Mrs. Bates proclaimed herself not hungry—until Mr. Bates had finished. Then she was hungry. It was certainly not going to improve my disposition if they had to be served one at a time.

Everything was finally back to normal the following day—except that Scoffield, who Mrs. Bates had assured me was expected, remained absent. Mrs. Bates went away on foot to visit the friend, Mr. Bates disappeared around noon, undoubtedly to avail himself of an unexpected holiday, and I took my reading to a shady nook on the south side of the graveyard.

Toward dusk, Vrijdag and I made another attempt to arrange work on the tavern sign brace with Schuppert, who was still ailing, swaddled in blankets in his backyard chair. Our negotiations—Harmanus was balking at sparing Vrijdag for more than one day a week—were disrupted by Machtel Schuppert, who broke in to demand whether we'd seen her slave girl. "Nobody appears to have laid eyes on the miserable little wench since early this afternoon," she stormed.

Vrijdag seemed quite startled. "Does she frequently attempt to shirk her duties?" I asked.

"Well, no," Vrouw Schuppert allowed.

Slaves weren't supposed to volunteer their observations without request, but I could tell Vrijdag was alarmed. "Is this a common thing for her to do?" I asked him.

"No. Not like Bette. She good girl."

The four of us looked at each other, stymied. "Perhaps you could go over to the quarter and look for the girl, Vrijdag? It would ... relieve Vrouw Schuppert if you found her."

He didn't need a second hint, and dashed away through the thicket of pines that separates the two sections of our town. But his absence left me unable to estimate the time to be scheduled. When he'd not returned after I'd finished the cider they provided, I thanked the Schupperts and returned home.

And I presently forgot about Vrijdag and Bette, because Mr. Scoffield was dropped off by a drayman just minutes after I got home. He seemed in fine spirits and while cursorily recounting his activities in the city over the past few days, surprised us all by extracting a small package from his valise, walking over to my Grootmoeder's rocking chair, kneeling on one knee, and presenting it to her.

Grootmoeder was sufficiently *compos mentis* to realize that a gift was intended. She opened the package and her face lit with delight.

"Crimson!" Anneke exclaimed. "Oh, she'll love that!"

It was a ball of yarn, not at all an outlandish present, but completely unexpected and thus rather overwhelming. The old lady patted his cheek.

"Very handsome of you, sir," Harmanus said enthusiastically.

"Thank you kindly, Mr. Scoffield," I added.

But Mother, who'd come back from the kitchen to observe the to-do, frowned in puzzlement before she shrugged and smiled.

When I served the three of them supper in the alcove a few minutes later, however, it was clear they were furious with each other and having difficulty keeping their arguments from boiling over into shouts.

*　　　*　　　*

"You're going your usual way, by Red Hook to get your canoe?" Mother asked as she put some porridge before me.

"Aye."

"Well, keep your eyes open for Bette."

Recollection took a second. "She's not found?"

"No. The slaves looked until the thunderstorms came through, well after dark—"

"I thought it was illegal for them to be abroad at night."

"It is, of course, at least in numbers. But … it's a special case. They're now in a perfect lather, as are the Schupperts, as is Constantija—"

"Constantija? What's she—"

"Roosje was too distressed to show up for work. And Anne and Jan are more addled than ever, so she's got no one to wait on her."

We shared a mocking glance at our neighbor's vexation. "Anne and Jan and Roosje are all related to the girl, right? That's why they're upset?"

"Anne and Jan are the grandparents. Roosje's her sister—or half-sister, I think."

"Ah. That's why Vrijdag was so concerned then."

"He wanted Harmanus to let him keep looking this morning, but Harmanus is in a hurry to sow.…"

It crossed my mind for a half-second that the girl might be trying to run away—but that was completely absurd. At fifteen?

Mother shook her head. "She'll probably turn up. Geertruid disappeared overnight once. Just being horribly willful, was all."

The current would already be north-bound, and time was wasting. Thanks to the holiday and to Mother's sojourn in Flatbush, it had been two weeks since my last trip, and I had a long list to shop. But I observed nothing out of the ordinary as I drove our horse and cart up the trail to Jacob's house on the Gowanus inlet.

The day was warm but overcast, with threatening showers that never quite seemed to arrive. But it was good to be busy with so many errands in New York. Once the family chores were accomplished, I managed to squeeze in a lesson with Mr. Fischl, and then loitered in the Society Library until four o'clock, its closing time. Jacob the ferryman shook his head when he saw the quantity of goods I was loading into my canoe. It was in fact the heaviest lading since my mate Nogert and I had come down from Albany last fall, and I had to reorganize the weight twice before I felt ready to face my two-mile voyage back. Jacob and I sometimes raced this trip and I usually won. Today, with a steady southwesterly, he won hands down. Good thing too, as I needed his help when offloading.

New Utrecht's problems, forgotten for ten hours, crowded back upon me as I drove into the strangely quiet town. Nobody was in the fields, though it was still light out. There were a number of horses tied in front of the kerk, but its doors were closed. My nephews and several other boys were playing nearby in the square. There were no slaves about at all.

"Hello?" I called, entering our house. No answer! Almost never happens. It appeared I'd have to unload the cart by myself. The first priority being to get the beef carcass down to our coolest spot in the cellar, I hoisted it onto my back and carefully walked down the not-too-sturdy steps. A little light gets in from above in the daytime, and I was startled to hear a low moaning as I hung the meat on its hook. I turned around and beheld Justus Bates glaring at me, his wrist in the same manacle that had recently constrained my father. "What the...?"

But I didn't want the explanation from him. Repulsed, I dashed upstairs. "Anyone home?" I shouted.

"Uncle Thomas?" My niece, from her room above. "Please don't yell, you'll wake the baby."

I took the stairs as noiselessly as I could ... two at a time. "Where is everybody, lass?"

At that moment, my sister Elisabeth emerged from the room vacated by Mr. Rockinham, looking very much out of sorts. "It's all right, sweetheart, I'll bring Uncle Thomas up to date. You watch the baby." The girl shrugged, and Lisa pulled me into the empty guest room and closed the door.

"What is Bates doing...? Lisa, you've been crying!"

She had. She was trembling still. "They don't want Berendina to know, Thomas."

That chilled me. "Know what?"

"Zwarte Anne found Bette about two hours ago."

"Oh god."

"Down by Coney Island Creek, in the swamps."

"She was—"

"Alive, but delirious. She'd been attacked and left for dead."

"Attacked by—"

"By a man, not a beast. Although...." She swallowed and straightened her back. "She was barely able to walk, but they presently came across Powles, in Loytinck's south field, and he carried her back to the quarter. And she revived a bit once they gave her some water. She hadn't had anything, they guess, for almost twenty-four hours." Another deep breath. "Somehow they got the notion that it was Wim who'd done this to her, and Jan, Powles, and Balt were getting ready to go hang him, when she rallied and said, no, it wasn't Wim."

"It wasn't?"

"No. Machtel Schuppert got there just as this was happening, and she pressed the girl for a name. And ... it was 'evil white man staying at *The Arms*.'"

It took my wind away. "Justus Bates raped a slave girl?"

"Aye, so it seems."

"Not Rockinham or Scoffield, of course?"

"Oh no no. She described him clearly enough. And ... everything he did to her." Lisa shivered and shook herself. "Well, Vrouw Schuppert charged off in a fury, and collected her husband, and Pa, and Dominie Van Voort, and they came back here to confront the three of them, Scoffield and Bates and his ... *wife*."

Not like my sister to pronounce that title with bitter sarcasm. "You were there?"

"Mother and Anneke and I were all starting with supper. The three of them had just gotten in from Flatlands—I think—and Mother had served them beer in the alcove when all this started."

"*Uh huh.*"

"Machtel Schuppert stormed in, threw their door open, pointed her finger at Bates, and yelled, 'My girl Bette says you attacked her and left her to die!' And Bates—I saw him—under his breath, he said, 'D—'" Lisa stammered.

"'Damn?'"

"Yes. Then he feigned righteousness and swore he'd no idea what she was talking about. But he wasn't able to answer any of their questions about what he'd been doing yesterday afternoon when Bette disappeared, and finally he gave up trying and pushed his chair back and sneered and said, 'Well, all right, so what? So what if I did ... *uh*—'"

I opened my mouth to provide the missing obscene verb ... and shut it again. Lisa may be assisting Mother with childbirth, but still....

"He said, so what if he did have his way with her, she was just a little black slave wench, and why shouldn't he have his fun."

"He confessed?"

"*Bragged,* Thomas! He.... Vrouw Schuppert—I've never seen any woman in such a rage—shrieked that the girl was her property, and he had no business having his fun with her, and he had a lot worse than fun, he nearly killed her, and she meant to see Bates pay for it! So she turned to Pa, and said, 'Very well, Schout! Do your duty!' And Pa"—Lisa managed a smile—"leant straight across the table, and whacked Bates on the nose!"

"*Pa?*"

"Aye. Didn't do him much harm. Bates put on a look of martyrdom for a few seconds, then made a try to butt his way out the entry. But there were far too many people. He ran directly into the dominie and Meneer Schuppert, and even Mister Scoffield pounced on him. 'Whose side are you on?' he demanded. And Scoffield said, 'You've really gone too far this time, Bates,' and he actually helped Pa and the others get him locked up in the cellar!"

"Huh!"

"And the instant all the men were down in the cellar, Ma suddenly looked hard at Mrs. Bates, and said, '*You* are not spending another night in this inn!' And she got all flustered and outraged—and Ma said, 'You are not spending another *hour* in this inn!' And then Scoffield and the other men came back up, and Mrs. Bates went whining to him, and Ma roared, "If this harlot is not off my property in five minutes, I shall throw her off bodily myself!' She was boiling!"

"Holy—" Lisa frowned a warning. "Gosh!" We both shook our heads, amazed at a side of our parents completely new to us. "What did—"

"Mr. Scoffield shook his head and said, 'You're quite right, Mrs. Dordrecht, quite right!' Then he assured Ma he'd immediately 'take the baggage to stay with her friend,' and vowed we'll never be troubled with her again. And Ma said it couldn't happen soon enough, so he pushed the woman back to her room and ordered her to pack; and five minutes later, by George, he was driving her down the highway towards the Ferry."

"Wow. And.... where is everyone now, Lisa?"

She sighed. "Well, you found out where Bates is. All the men of the town—they rang the assembly alarm—are in the kerk debating what to do next. They'll probably want you to join them. The boys went off with them.

Berendina's looking after the baby, I'm looking after Berendina. Mother and Anneke went off with the Schupperts. I think Mother is hoping she might be able to do something for Bette."

"What could Mother do for Bette? I mean, now?"

Lisa moaned and shrank. "Oh. I haven't told you the worst."

My stomach turned over. Lisa began trembling again. "He … cut her, Thomas. Cut her all over her body, then throttled her, then left her below the tide line. I know she's only a slave girl, but…. She never did me any harm and I…. I…." She burst into open tears and I pulled her to my side. "He *meant* to kill her, Thomas."

*　　　*　　　*

Ten minutes later—all my purchases still sitting in the cart—I arrived at the kerk just as the meeting was disbanding. Boys were still playing in the common, though the sun was getting low. A number of townspeople had congregated on one side of the entrance, and half a dozen slaves were gathered on the other.

Floris Van Klost, whose position as militia chief made him the presumptive spokesman for the Selectmen, was standing beside the dominie on the stoop, and saw me approaching Bertie for news. "Ah, Sergeant Dordrecht!" he called loudly.

"Sir?"

"You'll be wanting to know what has been decided, in view of this unfortunate incident?"

The townspeople, the boys, and the slaves all crowded as near as they dared to hear what Van Klost was ostensibly about to say to me. "Yes sir?"

"We have taken the magnitude of the crime under advisement. Actually, there are several crimes this man Bates stands convicted of by his own admission—fornication, blood pollution, theft, property damage—all serious affronts to God and the peace of our community. Therefore, we have concluded that he must be reprimanded here, with the most serious punishment that our township can legally administer, which is twenty-four hours in the stocks!" He looked over to the townsfolk as if he was hoping for applause.

"Might it not be better to remand him to the county seat, sir, for more—"

"The sentence will commence at noon tomorrow," Van Klost bellowed, "and I'm sure you'll agree that it's a most severe punishment?"

Well, that I could not doubt. "But—"

"Further, this man's owner, Mr. Robert Scoffield, is to be assessed a fine of ten pounds sterling for his negligence in allowing his servant to roam freely and commit such abominable mischief." He didn't pause to ascertain my opinion. "Eight pounds are to be paid to Meneer Schuppert as compensation, and two to the town for the disruption and humiliation Bates has brought upon us."

Van Klost slapped me on the back as if to congratulate me for my brilliant decision, then almost shoved me aside in his haste to speak with a vestryman who'd not attended the meeting. Bertie reached me at last, a look of perfect exasperation on his face. "They spent forty minutes, at least, trying to parse what *Leviticus* would have to say about Justus Bates!"

Dominie Van Voort joined us, shaking his head. "It's a terrible thing, Thomas, terrible!"

"Sir?"

"One wonders what the world is coming to, when Europeans can so demean themselves as to lie down with Africans!" My cousin turned beet-red as my brother glared at him. Bertie evaporated backwards, awkwardly stepping off the stoop into the ivy. Van Voort became distracted by another congregant. Harmanus moved aside to collect his sons.

Pa confidentially took my elbow. "I need a drink, boy, before these blowhards drive me to raving!"

"But—" Over his shoulder I was observing the agitated reaction of the slaves, talking among themselves. Lotje was gesticulating fiercely at Hans, who stood foursquare, scowling, with his arms across his chest. A boy a few years younger than myself was gleefully miming the process of a man being hanged by the neck. I heard Vrijdag's irritated hiss.

But my father pulled me away, and we began walking toward the house. "That damned whoremonger has his way with a black wench, and *I* have to sit out all tomorrow night to see that no one brains him with a tree branch!"

"Sir?"

"It's the schout's duty to protect the bastard from more punishment than they say he deserves."

"Ah, when the criminal's sons cannot, that is?" I asked rhetorically. It was a sore point. In three months Pa had never managed a hint of gratitude.

But sarcasm was in vain. "Aye. Blessed if I really care!"

Harmanus and his lads rejoined us at the threshold and did not object unreasonably when I begged them to assist in finally getting the cartload of purchases indoors. Mr. Scoffield pulled in just as we finished, just as a thunderstorm broke.

Having fortified himself with a glass of gin, Pa attacked our customer the instant he set foot indoors, berating him for the fact that he would be required to watch over Bates in the stocks.

"Oh I do apologize, Dordrecht, really," Scoffield protested unctuously. "I curse the day the man entered my life. And I am truly sorry for the hardship he's visited on you!" Scoffield caught my eye. "Ah young sir, I'd love a gin myself—and another for your outraged pater!"

"You've not heard what they want from *you!*" Pa nonetheless said with malicious glee. "A ten pound fine, my lad. Negligence!"

"Ten! That's a bit steep, isn't it? I mean, the wench isn't dead or anything, is she?"

"Ten it is. You'll have to take it to the Council if you want out of that one."

"Well. I suppose it could be—"

"Schuppert was angling for twenty!" Scoffield gagged on his gin. "But I seconded those who objected that he was blowing this all out of proportion."

"I am again in your debt, Mr. Dordrecht!" They clinked their glasses together. "I shall have to take comfort in the fact that I may be spared the further expense of boarding Bates and his wife in your excellent hostelry. Perhaps we can even arrange a refund for the remainder of the week?"

Pa looked at him innocently—as if he'd never heard of a refund. Then they both broke out in roaring laughter.

Mother and Anneke arrived ten minutes later, drenched by the storm, and immediately made their way to the kitchen, to see how Lisa and I were faring in supper preparations. Perhaps their simple bedragglement emphasized the extraordinary distress on their faces. "She may live, she may not," Mother summarized brutally.

My sister-in-law saw Lisa searching her pallid face. "Unspeakable," she shuddered.

*   *   *

In the morning Mr. Scoffield rose late. More from habit than any continuing necessity, it was I who brought in his breakfast. "Have all the children gone off to school?" he asked.

"Well, save the babe, yes," I replied, startled.

"And Bates is of course still incarcerated below?"

"Aye."

He held his fists together and set his jaw in a particularly grim cast. "I should like to have half an hour with him, alone," he said, "before all and sundry get their chance at noon."

"Indeed?"

"He remains in my charge, you see. What I mean to do … may bring some disruption to the peace of the household."

It did not require much imagination to guess his intention. The rights of masters to physically chastise slaves and indentured servants were detailed in law. "If you'll allow me to encourage my grandmother out of doors first, sir? It might derange her equilibrium, you see."

Ten minutes later, after I'd ushered Grootmoeder over to the square and forewarned Mother and Anneke, Scoffield returned from the stable carrying his horsewhip. He nodded to me and proceeded alone down to the cellar. I decided it was an excellent occasion to fetch my reading from the attic—I'd picked up Lord Bacon's *New Atlantis* yesterday—for an hour away from the house.

As I passed outside, I heard the awesome rhythm of a flogging—a grunt, a crack, a scream, over and over. But Bates, defiant as ever, seemed to be attempting to refuse his master the howl he expected, holding it in an instant longer than one would expect after every touch of the lash.

Horrible.

His session in the stocks was a considerable contrast to that of my father three months earlier. So far from being threatened with snowballs, the miscreant could justly fear perishing of the heat. And so far from standing in his defense, Bates' master had, Anneke informed me, abandoned him and resumed his business pursuits in Flatlands. Pushed by Mother, Pa managed to get Bates to the common on time—by deputizing Harmanus and myself to drag him there at the last minute. He read his commission as haltingly as Loytinck had, the dominie offered a prayer but no sermon, my brother and I locked Bates' ankles, and the children of New Utrecht had their fun.

It was not pretty. Pa ensconced himself in the shade fifteen yards behind the stocks, and ignored every torment visited on the prisoner. I decided to spend my afternoon elsewhere and returned to my reading.

Though hot, there was a refreshing breeze by my spot in the graveyard. I managed a good deal of reading and was thoroughly enjoying myself until old Vrouw Bilderbeek passed by with her market bag and cast a sour glance in response to my greeting. Clearly she did not, in her wisdom, approve of the indolent likes of Thomas Dordrecht, and thought him sure to follow his father into sloth and truancy. Her rebuke mortified me, on one level—and incensed me on another. Why couldn't she leave well enough alone? No business of hers!

Concentration ruined, I decided to make the best of it by taking myself off for a swim and a wash in the bay, which at least restored my good humor. Then I played the guitar in my room until called for supper.

Mr. Scoffield, returned from Flatlands, had decided henceforth to take his meals with the family and our other customers, and to release the alcove as well as the north bedroom. "Your mother generously calculated my refund at two shillings," he told me. "I'll need every penny to restore myself after settling that fine with Schuppert and Van Klost this morning."

"Very correct of you, sir. I'm sure it's appreciated."

"I don't know what the devil I'll do about Bates. Really should sell him. Not here."

"I fear his indenture wouldn't fetch even ten pounds in Kings County, Mr. Scoffield. Perhaps over in New Jersey?"

He made a face, but smiled when my father ambled in. "Ah Dordrecht, you look as though you need a drink!" I attempted a warning glance to the contrary, but Scoffield was not deterred, and Pa's enthusiasm for the idea was far too great. "Fetch us all three, please," he told me. "What'll you have?"

"Cider," I said quickly.

"I'll have a gin myself," he said.

"Gin," Pa said.

Several of the townspeople came in, having heard that we'd be serving beefsteak this evening, and a convivial neighborhood atmosphere grew. It is considered good fun to have a man in the stocks, the steak smelled wonderful, and no one queered the party by asking how Bates—much less the slave girl—was faring. Many had known that Scoffield had previously taken all his meals apart, and felt gratified to see him now joining the local gentry. Pa announced that the best jape of the day was when the Oosterhout boy had put a live mouse inside Bates' shirt. "You should've seen him squirm!"

Even I laughed. Chalk one up for the Oosterhout kid. Harmanus and Vrijdag came in, and Scoffield hailed my brother to partake, while Vrijdag proceeded back to the kitchen. "You're all new to slave-owning, right?" Scoffield asked. As we nodded, I wondered how he'd learned this, then recalled his studious absorption of local gossip. "Well, you don't *let* your slaves trail you through your main public room, you have them go outside and come in through the back." None of us had ever thought of this nicety. "Is he going to stand guard with you tonight?" he asked Pa.

Harmanus immediately looked vexed. "I need him fresh tomor—"

"Well, that's a good idea!" Pa said. "Should've thought of that too."

My brother hung his head in resignation—and I wouldn't protest if he wouldn't.

Anneke brought out the steaks, and we feasted handsomely on them. Presently my mother gave me a look that imperatively indicated there was sufficient traffic to constitute an emergency necessitating my assistance, so I finished up and left the table. Scoffield offered Harmanus and Pa more drink. Harmanus nursed his one ale; Pa knocked down several gins. Bertie came in for an after-supper tipple, and I was asking for his order when Harmanus said, "I thought you were spelling Pa? Wasn't that the idea?"

"*Uh*, I forgot, and he never asked."

"Well, who's watching Bates then, Pa?"

"Bates? I asked Hendrik to stand guard while I was at supper."

Harmanus stood up, clutching the table as his fury fought it out with the Fifth Commandment—which won, as usual. "You asked a seven-year-old to guard a violent criminal?" he rasped.

"He's in the stocks!" Pa shrugged. "What can happen?"

Harmanus vigorously shook his head, asked me to have Vrijdag relieve him as soon as dinner was finished, then bolted out the door.

"Such a worrier!" Pa said. Scoffield smiled indulgently. Hendrik came in five minutes later, little the worse for wear, but hungry and upset that he'd not been able to eat with his friends as planned. Some steak brought his grin back.

The bulk of the service being completed, the ladies sat down and chatted with Bertie while Vrijdag and I began clearing up. I saw Grootmoeder was already abed, and closed her door to avoid jarring her awake. In the main room, I presently noticed Willem crawling about on all fours near where Pa and Mr. Scoffield were seated. "What are you about, lad?"

"Vrijdag says there's a knife gone missing."

Everybody dutifully moved their feet. "You see it?"

"No."

"Well, we'll find it in the morning. Isn't it your bedtime?"

"Beyond that!" his mother said. "Off with you."

"Could it have been in the wash water?" I asked the slave, back in the kitchen.

"Don't think so. We checked before Miss Berendina took it out and dumped it in the privy."

Ugh. Possibly tomorrow I'd again have the privilege of raking the privy. "Pa wants you to stay out with him overnight," I observed. Vrijdag's startled, dismayed look suggested this was news to him. "Look, I'll finish up. You can run next door to the Van Klosts, and at least tell Roosje so she won't worry."

"Thank you, um.… Thank you." He hurried out the kitchen door. There was no offense in him calling me "Thomas," when we were working on the roof, I mused. But eyes would widen should he do that inside the house. And the usual "Mr. Dordrecht," "Mister Thomas," and "Sir," all seemed so wrong … the upshot was to cease to address me personally at all, which I tolerated rather than force him to say any variant of "Master"—an address to which Pa and Harmanus were welcome.

"A good evening to you, Mr. Dordrecht!" Scoffield's pleasant, resonant voice said. He was lighting a spare candle by the one on the hall bureau.

"Ah! The same to you, sir."

"It's been a long day, I'm turning in early."

"Very good, sir. We'll be done here in no time."

"Excellent meal!"

"Thank you, sir." He pulled his door closed after him.

Pa passed by, singing to himself, on the way to the outhouse. I walked out after him, still drying a platter, to get some fresh air. It was a bright night with a pleasant breeze scudding the few clouds across the sky. Vrijdag came back through the side gate and looked askance at how Pa was weaving. "Follow behind him, would you please," I said. "With the moon just past full, he probably won't trip between here and the square, but...." Vrijdag nodded, and I returned to complete my work. I heard Harmanus come back ten minutes later, but I'd already said goodnight to the ladies and retired. The house and town were soon still. I read for about an hour before blowing out my candle.

*   *   *

"No! No!" I protested. "No!" But the huge man had his whole weight on my chest, and continued to batter me mercilessly. I couldn't even make him out, only his red uniform, but I saw Justus Bates behind him, laughing evilly. He pushed upwards for a second, and I caught a glimpse....

It was Colonel Bradstreet! He raised his knife, a fierce expression on his grim, pale face, and I—

I woke up, my heart pounding, my chest heaving, my skin sweating.

It took seconds to think myself back into reality. It was a dream, another horrible nightmare. Had I shrieked? I didn't think so. Good thing. Certainly no one was rushing up to check on me.

Bradstreet! I shook my head. I was abashed that the man still loomed as an ogre inside my noggin, notwithstanding the fact that he'd made me rich last year, and offered me advancement. Little accounting for dreams!

My bed was sopping. The faint loom of light over the ridge to the west suggested the moon had just set, so dawn could not be too far away. Every time I thought of trying to sleep again, there he still was with Bates at his side. There's slander by association for you! I dressed to take a walk.

If I want to take a walk, I thought, I might as well go over to the common and check how Pa is doing.

I stopped in the kitchen to slice some bread for him. Grootmoeder's door was again ajar; I closed it to keep Mr. Scoffield's snoring from disturbing her.

By this time there was only starlight to guide me, but the night being clear and now perfectly calm, that was enough, and the route was of course as familiar as one could ever be. I crossed in front of the kerk and headed directly for Pa, who'd set his chair up on the south side.

He was snoring, every bit as loudly as Mr. Scoffield, and had his blanket over his head to boot. His musket was four feet out of reach on the ground. I suppose it would've been a mercy to leave him alone, but folks would be up and about in less than an hour, and such a situation would bring further embarrassment to our already embarrassed family. "Pa! Come on, Pa, you have to wake up."

"Oh go away, Harmanus, damn it!"

"It's Thomas, Pa. It's almost dawn. People will see you've put your blanket over your head, for heaven's sake."

"What blank—" A flurry of movement uncovered his head. "I didn't put the blanket over my head. Had it on my shoulders. Did you put it over me?"

"No Pa, I just got here. I had a bad dream, couldn't sleep." He grunted. "You're supposed to be watching Bates."

"Why? What's he doing? Is he pissing on the rosebushes again?"

My father, the jester. "You could lose your stipend if anything happened to—"

"Oh for god's sake, Thomas, what's going to happen?" We both looked over at the prisoner's inert form, slumped forward, almost bent double. "Why the hell should he get a better night's sleep than I do, eh?"

There was no arguing with him. "I brought you some bread."

"Oh? Good boy. But I think I'll wet my lips first."

He had the whole *jug* out here with him! "Pa!"

"Pa!" he parodied, setting me in my place.

"Where's Vrijdag?"

"Vrijdag?"

"He's supposed to be out here with you."

"Oh yeah. He was here ... for a while." He began indifferently to gnaw on the bread. I tried to think of something to talk about ... and couldn't. "Nothing's happened."

For a few minutes the two of us sat there in silence. Then, as the first hints of dawn appeared in the sky behind us, I decided I might as well try to go back to sleep, and rose. "Can I take the jug back to the house, Pa?"

Pa surprised me. "Give *him* a swig, boy, he needs it."

"No reason to have any sympathy for him, Pa."

"Dammit, Thomas, now do what I tell you! I've been in his seat, and a man needs a drink."

"Oh come on. He's asleep. A man needs his sleep too."

Pa grumbled unintelligibly for a few seconds, then rallied and said, "Well, check."

Finally deciding that whatever portion of the jug went into the prisoner would at least not be further polluting my father, I got up and walked over in front of him. "He's really out, Pa, he's...."

Something was wrong. Time in the stocks normally produces odd angles, but Bates' head was tilted far too sharply to one side. He didn't seem to be breathing. Alarmed, I rushed up to him, tried to push his clammy forehead back and—

I did not scream hysterically, as I fear I had last summer when I'd found my best friend scalped, but I did stagger to my knees and gasp desperately for air. "He's.... He's.... His throat's been cut! Pa, he's dead!"

CHAPTER 11

─────── ⋈ ───────

"Dead?" Pa seemed to be having trouble with the very word. "Can't be. I've been right here ever since supper."

Unable to quite accept it myself, I squatted down and again tried to push Bates' head back—and lost my balance, tumbled forward, and felt my palm land in viscous, sticky liquid. *"Aghh!"* I wailed, revolted. "Pa, there's no question. There's blood all over." I had just enough presence of mind to wipe it off on the grass rather than my breeches.

Pa finally heaved himself upright, retrieved his musket, and began lumbering toward me. "Can't be dead. I only shut my eyes for a minute!"

I stood as he joined me. His whole body was trembling. "See for yourself, Pa."

"I ... can't." He swayed on his feet, and I steadied him from behind. "I'm all right," he said after a minute.

"Well, there's no doubt about it, Pa. He's gone cold."

"Oh ... Jesus."

We stood immobilized, staring down at the corpse. I was struggling to think rationally, trying to seek out information in the gloom, when we both jumped, suddenly hearing a rustling sound in the trees behind the Arsenaults' house.

"What was that?" Pa whispered.

I was about to say I didn't know, when we heard it again. As I grabbed Pa's musket from his hands and tore off in that direction, footfalls were audible, fleeing toward the slave quarter. For a second I thought I'd lost them, but then I heard them again, heading more easterly, staying among the trees. They were not fast or nimble footsteps, and I sensed I was gaining quickly. Emboldened,

I didn't slow down when the sound ceased, and charged ahead for another twenty seconds, until....

He blocked my path, standing foursquare between two trees with his arms raised to heaven. *"I* do it! *I* kill!" he shouted at the top of his lungs. "Praise to God!"

Pa, wheezing far harder than I was, drew up beside me, and joined me in complete disbelief of our eyes.

"That man a curse!" the fugitive bellowed. With the pre-dawn light behind him, we could just make out the hunting knife in his hand, trembling under the strain of passionate conviction ... but we sensed little imminent danger to ourselves.

"Jan?" Pa panted. "What the hell? Jan?"

"He a curse!"

"Jan, put the ... put the knife down," I ordered, having to swallow to force my voice to a lower register.

"A curse to all!"

"No, Boudewyn!" I yelled at Boudewyn Voskuil, a neighbor to the Arsenaults, who'd come up behind us and was aiming his musket, full-cocked, directly at the slave. "Wait."

Not shifting his stance, Voskuil calmly inclined his head toward his grandson, a lad recently inducted into the militia, who was likewise aiming at old Jan, and repeated, "Wait."

"Jan, put the—"

"A curse! He die!" Zwarte Jan sank to his knees, arms still raised. "God forgive!" he roared.

"Put the knife down, Jan!" Five breathless seconds passed, then Jan abruptly plunged the knife into the soil, and the four of us were instantly on top of him.

"Oh thank god," Pa sighed in relief.

"What's going on?" Lukas Voskuil asked. "I heard him hollering and you running, and I called Grandfather, and—"

"We have to lock him up, Pa," I said, ignoring the boy. The town would be awake and about in a matter of minutes. "We have to do it right away."

"Yes. Right," Pa agreed. He nodded to the Voskuils, and the four of us hoisted Jan upright, forcing his arms behind him. "Jan! Walk! Don't try to run, they're ready to fire!" Jan simply hung his head. "Let's march!" With Pa and Voskuil each holding an arm, and Lukas Voskuil and me pointing muskets at Jan's back, we started off toward the common. I turned back and pulled the knife from the ground, thinking of it more as extra armament than as evidence.

There was still no one about on the common. Sensing no resistance in Zwarte Jan, I broke away from the others, picked up the blanket Pa had had about him, and threw it over Bates' corpse. "What…?" Voskuil asked.

"That's the matter," Pa said. "Jan cut his throat!"

"Oh no," Voskuil said. "Oh no, that's bad. We can't have—"

A woman's shriek pierced the air. One of the slave women, passing through the square bound for a field to the north, saw Jan under constraint and collapsed in howling dismay.

"Come on, hustle it," Pa said nervously.

It was barely two hundred yards further to our house, but half a dozen more people had been alarmed by the time we reached our door. Pa, Voskuil, and his grandson forced the unresisting slave into the cellar, but I didn't follow, thinking now of getting Bates' remains decently out of sight.

The rest of our family had been interrupted while saying grace over breakfast, and was looking up in confusion. "Harmanus! Need your help right away," I said.

My brother not only instantly intuited the urgency of the matter and complied, he called his eldest son. "No," I said, stopping Hendrik at the threshold and nodding him back to the table. "Men's work," I explained.

Bertie and our redoubtable militia captain were recruited from the gawkers gathering in the road outside. I set a quick pace to the common, ignoring all questions.

The first rays of direct sunlight lit the steeple as we approached the stocks. I immediately set about hammering my fist against the wooden pin that held the stocks shut, as the others, perceiving the blanket, deduced that something was amiss. "He … *died?*" Van Klost asked.

One side of the restraint came free and I moved to the opposite. "I fear it's worse than that," I said, preoccupied. This peg came loose more easily and I nodded to Bertie to help me lift the brace. As we secured it back in its open position, the unbalanced corpse tumbled over toward Bertie. The blanket was stuck on my side, however, and as the body pulled away, dark gore was revealed all over the stocks, the ground, and Bates' clothes … and hideous gashes were exposed on his neck. My brother—who has never been able to stand the sight of blood—blanched white, but the others also recoiled as the implication of foul play become obvious.

A woman's scream alerted us to a growing audience. "*Eew*," a boy exclaimed loudly. A burly slave folded his arms across his chest and spat contemptuously. Opposite him, my eyes met Vrijdag's for a startled second; he looked ill and rushed away toward the quarter. I hastily replaced the blanket.

"Steady!" Van Klost said to the reeling Harmanus, who clearly liked coming face to face with a corpse even less than I did.

"I think we should get him into the shed behind the kerk," I asserted, nodding toward the small structure used by the dominie ... and the gravedigger. No one having a better suggestion, we hauled the clumsy, already stiffened corpse across the common, worked it inside, propped it against the clapboard wall, and slammed the door shut with great relief.

"Do I dare ask," Harmanus said as we panted and began walking away, "did Zwarte Jan have something to do with this?" Van Klost and Bertie gasped, only then connecting the two anomalous events of the morning.

"Jan says he killed him," I said flatly. "He was waving his knife around"—I pulled it out, the familiar, dented knife that had cleaned the first fish I'd ever caught, from my jacket pocket—"and calling God to witness, when we subdued him."

"Oh no, that's a disaster," Harmanus groaned. "Oh dear heaven."

"*Jan?*" Van Klost objected. "I can't believe it. Why on earth would Jan—"

This point had been puzzling me in the half-hour since I'd first confronted the impassioned old slave, but I had a theory to hand. "Wasn't the girl his grandchild?"

*   *   *

Pa was attempting to convince a restive group of citizens that everything was all right, in hand, under control, as we arrived back at the house. But they weren't looking reassured. Van Klost proceeded vociferously to second everything Pa said. Our other neighbor, the widow Esselinkpas, looked imploringly at Harmanus, but he simply shrugged, unready to contribute further. Nobody, of course, requested an assessment from Bertie or me after such short shrift from our elders. Disgruntled, they eventually went about their morning's business.

Van Klost saw his wife scolding Roosje for her late arrival, at which point the heavily pregnant girl broke into tears, wailing about her Grootvader— Zwarte Jan. The militia captain impatiently commanded her to fetch a pail immediately and scrub up the town's stocks without delay, which set off a new flood of crying.

"She's useless!" Constantija Van Klost exclaimed.

I'd heard them arguing many times over how to get more work out of their slaves, but it seemed that Van Klost was in no mood for it. "Bertie, take a bucket of water over to the stocks, and we'll send Sander to wash them down. This has to be done right away."

Bertie cast me a grimace, but nodded obediently to his father-in-law. Van Klost proceeded to bark orders at his crippled slave boy, a permanently terrified little fellow of fourteen years who hated venturing away from the family's premises. Sander whined about the loathsome job until Van Klost impatiently raised a threatening hand—at which point the lad searched out a brush and hurried after Bertie.

I followed my father and brother into the house, and we each sat in our accustomed seats at the table in the hope that breakfast would magically materialize. Though clearly disconcerted, Mother and Anneke dutifully set food in front of us, and we'd just begun when Mr. Scoffield, dressed neatly as always, appeared through the hall entry. "Good morning, everybody," he said brightly, bringing conversation to a full stop. Frantically, we searched each other's eyes: *who would tell him?* It was Pa's duty, of course, but it was only when Mother prompted him that he rose, took our customer's elbow, and awkwardly tugged him back to the alcove.

Breathlessly, we tried to hear what they were saying, but the children disrupted any chance of success. I resumed eating my porridge. After two minutes, Pa and Scoffield returned, concluding a sober but placid discussion. "How do you handle this, here?" Scoffield was asking. He interrupted Pa's reply to request Anneke to prepare coffee and porridge for him in the alcove.

"There will be a trial in Brooklyn town, presently," Pa began.

"Very tiresome!" Scoffield sighed. "You can't just hang him here and be done with it?"

"I'll have to ask. I don't think so."

"But you say he's confessed, for heaven's sake!"

"Aye, but…."

"I'm sure you know best, but it seems odd to me to give all the other slaves ideas by expending due process on this … murdering fiend."

Pa helplessly spread his hands wide. The rest of us tried to cope with the realization that this characterization of the hitherto harmless Zwarte Jan was evidently correct. Scoffield shrugged and left as Anneke told him his breakfast awaited.

"I take it he was not devastated?" Harmanus asked drily as Pa resumed his seat.

"Just what you'd expect," Pa observed. "Bates must've been of some use, but…."

We finished eating in silence. "So what do we do now?" Harmanus asked.

"Jan has to be taken to Brooklyn town directly."

"Van Klost? It's his slave."

"He has no say in the matter," Pa observed with excessive satisfaction.

"Are you going—"

"I was hoping Thomas would volunteer to take him. I've been up all night already."

With some difficulty, I refrained from telling my father to go to hell ... and presently realized that whether he'd slept at his post or not, he'd never get Jan past the first tavern on the road anyway. "If you insist," I grumbled. "What about Bates?"

"Have to get Hans to dig him a hole in the south yard. Scoffield's not going to pay for any sort of funeral. I asked."

"Why should he, for that loathsome man?" Anneke interjected with sudden vehemence. "I almost sympathize with old—"

"We can't have slaves doing in white men whenever they please, woman!" Harmanus said firmly. Anneke flushed, picked up the porridge bowls and fled back to the kitchen.

*   *   *

An hour later, Harmanus having hitched up the wagon while Pa and I prodded the listless Zwarte Jan into it, I started off on the long trek to Brooklyn, going out of the way east in order to stay with the highway, which was at least cleared of stumps and boulders. Thinking mournfully of our many shopping trips together and of his attempts to teach me to fish, I'd decided not to put a gag on Jan—which I regretted directly, as he began to moan and sing and pray before we were out of New Utrecht.

We drew an inordinate amount of attention on the road. After I related the whole story to the first passer-by who'd asked—a Flatlands resident acquainted with my Uncle Claes—I told the next individual I simply couldn't stop to explain. Jan also caused a great stir among the slaves we passed, of course. Many dropped their tools on hearing his voice, ran over to the road, and fell into paroxysms of moaning on seeing him tied and helpless.

The worst came after I'd gone through Flatbush and was only a mile short of my goal. My bladder bursting, I'd tied up the horse on the side of the road, and dashed into a coppice of trees to relieve myself. "Jesus forgive me, I kill him!" I heard Jan bellow as I tucked myself back together and emerged to find five unfamiliar slaves staring at him in the cart.

"Who?" one of them demanded, ignoring my approach.

"That man evil!" They all gave me a very hard look. "I cut his throat!"

"Who?" the one fellow persisted. Glad that I had my musket slung over my shoulder but still eager to get moving, I hurried, missed my footing and gashed my shin. The horse shied as I leant against the cart to massage my leg. Unconcerned by all this, the slave repeated, "Whose throat you cut, Jan?"

Of course they know him, I thought as I finally regained the bench. Jan was the Pinkster king only days ago and now....

"Evil man hurt my girl!"

"Why you take him, mister?" a slave woman demanded aggressively. "Why?"

"White man, Jan?" Another male voice—very soft.

I flicked the reins and the horse pulled us on our way. "God forgive!" Jan roared.

"Good!" the woman said.

As soon as I had horse and cart firmly started down the road, I looked back. They'd all vanished.

A few minutes later I arrived in Brooklyn, a harborside town twice the size of New Utrecht boasting a few unusually handsome residences, and pulled into the enclosed yard of *The Mohican,* its largest inn. A big, swarthy, dirty fellow wearing a tawdry decorative ribbon approached. Seeing Jan under restraint, he yanked him off the cart and threw him to the ground the instant I halted. "What's it with this one?" he demanded blearily. "Insolence? Swearing? Thieving?" It was just past mid-morning, and he was already drunk.

"May I speak with the constable, please?"

"I'm the constable. Joe Wicklow is me. Who the devil are you?"

"Son of the schout of New Utrecht."

"Loytinck?" He placed one foot on Jan's prostrate back.

"No, his term's up. I'm Thomas Dordrecht, son of Rykert Dordrecht."

Wicklow required an inordinate, gaping half-minute to register this fact. "Oh, *Ryk!* You're Ryk's son. Yeah, he's all right!"

So: my father had made the acquaintance of high society in Brooklyn town. "This man is Jan, slave to Floris Van Klost, and—"

"How's he doing?"

"Van Klost?"

"Ryk!"

"Well, thank you." Trying to stay sober, I hope—and clearly to be steered far away from you! "*Um,* Mr. Wicklow, Jan here has confessed to—"

"Well, he'd better, hadn't he!"

"Evil! God forgive, I kill!" Jan roared.

Wicklow sobered. "Kill?"

I sighed, glad to have the man's full attention at last. "Jan has confessed to cutting the throat of a man—Justus Bates was his name—whom we'd put in the stocks overnight." Wicklow looked completely befuddled, so I explained everything I knew to him. Twice.

"Well, I'll let the Justice know this afternoon," Wicklow concluded. "He'll like this one. He'll handle it right away, on Monday. Don't often get hanging offenses in this county!"

His glee was making me ill. No matter that I concurred with the anticipated verdict and its sentence, I was glad that old Jan would suffer only two days with this man. "Trial will be Monday morning?"

"Oh yeah, I'm sure of it. Your town gets to hang him though! They figure you should make an example, see."

Something to which we can all look forward.

"Tell Ryk to come on back. He knows he's supposed to be here for the trial? We'll hoist another one at the corner!"

Feeling oddly guilty about leaving a confessed murderer in Wicklow's tender care, I backed the horse and cart out onto the highway, and left without farewells.

*   *   *

A lad hailed me as I came to the crossroads in Flatbush, and told me my sister and brother-in-law were expecting me for mid-day dinner. As I'd not infrequently made this trip before without garnering such an invitation, I suffered no illusion that they were eager to hear about my progress on the guitar, or my ruminations on Sir Francis Bacon.

Berend not being yet at home—the lad had proceeded to the fields to fetch him—I visited with my sister and her overwhelming foursome, an imp, a toddler, and the twin babes. Geertruid looks a bit like a female version of Harmanus, I'm afraid, and she has something of his tendency to bossiness as well, but we two have always gotten along. Unlike our parents' first-born, she's not a scold, and one can always appeal to her overriding benevolence. She let me hold the infants for a moment, but they presently broke into wailing, and that was that. A door slammed.

"Thomas?" her husband called. I yelled greetings in return, and left my sister to settle the infants back into their cradle. "Thomas, what's going on down there in New Utrecht?" Berend peremptorily demanded as I joined him—and two other local men. "This is Mr. Elijah Ellison," he said, remembering his manners and pointing to a slight, furtive little man, a stranger to me. "And you recall Armand LeChaudel?"

"Ah yes! How are you, sir? How is the lovely, *uh.*..."

"Nanette," LeChaudel supplied, irritated. All three men looked deeply preoccupied. "She's engaged," he couldn't help adding, however, clearly expecting me to be dismayed. I smothered my relief and muttered dutiful felicitations.

"Who was it that was killed?" Ellison hoarsely demanded.

"Were there any accomplices found, Thomas?" Berend wanted to know.

"What steps have the Selectmen taken?" LeChaudel added.

There was nought to do but relate every last thing that had happened in New Utrecht over the past week. The protracted task was made somewhat less tiresome by the fine dinner my sister laid out.

"That ancient black who drove through town just last Tuesday?" LeChaudel wheezed, shaking his head. "With the raucous entourage and the preposterous hat?"

Geertruid was distraught. "I can't imagine how old Jan could've done such a horrible thing to us!" she moaned.

Before I could put my finger on what was not quite right with her observation, the talk had taken another turn. "Why did you take him up the highway?" Ellison asked querulously. "You'd have been wiser to use the back roads, where nobody would've seen you. Now they're all in a froth!"

"Do you remember how gentle he always was with Grootmoeder?" Geertruid said, ignoring him. I did … but then, my sister hadn't seen Jan screaming and wildly brandishing his knife.

"The really smart thing would've been to move him by water, and not go through the county at all," Berend opined.

"Nobody else has any patience with Grootmoeder but Zwarte Jan and Zwarte Anne!"

"Well, I think your town ought to have strung him up on the spot!" LeChaudel asserted vehemently. "Mustn't jest about in cases like this. None of the Council officers in Brooklyn would've batted an eye!" The thought crossed my mind that Nanette's intended would probably prefer the likes of Bertie's father-in-law to this philistine. "Would have saved us all a lot of trouble!" he stormed. I'm sure my puzzlement read on my face. "You think this situation hasn't gotten around among *our* slaves?" he said, turning scarlet. "I'd wager there's not a black in Kings County who doesn't know of this—and it happened not twelve hours ago."

"Surely not as far as Bushwick?" the third man objected.

"Of course in Bushwick! And half of Long Island too!"

"Gentlemen," my brother-in-law reproved, rising at length from the table, "there's no way such a wager could ever judged and—"

"Oh but—"

"And I'm sure we all have better occupations anyway!" He moved to usher his guests out.

"This comes from mollycoddling the slaves, mark my words!" LeChaudel expostulated, walking out without even nodding to his hostess. "We allow them to live in their own quarters in this county, which is ridiculous. Each family should keep their bondsmen apart from all the others, as they do in Maryland. It's the only—"

"But we live in towns, LeChaudel," Ellison protested as he followed, "unlike…." It was a relief to be spared their disputation as the voices grew faint.

Berend distractedly returned inside. "I'm sorry, brother, I fear I must return to my fields directly. Thank you for dinner, my dear!" He left us—but popped back in yet again. "Oh, there's two new kegs you may as well take with you!"

"In the brewery shed, Thomas," Geertruid said morosely. "Pardon me if I don't go with you?"

"I know where it is, *Zus*." My sister looked nearly immobilized with sadness as I pecked her on the cheek, but shook herself when one of the babes cried. "Thanks for the meal!" I said.

"Nothing," she shrugged. "Give my love to all."

*   *   *

It was a good thing Berend's beer kegs were solidly constructed, as they both fell off the cart on the trail. I should've known better than to take produce over the short-cut, which is riven with holes the size of stew pots that the county never repairs, but I hoped to distress fewer people with the absence of my missing passenger.

The back road west from Flatbush eventually connects with the trail south from Red Hook, which is almost as rough, but finally I was driving into town. And something was radically altered. I sensed it as much as I saw it. There were fewer men in the fields, and the masters were warily standing behind the slaves, rather than among them. Waves from the householders, usually cheerful, were perfunctory. Nods from slaves were so brief, they'd normally be construed as an affront. Dogs were leashed near the thresholds. Gates were uniformly latched. It was a warm afternoon in June, but my homecoming was chilly. No one inquired how my business had progressed—possibly because everyone in New Utrecht knew exactly what Thomas Dordrecht's errand to Brooklyn had been.

It felt like another town.

There is only one other moment I can remember that felt as unhappy and grimly skittish as this: back when I was twelve. I'd been ordered to mind my own business at the time and only learned what it had all been about two years later. After a series of disasters for the Dordrecht family that had culminated in my younger brother's death, I'd spent an hour alone—I can't recall the circumstance—with my mother's mentor, the late Vrouw Zuykenaar. I'd always taken a shine to the old lady not simply because Mother admired her so, but because she always spoke to me seriously, as if I were a real, grown-up person. At that moment, overcoming the shock of Aalbert's demise, I was struggling for the first time to come to terms with the world outside my household.

What had given rise to our conversation? It had been the chatter that Vrijdag, then Loytinck's slave, was not expected to survive the fever that had attended the fierce whipping he'd received when he'd been apprehended. Ludicrously self-centered though most people would view it, I'd been upset over the prospect of losing yet another of my childhood mates. Vrouw Zuykenaar had explained with a sigh that it was "the way of the world" that runaway slaves were whipped within an inch of their lives upon recapture. It was only then that I'd realized that Vrijdag had in fact made a bid for his freedom; he'd fled on the very day Aalbert died. "Perhaps," she said softly, "it even happened then *because* of Aalbert's death—because he knew the entire town was too distraught and preoccupied to chase after him."

For a second, I'd felt indignant at the implication that our bereavement had been made the occasion of the slave's advantage ... but then sheer wonder at his audacious and disastrous exploit had overcome it. "But why did he do that, Vrouw Zuykenaar?" I'd asked. "Meneer Van Klost is always saying that the slaves here in New Utrecht are very happy!"

A curious play of emotions had passed over the old woman's lined but still beautiful face. She was far too genteel to suggest outright that Floris Van Klost was a nincompoop. "Slaves are never very happy, Thomas," she said. "They just never are."

"Never? Old Jan always seems so jolly and—"

"It's a myth, my lad," she declared succinctly. "A myth concocted by those of us who are slaveholders, to make us feel better."

Dominie Van Voort had talked to me of sin and redemption, but no adult had ever talked to me like *that*. For a minute, she took my breath away. Then I'd asked, "What was it that happened two years ago, Mevrouw? When all the slaves were suddenly confined to the quarter for a week? Nobody ever told me—"

"Ah. Another sad business, Thomas. But you're right, you should know. It started with a disastrous miscalculation on the part of Vrouw Van Klost."

"Oh yes?" I bit down on a smirk. Even back then my evaluation of the Van Klosts was presumptuous.

"You recall that Rozamond, Jenneken's older sister, was married to a man from Hempstead? That's way out on Long Island, over twenty miles."

"Yes?"

"The Van Klosts own old Jan and his woman Zwarte Anne, who had five children by him, all of whom of course also belonged to Van Klost. And in fact, he'd transferred ownership of four of them to Meneer Loytinck in order to repay a debt, but he'd retained the youngest, a woman named Mina."

"I remember Mina!" I exclaimed. She'd looked just like Lotje. Because she was Lotje's sister, of course, I realized.

"Yes. Well, Mina herself had children—Roosje, Jaap, Ernst, and Bette. And Vrouw Van Klost thought that, since there had been no repercussions when her husband had given Zwarte Anne's children to Meneer Loytinck, there would be no consequence if she gave the two boys to her son-in-law, as part of her daughter's dowry."

"But—" Of course there had been repercussions: *I'd* lost my playmates!

"She hadn't told anyone but her husband of this plan until the morning after the wedding, when Mrs. Coldcastle was packing up for the trip to her new home. When they tried to tell the boys they were just going on a little vacation, they didn't fool anyone, and the bridegroom had to tie the lads down, and finally gag them—all in front of Mina, Zwarte Anne, Roosje, and Bette. Mina attempted to pull the boys out of the cart, and was only prevented by Van Klost—and your father—who threatened the women with fixed bayonets. And the newlyweds left New Utrecht amid the shrieks and howls of the entire slave quarter."

"I … thought they just … went away," I mumbled, realizing how foolish the idea was as I'd said it. Where had I been? Oh—in school, of course.

"Things were tense for a few days, and the Van Klosts tried to pretend nothing had happened—until Mina attacked Vrouw Van Klost when they were alone in the house together, and came very close to strangling her."

"That was why?"

"Aye. It was your brother Brevoort who was the hero of the hour. He was passing by and he heard Constantija thrashing about, rushed in, and managed to break the woman's hold. Got a black eye for his trouble."

Right. Brevoort's moment of glory. "Mina…? I never saw her again."

"She was taken to Brooklyn town, Thomas, dragged away kicking and foaming at the mouth. And cursing the Van Klosts in a *voodoo* fashion that terrified old Aeltje Van Klost out of what was left of her wits. They tried and hanged her there, thank heaven. Things were in enough of an uproar here."

"They hanged Mina?"

"She attempted to murder her mistress, Thomas," Vrouw Zuykenaar said simply. "That was all there was to it. But it was months before anyone felt relaxed again, quite horrible. I remember we had two miscarriages that fall…."

I pulled into our yard, and Pa's greeting shook me out of my reverie. "What the devil took you so long?" he said.

*   *   *

The Dordrecht household was unusually placid. Pa—evidently shocked into sobriety, at least for the nonce—filled me in. Meneer Van Klost had spent the weekly militia muster haranguing the townsmen about vigilance rather than exercising them. Mother and Lisa had suddenly decided this day provided an excellent opportunity to consult with a young bride in the countryside north of town who was expecting her first child. Anneke had gathered all her progeny and marched them to the seashore. Harmanus had dithered about for some time when Vrijdag had not shown up for work, but finally gone off to the fields by himself. Grootmoeder was wandering about somewhere. Bates had been buried in the potter's field. Mr. Scoffield had again ridden away to Flatlands and was not expected for supper. The Selectmen had met for over an hour and debated whether to clamp down on the entire slave quarter, make "an example" of Jan's progeny, call up the militia to enforce a curfew, or to await the verdict—the execution, rather—before taking any general action. Indecision had won the day.

So I was in charge of the tavern again, which was again bereft of customers. I tried to read downstairs for an hour, gave up, and fetched my guitar. Nobody came in for a convivial tipple. Few people were abroad on the road at all. All of my family resurfaced only just before dusk, hungry, sunburned, and cross.

Sunday was even worse. Dominie Van Voort was at his most pedantic, and his peroration lasted half an hour longer than usual. Several of the gentry had actually brought their muskets to kerk and stacked them against the back wall. Harmanus browbeat me into joining a lengthy family Bible study, and the hitherto pleasant weather turned stormy just as he released us.

Mr. Scoffield paid for yet a third week at the inn, again remarking jocularly that one good thing about Bates' removal was that he'd no longer have to pay for his room and board. Rather tasteless sense of humor. Mother and Anneke talked of not only sweeping the north room and changing the sheets, but of scrubbing it down with caustic potash.

It had been decided that my presence was not needed at Zwarte Jan's trial on Monday morning. Only Pa, the schout; Van Klost, the slave's owner; and Meneer Voskuil, as independent witness, were required. As they set off, rather comically squeezed against each other on the seat of Van Klost's wagon, I commenced driving our own rig along the trail to Red Hook. There I waved to Jacob's wife, collected my canoe from his shed, and paddled on to the city as usual for my shopping trip. Although my list was extensive, I was able to satisfy it fully within Mr. Martin's emporium, but was then detained another quarter-hour by the grocer's unexpected interest in the news from Long Island. Finally released, I happily awarded myself a few hours at leisure before the current would turn. I perused the environs of Stone Street for a sighting of

Miss Chapman but, disappointed, began poking my way northward through the slightly quieter alleyways of the city.

"Tommy!"

The high-pitched squeal, delivered with the force of man's lungs, echoed through the narrow street, instantly shattering my equanimity. Lord, he was wearing that *wig* again! To my intense discomfiture he rushed up and attempted to kiss me on the cheek, which I barely avoided. "How do you do, Mr. Cooper?" I managed.

"'Mister Cooper' indeed, Tommy!" he yowled, clamping my shoulder with one hand and my jaw with the other. He was stronger than one might have supposed, and he'd pulled me off balance. I sensed he was deliberately trying to *keep* me off balance. "What a way to refer to your very own flesh and blood cousin!"

I regained my footing and scowled until he released my chin—only to slip his arm through mine and proceed to start walking in the direction I'd been heading. "Very well, Charles," I grumbled. "How fares my aunt?"

"Let me guess!" Cooper exclaimed. "You've been shopping at Martin's and now you're *en route* to Mr. Fischl's store on Pearl Street!" It irritated me intensely that he was precisely correct, and I'm sure it showed on my face. "How wonderful. I shall go with you, and we can catch up!"

Just before we reached the music store, however, we passed a pleasant-looking restaurant, and Cooper struck an attitude of distress. "Do you know, Tommy, I'm perishing peckish! Surely you'll join me for a luncheon?"

"Well, I—"

"Ah! You're embarrassed for funds!"

"No, I—"

"Allow me to treat you, dear boy!"

I was theorizing that my instant readiness to accept hospitality was due to my frugal Dutch heritage when I recalled that Cooper's lineage was equally half-Dutch, half-English as my own. A comely serving wench came to take our orders, and Cooper appalled me by paying her appearance an outrageously suggestive compliment that would have earned him instant eviction from any eatery on Long Island—but she tossed her head and laughed it off. Cooper kept up his bantering as we quaffed our ales, and I feared not even a free meal would recompense my irritation. When our meat was placed before us and the girl dismissed, however, he suddenly faced me directly and said in a low, settled tone, "What's going on in New Utrecht, Tommy?" It took me a few seconds to deal with my disrupted expectations. Cooper regarded me intently, his usually overactive person gone still. "Word has it that the entire slave quarter has risen in open defiance," he added.

"I ... don't think so, Charles, I—"

"People do get hysterical on this subject. They often assume the worst...."

"Indeed. For my part, I've seen no suggestion that anything more than communal unhappiness is afoot. Zwarte Jan was much liked by his fellow slaves. For that matter—though I doubt they'd credit it—until Saturday, he was well-regarded among the Dutch."

"You don't say?"

Ignoring the hint of a sneer in his tone, I said, "The Selectmen have ordered all of us in the militia to stand on general alert, but we think the town is really waiting for the result of the trial, which is taking place this morning over in—"

"He was convicted, of course. Barely an hour since."

"I beg your pardon?"

"Your father's testimony would've been sufficient, had he been completely sober, but with Mr. Voskuil's corroboration, the slave was doomed." I gaped at him. "He's to be hanged in New Utrecht on Thursday at noon."

I was speechless for at least five seconds. "Were you *there*, Charles? Did you rush back from Brooklyn just in time to accost me on Mill Street?"

He made an absurd twirling gesture with his hand—more in the character with which I associated him. "Oh no no no, dear boy. But ... I have my ways of learning what I want to find out."

"What on earth is your interest in this parochial matter?"

"Not parochial at all, my lad. New Utrecht's alarum has already raised hackles of fear from West Jersey to New Haven. In a week, I assure you, it will have upset the digestions of fine gentlemen from Boston to Williamsburg."

"You awaited the ferry and collared everybody aboard until you found one who'd attended?"

My cousin smiled inscrutably—and devoted a moment to his plate. "Was there any evidence of collusion in this murder? Wait. Who was the murdered man? He was not local, I gather?"

Cooper attended my recitation of events with a level of concentration I'd assumed beyond his capacity. "And Bates' master was not local either?" he persisted. I explained how Mr. Scoffield has been highly regarded about the county despite his unfortunate choice—or inheritance, rather—of a servant. Presently, Cooper's curiosity returned to the possibility of collusion; I examined the evidence that Zwarte Jan's motives were purely personal.

He snorted after I'd concluded. "Can you imagine?"

"What?"

"If the indentured servant's victim, and her grandfather, had been *white...?*" My jaw dropped. The speculation had crossed my mind just once—

but I'd instantly set it aside, unwilling to face the madness that would result. My cousin apparently had no such qualms. "Ah me!" he presently sighed.

The waitress presented the bill and Cooper teased her again as he paid it. He chortled briefly. "I hear the slave's owner—Van Kleist or something?—"

"Floris Van Klost, our next-door neighbor."

"*Ohhh* yes! The buffoon with whom Grootvader was always quarreling, the one with the two fat daughters?"

"*Er*, yes. The younger fat— The younger daughter married our mutual cousin Bertie Hampers."

Cooper's smirk suggested he was well aware of the attendant circumstances. "Right, right, last summer, while you were so gallantly defending His Majesty's claim to be the chief defrauder of the Iroquois."

I bristled. "That was hardly the—"

"Of course not, Tommy, oh certainly not! Well, you'll be glad to hear that Amherst has mustered an even greater force to attack Ticonderoga this year. They've already moved up to Lake George. That's why the governor went to Albany, in fact, and *that's* why New Utrecht's homicidal slave will have to wait until Thursday for someone else to sign his execution warrant."

I covered my confusion by concentrating on my food. "I haven't read a thing about the army's movements, Charles. How is it—"

Again, there was no response but a bland, rather chilling smile. "As I was saying, Van Klost made something of a fool of himself by pleading for clemency after the verdict, bawling that the slave had always been obedient and dutiful and such. Obviously desperate to preserve his investment. The Justice laughed in his face."

"Perhaps a more charitable construction might be put on that request? After all—"

"Not when the clown proceeded to demand compensation from the province! The only thing that shut him up was when the Justice threatened to arraign *him* for negligence in maintaining his slaves."

"*Sejanus* misses no details, I see?"

It was Cooper's turn to be disconcerted. "Only two people know *Sejanus'* identity, cousin. I'd appreciate it—"

What? I and Adelie Chapman were *it?* He'd shared that hazard-laden pseudonym with no one else? Was the man mad? My amazement and confusion must have shown.

"It would be most troublesome if—"

"I'll make you a deal, Charles!"

"I don't do deals, Tommy, not about—"

"I'll make you a deal," I reiterated, lowering my voice. "I'll never tell a soul that *Sejanus* and Charles Cooper are one and the same ... and *you* will never again call me 'Tommy' in public or private!"

He relaxed for an instant, then affected a pout that would have shamed Mr. Ingraham. I crossed my arms over my chest.

"Oh, if you insist, Tomm—"

"'Thomas,' if you please."

Five seconds passed in silence. "Thomas," he conceded.

"Thank you for the repast, Charles. Most kind of you!"

*   *   *

I normally bought the inn's newspapers at Fischl's, using that as another excuse to go there. A London journal was full of the military season's opening battle. The Germans and the English and the French had brought nearly two hundred thousand men-at-arms together—a staggering number, twice the total population of our province—at Bergen, in Hesse. Thousands were killed or wounded, but no one was victorious. Somehow this was the same war we were fighting in Canada. Mr. Fischl shrugged when I asked him where Hesse was. "Frankfurt area, Herr Dordrecht. Middle of Germany. One battle after the other!" He watched me read for another moment, then interrupted me. "You have not seen the truly terrible news?"

He turned the paper over and pointed to an obituary. I gasped, stricken.

The world's most famous composer, George Frederic Handel, was dead in London, aged seventy-four. I didn't honestly know much about Handel, but it seemed unjust that now I should never be able to behold him in person. When I begged Fischl to find me a piece of Handel's that I might be able to play on the guitar, he produced the *Largo*, a stately, deeply affecting anthem, and we spent our practice session on it. If I work on it every day for a month, I might be able to perform it passably.

On my long trip home, the insistent tune of the *Largo* endlessly repeated itself, amid random thoughts of my odd cousin, Ticonderoga, Hesse, *"Sejanus,"* Adelie Chapman, and poor, doomed Zwarte Jan.

And every time I thought of the latter, I had to upbraid myself. Jan was not "poor," but a confessed murderer.

When I arrived home, Pa was unusually irascible, having spent hours listening to Van Klost lecturing him on the criticality of his staying sober during this crisis, and clearly having tried to do so.

"What crisis, Pa?"

"He thinks all hell could break loose, any minute."

"You mean the slaves?"

"Of course, ninny. Did you hear we were attacked on our way back from Brooklyn?"

"Attacked?"

"Aye. Well, some stones were thrown at us as we were heading into Flatbush."

"After the verdict? They already knew?"

"I guess. Must have."

"You're sure it was slaves?" Could have been boys making sport of three portly burghers.

"Never saw them. Who else? Van Klost aimed his musket at one of the bushes they came from, but Voskuil pushed it up before he fired."

"Good thing. Wouldn't have helped."

"Well, Van Klost was furious. Now I think Voskuil finally realizes what I've endured from him all these years!"

"Oh right."

Most of the black and white residents of New Utrecht commenced a delicate minuet in each others' presence, avoiding physical and eye contact, but also mumbling or any relaxation of gesture or tongue that might be taken amiss. Most—not all. A few of the slaveowners decided this was the appropriate moment to reinforce the slaves' understanding of their place.

Ordinarily minuscule items of gossip loomed large. A family in Flatlands had been laid low overnight with food poisoning. Had they simply eaten some bad oysters, or had their slavewoman deliberately selected mollusks past their prime? When one of the local nannies had spoken harshly to an irascible toddler, had she not overstepped the bounds of allowable chastisement? When a field hand had managed only three-quarters of his usual hoeing, was this excusable due to the excessive heat of the day, or was it obduracy? Meneer Van Klost decided it was all worrisome enough that an unscheduled militia practice should be called, and the adult males dutifully showed up at seven o'clock Tuesday evening to be drilled back and forth by him. Surely the sight of a gaggle of farmers making this extra effort to remember which foot was their left one would terrify miscreants of all descriptions.

Or perhaps it would drive the wedge in deeper.

One might think any distraction from this suddenly uneasy situation of our home town would be welcome. The brief appearance of Corporal Nigel Hibbert, a sprightly young officer from the same regiment I'd joined last summer, however, was not. It happened that I was covering for Mother while she paid a call on an ailing friend. Hibbert came in modestly enough, but his familiar green uniform put me instantly on guard. He ordered an ale and I exclaimed over his accent. Entirely English, notwithstanding his employment by the province, he'd arrived with his parents in America only months ago.

His pleasant demeanor belied an intent concentration on his business, which was, as I'd feared, to recruit as many self-propelling militia age males as possible. "It's good to see that at least one family in this town is possessed of some patriotism!" he remarked. Presumably he'd made this deduction from the presence of Miss Chapman's sign. Still not properly hung, it was leaning against the entry doorframe.

It was said lightly enough that I took no umbrage at the disparagement of the town. "Why would you doubt—"

"I've not been met with open arms here. You wouldn't know a fellow by name of Thomas Door-dratch, by any chance?"

I confess I considered saying I'd never heard of him. "I would be Thomas Dordrecht, sir."

"Oh! Thought you'd be older, but, *uh.…* The regiment is very eager to retain your services for another campaign, Sergeant."

"I understood this year's campaign was well under way," I prevaricated.

"We have more than one offensive this year, I believe."

Niagara after all, I thought. "Ah. Well, I'm sorry, Corporal, but that's … not possible."

"But—"

"That's simply not possible."

He looked very put out, but I'd anticipated this moment and was determined to freeze any hope. He had news for me, though. "A strange name, yours. I came across it two weeks ago, when I was working in the north of Manhattan Island."

Oh no. "Brevoort Dordrecht, by any chance?"

"That's the one! He took the King's shilling in a heartbeat!"

Dismay warred with irritation in my breast. Two weeks, and we'd not had a word! "My elder brother, sir. Can you tell me which company he's attached himself to?" I was already dreading having to break this news to Mother.

"Eleventh. Seriously, why don't you join him?"

Remembering the dogged persistence of my recruiter last year, I took advantage of a feigned bladder emergency to escape and—trusting he was at least not larcenous—left him to finish his beer alone in the tavern.

He was back before suppertime, however, in far better humor, having convinced two bright sixteen-year-olds, a pair of best friends, sons of Ijsbrandts and Royan, to sign up. Unlike me, they'd at least have two days to say goodbye and be assured of their foolishness before having to take boat for Albany. As soon as I saw him approaching, I thrust my sister-in-law out to attend the bar and took over in her stead in the kitchen. Thus I learned only at second hand of Hibbert's expulsion from the temple by Van Klost. The latter, usually an indefatigable partisan of the imperial military, had burst in and collared the young corporal, jowls wobbling with Old Testament wrath. How was it, he'd demanded, that Mr. DeLancey was attacking the very marrow of Kings County's backbone, the New Utrecht militia, just when the threat of slave insurrection was rampant? Losing two young lads had been bad enough, but when Hibbert had presumed to accost the father of Van Klost's grandchild, it seems that all perspective had been thrown out the window—which is precisely where Hibbert soon fled to preserve his hide, Van Klost's fulminations having excited the ire of several other townsmen.

Van Klost needn't have gotten so fired about Bertie, of course. Having succumbed to marriage and fatherhood, my cousin was again honing his native expertise in avoiding any commitment that might involve actual exertion.

*   *   *

The glee that might have attended the town's anticipation of an execution was dampened by everyone's nervousness and mixed feelings. Bates had been universally loathed, and Zwarte Jan had long been patronized as one of the locality's most docile and agreeable slaves. Notwithstanding concurrence that the punishment was appropriate, real satisfaction seemed out of the question. Perhaps I was reading my own feelings into the expressions of others, but certainly the send-off of the detail to collect the condemned man and the execution order with the governor's signature on it—Pa, Van Klost, and no less than six militia members—was subdued. Thanks to my having transported Jan to Brooklyn in the first place, I was excused. Thanks to its being my regular shopping day, I would be spared the actual event.

Mr. Scoffield skipped breakfast and dressed hurriedly when he realized what was afoot. "I might as well avail myself of an armed escort to Flatlands," he explained. "One can't be too careful!"

They were all building their own nervousness into absurd phantasms of horrific disruption, I thought, pushing the barrow along the trail to the Red Hook ferry. If they'd actually watched the slaves over the past couple days, they'd not have seen anything more alarming than deep regret that Jan had allowed his rage and indignation to ruin him. Why our neighbors all feared that chaos would follow the law's just procedures I couldn't imagine.

My current list was shorter than its predecessor, but I nonetheless had three merchants to visit. I was on the alert lest I again be set upon by the effusive attentions of my cousin, but Cooper must have been uncovering dirt elsewhere today. When the bells rang at noon, I was in an apothecary's on John Street, purchasing a large order of willow bark—used for sore throats, among other ailments. Unconsciously I massaged my neck, until the proprietor kindly asked whether I needed some tea as a matter of urgency.

I lunched at a very cheap public house, had a lesson with Fischl, exchanged books at the library, and began walking back to Jacob's landing at Old Slip.

And suffered a true nightmare.

It was the hottest moment of the afternoon, so it was unsurprising that few were about in the glaring sun. I was unconcerned that no one was in sight as I headed down a side street of warehouses.

In an instant, I was disabled, gagged, and lifted bodily from the ground. I screamed, but a huge hand was firmly clamped over my mouth. I flailed, but only my left arm was free and it couldn't connect. I bucked and kicked, but strong arms were under my knees, compressing my legs against each other. Within seconds, we were hidden in a dark alley, where I gathered there were two of them and felt relieved I wasn't staring at a knife. Robbery was clearly the opportunistic object, and I expected a reach for my purse at any second. Though only seventeen pence were left there, I was far from eager to surrender it.

"Quiet, Dirt-Pusher, quiet!" one whispered. My eyes focused on a slight, wiry, white-haired man. "We're not wanting to hurt you," he panted. I recognized him! From where? A sailor. A Navy man. From that horrible boat that had taken me to Albany a year ago. "Quiet now!" Slowly, methodically, they loosened their grips on me one hold at a time. I got my footing, felt my right wrist freed, my left arm freed, my right arm loosened—all while the fellow was making conciliatory gestures.

I jabbed my right elbow backward into the other one's stomach, twisted free, slammed the white-haired man in the chest knocking him backwards, and bolted for the street, gasping too heavily to scream for help. But I must not have done as much damage as I'd hoped, as the other was presently on me again. Bigger and heavier than the white-hair, he instantly covered my mouth again and wrestled me to the ground, where I was still struggling when the other one joined him and added his weight on top of me. "He thinks we're the press, Nicholls," the larger one whispered.

Nicholls! Boatswain of the *Proserpine*. "No, lad, no!" he urged. "Dirt-Pusher … Samuel, we need you to be quiet. We—"

"It's not Samuel, it's Thomas!" the other hissed at him. I jerked to look backward. It was the ferocious black-beard—Jack—but … without the black beard.

"Thomas. We mean you no harm, lad. No harm! Look, I'm not touching your purse, eh? We just need to talk with you." My heart was still pounding, and my blood was still up with fury and humiliation, but they again cautiously began to loosen their hold over me. Memories came back: they'd befriended me during that dreary week-long trip. Nicholls was the hornpipe dancer who'd literally been around the world. He fixed me in the eye. "Promise you'll not call out?"

It took me half a minute before I nodded in agreement, then Jack slowly took his hand from my mouth. "Well, why the hell have you—"

The hand slammed right back. "*Shh!* Dirt-Pusher, you have to be quiet," Nicholls reiterated. And we went through it all again.

"Why the hell," I whispered, "could you not just have greeted me on the street like civilized Christians?"

Nicholls seemed to be seeking his mate's agreement. He took a deep breath. "Because we've jumped ship, Dirt—*er*, Thomas." He stared directly at me. "Jumped ship. We'll be missed by eight bells. If the Navy finds us, we'll likely be hanged for deserters."

"And if not, flogged," Jack said. "A hundred lashes at least."

This took a moment to absorb. And when I'd absorbed it … I rejoiced it was not my problem. "Look, mateys…. What do you want of me?"

They straightened up and relaxed further. "We've a promise, Thomas. A merchantman's in want of able seamen, offering real wages, real food."

"He's stealing the King's sailors?"

"We figure—twenty-seven years for me, fourteen for Jack—we has done our piece for the King. Not like I volunteered in the first place!"

"No time, Nicholls!" Jack prompted.

"Merchantman's going to haul into the Sheepshead Bay. That's near you?"

Three miles southeast of New Utrecht, and notorious. "Smuggler!"

Nicholls snorted derisively. "So they say. He'll call one night, when the wind's right and there's no moon."

"Yes? And?"

Nicholls shrugged. It was obvious. They needed to be ready and waiting. Nearby. Hidden. "We give him your name for the signal."

"You what! How'd you even know I was—"

"No time now, Nicholls!"

"Aye. Later, lad. Can you help us?"

"Can you at least get us across, onto Long Island?" Jack begged.

My mind instantly accommodated them by focusing on that problem. "Can't wait until dark. Current's already on the ebb."

"Aye, we know," Nicholls said. "But your ferryman will leave in another hour, right?"

"Unless he has an unusual delay, yes."

"We'll have to chance it in the light, an hour after that."

My indignation fought my admiration. "You've got this all thought out, I see!"

"Our necks are on the line, Thomas," Jack said. "We sail next week, or we swing next week."

Church bells rang half-past three—seven bells, sailor parlance. One noose was haunting me already. I capitulated, and we planned out the rest of the afternoon.

There's a chandlery on the quayside that boasts a large, paned window facing the river, and I dawdled there feigning an interest in cordage as I surreptitiously watched Jacob debark and the dock laborers thin out. I had plenty of time to ponder whether I was doing right in abetting desertion and smuggling, not to mention whether I was excusing their manhandling of myself, but I presently became in fact rather fascinated by the extraordinary variety of ropes that were available; a clerk was so kind as to explain their materials, provenance, and purposes to me notwithstanding my obvious lack of interest in purchasing anything.

But shortly after five, I decided to move. The two sailors appeared behind me, all of us hastening as unobtrusively as possible. I tossed a small chunk of wampum to the perpetually inebriated fellow who served as Jacob's excuse for a guard, and we retrieved my canoe and purchases from their usual spot behind the ferryman's shed. The canoe was lowered into the river and stowed within two minutes. Nicholls we covered over with a tablecloth, amidships, while Jack, whose strength would be needed to move the extra weight, donned my sun hat and my Indian winter coat. The first twenty minutes were very nervous, as I steered us as far from other boats as I could, but presently we were in the Buttermilk Channel with few others nearby. More relaxed, Nicholls sat up and I was brought up to date with their history and plans. They had, I was astounded to learn, worked me into their scheme for months. Merchants desiring to trade in the Caribbean with the French were eager to snatch up prime seamen whose skills were taken for granted by the Royal Navy. The agent who had suborned the sailors' flight from the *Proserpine* had apprised them that Sheepshead Bay, outside the city's main harbors, was a favored refuge for his master's small, fast, illicit boats. From the first moment they'd recognized me in the canoe this spring, Nicholls and Jack had determined that *I* was their main chance to manage their escape— extraordinarily presumptuous of them!—and begun to watch my movements intently, to the point of noting my biweekly shopping schedule.

Though they swore they'd never set foot in a canoe before, diligent study combined with ingrained seamanship made them sure-footed from the first. Instinctively they set their feet in the center and brought their weight carefully to the floor. Jack automatically knelt in the bow, kept his back straight, and paddled with the determination of an Oneida brave on the warpath. I noticed an oddity on his face: the skin was deeply tanned on his forehead and pasty white on his cheeks. He'd sacrificed the beard only today. And both he and Nicholls, I realized, had cropped the immense pigtails in which sailors invest inordinate vanity. If that didn't indicate the seriousness of their situation, nothing did.

At the mouth of Gowanus Creek we beached on the south shore, and the two men dashed for a grove of trees I'd pointed out, to which I promised to return after dark. I then took the canoe to Jacob's landing in Red Hook and offloaded into the wheelbarrow. Happily, the ferryman had been eating supper with his wife and hadn't noticed a thing out of ordinary. I replaced my canoe in his flimsy shelter and started for home. Working hard on the problem of how I'd retrieve, hide, and feed the sailors, I wasn't prepared when I turned the barrow onto the last leg of the trail into town, and....

And I beheld the corpse of Zwarte Jan swaying from a tree branch in the distance. There had been no other capital sentence executed in New Utrecht in my lifetime, and I'd assumed that, like stockings, whippings, and brandings, it'd be done on the common. But the notion was that the miscreant should remain a visible warning to all the county's malefactors for a matter of days, so it was most appropriate for the sentence to be executed at a crossroads. Therefore, he'd been hanged at the junction of the trail and the highway. During the twenty minutes it took me to reach the turn, I found it easier to concentrate on keeping the barrow's wheel out of ruts. When I came to the corner, I stopped and swallowed and forced myself to look. Grotesque, of course, particularly from the neck up. Hideous. But then I suppose Bates had been grotesque too. Human beings are never supposed to look like this.

The junction was deserted. No one was around to be queried for details of the event. Amid the refuse—apple cores, bread crusts, a child's toy—that indicated a crowd had recently congregated there was, improbably, a clutch of bluebells. I picked them up, wondering if my eyes had deceived me. No, the stems were tied with a piece of twine. I gently set them back down again.

Nothing to be done. Wryly, I noted that Jan's clean clothes still bore the mark of his woman's stubborn pride. He owned two frayed sets of togs made from old sail canvas. Anne had never let him wear either two days in a row. Sick to the heart, I proceeded the rest of the way to our house.

CHAPTER 12

The celebration had long been winding down. Meneer Van Klost, in an unusually tipsy state, was leaving just as I arrived, in the company of Mr. Traube, a Swiss-born man who now provided us and many other residents with most of our dairy needs. "Ah Sergeant Dordrecht," he effused, "you missed a fine ceremony. A huge crowd, people from all over. But no rowdiness at all. Matters proceeded without the least disturbance. Wonderful to see the majesty of the law in action!"

"I feel the town has surely turned a corner!" Mr. Traube—as well-oiled as Van Klost—exulted. "It's a great relief." They left, arms about each other's shoulders. Pa was still talking to Voskuil and Loytinck and Mr. Scoffield; Bertie was gabbing with Oosterhout; Harmanus was not around—still working, I presumed. The women were fixing supper, and the smell of it gave me strength to stow all the purchases away. When I returned Pa and Grootmoeder were staring into the empty fireplace, and Bertie was the only one left.

He brightened to see me fetching myself an ale. "What ho, cousin! The biggest event to occur in New Utrecht in many a moon, and you saw fit to skip it for just another shopping trip?"

"*Uhh*, yes." I took a deep draft of the ale and recollected my resolve to tell absolutely no one in New Utrecht how tumultuous my day had been. Until Nicholls and Jack were safely away, the fewer who knew of their presence, the better.

"Big excitement!" he said without much enthusiasm.

"Aye, well…. It sounds a tad pompous, I suppose, Bertie, but I really did see enough death and misery last summer to last me a lifetime."

"*Uh huh*," he grunted.

I hope he accepted that in the spirit I intended. "What, *uh*, happened?"

"Oh ... about what you'd expect. The detail got back with him just before noon. We rang the church bell and everyone came in from the fields. They stood him up in the cart and put the noose on him. Uncle Rykert read the governor's writ, my sainted father-in-law assured us this was the inevitable end result of all ungodly misbehavior, and the dominie offered an interminable prayer."

"Jan?"

"He just stood there like a rock, Thomas. Didn't wail, didn't protest, didn't curse. I'm not sure he knew what was happening." I looked sharply at him. "Well ... I suppose he did, but he was very, *uh* ... brave."

"Say anything?"

"Over and over: 'Praise God!' That was it. Van Voort got all excited and begged him to repent his sins at the last, but all he could be induced to say was, 'Praise God.'"

"The last words, eh?"

"Aye. Finally, your Pa'd had enough, and signaled Oosterhout to pull the horse away, and ... two minutes later ... it was all over. And we all went back to work."

Roosje was suddenly at Bertie's shoulder. "Master Bertie, Miss Jenneken says you're to come along home right away," she announced in a stentorian voice, looking at a corner of the ceiling.

"Ah, thank you, tell her I'll—" Roosje had spun on her heel and walked out. Bertie turned back to me, made a face, and rose. "I reckon I'll see you tomorrow, lad!"

*   *   *

It was past ten o'clock before the house was still enough for me to risk it. Carrying my boots, I sneaked down the protesting stairs and out the back door. Grootmoeder may have seen me, but Mr. Scoffield was a greater concern and he was snoring merrily away. I then set off through the fields trying to memorize paths and pitfalls in the moonlight. This being the last quarter phase of the moon, our path wouldn't be visible at all on our return. It would be folly to take the highway or the trail, for if one dog were to bark, the whole county would soon know of our movement—folk being unusually restive at the moment.

Nicholls and Jack in the same breath proclaimed their perfect faith that I'd return and their great relief at actually seeing me. We waited a moment while they consumed the morsels of bread I'd brought for them, then set back for home. "Glad to be away from there," Jack said, quietly slapping a mosquito. "Never saw so many bugs in my life! How do you land-folk stand them?"

It would not have been a kindness to inform them they were about to spend some time in the hayloft over a stable. As we walked I did, however, explain why they were asking this favor at a particularly bad moment for the town, and that even more caution than they'd anticipated was therefore in order. My notion was that, if the sailors kept quiet, they'd be less likely to be found in the stable than anywhere else. We had barns on our fields, but Harmanus and Pa and Vrijdag were constantly in and out of them. Pitching hay down from the stable's loft, however, was everybody's job and nobody's. If there happened to be plenty of hay on the ground, Pa, Harmanus, Vrijdag, or Hendrik would each assume that one of the others had obliged him. The boy was the only one who spent any serious amount of time in the stable at all, but that was because he loved the horses. How I'd get food and water to the men—was yet to be determined.

Shortly after midnight, we felt our way carefully back into our yard, into the stable, and up the ladder. As soon as the sailors were settled, I took my leave, retraced my barefoot steps to the attic, and collapsed, exhausted.

Unusual commotion downstairs roused me earlier than expected in the morning, and I trudged sleepily down to find out what was going on. Pa was sitting down to breakfast with his grandchildren—a rare occurrence—and answering Mother's questions. Meneer Halsema had been about on the highway before dawn and had discovered that Zwarte Jan's corpse had disappeared. He'd run to Van Klost, who'd gathered Bertie, Pa, and Harmanus for an investigation into the slave quarter that had proved fruitless. No one had seen or heard anything. "They're lying of course," Pa asserted. "They *all* know who cut him down and where they've buried him." Van Klost wanted to declare martial law, but Harmanus had argued him out of it, insisting that the farm work was behind schedule enough as it was. "For once, I was nearly ready to side with Van Klost!" Pa declared, thumping his fist on the table. Berendina looked at him in mock amazement. "But I couldn't go that far!" he added, with the shadow of a mischievous grin on his face—one I remembered from long back.

That afternoon I volunteered to do a water-fetch, to spare my sister a second pass—which had only become necessary because my sailors were drinking it up—and I stopped by the crossroads. Nobody had thought to retrieve the bit of rope still tied to the tree branch. It swung about in the breeze, useless. Depending on one's point of view, it symbolized the determination of law and order forces to see the penalties of crime paid in full—or the determination of Zwarte Jan's friends to see him decently buried in defiance of a heartless edict. Either way, it was a sore point, not to mention an eyesore. After fuddling myself with irritation that others hadn't removed it, the obvious solution occurred to me, and *I* climbed up the tree, out on the limb, and undid the rope.

*   *   *

With their hopes sinking, the burghers and their families began to realize that all had not instantly returned to normal after Zwarte Jan's execution. The other Selectmen had grumbled that Pa and Van Klost had no right unilaterally to acquiesce in the slaves' abstraction of Jan's corpse—a matter of obvious and illegal defiance—but, having no practical alternative, they let it drop. Householders who might also have objected became shy of escalating the conflict when word got around that the girl Bette, who'd been in and out of delirium since Bates' attack, had fallen into a coma.

Unobtrusively, I visited the stable and passed purloined food to Jack and Nicholls, managing to get in and out in less than two minutes. Still fatigued from the previous evening—while trying to pretend I felt perfectly normal—I stayed up long past the moment I desired.

And I suffered another bad dream, but this one left me feeling dizzy and nauseated, rather than terrified. I can't recall the specifics, but I woke disoriented in the dark, unsure of everything. Unhappy moments from the last many days wafted in and out of my awareness, from my horrific abduction to my perplexing cousin Charles to Herr Fischl's impatience with my clumsy fingering. Then one incongruous thought abruptly shook me fully awake: *How was it that when we found Bates' body, it was already stiff?*

He shouldn't have been stiff. It was too soon for him to be stiff, for *rigor* to have set in. We'd found Jan within minutes of finding the corpse, and it had seemed unquestionable not only that he'd killed Bates, but that he'd *just then* killed him, only minutes before I'd come out and wakened Pa. Jan had clearly been still in the grip of an immense passion, and I'd instantly concluded that the righteous fury he'd visited upon the man in the stocks had stayed with him as he waited for Pa or me to make the discovery of his lethal handiwork.

Jan was no thespian able to dissemble a frenzy of emotion on command. How was it that the processes that freeze a corpse's bones in one position had already taken hold? From my forced observations last summer, I knew it took a couple hours, at least. And—I slapped my palm against my forehead to think of it—I'd said to Pa at the time that Bates was already cold. I'd even said that!

But if Jan had attacked Bates much earlier, the moon would still have been up, lighting the common for all to see. Could Jan have been so resigned to his own discovery and the obvious consequence from the very moment he'd decided to act? By the time we'd chased and collared him, he was ready to shout triumphant defiance to the whole town, but had that been his plan hours before? There was no question in my mind that Jan had cut Bates' throat and that he was resigned to face the law's wrath, but … *how* could he have done it at the time I'd assumed he'd done it?

*   *   *

I couldn't shake the question. Through breakfast and the interminable regular weekly militia exercise, it kept coming back to me that, even though I'd been present in the midst of it, the story of Bates' murder just didn't make sense as I had imagined it. If Jan had killed him in the middle of the night, how had he managed such a fit, hours later? And why had he stayed at all, when he obviously had some opportunity to preserve himself by creating a mystery?

None of it made sense, so I inexorably went back to the beginning and thought it all through again.

"Could we possibly have your full attention, *Sergeant* Dordrecht?"

"Yes sir!" *Ugh*, I must really be slipping. Not like Van Klost to berate me—at least not since I got back from the North.

When practice was finally over I spent another hour dithering, and then decided I had to satisfy myself as far as I could to keep from going mad. But how? With whom? The others who'd seen Bates? Pa, I was sure, would instantly assure me I was crazy and walk away. Van Klost was on a high horse at the moment. My brother would be furious that I'd dare to interrupt his *real* work with a query so frivolous. Bertie would *be* frivolous.

Then I thought of the logical person, the only one with a professional interest in the remains of Justus Bates: the gravedigger. The town's gravedigger, however, is the slave Hans—who happens to be Zwarte Jan's eldest son, and uncle to the assaulted girl. Hans belongs to Loytinck and spends most of his time in the fields, but when someone dies, Loytinck pays down some of his tithe by seconding Hans to Dominie Van Voort's command. He is a big, stolid, strong man of middle years, not as genial as his sire was but never surly either. I've known him my entire life—but our paths tend not to cross and I doubt we've exchanged ten words a year in all that time. Where would I even find him? The sun was approaching its zenith, so Loytinck's hands would soon be breaking for dinner. I set off to the Loytinck property, hoping to be directed to him before he returned to the quarter—where I imagined the presence of any Dutchman would be unwelcome at the moment. Happily I encountered Mr. Stanley; though mystified by my request, he duly directed me to the south field.

Hans was plowing. The plow was triced to an ox, and Hans was directing it into straight, even furrows. One of the younger slaves was following, planting corn at careful intervals. On the far side of the field, Hans' brother Balt was directing another team. I hadn't recalled Hans as surly … but he seemed peevishly resistant to the obvious fact that I wished to speak with him. Finally he could evade me no longer and reined back the ox. "Master Thomas?" he said evenly. Before I could state my business, however, he quickly and somewhat angrily added, "I told Schout everything! I don't know who cut Jan down. I don't know what they done with body. I sleep through all that night."

He was lying, I knew—necessary lies that neither of us could help. I cast my eyes downward, unable to bear watching it. "Hans—"

"You ask my woman. She tell you!" I nodded to the following seeder, who somehow recognized my desire for privacy and walked over to join the other pair, who'd halted and were staring at us. Not much privacy in an open field at high noon!

"Hans, I wanted to ask you about Justus Bates, not your.… Not Jan."

It took him half a minute to get possession of himself. "What about?"

"When you got him, was he—"

"Evil man! Dominie don't want him in graveyard with decent."

"Ah. When you first saw him, Hans.… When was that?"

"That Bates? I hear him beat Mister Eben too."

"When were you asked to dig a grave for him, Hans?"

"Oh. Right away. Vrijdag find me in quarter before work. I go to common. Dominie tell me bury body in shed. I get horse and cart and take to potter's."

"Was anyone assisting you?"

Hans looked at me uncomprehendingly for two seconds, then shook his head. "I manage. If heavy man, or person go in casket, I get Balt help. Not this. This I put under my own self." I pondered my next query. "I done and back here on field mid-morning."

"*Uh huh.* How long would you say he'd been dead, Hans?"

He stared for a second, clearly registering that our interview was the result of some unease on my part—and clearly wondering what that was. "Him stiff. Him dead five, six hours. Him never straighten."

Aha. I tried to think of an easy way to ask my next question. Couldn't. "That night, Hans. When did you last see Zwarte Jan?"

Hans looked away and gulped. "Sun go down. I say good night. He go in with Anne."

"Did you hear any commotion overnight?"

Now he was truly mystified. "I hear Anne talk quiet outside to friend, long time, middle night." He thought more. "That all."

What else had I meant to ask? Oh. How could I forget? "Did you look at the corpse's neck, Hans? Could you tell—"

"Him cut twice."

"I beg your pardon?"

"Twice. Low cut"—he gestured just above his collarbone—"deep, smooth. Much, much blood. Blood all over neck, shirt, breeches."

Yes. I remember having difficulty looking at the horrible gashes. "Another cut?"

"Up here." Just under the chin. "Rough, jagged. But no blood."

"*No* blood?"

He closed his eyes briefly. "Very little blood. Almost no blood."

"Was it as deep a cut?"

He pondered. "I don't think, Master Thomas. But … I don't worry about. I want him under, that all I want."

I was as stumped as he. Unable to think of anything more, I sheepishly thanked him and left. I could sense his eyes following me as I regained the road and finally put some trees between us.

*   *   *

The controversy—whether it was still necessary for me alone to service Mr. Scoffield's room now that the disreputable Mr. and Mrs. Bates had departed life and New Utrecht, respectively—had been raised to my mother once, and decided with a resounding affirmative. When she gets a notion going, very little will change her. So when I got home, she reminded me there was no time like mid-day to locate untoward dust and debris, and therefore my chaotic thoughts were necessarily postponed pending completion of this tiresome chore. First I stripped the bed and reversed the mattress, then reset it with clean sheets. Finally, I commenced dusting the window sill and the two items of furniture.…

There was a handsome folded knife on the bureau. It had been there all along, but … curiosity got to me. No one was about—Scoffield himself had said he was going all the way to Bushwick today—so I pushed the door almost closed. I took the knife to the window and opened it out in direct sunlight. The handle was carved oak with etched filigree decorations. Its polished steel blade gleaming, it looked as if it had never once been used. I looked very carefully and found, with vague relief, that the item looked perfectly ready to set back on a respectable merchant's shelf.

Mother begged one more favor as I reported the room readied. Would I bring in a bushel of apples from the stable? Of course. The bushels were stacked high. I looked about, hissed quietly, and pitched four up to Nicholls. But as I again hefted the bushel, I spied, stuck in a rafter over the tool bench,

Zwarte Jan's knife. I'd wondered what Pa had done with it. I'd given it to him on Sunday, suggesting he should take it to Brooklyn as evidence, and that was the last I'd known of it. He'd probably "forgotten." I pried it out and examined it in the sunlight. It was in worse shape than I recalled, the blade nicked and badly scratched. There was a dark streak along the edge that was probably blood. But there was not a lot of blood. Grime perhaps—Jan wouldn't have had access to anything better than sand with which to clean it—but no great accumulation of dried gore. I stuck it back in the rafter, and carried the apples to the kitchen.

My chores complete, I took my reading outside, as normal, but was again unable to concentrate. No matter which way I turned the problem, I made no headway. Twice I tried to put it out of my mind and absorb some wisdom, but I couldn't. Perhaps, I decided with a sigh, if I could unburden these doubts, they'd at least let me alone. A vision of the stony reception I might receive from Meneer Van Klost brought me up short. Speculations on the details of Bates' last moments would be unwelcome to anybody in New Utrecht. The town had just hanged a man and was hoping that the rebellious spirit of the last weeks had died with him. Not a soul would care for the intellectual exercise that was distracting me. What I needed was someone like Mr. Glasby, who would be a patient, intelligent listener to this conundrum. So would Miss Chapman, for that matter. Or my friend Marinus Willett, whom I'd seen only once since his recovery. But they were all far away, and....

The dominie, of course! He was no stranger to controversy, and was adept at managing it. And it was the perfect time to consult him, too, as he made a practice of being available to his communicants on Saturday afternoons. I fretted for twenty minutes more whether I really needed to impose on him before finally resolving that there was no alternative.

Just as I was passing in front of the kerk toward the dominie's residence, however, I spotted my youngest nephew running flat out toward our house with an unsheathed knife in his grubby little paw. "Petrus! *Stop!*" He lurched to a halt as I yelled, and my heart skipped a beat. "Boy, you must never run like that with a knife in your hand! If you trip, you could—"

"Isn't this our knife, Uncle Thomas? I found it!" I squatted beside him and looked at it dumbly. "It's the one that went missing, isn't it? Hendrik said I should wash it off and give it to Grandmother. I have to get back to the game—"

"No, wait, wait! Let me see." Distractedly, Petrus handed me his find, nearly stabbing me in the process. "The one that we couldn't locate after supper last week?" I'd forgotten all about it ... because I'd been delegated to take Jan to Brooklyn. "I'll take care of this, Petrus, but ... show me where you found it."

"I have to get back to the game!"

"Well this won't take a minute. Now come on."

Petrus looked as guilty as a four-year-old can manage. "It was in the well, Uncle Thomas."

"The well! Hasn't your father told you never to go down into that well?" Of course he had. "Show me."

The well in the common next to the kerk is dry most of the time. Every now and then, usually in the early spring, there's enough brackish water to use for cleaning, so the town has never filled it in.

Hendrik and Willem joined us as we approached it. "Hendrik threw the ball so hard it bounced off my hand and went into the well," Willem protested even before being asked.

"You found the knife on the ground at the bottom, along with the ball?" I asked Petrus.

"Yes sir."

"Right out on top? No leaves or anything over it?" He shook his head— and I shook mine. "You be careful with this well, lads. It's very dangerous!"

In chorus: "Oh, we were careful, Uncle Thomas!"

"It's not like the new well, there's no ratchet on this one. If the handle got out of control, he'd fall straight to the bottom."

"Oh we know that!" They dashed off, grinning, as I sighed. Anger would do no good. I'd been just as glib myself when Meneer Nijenhuis had reproved me for lowering Aalbert down the well a dozen years ago. After all, Brevoort had lowered *me* when I'd been youngest and smallest.

I took a good look at the knife. A thin, sharp blade like its mates in our dining room, but it was filthy. Sticky! Could it be dirt of some kind?

No. Blood.

*   *   *

"Thomas?"

"Good afternoon, Dominie."

Van Voort's smooth, untroubled face looked up at me in his doorway, surprised but smiling. "Well come in, come in." He led me back to his study, a large, airy room familiar to me from years of my schooling. Reuben, the elderly valet who is actually owned by the kerk rather than the dominie personally, was busy in the adjacent pantry, cleaning tableware for the morrow's consistory meeting. "Sit you down, lad. Is something wrong? What can I do for you?"

I prevaricated with small talk for a moment, hoping Reuben would leave, or the dominie would dismiss him, but he hauled out a new stack of bowls and proceeded to examine and clean them one by one. Finally I admitted that I had a problem that was greatly troubling me....

"Ah. I imagined as much. Your attendance has been irregular, young Thomas!"

"Yes sir."

"But we shall let that pass for the moment." He sat back and waited for me to explain myself. I felt inhibited because Reuben was still within hearing distance, twenty feet away. I kept expecting Van Voort to send him out of the room. Finally, I nodded directly in the slave's direction, as an unmistakable hint. "Ah, you needn't worry. Reuben is extraordinarily discreet; I've observed that on many occasions. He is quite reliable. Now, is it your father?"

My father? Oh. "Oh, no sir."

"Aha. You are finding yourself in conflict with your elder brother, perhaps?"

"No sir, I—"

"Oh dear. I hope we're not contemplating a situation such as your cousin faced a year ago?"

What? Oh. Bertie—finding he'd got Jenneken with child. I felt myself flushing. "No no, sir, I—" I nearly laughed.

"What then, lad? What could be so terrible?"

Once more, I attempted indirectly to plead for privacy. Dominie Van Voort shrugged impatiently, and I gave up. "I've been thinking a lot, sir, about the town's problems, and I want—"

"The *town's* problems?"

"Yes sir. What happened a week ago, sir, it troubles me, and—"

"Well, I'm pleased that you trouble yourself with the town's problems at all, Thomas. We had worried that you were planning to dissociate yourself completely from the town of your forebears." I was speechless. "I've been most distressed that your brother Brevoort did not even see fit to attend your niece's christening!"

Should I tell him Brevoort's children are being raised as Baptists?

"That was really quite irresponsible. I am very disap—"

"Dominie, what's worrying me is that I can't make sense out of how Zwarte Jan did in Justus Bates. There are too many discrepancies in the narrative."

The dominie stared at me, open-mouthed. The clatter of which I'd been dimly aware, of tableware and cutlery, suddenly went quiet as well. "Such as?"

"Well, when we captured Jan, he was suffused with enthusiasm, sir, as if he'd just walked out of a revival tent." Van Voort shook his head in synodal horror. "So we assumed he'd attacked Bates scant minutes before my father and I found him, Jan being a most simple slave, and—"

"I must say, your father was most remiss in allowing this to come to pass, really."

"Indeed, sir, I fear so. But the point is, we ignored—or at least forgot—the evidence of our own senses, which was—"

"What?"

"That the body of Justus Bates was already cold, sir. In fact, the *rigor* had already set in when we removed it from the stocks."

The dominie sat still in thought for a moment. "I see, and the implication of—" He broke off for a second. "Reuben, leave us, please! You can finish that in an hour." He waited until we heard a door close. "But Jan did confess, Thomas? He avowed he'd cut the wretch's throat, did he not?"

"Aye sir, most convincingly. But he would have had to have done it hours before. Not just before dawn, but in the middle of the night."

"*Um hmm.*"

"And if he did do that, his mere presence near the green becomes hard to explain."

"Ah. Perhaps he returned to view his abominable handiwork in the light?"

"Or perhaps, sir … perhaps he had an accomplice."

Dominie Van Voort shuddered. "That's a most alarming thought, Thomas. But is there really anything to suggest that?"

I explained about the two cuts on the neck, and the second knife that had just come into my possession as I had approached the kerk. "You see why I find it all confusing, sir?"

He sighed. "Ah yes, well of course. But we must all live with a certain amount of disorder in our lives. It is not given to us to know God's mind, Thomas."

"Of course not, sir, but—"

"And you know…. This is a very dangerous line of inquiry, Thomas. The citizens of the town, the whole county—I've even heard men assert the entire province is concerned—are most nervous, unsteady, mercurial in the instance of violence by the bondsmen. It is a subject properly to be considered only by the most mature and settled minds, and that in absolute privacy."

"Well, yes sir, I do realize this. That's why I came to you, sir!"

He smiled briefly. "Ah, well, you flatter even me, lad. But this is a proper subject for authority, not idle surmise, and I shall remand it to the Selectmen of the town to judge."

The Selectmen include Meneer Van Klost and my sorry father. "But sir—"

He raised his hand to halt my objections. "All will be handled in due time, my friend. You must remember that the slightest indiscretion in a matter of such delicacy can have catastrophic consequences." Feeling queasy, I nodded. "And I think you should cease torturing yourself, Thomas." He smiled knowingly. "You really need to bring your own affairs to maturation, young man!"

This I interpreted as more than another hint that I ought to find work. "So say everyone," I grumbled, trying to correct my insolence as the syllables passed my lips. But it really was infuriating to hear the county's most eligible bachelor—twice my age—drop suggestions that a nineteen-year-old was overdue for wedlock! Especially when—

"And you must guard against the sin of pride, Thomas, against intellectual arrogance. I fear you are sometimes importunate with your betters."

It took considerable willpower to conclude the interview a few minutes later without exploding in irritation. I'd thought the man my friend, but at the moment I was finding him completely insufferable.

*　　　*　　　*

"The missing knife's been found, Mother." I set down the buckets of water she'd commanded me to fetch the instant I'd returned from the kerk.

"Oh thank heaven, we really need it. Where on earth was it?"

"Petrus found it at the bottom of the old well."

"The bottom of the.... What was it doing *there?*" I pulled it from my vest and showed it to her. "*Ugh!* Let me clean that up right away."

"Wait, wait. Do you see what I see?"

She halted, brought it closer to her eyes, and turned it over in the light of the kitchen window. "Is that ... blood?"

"You tell me."

She shrugged. "It's all over the handle, not just the blade. The bottom of the *well?*"

"Aye. The boys lost a ball."

Her scowl deepened. "You reprimanded them, I trust?"

"Oh yes."

She grunted, dropped the knife into a wash bucket, and promptly began cleaning it with a rag. "The well! I'll never understand how things end up where they do! Would you bring me a peck of turnips from the cellar, please?"

Was life in New Utrecht finally returning to normal? Hints that it might be made me all the more hesitant to voice my doubts to anyone else. We had a goodly amount of custom that night, and Mother even asked me to play my guitar, and that in turn profited us by a few more sales.

At kerk the next morning the dominie expounded on a theological subject that had nothing whatever to do with the problems of life in Kings County, New York. Again, back to normal. If he later detained the Selectmen after the Consistory meeting to debate the issues I'd raised, Pa gave me no indication of it.

But when I joined the family at supper, Mr. Scoffield—just returned from Gravesend—looked up sharply, and said, "Well, *you've* put your foot in it, my boy!" Everyone looked at each of us, curious at this outburst.

"I beg your pardon, sir?"

"All of Gravesend is agog with your contention that the old slave had an accomplice when he did Bates in!"

The clamor of my family was matched only by my own inability to breathe. "That was only a surmise, sir, the merest hypothesis," I finally gasped out. "And it was voiced in strictest confidence. How—"

"Really? Oh, then I do apologize. But I'm afraid it's all over Gravesend, and...."

And all over Kings County.

"My host there queried me this afternoon about a rumor among his servants, and I had to tell him I knew nothing of it."

As I frantically considered how this might've happened, my brother angrily slammed his fist on the table, and groaned, "Oh not again!"

"Damn it, Thomas," my father shouted. "When will you learn to keep your fool trap shut?"

Unable to reply, I.... Oh yes. Reuben, the kerk's bondsman, actually lives with his family in the Gravesend slave quarter. He has a special pass he carries with him at all times. So much for his reliable discretion!

Mother suddenly looked up with a startled thought—that she unfortunately blurted out. "Does this have anything to do.... Is that why you wanted me to examine that knife yesterday, Thomas?"

"What knife?" Harmanus demanded.

"The knife I found in the well?" Petrus squawked, delighted.

Mother sensed she was on dangerous ground. "Oh never mind."

Pa's curiosity was aroused. "What, Chastity?"

"Our table knife. We had one go missing a week ago, and Petrus found it yesterday in the old well."

"So?"

"It was covered with blood."

The entire room was quiet. "So?"

"Well, that's just thirty yards from the stocks, isn't it."

CHAPTER 13

Deafeningly loud and insistent, the church bell woke me from a sound sleep. I sat up and looked out the window: pitch black. But the bell kept ringing. This was not a nightmare.

"Thomas!"

"Aye, I'll be right there, Harmanus." I dressed and rushed downstairs in the dark, nearly colliding with half a dozen other Dordrechts. "What is it?" I asked.

"Fire," Mother replied. "Can't see what. Somewhere near the crossroads."

Mr. Scoffield was asking the same question as we reached the bottom, and immediately volunteered to assist. An orange glow greeted us as we left the house. As we passed the kerk, there was no question what was amiss: the Oosterhouts' barn was ablaze.

There had been enough fires in the past that everyone knew what to do. Male and female, free and slave, adult and child all sorted themselves with little fuss according to physical strength. A few of the strongest were needed to draw water at the well, while the majority of men would throw it on the site and pull such goods from harm as might be saved. Most of the womenfolk formed a chain to pass the full buckets while children returned empty ones.

"You take my bucket!" Harmanus commanded, thrusting it, full, into my hands as I rounded the Oosterhout house and beheld the horror. "I've got to help get that beast under control!" A panicked horse was loose, threatening to run riot through the town, and three men were struggling to calm it. I turned back to the conflagration. It was reaching a peak, flames having already engulfed half the building.

"Over here!" It was Meneer ter Oonck, calling me to throw a bucket at the doors. I ran up within six feet of it, heaved, and got the water onto the flames, but I couldn't even hear the hiss of it boiling off, the noise was so great. I backed away from the heat and one of the boys pulled the bucket from my hands. For half a minute, waiting my turn for another bucket, I tried to assess the problem. The wind was light, but steadily from the south. The barn was oriented in line with the house, only twenty feet north of it. Just as I was about to make a suggestion, ter Oonck shouted my thought, "The barn is lost. Save the house!"

The ladder we'd used when roofing arrived as I was handed another full bucket, and I was the first to carry water to the top, where I poured it along the edge nearest the fire. Fortunately, their roof was not as steeply pitched as ours, and there was no false wooden front to catch the flames. Bertie, Vrijdag, and Balt formed a chain to lift buckets up to me; others threw water from the ground up onto the exposed south wall of the house. The crisis lasted near an hour. At one point the heat and smoke became so intense I backed away to the middle of the roof, but still managed to pitch the water forward to the edge. Presently, however, the barn collapsed, ending the worst of the threat.

I only realized how badly my muscles were aching as I touched the ground and stood up straight. I grinned at my three immediate companions who grinned tiredly back in the light of early dawn. Activity near the barn had virtually ceased.

Oosterhout was frantically gesturing and apparently arguing with Voskuil, his neighbor. "This wasn't any act of Providence, Boudewyn," he shouted. "This was set by the slaves! This was set by"—he looked wildly about and focused on Balt and Vrijdag—"by *them!*" The palpably unjust accusation outraged us all.

Before we could manage a protest, however, ter Oonck called the man sharply. "Oosterhout! Look to your family, man!" Vrouw Oosterhout was shrieking hysterically despite Vrouw Nijenhuis' efforts to calm and console her. Oosterhout obediently moved to join them. "He's ... overwrought," ter Oonck pronounced, looking at our group. "Not himself."

"He should be counting his blessings," Bertie said, not quite looking the slaves in the eye. "He could've lost a lot more than a barn and a few pigs!"

"Voskuil say that," Balt observed. "He no listen."

Along with everyone else, we turned to leave. As I'd often done following a hard day on our own roof, I squeezed Vrijdag's elbow.

He jerked his arm away.

*   *   *

Loud exchanges from two floors below roused me from my exhausted nap. Long shadows across the property indicated it was still early, but I was sweating in the already terrible heat and had no hope of further rest. I dressed, fetched myself some water from the kitchen, and went to the tavern room. The five Selectmen—Pa, Van Klost, Van Voort, Loytinck, and ter Oonck—were sitting together, with Harmanus and Mr. Scoffield on either side, openly listening. Harmanus, whose mere presence at this late hour indicated a serious disruption of routine, nodded me to sit next to him. "They've found evidence the fire *was* deliberately set," he whispered.

"We're resolved, I take it," ter Oonck was saying, "that the slaves must be placed under curfew?"

Ayes, reluctantly, all round.

"Dusk to dawn?"

Ayes—grudging.

"But for how long?" Loytinck said testily. "I need some of my bucks up and about before dawn."

"As long as necessary!" Van Klost said, irritated.

"Well, really, how long do you think that will be?" Van Voort asked mildly.

Thoughtful deep puffs were taken on the clay pipes. "We have to resolve the issue that's riling them," ter Oonck observed. "I think they're convinced we're going to punish all of them for what Zwarte Jan's accomplice did."

"That's what we'll have to do," Van Klost said, "if we don't think he acted alone and we can't determine the guilty one."

"It really doesn't make sense that Jan acted alone," the dominie observed, "and the implication of that is there's another murderer over in our slave quarter."

"Well, we can't live with that," ter Oonck said, "no matter what we thought of that fool in the stocks."

"Really have to apologize—" Scoffield interjected.

"Water over the dam, man," ter Oonck rejoined, looking annoyed by the interruption. Meetings of the Selectmen were generally not held in public, and we observers were being suffered only in view of the developing emergency. "Point is, we have to find out who it is before we have to call in the redcoats!"

"We'll never need them," Van Klost said angrily. "There's nothing the militia can't handle!"

"We'll see," ter Oonck said, frowning.

"We also have to find and punish the arsonist!" Loytinck insisted. "That's the critical matter right now."

"The other is perhaps the root cause of—"

"I think, Schout," the dominie said quickly, "that you should initiate some investigations."

Pa started. "I … can't do that. I've got my farm work, and … we'll all be called for curfew duty."

His four colleagues stared at him, horrified. "So we just have to let this go on, until the quick are judged with the dead?" Loytinck demanded sarcastically. "Or at least until tempers cool in the autumn?"

My father looked extremely uncomfortable for a minute. "Perhaps I could deputize my son."

Harmanus flushed and groaned, and the others looked exasperated. "Harmanus is far too busy for this, Dordrecht!" ter Oonck objected. He and Pa had long trod carefully about each other, but now he evidently thought their mutual grandchildren at risk. "We all know Harmanus is working your farms practically without assistance, and—"

"Oh. Not Harmanus, Thomas."

I blanched as they turned balefully in my direction. "He's very young," the dominie sniffed.

"He was a sergeant in the regiment last year," Van Klost stated. "Perhaps it would be acceptable."

"He's got too much time on his hands," Pa asserted. I was not the only one who rolled his eyes at that!

Loytinck grunted. "Well, what about this curfew, Van Klost?"

Van Klost announced that he and Bertie would take the first night's watch, and that further assignments would be forthcoming. He asked the others to ensure that all slaveholders understood that it was their duty to instruct their slaves that any Negro discovered abroad after dusk would risk being shot on sight, and that the Selectmen were deadly serious in their resolve to preserve the peace.

"I recommend we meet again tomorrow at dawn," ter Oonck said, "to consider the effect of the curfew and learn of the progress of the deputy schout."

They all mumbled assent, the dominie pronounced a quick benediction, and they rose.

Stunned, I realized my agreement had been presumed without even being requested, and without any discussion of terms. "Gentlemen!" I said hastily, rising. "I trust I may at least rely on the cooperation of each of you as needed?"

They seemed a trifle startled, but each murmured his "Of course," and walked out.

"You will remember that this matter requires the utmost prudence, Thomas," Van Voort said meaningfully as he reached the threshold—calling on all my prudence to keep me from punching him.

I looked back to the table to see Pa, Harmanus, and Mr. Scoffield looking momentarily spent. The latter two quickly stood, however. Mr. Scoffield announced he would again be traveling to Gravesend, and would saddle his horse himself. Harmanus, looking quite shaken, touched my arm as he reached the door. "Thomas, I.... This is a terrible business, brother. Let me know how I can help." He went outside and rushed off toward the north field.

Pa stood. "I'd best be going too," he mumbled.

"Pa!" He halted. "The least you can do is answer some questions for me!"

"Very well. But I've had no breakfast."

"Nor have I. Wait, I'll get us some. Where's Mother?"

"She's not allowed to observe the meetings, so she leaves the house altogether. Says she can't bear any of us anyway."

Not entirely unreasonable, I thought grimly. I cut bread and cheese for two. Pa poured himself an ale; I had to go back and pour my own. Digging in, I said, "First of all, how'd they become convinced this was arson?"

"Hay and kindling by the south side of the barn," Pa said. "Oosterhout swears it was never left there."

"You're sure it wasn't part of the barn itself, that just fell in that direction?"

"Think not. Small logs, not planks. Fire began from the south end and the whole barn collapsed toward the north."

"*Uh huh*. That's fairly convincing. Is anyone feuding with the Oosterhouts?"

"Well, I don't think anyone particularly likes him, but they've not been here long enough to raise really bad blood."

"*Hmm*."

"Then there was the totem."

"Totem?"

"Aye, a voodoo doll. That's why they think it was slaves. On the sycamore by the corner of their fence. Man of straw."

On the far side of the fire, no one would have noticed the object during the night. "Well, anyone can make a straw doll, Pa. Berendina still takes hers to bed every night."

"This one was hanging by its neck."

"Ah. Any of the blacks have special enmity for Oosterhout?"

Pa shrugged. "Not that I know. He's rough with his own slave, but no more than Smilda or Meerdink. He is the closest to the quarter, however. And the way the wind was blowing, they might've gotten two buildings with the same fire."

"Wasn't Oosterhout the one who controlled the cart at the execution?"

Pa froze for a second. "Aye. Hadn't thought of that. But Van Klost and I were in charge, and...."

We blinked at each other: *And if that were the motive, it might as easily have been us.* I was further distracted, imagining what might've happened to the two sailors in such a conflagration. "Did you make inquiries in the—"

"Why even bother asking, Thomas? We know what we'd get. Nobody will know anything."

"I should think you'd find less support for arson than for spiriting Jan's body away."

"Nonetheless, we were too tired to pursue it."

"You fulfill your own prophecies that way, Pa."

"If you're going to preach at me—" Pa flared, rising. He relented and sat again after a pout. "It'll be easier to figure out who Jan's accomplice was than who set the fire."

I sighed and pushed my empty plate away. He might be right on that point. "Pa, have you any idea when you fell asleep that night?"

"I was only asleep for a minute!"

"Oh Pa! You had the blanket completely over your head when I found you!"

"I did? Well, I never put it over my head. Over my legs or around my shoulders, maybe. I never put it over my head."

"Well that's where I found it."

"I'm telling you, I never put it there."

"Well, have you any idea when you fell asleep?"

Pa shook his head. "I may have dozed on and off."

"Did you see anybody at all, all night?"

"Oh sure. Westerhof came out just after I got there, and we chatted half an hour while he had a pipe before turning in."

"Was Vrijdag there, then? He was supposed to be there."

"Yes yes, he was there."

"And Bates was alive, of course?"

"Wouldn't quit moaning." Pa swallowed a draft of ale. "Scoffield thinks Vrijdag is the accomplice."

"He what?"

"Yeah. I heard him telling Van Klost and Van Voort before ter Oonck arrived."

For seconds, I was too stunned to speak. "On what ... basis does he make this contention?"

"Well, Vrijdag was out there with me—at least for some part of the night."

"Yes?"

"And he was here at supper, when the knife disappeared."

"So were a lot of people. And he was the one who called our attention to it."

"You always defend your slave!"

My slave? "Pa, this is absurd!"

"That's what Scoffield was saying, anyway. I don't think the others believed him."

"What did they say?"

"They said they thought Vrijdag had learned his lesson five years ago."

"When he'd been whipped for running away?"

"Aye."

"Well…. Vrijdag wasn't with you when I came out just before dawn, so do you have any notion when he left you, or where he went?"

"No, I don't know. He went home to his woman, of course."

My assumption, too. But I'd have to check. "Did you see anyone at all, the whole night, white or black?"

"*Uh*, right after Westerhof left, Bilderbeek and his wife walked by. Nightly exercise. They walked back. Waved both times, but didn't stop to chat. That was it. It was a bright night, but there was nobody about. Everybody'd had their fun with Bates during the afternoon."

"You saw no one?"

"No…. Yes! I must have been dozing—"

Read *asleep.*

"… and Bates squawked or was spitting or something and seemed to be shaking his head back and forth. I looked around and I saw a small man going around behind the kerk."

"Ah. And … did you recognize him?"

"Well, I wasn't positive. Cloud came over at just that instant. But I thought it was Loytinck's gutless wonder of a foreman, though what the devil he'd be doing there, I couldn't imagine."

"Eben Stanley?"

"That's what I thought."

"Did you go check to see that Bates was all right?"

"Huh? No. Why? Still spitting and cussing. Just another citizen having a little fun."

Then I guess this bit of fun had not involved cutting his throat! "This was about what time, Pa?"

"Come on, Thomas. How should I know?"

"Where was the moon, Pa?"

"Oh. Moon was almost overhead, slightly to the east."

Two nights after full: that'd be just past midnight. "Was Vrijdag with you then?"

"Vrijdag? *Uh....* You know, I don't think I ever turned to look."

"What happened next, Pa?"

"Next? Nothing. Lots and lots of it!"

"You fell asleep?"

"Well, it seems I must have at some point, Thomas."

"And Bates?"

"He stayed quiet."

We sat silently for a moment. Obviously, I needed to talk to Stanley and to Vrijdag. "If you think of anything else, Pa, I trust you'll let me know?"

"Oh sure, Thomas, sure."

It's very awkward to be placed in such a reversed position relative to one's father. I can't imagine I'm the first in all history, but it's not easy to accommodate. But the rather cold and bitter resolution came to me that, whatever Rykert Dordrecht intended to make of his life and his responsibilities was now a separate issue from what Thomas Dordrecht intended to make of his. Pa ambled out the front door. I collected the dishes, returned them to the kitchen, cut some of the cheese for Nicholls and Jack, and proceeded out the back.

*   *   *

Leaving the stable, I saw my cousin's wife sitting under a tree nursing her baby, now nearly six months old. It occurred to me that if I spoke with her slave girl Roosje, Vrijdag's woman, first, before Vrijdag himself, I'd have less concern about any collusion between them.

"Good morning, Tommy!" she called, setting my teeth on edge as always.

"Good day, Vrouw Hampers," I said, returning her wave as I approached the fence.

She pouted for a second at my formal address. "I hear you've been made the deputy schout. That's so exciting, Tommy!"

"Yes, well.... I'd like to talk to Roosje, Jenneken." I couldn't maintain the formality with a next door neighbor my kid sister's age.

"Roosje? Whatever for? Oh, because you think her man was the one who—"

"I just need to talk to her, please."

"Well, she's inside. I'll go fetch her." She put Maurits down in his cradle and slowly got herself upright. "She's shamming illness right now, the lazy wench. Nothing wrong with her. I never shirked my chores when I was seven months gone!"

"I need to talk to her."

"Oh very well." She disappeared indoors. A minute later she reappeared, prodding the slave before her.

The instant I saw Roosje I despaired of my immediate purpose. She was the picture of misery, her head hung down facing the ground. When they reached me by the fence I saw she was trembling from head to foot. "Yes?"

"Say 'Yes, Master Thomas!'" Jenneken demanded.

"Yes, Master—"

"Jenneken, I'd like to talk with her alone, if I may."

She looked baffled. "Why, Tommy? She's our girl, she's—"

"This is in my capacity as deputy schout, Jenneken."

"Well, if you insist!" She waited another few seconds—as did I, and Roosje, standing openly in the sun—before realizing that I did insist, and petulantly returning to her infant under the tree.

"Roosje, I need to ask just a couple questions. It's about the night that Bates—" She flinched and whimpered as if I'd struck her. But I needed to hear her answer. I pitched my voice lower and softer. "The night Bates was ... in the stocks, at what time did Vrijdag come back to you?" She looked up quickly, panic written across her face, and I realized how impossible a position she was in—and that I'd never be able to frame a question that didn't make her man either disobedient, for leaving Pa, or a murder suspect, if he'd stayed. But there was no help for it. "I know he was supposed to stay with my father, Roosje, but that's not important. Please just tell me when he got back to you."

She sighed heavily. "Soon," she whispered. "Two hour after dark. Surprise."

"Did he go out again, at all, before dawn?"

"No. He look at children, then lie down. All night. He mad I not wake before dawn."

I tried to catch her eye, but she was unable—or unwilling—to lift her head. This was exactly what I assumed to be the case, but unfortunately it was also what served her best, if one was inclined to think the worst. There was no reason to belabor the issue. "Have you any idea who set the fire, Roosje?"

"No," she moaned, shaking her head slowly, "no."

Well, what did I expect? I thought it more likely she'd know who buried Jan but happily that had not been made part of my assignment, so I didn't pursue it.

She crossed her arms protectively over the unborn child in her belly. "Anne think maybe Bette die."

It silenced me. Like all the others, I'd given little thought to Bates' victim since the attack. That the girl's wounds might've become infected was completely plausible. Though I instantly denigrated the thought as self-centered, it occurred to me that matters would worsen in the town should the girl expire. No wonder her sister was in such a state. "Thank you Roosje, that's all."

She looked at me for a second, with the briefest flash of hope in her terrified eyes, then started back for the house. Jenneken rushed to her to demand what had been said, and she collapsed into tears as she crossed the threshold.

When I found them, Harmanus and Vrijdag were plowing the north field, exactly as I'd seen Hans and Balt do on Saturday. Except that they lacked seeders. So as each finished a row, he halted his ox and retraced his steps to plant the seeds. "Of course," Harmanus said nervously when I asked his permission to question Vrijdag. He kept right on going as I stopped the slave in the middle of a row.

"Look, Vrijdag," I began directly, "where the devil were you the night Bates was killed?"

"Home with Roosje."

"All night?"

"All night. Late getting back, didn't wake with the light."

"Did Pa let you go? He didn't tell me he gave you permission." Vrijdag stared at me stubbornly, inviting me to make the most of the obvious. "All right, when did you leave the common?"

"Before midnight. Moon still in east." I waited. "No one come by square, over an hour. Meneer Rykert sleep. Prisoner sleep. I go home, I go sleep."

"Did you see anyone after dark?"

"Meneer Westerhof stop and talk with Meneer Rykert. Meneer, Vrouw Bilderbeek walk back and forth. That all. No one else."

"Did you see anyone when you got to the slave quarter?"

He furrowed his brows. "All quiet, all sleep. I hear Jan and Anne with Bette, but I not see. I see Roosje, Kaspar, Toontje."

His children. I took a deep breath. "Did you kill Bates, Vrijdag?"

It took him aback, as I'd hoped, but his answer rattled me. His hands clenched repeatedly around the traces he was holding. "I wanted to kill. I thought about, long, when schout fall asleep. I want dead. I thought: take musket bayonet, cut him as he cut Bette. I…." He shook himself. "I go back to Roosje so I *not* kill Bates."

I watched him for a minute. He didn't relent. "Some people suspect that you—"

"I wish I *had* kill Bates!" he exploded. "Then Jan still be alive."

Perhaps I'm just a nineteen-year-old stripling sent to do a man's job, but if he was lying, it was beyond any experience of falsehood I've ever known. When I asked him if he knew who'd cut Jan down from his gibbet, and he said he'd no idea, all my senses told me he was lying straight at me. But not when he talked about Bates.

When I asked if he knew who'd set the fire, he said no, and I believed him. When I asked if he had any suspicions, he said no, and I had my doubts. As a circumspect deputy schout, however, I thought it wisest to keep all my thoughts to myself, so—although it made me feel pompous and self-inflated as Van Klost—I walked away without another word.

*   *   *

"A good day to thee, Mr. Dordrecht."

"A perishing hot day, though, is it not, Mr. Stanley?"

"Aye, that's so. At least come into the stable."

It was stifling inside the stable, but the relief from direct sunlight was great. "Mr. Stanley—"

"The master told me of thy errand, Mr. Dordrecht. I fear I know nothing of what happened last night. I never even saw the heathen doll he speaks of."

"Yes, that's part of my mission. Tell me, did you see all of your slave charges helping out last night?"

"Ah, we were all spread out, in no special order, Mr. Dordrecht." I waited. "But, *uh*, I was near the well with the master and Miss Katelaar, and Lotje was next to us in the chain, and all four of her late daughter's brood were right there in the return chain, she always keeps them close."

"Aye?"

"Old Jermyn and Virginia, his woman, arrived a little later; I saw them join the chain twenty yards down. Hans was working the well. I don't recall seeing Powles or Balt or Wim."

"Balt was near me, by the fire itself."

"Ah. Well, there was great confusion."

"I'm also charged to learn all I can of the night Justus Bates was murdered. Can you—"

The slight little fellow shuddered, looked away, and seemed to draw all his reserves. "Ah, then I would make a confession to thee, Mr. Dordrecht."

Him? My jaw dropped open. "Yes?"

"It is a sin, Mr. Dordrecht, to hold hatred in one's heart. We are all God's creatures and fallible mortals." He swallowed again, and spoke slowly and haltingly. "But I fear I did hate Mr. Justus Bates most shamefully, to the degree that I felt a great violence toward him ... to the degree that I exercised great violence upon him." With some effort, I waited silently. "I restrained myself far from the common all during the day, but it happened that was the night Miss Katelaar and I stayed up awaiting the birth of the foal." He nodded his head at a filly in a nearby stall. "Hours had gone by, yet the mare had still not given her signs, and I begged some minutes for a walk. But as I was leaving, I saw a stack of rotten pumpkins—since used for fertilizer—and I was wickedly inspired to take one. And I carried it in my hands to the common, where I saw both the prisoner and the schout asleep. I … broke into that pumpkin and I carried its seeds to the stocks and I … I smeared them into the face of the prisoner!"

Had the man not been shaking like a leaf, I'd have fallen to pieces laughing. Almost did, anyway.

"He woke up and he cursed me, Mr. Dordrecht, and I felt so ashamed, I left him and fled into the graveyard to pray for forgiveness on sacred ground."

"My father did see you pass, Mr. Stanley. He woke up as well."

"Ah. I am sorry to have disturbed his repose. It is all so unforgiveable!"

Had my father's *repose* been more often disturbed, perhaps we might have returned to normal life by now! "You went over into the graveyard?"

"Aye. I went behind the church, fearing to be seen by any decent Christian who might be on the highway, for I was so—"

"Had you seen anyone up to that point?"

"No."

"Only Justus Bates and my father, the schout?"

"Yes."

"You never saw, for instance, the slave Vrijdag?"

"No. I know Vrijdag of course."

"Or Zwarte Jan?"

"No, nor he."

"And the prisoner was alive and uninjured?"

"Yes. Oh I see!"

Could this man be such an innocent that he only now perceived the drift of my questions? It seemed implausible and yet … how could any normal criminal have concocted such a preposterous fable—mashing a pumpkin's guts into Bates' ugly craw and then falling on his knees in a paroxysm of guilt? "Can you estimate what time of night this was, Mr. Stanley?"

"Oh yes, easily. One can hear Mr. Loytinck's hall clock in the stable, and it had struck a quarter past midnight before I left. It struck the three-quarter chime shortly after I returned."

"And you saw no one save Bates and my father the whole time?"

"Ah." He blushed scarlet, looked away, and again gulped. Surely he'd not committed another peccadillo as shocking as the pumpkin punch? "I did, Mr. Dordrecht, I did. I remained in prayer for perhaps ten minutes, but finally was moved to recollect my obligation to Miss Katelaar, who might be coping alone with the mare. So I brushed myself off and came out to the highway, where I saw *her* on the far side of the road, down near *The Arms*. In front of your neighbor's, Mrs. Esse—"

"Vrouw Esselinkpas?"

"Yes, that house, in fact. It was that ... horrid woman, the wife of the prisoner, who I'd been told was gone from us for good."

"*Mrs. Bates* was on the Kings Highway in New Utrecht, at twelve-thirty that morning?" I exclaimed incredulously.

"Aye, sir. That dark red gown can be confused with none other."

"*Um....* Did she see you, do you think?"

"I don't believe so, Mr. Dordrecht. She was looking back and forth along the highway, not across it. I hurried away, fearing that she might ... that I might be tempted ... *uh*, to be even more remiss in my duty to my employers."

"She was looking back and forth?"

"That seemed to be what she was doing. The breeze was up at that hour, and there was a cloud over the moon just at that moment."

"Did you hear anything?"

"*Uh*, yes, actually, just as I'd regained the road beyond the church, but it seemed as bewildering as everything else about that woman."

"What, pray?"

"What I thought I heard her say was, 'Well hello there my robin.' But of course that makes no sense."

"I confess I might've been tempted to stay and spy on her, Mr. Stanley!"

He blushed yet again. "Ah, perhaps I might have too, Mr. Dordrecht ... but happily the holy spirit recalled me to my duty."

"Were you tardy for the birth of the foal?"

"No, thank heaven. We still had over an hour to wait."

*   *   *

"Juffrouw Katelaar, I pray you will forgive me for disrupting your afternoon." The imposing woman, near as tall as myself, had come to the door, not waiting for the manservant.

"No need, Master Thom– ... Meneer Dordrecht. Do come in. I fear my grandfather is taking his nap at the moment, however."

"Oh, but I came to see yourself, ma'am, not him. You may know I've been appointed the deputy schout?"

We sat down in the parlor and she instructed her maid to bring refreshments. "So Grootvader said, Meneer Dordrecht. He said we must all rally to your assistance now, as we did for the Oosterhouts last night."

For a second I was tongue-tied, always feeling somewhat intimidated by this woman. I wondered if she felt as awkward with me as I did with her—there was something stilted and ungainly in her recitation, as if she felt constrained to present herself as a demure, obedient grandchild. Oh, no matter! "Ah yes, ma'am. Well, that brings one thing to mind that I'm just endeavoring to check. I asked Mr. Stanley whether he had seen all of your servants assisting in the effort to put the fire out last night, and he had—with the exception of Wim and Powles."

"Aha. Well, Powles, I know, got there very early, and he took charge of the two oxen in the barn and managed to lead them to safety over here in our yard, where they still remain. It was a difficult job, because they had no harness, and he had to go behind the Schupperts' house to avoid the crowd."

"*Uh huh.* And Wim?"

She shrugged. "I didn't see Wim last night, but then ... I didn't see *you* last night, either!"

This was reasonable enough but, coupled with my aversion to the slave, it occurred to me to pose another question. "On the morning after the murder of the prisoner, Juffrouw, did Wim report for work as usual?"

"Wim? Let me think. Oh no, that was the week after Pinkster, and we had hired him out to my cousin's husband in Bushwick. He wasn't even in New Utrecht."

"Aha. There's no way he could have come back here on his own recognizance?"

"From Bushwick? No. Especially as they're very strict about locking their slaves up at night."

"I see. Well, also regarding that night, the night your foal was born—"

"That's how I remember it, you know," she exclaimed, her face relaxing for the first time. "I was very sorry for the town's distress, but I'd never met the indentured servant or his master, and I was overjoyed with the foal!"

"Indeed. Mr. Stanley said he left you for a recess shortly after midnight?"

"Yes. And I became rather cross with him, as it was nearly half an hour before he returned and, well, one never knows when the spirit will move the horse. Once things get started, it's usually rather quick, as I'm sure you're aware."

"*Uh huh.*" Not really. "Was his behavior odd, in any way?"

"Eben's? Mr. Stanley's? Oh, well, he was a trifle subdued, I thought, which is not his characteristic ... but when the foal was finally delivered, he gladly joined me in prayerful thanksgiving!"

"About what time was that, then?"

"Oh, very late. It was nearly three o'clock before we left the stable." This was all the information I'd come for, so I proffered my thanks and rose to leave. "If I may ask, Meneer Dordrecht, is your mother at home today?"

Mother? "Yes, ma'am, it's been some time since she's had a call for her midwifery."

"She has always seemed to me the most sensible woman in New Utrecht."

"I ... wouldn't deny it, ma'am—though it would surely be prejudicial for me to say!"

"I should like to pay her a social call."

After some fifteen years of living half a mile apart? "I'm ... sure she'd be delighted, Juffrouw Katelaar."

"Would four o'clock be a good time, do you think?" I agreed that that hour was well before Mother normally began work on supper. "And I suppose," she said, blushing, "that your father would still be working his fields?"

A polite and delicate effort of checking, I surmised. One could hardly blame her for wishing to avoid my father. "He is seldom home before suppertime, ma'am."

This appeared to be satisfactory. Rather at a loss, I left the house.

I'd just turned westward onto the highway, when I heard a musket report. At first I feared it might be back from the Loytinck establishment, but I quickly revised that: more in the direction of the well at the north edge of town. This was alarming. Hunters fire their pieces in the fields from time to time, and the militia fire ceremonially, but a single report within the town precincts was very rare. I ran back toward the well, in company with several other townsfolk.

Gosselick ter Oonck was standing by the well, trying to reload his musket, which was jammed. Vrijdag was lying on the ground in the clearing there, doubled up and groaning. I saw blood on his cheek and forearm. "Ah good," ter Oonck said calmly. "The young fools won't come back now. Better see how he's doing."

I knelt beside Vrijdag, who was coughing and massaging his throat. "Are you wounded?"

"No. They has no weapons."

"How many were there?"

"Four."

"I know who they were," ter Oonck said disgustedly. "Smilda's pair, the Oosterhout boy, and Lukas Voskuil."

Van Klost arrived, his chest heaving. "They attacked him right here, in broad daylight?"

"Aye."

"Well, leave the Voskuil lad to me. He's militia now."

"One might've hoped that would have prevented this, Van Klost!" the older man snapped.

"I've only had him two months, ter Oonck," Van Klost rejoined hotly. "You're going to have to take that gun apart to clear the wadding," he added, masking his officiousness as concern. He was correct, but I could tell he was enraging ter Oonck.

Pulling heavily against me, and favoring his left leg, Vrijdag got himself upright just as Harmanus arrived. "Sorry about bucket," Vrijdag said as my brother took in the miserable scene. Harmanus had sent him to fetch two buckets of water, and he'd been set upon by four of the town rowdies when he'd just hoisted two full buckets onto the yoke. One bucket had been crushed when he'd fallen.

"No bones broken?" Harmanus asked me—about Vrijdag.

"Don't think so. We're lucky the bucket gave way."

Most of the other citizens had quickly seen their fill and were leaving. Ter Oonck came over to us and spoke quietly. "I think it might be wise to keep this fellow out of sight a few days, Harmanus."

"Oh no," my brother groaned. "I've got to finish the seeding!"

"Well, enough people think he's the one who set the fire—"

"I don't set fire!" Vrijdag shouted furiously, moving forward and nearly tumbling as he put weight on his right leg.

"He was *fighting* the fire all night, right next to us!" I yelled.

Ter Oonck was unperturbed. "I'm afraid the truth of the matter is neither here nor there, Thomas. It'd be safer—"

"I think they've confused the arson with the murder," Van Klost opined, "and they all know he was out on the common with your father that night. I'd lock him up, if I were you."

"I want go home," Vrijdag moaned. Nobody paid any attention.

"We could put him in the hayloft over the stable," Harmanus said. My heart stopped as I instantly tried to concoct some reasonable objection.

"No no, Harmanus, you'd be inviting the same thing that happened to Oosterhout!" his father-in-law scolded—saving my backside. "He has to be kept down in your cellar!"

"For his own good, Dordrecht," Van Klost added.

"He needs to stay off that leg a couple days anyway," ter Oonck said, defeating the last of my brother's objections. After much discussion, we decided it'd be better to have Vrijdag hop the half-mile to the inn bracing on both our shoulders, than to go home, hitch the horse and cart, return, and carry him. This we effected in twenty exhausting—and for Vrijdag, very painful—minutes, Meneer Van Klost bringing up the rear carrying the buckets and the muskets.

"Maybe we could just leave him down here, rather than shackle him," I suggested as we struggled down the cellar staircase. "He'd be safe, and—"

"And he'd go home to his woman the first moment you weren't looking," Van Klost said. "What are you thinking, deputy schout? The whole town would know he'd broken free of you, and there'd be pandemonium!"

We shackled him. He repeatedly slammed his fist into the dirt floor, just as he had in Loytinck's cart. Van Klost led off toward the stairs. "Tell Roosje I safe here!" Vrijdag called to him. Van Klost halted for a second, then, without acknowledgment, continued out. I stayed to pick up a keg of cider I knew we needed upstairs. "He no tell her!" Vrijdag roared angrily, looking at me peremptorily.

White men are not supposed to let slaves make demands on them.

"I'll tell her, Vrijdag," I promised.

CHAPTER 14

⊰⊱

Given that our house, like all others in our rural locality, is devoid of security locks and protected only by the errant vigilance of its inhabitants, it was particularly slovenly of my father to leave his militia musket atop a table in the public room—especially when the militia is officially on alert and therefore expected to be bearing arms at all times. Noticing the musket, I automatically picked it up to replace it in the back closet where they are normally kept. But I stopped by the window, and removed the bayonet to examine it. Our manual instructs us to polish and oil the blade weekly, but Van Klost long ago gave up any hope of that. Pa's showed no evidence of attention since the last parade day in October. But while it was tarnished, there was no evidence that it had recently—or ever—been blooded.

Roosje had heard us bring Vrijdag in; craving news, she was painstakingly hanging laundry in our neighbors' backyard. Though relieved to learn he had no major injuries, she was suspicious of my assertion that he was being detained for his own protection.

Anneke, nursing her baby under the elm in our yard, told me Mother was napping upstairs, prostrated by the heat and last night's excitement. I let her know of Vrijdag's presence and my plans, and departed to seek out the trail of Yvette Bates at Denyse's Ferry.

There can't be but a dozen isolated structures between New Utrecht and the spot on the shore, two miles to the west, where the road ends and the Denyse family has long operated a ferry to Staten Island. Which of them might harbor the likes of Yvette Bates? I ignored the first four houses; I knew the residents and felt sure they would as soon entertain the handmaid of the devil. In sight of the Narrows, however, were a few huts with which I was unfamiliar. I made my way to one in the marshes to the south of the road. It showed evidence of occupation, but no one was about. Oystermen, I guessed. How on earth did they survive the winters in such a hovel, without even trees nearby to break the gales? Another hut, two hundred yards away, was completely derelict, but a third, barely above the high water mark, was inhabited but empty at the moment. I spotted a woman further down the beach, squatting down as she smoked fish on piles of rocks, and approached noisily to avoid startling her.

She stood as I drew near—a stocky, ruddy-faced dame well past her prime, not familiar to me. "God be with you, sir," she said pleasantly, in English accented by something other than Dutch—Irish, perhaps.

"And with you, Madam," I returned. I introduced myself and stated my mission. As she'd never heard of Yvette Bates, I began to describe her—and her congenial attitude quickly soured.

"What's your wife ever done to you, young man," she said contemptuously, "that you're seeking out that shameless whore?"

Vexing to have my purpose so completely misread! Hastily, I repeated that I was the town's deputy schout, and that I sought the woman as a witness.

"What's a *schout?*"

Oh. I explained I was temporarily commissioned by the Selectmen as an officer of the law. She still hesitated. "Perhaps I shall inquire at the ferry house," I said, my patience growing thin.

"No," she said, "they'll not help you. They profit of her." I waited another half-minute while she decided to risk my virtue. "You see the boat down there?" she said, pointing further to the south.

"The wreck?" I said, focusing on the mastless hulk a half-mile away, and recalling the terrible storm that had washed it onto our shore nearly two years ago. "She's living on the wreck?"

The fishwife shrugged uneasily. I thanked her and turned, but she caught my sleeve. "Sir, you're from the town?" I nodded. "Is it true the blacks are set to go on a rampage?" she asked anxiously. "My husband thinks we ought to move to the other side"—she pointed over at the Staten Island shore—"until there's peace, even though we've no roof there."

"There's no reason to expect any violence, ma'am," I said with more assurance than I felt. "No need to pull up your stakes. The commotion stems only from private grievances, I think—it's not a conspiracy or a revolt." She stared at me uncertainly as I proceeded down the beach. *She* needn't anticipate violence, I thought. The bondsmen were another matter.

I recalled the name of the sorry relic as I approached it: the *Anthea Rudge*, a coastal shipper out of New London. Survivors claimed she'd done everything right. Bound for Baltimore and sensing bad weather, she'd taken the long route through the Sound rather than risk open water; nonetheless she'd come to grief here in the lower bay. Over half the boat was now missing, scavenged no doubt for firewood over last winter. The port quarter mostly survived, however, sitting slightly askew in the bay. It took a minute to find a means to board it. The starboard bow was completely gone, but a few planks led over the sand into the hull. "Mrs. Bates?" I called, looking aft, where there was the remains of a cabin. "Mrs.—"

The cabin door screeched open, and the woman herself stepped out, looking worse than ever. The sun mercilessly exposed every flaw in her person, grooming, and dress. The gown had faded and her skin had reddened horribly in the absence of cosmetics. "Well, well, well, the boy sergeant," she cooed, evidently neither surprised nor abashed to see me. "Hello there, my pretty lad!" She took a few steps toward me, sat on what might once have been the scuttle, and patted a spot next to her. I refrained from joining her and surreptitiously checked that I was in the fishwife's line of sight; certain she'd be watching, I wished to avoid unnecessary gossip. "Has your mamma loosed you from her apron strings, then?"

"Mrs. Bates, the Selectmen of New Utrecht have nominated me a deputy schout, to inquire into the death of your…." I stopped short. Did she even know? "You are aware, ma'am, that your husband, Justus Bates, was—"

"Murdered? Foully murdered? Of course I am! Of course." She pulled up a corner of her shift to dab her eye—coincidentally exposing her right calf. "Poor dear Justus!"

I shuddered to think how *Sejanus* might demolish this thespian performance. "Very well, ma'am. I am directed to examine the facts of the matter, and—"

"I know nothing about it, Sergeant Dordrecht," she stated emphatically, "nothing at all. I hadn't even known that your wretched town was putting him in the stocks, much less that he'd almost survived it when some horrible old slave came up and strangled him while he was unable to defend himself! What had Justus ever done to deserve that fate, I ask you!"

I stared at her and held my tongue.

"I confess there were times when I'd have liked to strangle him myself—not that my delicate hands could be capable of such a thing!"

She held them out for my inspection. They were reddened and chapped, not delicate at all; but they did not look like a strong woman's hands—unlike Juffrouw Katelaar's or even Mother's. But the real issue was whether she was shamming her understanding of how Bates had died. I couldn't see it, even though her bereavement was transparently false. I looked again, sensing that the judgment was critical. "Justus Bates died when his throat was cut, ma'am."

She froze and looked at me blankly. "His throat was cut?"

"Yes."

"I thought…. Well, that's even worse!" The histrionics began anew. "Slaughtered like a pig! Outrageous! Such things ought not to be allowed in a civilized province in this day and—"

"We have reason to believe he actually met his end in the middle of the night."

Her flow of false hysterics abruptly stopped. She looked startled and briefly discomfited. "Really? But you've caught the beast who did it? I heard he'd confessed."

"A slave was tried, condemned, and hanged, ma'am, but—"

"Good!"

"But we have come to think he may perhaps have had an accomplice."

She fixed me with a look of indifference and impatience—that struck me false. "Indeed? Well, I don't see how I can possibly be of any help to you, Sergeant Dordrecht, I—"

"A citizen of the town saw you in New Utrecht around twelve-thirty that morning, ma'am."

She trembled for a second, but quickly recovered, and her shamming became emphasized to an absurd degree. "No! Oh, but that's impossible, Mister—Sergeant—Dordrecht, I couldn't have been there because, of course, I was here! Good heavens, would any lady alone venture on the public highways hereabouts in the middle of the night?"

Other than my mother, who is decidedly a special case, no *lady* would, no. "He was quite positive in his identification, ma'am."

"He was mistaken, Sergeant Dordrecht."

"He identified your frock, Mrs. Bates, which is unlike any other in—"

"Then he's lying, Sergeant Dordrecht, he's lying! Who is this horrible man that's saying this?"

"Meneer Teunis Loytinck's foreman, ma'am, Eben Stanley."

"I know that name. Is he not the one whom Justus had to chastise for his insolence? Well, there you have it, Sergeant Dordrecht! I am maligned!"

Eben Stanley had once received an excess farthing from Mother in change for a cider, and had immediately walked back across town to return it. "I am merely trying to discover whether anything you may have observed might lead us—"

"But I was not *there* that night, sir! I have not set foot in your miserable town since your mother so cruelly thrust me away!"

Now what? "I have little reason to doubt Mr. Stanley's honor or his eyesight, Mrs. Bates."

"He is lying, Mr. Dordrecht!"

She'd have tried Job's patience. "I only wish to ask whether you saw anyone else that night, Mrs. Bates!"

"How could I, sir, I was not there!"

Did I dare mention the preposterous words Stanley claimed he'd heard from her lips? It seemed to me that Stanley must have heard her say *something*, but that he'd somehow garbled it up; and that she'd only use the inane reference to birds to proclaim his entire witness unreliable. "Then you refuse to provide any assistance to the investigation, Mrs. Bates?" I demanded, my anger getting the better of me.

"I do, Sergeant Dordrecht."

At this juncture I definitely felt the lack of the advice of someone older and wiser. The woman was deliberately resisting me, but how was I to combat it? I suddenly wondered whether I was even within the jurisdiction of New Utrecht. The town's border with Gravesend was nearby—likely a few hundred yards further down the beach. Did that matter? Had I the power to arrest her? What would I do with her if I did? The Selectmen had trusted overmuch of my casual commission to worldly knowledge I did not possess, I thought, irritated. Would it even do to *threaten* her with the law? I thought better of it, given that she'd be likely simply to abscond to Staten Island or New Jersey, or back to the port, from which I assumed she'd ventured in the first place. "I shall take my leave, Mrs. Bates," I announced, striving to sound stern and dignified. Van Klost would laugh.

"Oh, why be so hasty, lad?" she teased—all stubbornness evaporated. "There's no rush, is—"

"Good day to you, ma'am."

I quickly made my way off the wreck and struck out northward over the fields. Should I ever succumb to the wicked blandishments of a harlot, I trust she'll be better looking than that one! As I tramped my way home in the sun, my anger cooled and I began to regret my failure to challenge her stubbornness. An honest woman's response, obviously, would have been *I cannot* rather than *I will not*.

*   *   *

The premises seeming quiet as I returned, I entered through the kitchen door, aiming to pilfer some more food for my ravenous sailors. While locating slabs of bread, cheese, and ham for them, I overheard women's voices through the open door of the alcove: Mother and Marijke Katelaar, having what sounded to be a famously agreeable time together! Who would ever have imagined it?

The sailors eagerly and gratefully accepted the food—which I intended covertly to replace out of my own pocket on my next shopping trip—but were desperate for news of their call. Or for any excuse to vacate the stable loft. They regarded me with such disbelief when I told them I didn't know which way the wind was blowing, that I racked my brain to recall the breeze at the shoreline. "Easterly, but very light," I finally concluded.

"Ah. They'll wait for the prevailing Southwest, I think," Nicholls said.

"Perhaps an on-shore breeze will suffice," Jack said. "And the moon sets early now. Perhaps even tonight!"

"We'll pray for Southwest, then," I said. "But you must excuse me, lads, lest I betray your presence."

It was with obvious reluctance that the tars, inured to constant fellowship, allowed me to depart.

I returned through the front door of the house, fetched myself a beer, and sat down to enjoy it and compose my thoughts. Anneke had been conscripted by Mother to mind the business, and was glad that I volunteered to relieve her.

About ten minutes later, Mr. Scoffield came in, fell into the seat opposite me complaining of the heat, and begged an ale. "And how fare your famous investigations, young mister deputy *schout*?" he asked after his first swallow—pleased to be showing off his Dutch word.

He found me off guard. "Nothing conclusive yet, I'm afraid, sir," I replied cautiously.

"Ah well, Rome wasn't built in a day!"

"Indeed. Perhaps you can help me? Can you recall if you saw or heard anything on the night Bates was killed?" Now I'd caught him off guard—served him right! "I do recall our saying goodnight, just after supper...."

"Yes. Yes, that's so. *Um*, I'm afraid I'll be no assistance, Mr. Dordrecht," he said placidly, "as I slept quite soundly all through that night without interruption. The first I knew of any irregularity was when your father took me aside at breakfast."

I sighed. "I wonder, then, if you can speculate on who might have wished Bates dead."

"Which of the slaves, you mean?"

It was only at that moment that I realized that was not what I meant, that the word *accomplice* had perhaps generated a distraction, and that it was not inconceivable that a third party had acted independently of Zwarte Jan. "Anyone, slave or free, Mr. Scoffield."

"Well, aside from the obvious, then?" I waited. "Your own family's bondsman, that is?"

"Why do you suspect Vrijdag, sir?"

He looked slightly disconcerted. "Well, he obviously had the opportunity, staying out overnight with your father. And he could easily have purloined the knife from the table or the scullery."

"Yes?"

"And well, I admit that Bates was perfectly horrible to him, that one time in the stable. One might expect such provocation to enrage the most servile of curs. And did he not have some sort of family relationship to the wench with whom Bates had his filthy way?" He regarded me with the confidence of one who has adduced an exceedingly challenging syllogism. "I have to apologize yet again for the fool, but certainly all indications point to your man as the accomplice, my friend."

I felt the odd, unjustifiable premonition I'd once felt in Colonel Bradstreet's office: that despite all indications to the contrary, the man was *not* my friend. But such omens were not admissible in a rational world. "I have strong reason to believe that Vrijdag had nothing to do with this, Mr. Scoffield," I stated with rather more vehemence than was justified.

"Well … we must all learn to avoid asserting our personal feelings into such public matters, Mr. Dordrecht." I imagine my irritation showed. "He is your family's man, and the consequences of his meeting the same fate the other one would no doubt be dire on a financial level. And of course," he added delicately, "I understand it was you personally who purchased him on your father's behalf."

"I have testimony that Bates was alive long after Vrijdag had abandoned my father and retired to the slave quarter."

He sniffed. "Is that so?"

"It might have been more prudent, if I may say so, sir, to have withheld your suspicions from all and sundry pending more conclusive evidence or conviction. The town is rife with rumor as it is, and such speculations may have contributed to the attack Vrijdag suffered earlier this afternoon."

"He was attacked? Oh I am sorry. But I fear such things are not entirely unpredictable."

Precisely. But this was getting us nowhere. I wanted an explanation of the baffling relationship of Mr. and Mrs. Bates, but I was suddenly concerned not to reveal everything I had learned—I was regretting having told Mrs. Bates that it was Eben Stanley who'd observed her. I cast about for a new line of inquiry. "How have you been managing, Mr. Scoffield, without the benefit of your manservant?"

The question startled him—much to my gratification—but he quickly responded. "Ah, well, there are some observations that sudden change make real, and it's only since Bates has been taken from me that I realize what a worthless sod he'd been all along!"

"Indeed?"

"It was convenient, of course, to have the wagon hitched or the horse saddled as needed, but the fool was always getting into difficulties that were most embarrassing. As if his pugilism weren't enough, he gambled constantly, and I twice had to salvage him from debtor's prison...."

Though stated with perfect, simple assurance, the sentence struck me as highly improbable; but no matter. "How did he come by Mrs. Bates?"

Scoffield colored briefly. "Ah. In Philadelphia, just last year, before we removed to New York."

"You agreed to the marriage, knowing you'd have to bring her as well?"

"No, it was just before I'd determined on the move."

"What led you to leave Philadelphia?"

"Mr. Dordrecht, I don't see what possible relation that might have to your present inquiry!"

Ah! He was right—up to a point. "I'm sorry, sir, it's just that.... Their marriage seemed so extraordinarily peculiar."

"Well, I grant you, it did that! I never remotely comprehended what she perceived in him!"

It was finally dawning on me that Mr. Scoffield had the capacity of making disingenuousness appear perfectly reasonable. "Have you seen Mrs. Bates at all since she left New Utrecht?"

"Mrs. Bates? No."

"Where was it you took her, the afternoon Bates was apprehended?"

"I took her to the ferry, Mr. Dordrecht, and that was the last I saw of her. The last I ever hope to see of her, in fact."

"I'm sorry, which ferry, Mr. Scoffield?"

"Oh. Denyse's ferry. She expressed a desire to return to Pennsylvania."

As I was contemplating what to make of this, Mr. Scoffield, his beer half finished, begged an excuse to visit the privy. Anneke and Harmanus' foursome tramped in, full of the news of their day, so I'd not made up my mind by the time he rejoined me.

"I say, who is the lady with your mother in the alcove? Is that your sister?"

"My sister? Oh, you mean Geertruid, my elder sister. No no, that's Juffrouw Marijke Katelaar."

"*That's* Loytinck's granddaughter?" he exclaimed loudly. "Well, she's not that bad-looking at all!" Before I could protest, he blared on. "You'd think the woman was one of the weird sisters out of *Macbeth*, the way the lads hereabouts describe her!" The children looked at him curiously—especially my niece, who is already skittish about her appearance. He lowered his voice slightly and continued. "Sure, she may be bigger than half the men in the county, yet she's not *deformed,* for heaven's sake!"

Although one could not quarrel with the truth of these statements, the outburst was oddly unsettling. "How has your business been progressing, Mr. Scoffield?" I asked, to change the subject.

For a couple of seconds, my query appeared to have fallen on deaf ears. "What? Oh, well enough, thank you, Mr. Dordrecht, well enough. I have lined up a great quantity of grains for this fall, mostly at good rates—though none as generous as your brother's." He seemed completely unaware that he was rubbing a sore point. "However, I'd been hoping to acquire some parcels of land for my principal and, aside from a small plot in Gravesend, I've had no luck."

"No one's willing to sell?"

"It would appear so. The sale in Gravesend was due only to particular family circumstances, and—"

Floris Van Klost came in and stood beside us, looking harried. "Is your father about, Thomas?" he demanded.

"I've not seen him since this morning, sir."

Van Klost looked deflated and unable to decide his next move. Scoffield hailed him. "Do sit down, Van Klost, you seem all in. Dordrecht, I shall buy this excellent public servant a drink. What will you, sir?"

Our neighbor seemed flattered—and relieved to have his next move decided for him. "Very kind, Mr. Scoffield. An ale, please, lad."

"What is it so very amiss, Van Klost?" Scoffield inquired as I moved to the tap.

"Ah, everything," was his reply. "I've spent the whole afternoon remonstrating with Smilda and Voskuil and Oosterhout concerning the frolics of their sons, and haven't made headway with any of them. If your father wants any compensation for damage to the slave, Thomas, I'm afraid he's going to have to sue them. They're certainly not ready to volunteer anything!"

The notion of my addled father organizing a lawsuit against his neighbors was ludicrous. Harmanus or Mother might do it—*I* might do it—if sufficiently provoked or if the slave had been hobbled; Pa, never. Vrijdag's known attackers would face no legal consequences. The situation was infuriating. "That's...." Words failed me. "They're being very irresponsible, countenancing such wantonness!"

"So I did suggest, Thomas. But they see it as defending the community."

"Destroying it, rather!"

"It could be argued either way," Scoffield observed reasonably.

"Indeed," Van Klost shrugged. "Even as normally calm a fellow as Meerdink told me he's planning to lock his males in his stable overnight, until this is over." Scoffield nodded sagely as I shook my head in disbelief. "And Oosterhout was whipping his slave when I arrived. 'Five strokes for insolence,' he told me."

"But Oosterhout's slave was one of the men trying to get the animals under control, wasn't he?"

"I believe he was, yes."

"He was there when I arrived, and he was still sweating to get that pig into Voskuil's pen as I left!"

"My recollection too."

"So why—"

"Hardly encouraging of good behavior in the slave," Scoffield observed.

"I told him that," Van Klost said, "but there's no reasoning with him—at least, not at the moment."

"Preparing for the worst!" Scoffield exclaimed, with grim ... satisfaction.

"It may come to that."

"All-out war, you think?"

"I do fear the worst, yes."

Perhaps it's indicative of excess temerity for a lad my age to challenge his militia captain and a worldly man of affairs, but my impatience with this line of thinking overwhelmed me. "Could we not be overreacting, gentlemen?" I spluttered. "Surely matters have not remotely come to such a pass?"

"On the other hand, it might be wise to pre-empt matters lest they do!" Scoffield countered cheerfully.

Van Klost nodded vigorously. I was struggling for a rejoinder when Mother and Juffrouw Katelaar, still conversing, walked past us to the door. To everyone's surprise, Mr. Scoffield leapt from his seat and bowed to them with a great flourish. "Miss Katelaar, good day to you," he said effusively—barely nodding to my mother. "I'm Robert Scoffield, and I hope you'll excuse my presumption, but I'm most eager to introduce myself. I've called several times on your grandfather, but never until now encountered your fair person!"

At first, knowing the lady more from reputation than observation, I half-expected her to faint of confusion. She did in fact seem disoriented for some seconds; then to my further wonderment I noticed a glance in my mother's direction, as if soliciting advice in the etiquette of the situation. Mother merely raised her eyebrows and a shoulder. Juffrouw Katelaar rallied and proffered her hand. "I'm pleased, Mr. Scoffield. Grandfather has often spoken of you."

"Ah, has he, indeed?" Scoffield suavely scooped up her hand and raised it to his lips, courtier fashion. I'm not sure she truly cared for that, but if Scoffield sensed any distaste, it hardly dissuaded him. "I've often wished for your direct observations, ma'am, concerning the business issues we have been discussing."

Juffrouw Katelaar looked flattered, perplexed, distrustful—confused. "I'm sure Grandfather can provide whatever information you may need, sir," she said carefully.

"Ah yes, but.... May I offer you a lift home, Miss Katelaar? My wagon's not yet been unhitched, and I'd be honored to escort you!"

The lady looked more dumbfounded than ever, and odd glances again passed between her and my mother. "Very well, I see no reason why not, sir," she said at length. "Thank you!" Scoffield held the door open, but Juffrouw Katelaar turned back to Mother with a modest but real smile. "Thank you again, Vrouw Dordrecht. I'm only sorry I've waited so long!"

"A very good evening to you, my dear!" Mother replied warmly. She remained at the threshold as they proceeded to climb into the wagon— smiling when they looked back, seeming rather bemused when they weren't. She walked quickly back to the kitchen with a casual nod of greeting to Meneer Van Klost. The knowledge that my intense curiosity regarding the proceeds of the women's long conversation would never, ever be satisfied ... encouraged me to take a long pull of my ale to forget about it.

"A splendid fellow, really, Scoffield," Van Klost observed.

"Assuredly, sir," I agreed automatically.

"Though I doubt he'll find the granddaughter any less tough a customer than Loytinck himself."

"I daresay not."

Van Klost sighed and seemed unusually pensive. "Curious. Usually, you know, when a town's women find some passing male to their fancy, the men find him unbearable...." He drained the last of his brew and sighed heavily. "Ah. I'm exhausted, and yet Bertie and I are to stand watch tonight," he said. "I think it would help greatly if you could come to some conclusion regarding the mysteries with which you've been charged, Sergeant Dordrecht!"

"I'm doing my best, sir."

"That might be our only chance of averting riot and mayhem, you see." He rose.

"Well, of course I'm devoting my utmost, sir, but I see no reason why it should come to—"

"We're depending on you!"

*   *   *

Sometime after supper, I took an unexpected opportunity to hustle some more victuals up to the sailors. Though glad of the food, they were again upset there'd been no call for them, and that the wind had gone completely calm.

They were, however, models of stoic manly fortitude, when it came to the weather, and grimly resolved to await the morrow.

Quietly shutting the stable door, I heard an eerie sound coming from the direction of the slave quarter a scant two hundred yards away. It was an agonized, high-pitched wail, at first steady, but soon varying and broken. First one voice, then many, then fewer, then others, keening with an intensity not known to the Dutch. I walked the few paces to the house, wanting to get inside and shut it out, but I halted, frozen, at the entry.

"What is that?" my sister asked. She was bound for the privy when she saw me frozen and was also chained by the sound.

"The slaves," I said.

"Something's awfully wrong."

"Aye."

"Vrijdag being here, do you think?" I shook my head. "Oh. I know."

"Aye."

"The slave girl."

"Aye."

"Poor soul." Lisa had clearly never been told there was scholarly debate whether the blacks *had* souls. She trembled briefly, then shook herself. "Thomas, will you wait for me? I'll just be a minute. I know it's silly but I ... don't feel safe."

I nodded and she hurried away. I gulped, soaking in dread.

In her own back yard, my sister didn't feel safe.

CHAPTER 15

At the first crow of the cock, I pushed myself out of a damp bed to get my chores done before the Selectmen made their appearance. I cleared the kitchen hearth, brought in new wood, and started the day's water to boil. Harmanus appeared. "Have you seen Pa? Loytinck's already here."

Oh not again. "He's not in the stable, I've just been to the woodpile."

"Did you look in the hayloft?"

It took me a second to concoct a fable. "I did, actually. Thought I heard a raccoon."

Hendrik came sleepwalking in, hoping for a morsel of breakfast. His father instructed him to saddle the horse immediately. "He couldn't be in the attic?" I shook my head. We split the search of the remainder of the house. Three minutes later, it was clear Pa was not on the premises. "In the north barn, I'd wager," my brother said bitterly.

"Can we send Hendrik?"

"Can't ask a seven-year-old to retrieve his souse of a grandpa. Indecent."

"I'll go."

Loytinck had overheard. "Nay, Thomas, you're required here. Send the slave." For an instant that seemed a solution....

Harmanus shook his head. "We have Vrijdag chained in the basement for his own safety. I'll go. I'll put Pa on the horse and walk back as quickly as I can." He cantered off two minutes later. I busied myself preparing the table as Mother appeared to tend the kitchen.

Van Klost and ter Oonck arrived, and Dominie Van Voort shortly thereafter. "I was very glad to know you were on watch last night, Van Klost," the dominie said. "I barely slept as it was, with all that caterwauling."

"The girl expired. Vrouw Schuppert told me."

"I expected as much. I half feared I'd be called to sound the tocsin to prevent their torching the entire village."

"Dominie, with all respect," ter Oonck began, "the slaves would have to be suicidal to contemplate such an—"

"Well, do you think that's so completely far-fetched?" Van Klost challenged. The dominie nodded.

"Nonsense!" Loytinck objected. "Slaves wouldn't dream of such a thing. They like their dinner as much as anyone. Trust me, they eat me out of house and home!"

"Where is the schout?" Van Voort asked—perhaps eager to change the subject. I then had to endure the familial humiliation of listening mutely as Loytinck explained that nobody knew.

Meneer ter Oonck broke the seconds of icy disdain that followed by kindly inquiring how my investigations were progressing. I was opening my mouth to reply when the rumble of horses' hooves was heard outside. Not the single horse I expected—a great number of horses.

"What the ... devil?" Loytinck said, remembering in whose presence he was speaking as he rose to look down the road. "My god!"

We all rose and walked out the front door. I heard Mother gasp from the side yard as she too beheld about a dozen armed men clattering down the highway in our direction. Almost as soon as we saw them, we were slightly reassured to begin to recognize them as men of the Flatbush militia. At their head was none other than my briefly prospective father-in-law, Armand LeChaudel. I searched hopefully for my brother-in-law, but he must have been spared this muster. Silently LeChaudel, followed by all the others, dismounted and tied his horse to our hitching post. "I hear you have trouble here," he said to Van Klost without preliminaries.

Van Klost was clearly still fatigued from his nocturnal perambulations. "*Uhh....*"

"We thought we'd best come before matters got out of hand and the entire county goes up in flame." The other militiamen stared at us blankly.

Van Klost seemed immobilized, unable to respond. Loytinck, however, was not restrained. "Of all the idiot notions, LeChaudel," he began, "this crowns the list. Why couldn't you wait to see if a summons were forthcoming, like any sane—"

"Meneer Loytinck, Meneer Loytinck!" the dominie expostulated. "Our neighbors have come to our assistance out of their deep sense of Christian duty. It is hardly hospitable to—"

"Yes yes," Van Klost concurred, shaking himself awake. "Come in, gentlemen, come in. I'm sure Vrouw Dordrecht will be able to offer some refreshment...?" He looked at me expectantly as everyone lumbered inside.

I scanned about and saw that Mother had bestirred the laggards of the household for the emergency and already had matters under control. A great clattering of mugs, bowls, spoons, and conversation now made it difficult for anything to be heard. The Flatbush militiamen automatically sat together at one of the trestle tables, while our Selectmen ensconced themselves with LeChaudel at the other.

Striving to miss nothing, I moved about with the cider pitcher hoping to fathom the true cause for this visit—and was briefly but sharply vexed to note that our dominie was among the many males distracted by Lisa's fleeting appearance with a tureen of porridge. But as I was pouring into Meneer ter Oonck's mug, he pulled on my shirt sleeve, commanding, "Leave that. Sit." All without taking his eyes from the discussion. Anneke saw her father's gesture and deftly picked up the pitcher to finish my round.

"None of mine had shown up by the time I left this morning," Loytinck was saying.

"Nor mine," ter Oonck added. "Nor Arsenault's—I just saw him."

"Have they not buried the wench already?" LeChaudel asked. "They had all night."

"They were under curfew," ter Oonck stated.

"And I would have noticed, of course," Van Klost added. "We've set overnight watches until this is past."

"Might be all summer, at this rate," LeChaudel said dourly.

"Well, do we make an issue of it?" Van Voort asked. "Or rather, *when* do we make an issue of it?"

"You can't just let them decide when they please to avoid work!" LeChaudel exclaimed.

"Well, of course not," Loytinck agreed, "but—"

"I'd tell the gravedigger to bury the girl as fast as he can, but the rest of them should be dispersed to the fields right away," LeChaudel imperiously advised. "Delay only gives them a chance to conspire, you see."

At that moment, Pa slouched through the door and staggered over to join us. Mortification was made perfect by the effusive reek of gin off his clothes. I could even tell he'd gotten hold of the good stuff from Holland. Van Klost laboriously brought him up to date as the rest of us glumly ate the bread Berendina had set before us.

"When Meerdink's old Rachel died, we gave them all two hours for the interment, rather than see them gather by stealth in the night," ter Oonck resumed. "I really think that's the best—"

"But *we* decided that, ter Oonck, we didn't let them decide!" Van Klost objected.

"And it was in the middle of winter, too," Pa added. "I remember all of you saying, who the hell needed 'em in February anyway!" He cackled loudly, to my dismay and the discomfiture of the others.

"Our best hope of keeping them calm will be to apply the same policy for this girl that we did for old Rachel," ter Oonck asserted stubbornly.

"Oh, and then every time one of them drops, we all lose two hours' work?" Van Klost jeered.

"The alternative's having them gather in the middle of the night, as they obviously did for Zwarte Jan. Forces them to disobey the law. I think that's infinitely more dangerous."

"You only say that because you have just the one. My family's far more dependent on our slaves, and we can't afford to—"

The Flatbush lads had finished their breakfast and one of their number, a burly young farmer, had evidently been delegated to speak to their captain. Having hovered behind LeChaudel for a minute and been ignored, he finally tapped his shoulder. "What is it, for heaven's sake, Polden?" LeChaudel demanded testily.

"Captain, if we're not really needed here, we lads have got to get back to our fields."

"We are discussing what's to be done, can't you see? Just sit down and wait 'til I call you."

Polden flushed and reared back, his jaw clenched. After a few seconds of labored breathing, he moved stiffly back to the other table and sat.

"Man's such a fool," LeChaudel exclaimed.

"I thought you handled him well," Van Klost said unctuously. The two eldest men—who seldom agreed—shook their heads in disbelief. Pa rolled his eyes. I wondered whether LeChaudel's chances of being renominated to his post were non-existent or merely dismal; for that matter, I began to wonder how it was that Van Klost kept getting reinstated here in New Utrecht.

"How many guns do they have in your slave quarter?" LeChaudel suddenly asked, looking at Loytinck.

"Guns?"

"Aye. Guns and all weapons."

"I bought a used musket for Powles when he proved a good hunter. He bags more deer than anybody. I'm not sure who else—"

"There are three guns," Van Klost said. "Both Powles and Ijsbrandts' Saal have muskets, and I think Wim has a pistol, does he not?"

"Yes, that's right," Loytinck said.

"Oh!" the dominie exclaimed. "Well, Reuben carries a pistol … but he belongs to the kerk, and he lives in Gravesend. Does that matter?"

"Of course it matters!"

Loytinck suddenly recalled something. "I gave Jermyn my old militia musket twenty years ago. Haven't seen it since."

LeChaudel regarded him with shocking contemptuousness. "And you've no idea what he's done with it, I suppose?"

Loytinck colored briefly, and seemed to call on his stores of forbearance. "No, Mr. LeChaudel, I don't."

"Well, that's five, not three. What about knives? Any of the muskets have a bayonet? Axes? What about pikes or spears or halberds?"

"There never was a bayonet on either of my muskets," Loytinck said.

"I don't think Saal's has one either," ter Oonck noted. "Look, Mr. LeChaudel, what is this about? What are you intending?"

"Obviously, you should disarm your slaves before they can use those weapons on you!"

Loytinck, ter Oonck, Pa, and even the dominie all jumped on him at once, protesting that their slaves—though perhaps not everyone else's—absolutely needed their weapons, to bring in the wild game that helped keep the whole quarter alive, for defense against animal predation on the crops, to subdue unruly members of their own community ... and, besides, they'd never surrender the guns without a fight. A real fight, that was.

Van Klost—none of whose slaves had any tools or weapons, Jan's hunting knife having been confiscated—alone seemed to accept LeChaudel's thinking. "That's why Flatbush has come to our aid, you see," he explained. "To ensure that we prevail in this."

"The entire idea is preposterous, Van Klost," ter Oonck objected. "They've had the guns for years and never raised them against us."

"I agree!" Loytinck exclaimed.

"Well, I don't really like it, but—" the dominie moaned. They all suddenly focused on Pa, whose vote would break the impasse. "Dordrecht?" My spirits sank as I saw my father shake himself awake.

"I think we should get this over with!" Pa blustered.

"Exactly," LeChaudel crowed, not waiting for further deliberation. Loytinck and ter Oonck looked momentarily defeated. Harmanus walked back in, and I felt a pang of hope that he might be allowed to offer some common sense, but he was hailed by an acquaintance from the other table. "So...."

"What's the next step, Mr. LeChaudel?" the dominie asked.

"Why is it his prerogative to decide the next step?" Loytinck protested angrily. "This is our business, it's at least up to—"

Van Klost rallied and inflated his chest. "Right! Well, *I* say the next step is to summon our militia. Then we take advantage of the Flatbush militia's kind assistance and move together into the quarter, where we confiscate all dangerous weaponry and order them back to work."

Ter Oonck exhaled, shaking his head. "For how long, Van Klost? Forever? Are we going to confiscate the butcher's cleaver and boning knife? How do you hope to get any meat dressed?"

"It won't be forever, of course not. It'll just be … until things calm down, that's all."

"And invading the quarter and confiscating the guns and knives is going to calm things down?"

"I don't see any alternative!"

The five Selectmen scowled at each other in great mutual irritation for ten seconds. Dominie Van Voort rose and announced that he would have the bell rung to call the militia. "Excellent," LeChaudel said. "I fear my lads are on the point of mutiny!" I think he was attempting to be humorous.

Mr. Scoffield walked in from the back and appeared startled at the size of the assemblage. "My word!" he exclaimed to my sister-in-law. But he saw a man he knew from Flatbush—Mr. Ellison, the third fellow who was at the Kloppens' luncheon a week ago. I'd not noticed him before. Scoffield moved to greet him, and they immediately drew together in earnest private conversation.

"I do believe you'll come to regret this action," ter Oonck said, his voice choking.

"We can't sit back and do nothing, ter Oonck!" Van Klost protested, LeChaudel nodding—and sneering.

Loytinck seemed on the verge of asking *Why not?* when the alarum sounded.

Van Klost and LeChaudel hastily stood, and the rest followed and began moving toward the door.

"Just a moment, gentlemen!" said my mother, detaining the first. "Breakfast was tuppence apiece, if you please."

The militiaman looked to Polden, who looked to LeChaudel, who looked to Pa. "Surely this can be worked out at a later date?" LeChaudel said. "We have urgent business at the—"

"No, I'm sorry," Mother insisted, overruling Pa's shrug. "Unless we have a clear commitment to—"

"The town will take care of it, Vrouw Dordrecht," Van Klost asserted, ignoring his colleagues' frowns. "We can cover that."

Mother let the men pass, and even smiled and thanked them for their patronage, but she shook her head as the Selectmen filed out. "The town will, *eh?*" she said sardonically. "And who will pay for the town?"

*   *   *

Our militia quickly mustered on the common. "Wasn't getting anything accomplished anyway," Lodewyk Nijenhuis said to Harmanus, "because none of my people have stirred themselves out to the fields."

"Bad," my brother said tersely.

Van Klost and LeChaudel seemed to have worked out an order of procedure that nominally left the former in charge. Fully armed, the New Utrecht militia, twenty-eight strong, moved to encircle the town's slave quarter from the east and north; while the Flatbush lads—augmented by Mr. Scoffield, who declared he "wouldn't miss the sport for the world"—proceeded along the western perimeter.

The quarter was nearly empty save for a few women minding very young children. Though I'd often run through it, playing as a child, it had been some time since I'd really looked at it. I knew which hut belonged to whom as well as I knew the common-law family relations of all the slaves. The meagerness of the habitations suddenly struck me afresh, as if I'd never seen them before. My attic room, in wintertime, is barely warmer than the outside, but the walls are proof against wind and rain, at the least. And we have a floor to keep us off the ground....

There was no time for idle contemplation. Positions were taken along a wooded trail to the south that led to the quarter's little graveyard. Meanwhile, Van Klost sent men into the various hovels in search of weaponry. Meerdink's son thrust Saal's woman to the ground as he and Oosterhout stormed in to search. Cheers were given when they emerged brandishing the musket. Almost immediately afterward, Voskuil stepped from Powles' house—possibly the sturdiest in the quarter—with another trophy, an Indian bow. But shrieks were then heard as the slaves encountered militiamen on returning from the gravesite.

The eight dozen bondsmen of New Utrecht were herded at bayonet-point into the center of the quarter, surrounded by men at arms. Vrijdag's woman Roosje fell to her knees, clutching her belly in a paroxysm of weeping and despair that tore at me so that I—

"All right now!" Van Klost barked. "Listen to me, you have to get back to work, here. It's the gravedigger's business to put the dead girl under. The rest of you should be working."

Loytinck's old Jermyn stepped forward. "We already buried Bette, Meneer Van Klost. She's gone. We'll go to work now. What more do you want?"

Van Klost was unsettled to realize the slaves had buried the girl in the time it had taken the Selectmen to decide they shouldn't be allowed to do so. "Well, that's good. *Um*, however.... We don't want to hurt anybody, but for your own good, we're taking all the weapons out of the quarter."

A storm of protest, objection, and howling ensued that Van Klost couldn't shout over … until LeChaudel, standing behind him, fired his musket into the air, making our militia captain jump in a manner I might someday find amusing to recollect.

"Right!" he said, recovering. "This is for your own good. The weapons will be returned when—"

"Don't promise that!" LeChaudel warned.

"We never agreed on that," Van Voort added.

Disconcerted, Van Klost lost his train of thought for seconds. "We know there's two pistols and a musket we haven't found. And we want all the knives. We want them now."

"*All* the knives?" Hans asked boldly after seconds of disbelieving silence. "All of them? You want this, I suppose?" He wrested an implement from the hands of a toddler who'd been scraping at the ground: a flat piece of metal that would barely halve a mound of lard. He tossed it disdainfully at Van Klost's feet. Nobody laughed.

"We want all the knives!" Van Klost shouted, striving for authority. "And the guns. Wim, your pistol. Find it and hand it over! Where's Reuben now?"

Van Voort coughed and said, "Well, Reuben's in the kerk, of course. He rang the alarm. He's not part of this at all."

"Get it later!" LeChaudel urged.

"Very well," Van Klost agreed. Wim hadn't budged; the huge slave stood erect with his arms crossed, his scarred face glowering at Van Klost—a figure that might well affright anyone who met him on an equally disarmed basis. Van Klost pointed to Smilda and two others carrying fixed bayonets. "You three help Wim find his pistol!" he ordered. As the steel pressed directly against his shirt, Wim finally moved away toward his hut.

Van Klost turned to Loytinck's butler. "Jermyn, your master gave you a musket some time back. Where is it? We didn't find it."

"Musket?" Jermyn said, looking about for Loytinck. "I remember no—" The biggest of the Flatbush men took it upon himself to deal with Jermyn by impatiently kicking him sharply in the back, knocking him flat into the dust, causing a huge outcry of outrage and dismay.

Loytinck arrived and thrust his bony arm up against the man's chest, screaming that if he chose to hobble his own slaves, that might be his business, but he had none hobbling other men's … all of which, bellowed in Dutch, only further enraged the fellow, who clearly spoke only English. He was restrained from battering the oldest and wealthiest man in New Utrecht only by Polden's quick intervention.

Jermyn rose with difficulty and dusted himself off. "I remember the musket now. I sold it, years ago, a dozen years ago, to a white man from Flatlands. Master gave it to me, I had no use for it anymore, so I sold it."

"Oh I remember," Loytinck said, puffing, "you even asked whether I'd mind if you sold it. I forgot."

"All right, well, we still have to get the knives. Yes?"

Wim was being escorted back. "He had two knives besides the pistol!" Smilda said, tossing the knives—ordinary utility blades—toward Van Klost's pile, eight feet away. "Where the heck he got this, I'll never know." Before I or anyone else could say *No!*, he lobbed the gun.

It fired with a devastating report on hitting the ground. Half the guns I dealt with last summer refused to fire when you wanted them to, I reflected abstractedly. "Idiot!" Van Klost yelled over the shrieks of everyone present— screams that died down quickly … except for a group thirty feet to the side. A slave boy, about twelve, had collapsed onto his back, jerked spasmodically a few times, and fallen still. A woman and two girls were beside themselves with grief and horror. Everyone stared in disbelief as this completely unexpected and unintended event sunk in.

Mr. Edwards—the boy's owner, I recalled—rushed over, took one look, and began to curse. "Damn, god damn, god *damn!*" he hollered.

"Mr. Edwards, please!" Van Voort protested.

"Oh shut up!" Edwards said, shocking the dominie into silence. Edwards shook his fist and bared his teeth at Van Klost. "Twelve years I put food into this kid, and just when he's about ready to be of real use, you take it on yourself to invade the slave quarter!"

"Well, we thought it was for the best, Edwards!" Van Klost whined. "We all voted—"

"Gentlemen, not in front of—" LeChaudel remonstrated.

Edwards let loose a great roar of frustration, angrily flung his hat onto the ground, and stalked away. The family and friends of the dead boy continued to wail. "Smilda, you bloody jackass," Van Klost hollered, "whatever got into you to—"

"How was I supposed to know it was loaded?"

"Well, any fool could see—"

"Enough!" Loytinck commanded, silencing them both. "Surely we have gotten everything we came here for? We need all to get back to work, that's what. Enough of this!"

"Right," Van Klost agreed, now thoroughly disoriented. "Militia, right face!" The response, comically inept during routine practice, was utterly pathetic now. Most of the men simply began walking back toward their homes. The Flatbush lads followed in little better fashion. Van Klost turned back to the slaves. "Right, so everybody, get back to the fields now!"

"No," Hans said.

"What!" Van Klost and LeChaudel exclaimed simultaneously.

"No," Hans reiterated simply, thrusting his chin forward. "We have new child to bury. We bury him, then go to fields."

"You can't let that—"

"Mr. LeChaudel," Loytinck said, mustering an unnerving sarcastic intensity as he steered the man out of the quarter, "thank you so much for your help today. I'm sure you're urgently required back in Flatbush, and I do believe we can handle our own problems here in New Utrecht, so there's really no reason for us to detain you any longer."

"But—" Van Klost spluttered. Only half a dozen whites were still in the quarter. Bertie and I quickly gathered up the dearly bought weaponry, lest forgetting it should occasion another calamity.

"I really think there's nothing we can do that'll make things any better, father-in-law," Bertie said.

Bertie? Yet another unexpected surprising apostle of calm reason. For who would have thought one might ever have been glad of the presence of Teunis Loytinck?

*   *   *

Meneer Gosselick ter Oonck, Anneke, and my mother, having heard shots and renewed keening, were anxiously awaiting our return in the tavern. They encircled Harmanus for the news and seemed to find it even more dire than I had as the events had transpired right in front of me. Anneke collapsed into tears on hearing of the boy's death, moaning, "Poor Nonna, oh poor Nonna!"

"An accident?" ter Oonck demanded. "You're saying it was an *accident?*"

Harmanus quailed with the implied rebuke. "Well, certainly not even Smilda had any intent to—"

"An accident!"

Harmanus patted his wife's hand and excused himself to the fields.

"Horrible!" Mother summarized. "Just makes one ill." She walked back toward the kitchen shaking her head. Belatedly realizing how disastrous the episode had been, I struggled upright, preparing to do more of my regular chores.

Ter Oonck called me back. "Lad, we never heard your report. I'd still like to hear it."

"Sir, even without the others?"

"Right now, if you please."

"Would you care for a cider?"

"No. Get on with it!"

I sat on the bench and tried to thrust the most recent events away. "It seems a great many people were abroad that night, Meneer, including.... I'm convinced Justus Bates actually died shortly after midnight, you see, not at dawn."

"Indeed?" Ter Oonck listened patiently and attentively—though evidently in some confusion—as I related my talks with Hans, Pa, Roosje, Vrijdag, Mr. Stanley, Juffrouw Katelaar, Mrs. Bates, and Mr. Scoffield. At length he sighed, expressed the hope that I was on the right path, and suggested I try to list events in a chronological order—making me wonder dully why this had not already occurred to me. "And what will be your next step then?" he demanded.

That next step was suddenly revealed to me, as if by virtue of his asking for it. There was only one person who might be expected to be able to tell me more about Zwarte Jan's movements that night, whether he had conspired with others, and what had been preying on his mind. And I'd never even thought of examining her—she's as dotty as he was, for one thing. His woman, of course, old Anne.

Meneer ter Oonck raised an eyebrow. "Really? Well, it can't hurt, I suppose." I waited in the hope that he had a better suggestion. "You must keep at it, lad," he ordered, rising. "Van Klost's at least right that we'll not know peace again until this question is put to rest." He strode out the door without another word.

*   *   *

As Constantija Van Klost would happily complain to everyone, old Zwarte Anne worked only when she felt like it. Ever since Jan had been taken away, she had *not* felt like it, but Constantija's husband had avoided any application of duress for fear of making her mercurial and fractious personality even more balky. Therefore, I would have to go back to the slave quarter to talk to her.

Apprehending that my presence would hardly be welcome under any circumstances today, I at least waited two hours until I saw the bulk of the slaves, presumably having buried Nonna's fatally unlucky boy, heading back out to the fields. For some time, I debated whether to carry my musket. Though venturing out disarmed suddenly scared me—and was actually illegal for a militiaman, given the declared state of alarms—the goal of learning something from an angry and frightened old slave woman seemed problematic at best, so I finally opted to leave it.

As I cautiously approached through the row of trees that separated the quarter from the south end of the common, the quarter looked as placid as it had before our intrusion, with perhaps a few more children playing quietly in the growing heat. They scattered, affrighted, when I walked across the open space toward Jan's hut. Anne stood and turned about, scowling. "What you want now, boy?" she demanded. A three-year-old lad cowered behind her skirts. "What now?"

I sat opposite her on a log clearly intended for sitting, thinking myself a fool and a coward for being so nervous in such company—further embarrassed that I was barely two hundred yards from the house in which I'd been born and raised—and mastered my thoughts. "I need to talk with you, Zwarte Anne. The Selectmen have asked me to do further investigation into the death of Justus Bates."

At first I thought she was making the sign of the cross. No. But the hand gestures were undoubtedly ritualistic ... and they ended with her spitting on the ground. "Him evil!" she said. I was about to make a conciliatory response, when she demanded, "Where Roosje man? Where this boy papa?"

So that's Kaspar, I thought, distracted. While we were on the roof Vrijdag had bragged of his son's propensity to climb trees. "Vrijdag's safe in our cellar, Anne. I took him breakfast this morning."

"You no take him sell?"

"No. Of course not!"

"Why he not here?"

"He's all right."

"Why—"

"He's all right. None of his bones were broken." Her lips curled back in dissatisfaction. "I need to talk with you because—"

"I no want talk. I no have talk you, you not Van Klost."

The prospect of trying to explain that ownership didn't matter when the local officials had appointed me ... was too daunting. "If we could clear up what happened to Bates, it might reduce some passions in the town, Anne, some ... bad passions." She continued to stare at me. The lad attempted to move forward, and she pushed him back. Had I made any sense to her? I wasn't positive it made any sense, myself. Learning the truth might make matters worse.

"Show him me," she said. "Show Vrijdag me, then talk."

Her bargaining rattled me. As I scanned the quarter, trying to think, my eyes stopped on the mound of blue flowers that lay on the spot where Nonna's boy had just this morning met his senseless, horrible death. Was it any wonder Anne distrusted me? I suddenly yearned to release Vrijdag back to the quarter, but did I dare? If anything else were to happen.... "I'll take you to him, if you'll come with me."

An even more ancient slave woman had been watching intently, surrounded by a clutch of toddlers. Anne nodded to her and pushed Kaspar in her direction. With no further word, she stood and followed me back to the house.

Intent on my purpose, I led her in through the front door—once again scandalizing the senior Vrouw Bilderbeek. I saw Anne to the cellar steps, closed the door behind her, and elected to wait in the empty tavern room. Even if Anne could manage to release Vrijdag, the notion that they'd attempt to bolt was preposterous. It's not that Kings County slaveholders "trust" their chattels, any more than the slaves enjoy their bondage; it's the near impossibility, plain to all, of escaping from a flat island with few places to hide.

She emerged twenty minutes later, just as I finished washing the inside of the windows. "I talk Roosje now," she announced. Before I could object, she was through the door, headed over to the Van Klosts'. When I arrived, I had to assert all the authority her husband had given me to prevail on Vrouw Van Klost to permit Roosje and Anne ten minutes. My guess is that quite a few more minutes than that passed before Jenneken came out and imperiously demanded a lemon-water. Roosje kissed Anne and went inside. Anne then shrugged and simply began trudging back to the quarter. Aware that others would find it reprehensible for me to be seen tagging after a slave woman, I awkwardly rushed up to walk beside her. Nothing feels normal or relaxed when you're around slaves, of course, but it was only for five minutes.

We returned to the hut she and Jan had shared. I sat while she went inside to check on the baby. Kaspar made a wide circle around me and again hid behind her skirts as she came out and sat. "What?" she demanded.

Startled despite all the time that had passed, I shook myself into an investigative mode. "The Friday before last, Anne, two nights after the full moon, when Jan killed the man in the stocks.... Did he ever come back here to sleep?"

She looked puzzled. "What mean?"

"The night Bates was in the stocks?"

"Yes yes?"

"Did Jan come home that night?"

"Jan home. He always home, dark."

"So he ... went to sleep?"

She nodded. "Him always sleep soon dark."

I tried to keep my voice neutral. "And when did he rise, Anne?"

"Rise? I get him up before sun, always."

She couldn't be lying, could she? Her voice and manner were perfectly flat. No one had ever accused her of deviousness. She might have some convoluted motive for protecting someone, but I couldn't imagine it. "Even that night? He didn't rise in the middle of the night, not once?" Zwarte Anne remained perfectly still, not quite looking directly at me—slaves are often chastised for effrontery—but not evading me either. "When did you retire, Anne? How were you able to wake Jan?"

"I don't sleep."

"You ... don't sleep?"

"I don't sleep full moon night."

Aha! "Why is that, Anne?"

"Friend."

Yes! The friend. Hans had mentioned a friend. Perhaps the friend was Jan's accomplice! *"Uh huh.* When did the friend arrive, Anne?"

"Eh?"

"About what time of night did he get here?"

"He? Woman."

That chilled me. I quickly conjured an image of Lotje taking an even bloodier revenge on Bates than her sister Mina had attempted on Constantija. "A woman friend?"

"Yes. We talk."

"Wait. When did she come?"

"Before middle night. Moon high. Fire still burn."

"Yes? And how long did she stay?"

"Most night. 'Til she tired."

"You and she were together most of the night?"

"Yes. Very late, she want sleep. I get Jan to walk home. Last I see him ever."

I failed to observe the pathos of that remark in my haste to parse the plausibility of its predecessor. The slave quarter is not a large place; one can easily view almost all the huts in a single glance. It seemed a curious excess of chivalry to rouse an old man to see a female to a door not thirty yards away. "Who was the friend, Anne?"

She shook her head. I wasn't sure whether I felt it was obstinacy or fear or amusement.

"You must tell me, Anne! Who was—"

"You know!"

No, I surely did not. And she was trying my patience. "Please now! Who—"

"White woman!"

I was thunderstruck. But then ... of course! *"Mrs.* Bates?"

"Evil man hussy?" She spat again. "No!"

My imagination deflated as quickly as it had ballooned. "Well, who then?"

"Emke."

CHAPTER 16

Ten seconds elapsed before my vertigo passed. Emke. Anne couldn't possibly have made *that* up. My own Grootmoeder had spent that night, of all nights, in the slave quarter, chatting companionably with a black slave woman. For a second I almost imagined Grootmoeder flaunting a knife, shambling up to Bates in some demented state ... but it was too absurd. Could she have been the accomplice? I laughed aloud at that thought too, and stumbled to apologize, thank, and excuse myself to the bondswoman.

Talking to my grandmother—something I'd not really done since I was twelve—was suddenly a matter of urgency. But communicating with her would be even more daunting than talking to Zwarte Anne. Though Grootmoeder somehow manages to maintain herself, and to put in a decent weekly appearance in kerk, she has no more apparent comprehension of sentences than a two-year-old. She can mumble individual words and will occasionally respond to suggestions, but not in any way most of us can recognize. Before I reached the house, I decided to hurry over to Flatbush in the hope of rushing my sister back to serve as an intermediary.

Spurred though I was by Meneer ter Oonck's admonitions, it still took over three hours to borrow a horse, ride over, convince Geertruid to drop everything and help me, find someone to mind her children, hitch up the Kloppens' horse and trap, and return. As we drove back—taking the bumpy short-cut—*Zus* and I worked out our approach and the questions that most needed to be answered. Geertruid high-handedly insisted that I should be completely out of sight while her discussion proceeded, but we compromised by deciding the interview might take place in Grootmoeder's tiny sleeping pew, where I could listen in through the thin walls of the north guest room.

One problem we had dreaded on arrival back in New Utrecht—finding her—was luckily obviated by her being asleep right there.

As a sweetener, *Zus* had thought to bring a ball of white yarn she'd meant to use herself. Waving me away, she immediately knelt down by the cot and rubbed it gently against the old lady's chin. I hastily tiptoed around the walls and arranged myself on the guest bed with my ear next to the wall. With the house unusually peaceful in mid-afternoon, and my sister deliberately speaking up, I could overhear a good deal of their conversation.

That "conversation" was mostly one-sided, and mostly maddening to me. Whenever was my sister going to come to the point? She was relating childhood memories of Grootvader that we'd all heard a thousand times. Grootmoeder would grunt or say, "Oh yes," and Geertruid would proceed onto another unrelated story. I was constantly on the verge of screaming out in frustration. But my ears pricked up when she began a reminiscence of a trip she and Grootmoeder had taken to visit Aunt Betje in Flatlands; it had been arranged that Zwarte Jan had driven them in the old red trap. "Whatever happened to Zwarte Jan, Grootmoeder?" Geertruid said.

I nearly howled. "Oh come on, Geertruid!" I thought. "You know perfectly well what—"

"You don't know? I haven't seen him for a long while. When was the last time you saw him?" I held my breath. "Oh, I've seen him since then, Grootmoeder. I saw him at Pinkster! He was all dressed up. Remember his green hat? They made him the king!" Muttering from Grootmoeder. "Did you ever go and visit with him and Anne?"

"Oh yes."

I can just imagine how Harmanus would have reacted to that admission. My elder sister, however, said mildly, "Really! When was that?" No answer. "Was that back when we had the full moon after Pinkster? Just over a week ago?" I couldn't hear. "You did? Was that the night that horrible man was in the stocks, the man who stayed here?"

He had slept in the very bed on which I was now reclining, I thought uncomfortably.

"Why did you go to visit her that night?"

"Moon."

"Oh, to look at the moon. How lovely!" Geertruid enthused—while I shuddered to think how Dominie Van Voort would react. "But Grootmoeder, the moon was already past full that night. Why—"

"Rain."

"Oh, it had rained the night it was full? I see!"

Between marveling at Geertruid's persistence and Grootmoeder's recollection, I had to strain my mental muscles to recall that there were indeed great thunderstorms on the nights in question.

"Did you go to visit before dark?" I heard a rustle, and imagined she'd shaken her head. "You went by yourself, in the middle of the night? Grootmoeder, that's dangerous!"

"Bright out!"

"Oh. I guess it would be. Did you see Papa on the green?"

"Sleeping."

"Oh my! Well … what about the man in the stocks?" There was a garbled exchange, and they both chuckled. "He snores funny! What do you mean, he snores funny? Oh … you recognized it because he slept right next door, here. How about that!" Grootmoeder made some rather repulsive noises—I'll pass on describing them—and they both laughed again. "Was Vrijdag there, Grootmoeder?"

"Vrijdag?"

"The slave man, Grootmoeder. Vrijdag. Tall. He was supposed to be helping Papa." I desperately wished I could be there to see what was happening … but I didn't dare disrupt what was undoubtedly the most miraculously sustained talk anyone had had with Grootmoeder in years. "You didn't see him, then? Oh that's bad, he was supposed to be helping!"

Vrijdag was gone, and Bates was still alive! But had this happened before or after Mr. Stanley had paid his visit?

"So you just walked over to the quarter by yourself! You're too brave for your own good, Grootmoeder! But were you in time? Did you get there before the moon was highest?"

"Oh yes." There was more.

"It was *almost* at the highest point in the sky?"

"Yes."

"It was so bright, you could see your knitting? Aren't you smart! And was it all very beautiful?"

Oh Geertruid, who *cares* whether it was beautiful or not!

"Yes."

"Ah. Does Anne like that too?"

"Yes."

"Oh, that's nice that you have a friend. Did Jan see it too?"

"Sleeping."

"Oh. So he missed it? That's sad."

"Sad."

There was a long pause. "Did you *see* Jan sleeping, Grootmoeder, or did Anne tell you he was sleeping?"

Again a pause. "Door open."

"Aha. So you could see inside their hut? And he was there?"

"He come out."

"Oh! When was that?"

"I go home."

"When you were ready to go home? Had the sun come up by then?"

"Still dark."

"But you were tired?"

"Yes. Moon low. Anne tired."

"So you came on back home. By yourself?"

"Jan."

"I see. Jan escorted you home. How very nice of him." More. "Your knee was hurting? Still? Let me see. Oh my heavens, when did that happen? That night? When you were leaving? You dropped the needles right out here in the hall! You knelt on the head of it while you were picking them up? *Ow!* Hurts me even to think about it!" There were little smacking sounds; I gathered my sister was kissing the sore spot to make it well. "But it's black as pitch in this hall at night. How could you even see where they were?" I couldn't hear. "Mr. Scoffield had his candle lit, I see. That was fortunate.... Well, you'd already found them by then, and you can feel your way to the door even if he did blow the candle out, right?" An interminable discussion of whether cats can see in the dark followed. Finally: "Did you and Jan pass Papa on your way home?"

"Sleeping."

"He was sleeping. *Still.*" Geertruid couldn't disguise the coldness in her voice. "And the man in the stocks? You didn't notice? And Vrijdag? No. No one. Well, I guess I wouldn't expect to see anyone about at that hour either, Grootmoeder." They shared a little laugh. "What's that? Papa's blanket? Oh that's nice, you got Jan to pick it up and cover him with it? Yes, you can get chilly even on a warm night."

Another mystery solved—one that I'd forgotten even to mention to Geertruid.

"Did you go right back to bed? The house was quiet, yes. He left you here at the back door? Very sweet. So much more than you ever expect from a slave, you know! What's that?" Grootmoeder was asking something in an agitated voice. "Where *is* he? Grootmoeder, I.... I...."

I felt my sister's consternation—and my own.

"Grootmoeder, I'm sorry, I thought you knew." The old lady had called us on our little fiction. "He's, *uh* ... he ... died, Grootmoeder. Last week. Oh I'm sorry, sweetheart!" There were tears. I had to swallow hard to stifle my own.

While *Zus* took several more minutes to console Grootmoeder and end her visit on a cheerful note, I pondered the implications of Grootmoeder's "testimony." While Jan's innocence of Bates' actual extinction had been corroborated and many peculiar events had been explained, one anomaly stuck glaringly out.

Robert Scoffield had lied to me when he said he'd slept soundly through the night.

"Can I fetch you a drink, Zus?"

My sister looked somewhat drained by her effort, but she shook her head. "No thank you, Thomas, we have to get right back. But what you can do for me, Mr. Deputy Schout—"

"Aye?"

"The next time you're in the city, you can certainly buy me a new hank of white yarn!"

*   *   *

Returning from my second trip to Flatbush, I passed by Loytinck's north field and saw Hans, among others, in the distance. I halted the horse to ponder whether there was any further question I had for him and presently decided there was. Thinking it would be bad form to walk the horse across the newly seeded field, it took me several minutes to hobble him, there being nothing around to which the reins could be attached. I finally simply tied them to a branch that a dog must have carried out from someone's yard, which would at least prevent the beast from getting far.

Notwithstanding all the time this took, Hans seemed even more reluctant to acknowledge my presence than he had three days before. Despite all my awareness of reasons why he might detest the sight of me at the moment, I still felt irked that he refused to see that *I,* who'd done all I could to restrain the likes of LeChaudel and Van Klost, should have to raise my voice to demand his attention. There was no greeting when he finally looked up, so I elected to be equally direct. "I have just one question for you, Hans. Bates, again. You handled his corpse. Was there anything unusual about his back?"

"Back?"

"Aye."

"Didn't see."

"Because there wasn't anything, or because you didn't look?"

He flared up angrily. "I don't see 'cause I seen all I need and I want get him under. I never take shirt off."

"All right, all right. Sorry." I stood irresolute for a few seconds, then turned away.

"I drop him in, shirt come up little," Hans offered. "I see nothing."

"No tattoos, no scars?" He crossed his arms and refused to repeat himself. I'd irritated him again. "So. Thank you, Hans."

No marks of a recent whipping, I thought, walking back to the road.

Willem was temporarily in charge as I finally entered the tavern—having returned, stabled, curried, and fed the horse, and expressed due gratitude to widow Esselinkpas, its owner. "You got a letter, Uncle Thomas!" he squawked as I pulled the lower door shut. This was startling. *The Arms* served as a postal depot for the town, to be sure, but I had received barely a dozen letters in my life. "They don't know how to spell!" Willem exclaimed, handing it over with profound superiority.

"That so?" Well, it was so. The paper, folded twice and messily sealed with red wax, was inscribed to "T. Dorrdrick, New Uttreck." Willem crawled onto the bar to read over my shoulder. "Excuse me?" I demanded. He shrugged, smirking, and I lifted him back down to the floor and gave him his leave. "Your grandmother and Aunt Lisa aren't back yet?" I called. Shaking his head, he scurried outdoors.

The missive contained but one alarming scrawl: "Tooneight." My mind raced from possible insurrections to slave massacres to watch schedules to grocery deliveries before the obvious explanation overtook me: *the sailors.* Nicholls and Jack were to sail from Sheepshead Bay in Gravesend tonight. Lord, that meant I'd have to lead them there, three miles going and coming, evading the night watch. At least—the moon's phase now being late in the last quarter—it would be truly dark.

With a shock, I realized I'd not taken them any food. Nobody being around, I again raided the larder, dashed out to the stable, and handed it up with an admonition to be ready an hour after dark. "Wait, we've got a story for you, lad!" Nicholls said—as I heard Harmanus calling for me and Mother and Lisa returning, simultaneously.

"Not now, friend!"

"But—"

"We'll have plenty of time in a very short while."

Harmanus, the boys, and I unloaded the groceries, but Harmanus stopped Hendrik as he was preparing to undo the wagon. "Thomas, it seems that Pa and I are on watch tonight."

"You're jesting!"

"I wish I were. Van Klost insists that it was simple bad luck and that the dominie vouchsafed the drawing process, so.... I found out only an hour ago. He told Pa this morning, but Pa only told me—"

"He might as well put you on watch by yourself, for all the help Pa will be!"

"Well—" Harmanus took me aside, where his son couldn't hear. "What Van Klost wants is for both watchmen to circle the quarter separately for the first three hours, then to take turns for the remainder of the night, but I'll keep Pa with me lest he simply fall away—"

"In which event you'd have to drop everything and locate *him!*"

"Right." My brother sighed heavily. "Do me a favor? I'm going to skip supper and try to get a little sleep. Pa got away from me again. Can you take the wagon and retrieve him, then try to put some food in him without too much to wash it down, and hold onto him until it's dark?"

I was in no position to explain that I was equally unlikely to get much rest. "Sure. Are the other towns going to all this trouble, do you know?"

"*Eh?* Oh, well, Flatbush and Brooklyn are, for sure, and I think Flatlands too. Don't know about Gravesend. They always go their own way."

"They have fewer slaves about, too."

"So I understand. Can you do that?" I nodded. "He's probably in the north barn, but you'd better check Bilderbeek's hayrick on the way."

To give him the best chance for a rest, I piled Berendina and the three boys into the cart, and we all set out to locate Pa. Took us three-quarters of an hour. I think the children were in too gleeful a mood to understand how embarrassing it all was.

After supper clean-up, quite tired but determined not to fall asleep, I climbed to my attic room, and was surprised to find my sister-in-law. "Anneke?"

"Oh! Hello, Thomas. I'm sorry, I thought you'd be longer. I'll be finished in a minute." I sat beside her on my bed. "I've one tiny bit of mending, and I need the last of the sunlight. This room has light for ten minutes after the floor below, you know!"

"*Uh huh.* That's Scoffield's coat, isn't it?"

"Aye. Constantija called me over this afternoon, and asked if this weren't his button. Said her boy had found it."

"Sander?"

"Of course."

"Where?"

"In the road, she presumed. I think she was upset because he hadn't given it over directly."

"Ah."

"So I showed it to Mr. Scoffield and volunteered to fix it back on for him. He said he hadn't even noticed, but I certainly had. It's been missing for a week!"

"That's just one of the cuff buttons. Not sure I'd have noticed one missing either!"

"Oh you men, so unobservant! Such a handsome coat and it looked just terrible! Ha, there, much better." She stood up and began collecting her tools.

Something about this suddenly piqued my curiosity. "May I see?" She shrugged and I picked it up. The missing button had been the bottom one on the right cuff. I held it up to direct sunlight—now almost to my eye height. There were faint but widespread stains on the sleeve and its lining. "It's been washed recently."

"And not too well, either! So, you can see that, at least!"

"What is that, Anneke? Plain dirt?"

"Could be anything, Thomas. Mud, wine, mashed beets. Hand it back, please. I've got to summon your brother to his watch duty." Wishing me a good night, she quickly made her way out.

The stain could also, in my humble estimation, be blood.

*   *   *

"Can we talk now?"

"Yes. But softly, if you please, Nicholls."

We were finally out of earshot of any habitation, and I felt secure that we'd successfully evaded my brother and ever-watchful Pa. The most direct route to Sheepshead Bay would've gone right past them, and been about three miles, but I'd headed through fields well north of town, a far longer trek. We were presently trudging two miles to the east; at some point ahead I planned to cross the highway and cut south below Gravesend, and finally into our rendezvous. Given the state of nerves in the entire county and the illicitness of our mission, I'd no intention of letting my guard down.

Nicholls, however, was primed to explode with some revelation, and blurted it right out. "You had guests beside us in that stable last night!"

"*Eh?*" Vagrancy was no great problem in New Utrecht, but we had known a few in recent years—often sailors, just like Nicholls and Jack. "More than one? Nothing seemed disturbed there, this morning."

"A man *and a woman*, lad! In the middle of the night!"

"A woman!" Instantly it became a strain to concentrate on both his story and our present circumstances. "Surely not. A boy with a high voice?"

"What'd he call her, Jack? *Eva?*"

"I thought it was *Annette*, Nicholls."

And I was unable to avoid the assumption it was that of another woman once reported alone in town in the middle of the night. "You didn't see them?"

"Oh no. Course not. But they wasn't keeping their voices that low."

"I think he shut the stable door when he came in."

"She use his name?"

"No. But we knowed who it was."

"The toff what keeps his horse and cart with you," Jack said. "We hear him all the time bossing your lad about."

"Not my brother or my Pa?"

"No, we knows them. They talk in Dutchy most the time. This one only talks English."

Well, that settled that.

"They had theirselves a *very* good time!" Nicholls chortled.

"How's that?"

"Lordy, boy, you'll abash a sailor! He fucked her, in the King's plain language."

"Twice," Jack noted dispassionately.

I nearly reeled. "In the *stable?*"

"Mustn't be choosy!" Nicholls said brightly. "She must be some looker, *eh?* The lass?"

A raccoon scurried across our path, froze us for half a minute, and spared me having to disappoint his lustful imaginings.

"This was when?"

"Can't say certain. No moon. Woke us up."

"Can't have been all that late, 'cause we went back to sleep."

"Uh huh."

We were approaching the highway. The entire treeless area seemed as desolate as I imagined the middle of the ocean. The crops were close to the ground at this point in the season, so there was nowhere for us to hide should anyone unexpectedly come riding along. Had it been daytime, we could probably have made out Meneer Loytinck's roof back in town. "You ain't told him nothing about what they *said*, Nicholls!" Jack remarked once we were well across.

"Didn't make no sense, Jack."

"Well, it sounds rum enough!"

By this point, it all sounded queer enough to me that I insisted on hearing every detail of Scoffield's tryst with Yvette Bates, repeatedly, from both men. Though I would have been glad to learn their own future plans, what they'd overheard was the sole topic of our remaining minutes together. By the moment we sat down in the extraordinarily disreputable tavern—Open for business in the middle of the night!—on the waterfront, I was determined to get it in writing. It took an effort to locate the materials, but I had finally written down the salient phrases they'd overheard—which were damning—when their new captain walked in.

"You're on time, that's good," said this worthy, squeezing his ample bulk in beside us. "Time for a nip before we slip, eh?" He was a gruff fellow of late middle years, and he nearly crushed my hand in greeting.

"Thomas Dordrecht, at your service, sir! And you are…?"

"Best ye don't know, lad!" The three roared with laughter.

"Begging your pardon, sir, I was hoping for a favor, that you might certify this deposition that I've made out for Nicholls and Jack."

"Eh?" He grabbed the paper, held it beside the candle flame and, unlike the two sailors and the taverner, was obviously able to read it. "This important?"

"Very important to me and the town of New Utrecht, sir."

"Not sure my name carries much weight in this county, lad, but if the inscription of Zechariah Jameson, master of the *Hasty* of Newport, is worth aught to you, I owe you something for preserving these two bilge rats, and it's naught to me. Suit yourself." I hastened to have him read my paper aloud to the two men. They avowed it acceptable, and I had them make their marks below it. "You have a Christian name, Nicholls?"

"Aye." But he had to think. "Shadrach!"

"Aha. And Jack, I trust you have a surname?"

"Well, you know." I was mystified. *"Nicholls!"*

"You two are related?" This time the hilarity was so great I feared we'd wake the entire town.

"He's my pa, Thomas!"

Thrown, I could only confess I'd had no idea. Jameson witnessed their signatures and appended his own, then looked me in the eye. "You're a likely lad, it seems, Mr. Dorrdrick—"

"Dordrecht, if you please, sir."

"Yes. I could make a sailor of you, I'll wager!"

"I beg your pardon?"

"I need men badly, *um,* Dorr– … *um,* so why don't you forget all this"—he waved the paper about so that I felt impelled to rescue it from the flame—"and come away with us, *eh?* We're bound to Grenada, and should get there before the winds go nasty."

Nicholls and Jack jumped with enthusiasm as my head swam with a confusion of excitement, yearning, horror, and guilt. I was astounded by how strongly my heart was beating and how entrancing the offer struck me. "You mean … *tonight,* sir?"

"Of course, lad! Directly. We've just time to drink up, and the tide begins to fall. With any luck, we'll have sunk the land before dawn!"

"He followed Jack right up to the crow's nest on *Proserpine,* Mr. Jameson," Nicholls avowed.

"They never heard of snow in Grenada, Thomas," Jack tempted.

Coming so unexpectedly, it took all my reserves to recall that this was precisely what I'd vowed never to do again. Clutching the table, I drew up my chest and said, "Sir, I thank ye, but I may not join you, however you may entice me."

Jameson looked at me dubiously as he swallowed the last of his ale. "Sure, lad? Not all skippers are eager to take landsmen on, y'know."

Again I came near to panic. Was I dooming myself to plowing the soil of Kings County for the rest of my life? Would I never set foot outside the province of New York? On the contrary hand ... what sort of reprobate disowns his solemn word to his mother? Though mortified by the tremor in my voice, I said, "Thank ye, sir, but I ... I may not."

They stared, disappointed and motionless, for a few seconds, before Jameson shrugged and said, "Well then, bottoms up, lads! Time to be off."

Nicholls and Jack thanked me profusely and vowed they'd seek me out on their return—and I suddenly concluded I'd be unlikely ever to hear from them again in my life. "You'll not again waylay me on the street?" I jested. Their raucous denials made me suddenly nervous: had I never heard of lads being kidnapped into marine service? If the King's own navy pressed lads like me, what was to prevent this unconvicted felon who'd hesitated even to state his name? I straightened into heightened alertness and cursed the fact that I'd ventured out lacking even a knife.

My sudden suspiciousness proved unwarranted, and I fear it may have dampened our farewells. Outside, I kept my back to the wall of the tavern as I listened to the keeper locking up after us; then I declined to accompany them over to the wharf, pleading my genuine need to return. We parted friends, but I remained cautious as I edged around the building and regained my path out of the hamlet. Then, of course, I felt ashamed that I could think so ill of my honest comrades.

*   *   *

With so much to sort out, it was perhaps a good thing that it took near two hours to make my way back. After some time it occurred to me that the *Hasty* would expect to reach her destination in August, the very time of year Mr. Glasby had told me all prudent mariners avoid the Caribbean. Then so far from feeling distressed that I'd not sailed with Captain Jameson, I began to feel guilty for having allowed him to make off with Nicholls and Jack.

My emotional flurry finally calmed to the point where I could reconsider the matter tormenting my home town. Thanks to Grootmoeder, I believed I understood what Zwarte Jan had actually done. And thanks to what the sailors had fortuitously overheard, I knew for certain who had killed Bates and how it had been done.

What mystified me was *why* Bates should have been killed, when appearance suggested the action to be so contrary to interest. But the deeply urgent matter was to relieve the tension of the community by exposing the author of our current chaos, no matter what his motive.

Walking westward, absorbed in my thoughts, I failed to notice the crescent moon rising behind me.

"Stand there! Hold still or be shot!" These words caused less terror than one might suppose. I did, of course, halt all motion, but when Harmanus approached to a point where he could make out my features.... "What in the name of all that's holy—"

"Sorry, brother."

"You gave me such a fright, I can't tell you! I've a good mind to—"

To beat me? "Harmanus, we're surely beyond that, aren't we?"

"It must be two in the morning!"

"Aye."

"What the—"

"A very long story, Harmanus."

"I've got all night, Thomas!"

I laughed, appreciating the fortitude that could make a jest. "Can I promise to tell you tomorrow, brother? I've learned much that pertains to my mission for the Selectmen, and I believe that it will soon give rise to a conclusion."

Harmanus' complete perplexity, or perhaps his exhaustion, rooted him to the spot. "I suppose I've no alternative but to trust you."

Only months ago, the statement would have made me livid; now, it merely amused me that this was the highest vote of confidence I'd ever gained from him. "Where's Pa?"

"Oh I put him up in the stable's hayloft hours back."

I dully imagined the consequences, had the day's breezes not blown from the southwest. "Ah? Any disturbance? Besides me, that is?"

"No. Probably quieter than normal, if anything. People too nervous to venture out. *Some* people, anyway," he added pointedly.

"Uh huh. Well, good night to you, Harmanus." I started on toward the house but looked back, hoping for some acknowledgment.

It took a few seconds. "And to you, Thomas."

CHAPTER 17

⟨✦⟩

Willem shook me awake not three hours later. "Meneer Loytinck and the dominie are already here, Uncle Thomas. Grandmother says to come directly!"

Within five minutes, I made my appearance. The Selectmen were now all present, Harmanus having come off watch in time to send Hendrik scurrying to the stable for Pa.

"We have bad news from the county seat, gentlemen," Van Voort began. "It's admittedly at third hand, but there appears to have been what can only be called a riot in Brooklyn last night. Over two hours passed before the militia was able to stifle it. Two whites and five blacks killed!"

There were groans all around. "It gets worse and worse," Van Klost wailed.

"And there was a suspicious fire in Bushwick. A mound of hay, not a building."

"Still...." Pa said ominously, after a silence.

"But there was no incident here, overnight?" Van Klost asked hopefully, looking at Pa. Pa looked to Harmanus; Harmanus looked to me. I shook my head; Harmanus shook his head. "No," Pa affirmed.

They all relaxed slightly. "Well, Powles is upset, I can tell you," Loytinck announced acerbically, "because he saw a fat buck early on, and wanted to shoot it, but all he could do was to drive it off with a stick."

"Must be the same deer I saw later," Harmanus said. "I used the stock of my musket."

"No reason *you* shouldn't have shot it, Harmanus!" Van Klost said. "Good meat and good riddance!"

Harmanus sighed. "Didn't want to wake the town … given the circumstances."

They all seemed evasive, as if unwilling to admit they were just as glad their rest had not been disrupted. "What next?" Van Voort demanded at length. "I think it's time we asked the province to—"

"We haven't heard from our deputy schout as yet," ter Oonck intervened.

They all turned dubiously in my direction. "You have anything to say?" Loytinck asked.

"I do, gentlemen," I avowed. "I have become quite sure in my own mind that it was not Zwarte Jan who killed Justus Bates, no matter that he claimed he had. And furthermore, I know who did kill Bates."

They were dumbstruck only for a second. "Well, out with it, lad!" Loytinck demanded.

"If you'll forgive me, sir, I prefer to keep my counsel—"

"What!"

"—until such time—perhaps this evening, I'd suggest—that we may gather many of those whom I've interrogated so that their collective witness may make the events clear to everyone at once."

"Well now, lad," Van Voort demurred, "you do understand, first of all, that we cannot simply constitute ourselves as a public trial? This is a civilized territory—not like your northern wilds—and there are forms to be followed."

"I understand that, Dominie," I agreed, rather flattered that he recollected the unorthodox proceeding I'd led on the frontier last summer. "But I believe our most important goal is to settle matters as quickly as possible to the satisfaction of everyone here in New Utrecht. Particularly as I think it will become plain that there's never been the remotest hint of a slave rebellion in all of this."

That woke them up. Harmanus' face showed a slight lift of hope. "You think not?"

"None at all."

"Then what's the harm," Van Klost said, "of telling us whom you—"

"Were I to name the individual I suspect, sir," I replied, keeping my voice down, "it would most likely get public, and then it would be easy for the individual to flee the province even before this evening arrives." Pa and Van Klost looked puzzled, but the others glanced toward the back of the house, wide-eyed, having had no trouble deducing which individual connected to this case would find it easiest to show his back to the crown colony of New York. "It would be optimal, I think, if no word of this were to be—"

Disruptive shrieks and yells were suddenly emanating from the vicinity of the slave quarter. We all rose. Mother came in, pale, and joined us in listening. "Oh my god," Loytinck moaned. The noise kept growing.

"Ring the alarm!" Van Klost cried to the dominie.

"Oh no, wait," ter Oonck said.

"Do it!" Van Klost urged. "Better safe than sorry!" Van Voort rushed out. The disturbance continued. All of us filed out the door onto the highway, where other nervous citizens were gathering. The church bell resounded with the militia summons. Pa still had his musket to hand, and set off directly to the green with the older men. Harmanus and I went back to fetch ours from the closet. Mr. Scoffield appeared at his door, rubbing his eyes. "Something gone wrong again?" he asked … with a faint trace of amusement in his voice.

"A commotion among the slaves," I said, checking my haversack for extra shot.

Seeing no women present, Scoffield stepped out into the hall, clad only in a summer nightshirt, and stretched. "May I again offer my assistance?" he asked my brother. Though leery of making the slightest unexpected move in front of him, I could hardly avoid noticing the livid scar on his upper left thigh. One would not imagine such as he to be party to a recent knife fight.

Disconcerted, Harmanus looked back at me. A memory of one of Mr. Ingraham's better moments—feigning an indifference Hamlet did not truly feel—flashed through my mind. "As you please, Mr. Scoffield," I said levelly. "We've no idea what will happen." I nodded to Harmanus and we hurried out to join the others.

"That's a dozen," Van Klost exclaimed as we mustered into the line, "I'm not waiting for the rest. Let's go." He started off without even commanding a *Forward March*, and we forged irregularly through the trees toward the slave quarter.

The yelling died down, however, just as we set out. When we arrived in the dusty little clearing that constituted the quarter's effective public space, the population appeared quite subdued. Several were panting heavily. All were staring at each other and an inert figure sprawled on the ground. Balt was kneeling on one knee, holding his opposite forearm, which was bleeding copiously into the dust. Taking no notice of Van Klost, Hans kept staring at the individual on his back, hatred palpable across his visage. Wim. Not moving. A strand of climbing vine was twisted about his neck, and blood was seeping from fresh scars on his forehead and arms. "Check him!" Van Klost ordered everyone and no one. Then he looked down his line and nodded at me, to my quickly stifled irritation.

Hesitantly, I knelt beside the prostrate slave, watched and then listened for breath, then felt his wrist—the carotid being obscured—for a pulse. "He's gone," I observed a minute later, fighting revulsion. "He's dead."

A woman howled from the far side of the quarter and Lotje, whom I'd always thought very gentle, viciously clamped her arm over her mouth and wrestled her to the ground. Another woman leant on the victim's legs to keep her from thrashing.

"What's going on here?" Van Klost demanded, somewhat tardily.

Silence. Hans, I noticed, was threateningly scanning the eyes of everyone in the quarter.

"Who killed this slave?" Van Klost insisted. "We have to know!"

Silence. A squealing toddler escaped her mother's grip and ran two yards, garnering the attention of a hundred pairs of eyes before being nabbed again.

"Well, somebody's got to pay for this, you understand!"

Silence. An interminable solid minute of it.

"You! Hans! Who did this?"

It was achingly clear to me that Hans and Balt had garroted the vicious and unpopular Wim, probably abetted by several others. Because it was his loaded gun that had killed the boy? Guessing was futile. None but the one female Lotje was holding down—probably Wim's woman—seemed distressed by anything other than our presence in the quarter. If Van Klost thought he'd get at the facts by selecting out a single individual … he'd certainly chosen the wrong one, Hans being as stubborn as his sire had been docile. Silence reigned supreme for another minute. I noticed Zwarte Anne and Roosje standing motionless off to the side. Finally Loytinck had had enough. From behind, he touched Van Klost's elbow, making our captain jump again—I nearly snickered aloud this time—and closed for a conference. "Yes yes," I heard him hiss at the militia captain, "and the somebody is me, obviously. Who's done in my slave? My *other* slaves! I lose no matter what, so let's get out of here!"

Though far more curious than the aggrieved slaveholder, like all the other militiamen, I was very glad for the suggestion.

After squalling that everyone had to be out working on the fields in ten minutes, Van Klost abruptly took it.

*   *   *

"I submit again," the dominie stated, as the Selectmen reconvened, "that it is time we admit ourselves to be out beyond our depths, and secure the assistance of the province. We pay the crown a great deal for our protection, after all; it's time we—"

"Oh all right, all right," Van Klost acquiesced, "perhaps we should." The others seemed a little dubious at this concession. "Before we're driven mad, if nought else."

Ter Oonck was shaking his head. "I'm not sure the province will be any help at all. Flatbush certainly wasn't!"

"Meneer Loytinck?" Van Klost asked.

The old man appeared lost in some very unhappy thoughts of his own. "*Eh?* I'm sorry, gentlemen, I've been brooding over my luck. Possibly my most valuable field slave...."

His colleagues made suitable noises in sympathy for his terrible loss.

"Perhaps I should volunteer to go into New York this time," Van Voort announced. "It should be one of us five."

"Certainly no one could present our case any better!" Van Klost flattered—looking relieved that there'd be no pressure on him.

"Oh, but is this really necessary at all, gentlemen?" ter Oonck persisted. "We've no idea what occasioned this morning's incident. It might have nothing to do with—"

Pa spoke up. "Seems pretty suspicious to me!"

Meneer ter Oonck grimaced and looked to Loytinck for support, but Loytinck failed even to acknowledge him.

"Well, thank you, Dominie," Van Klost presently said. "I suggest we adjourn, gentlemen, pending the dominie's return. Which way will you be traveling, sir? I'd suggest the Red Hook ferry. Steer clear of Brooklyn for your safety's sake!"

"Excellent advice," the dominie agreed as they all rose, ter Oonck shaking his head in apparent disbelief.

They were almost out the door when I recalled my own motion. "Gentlemen, can we be thinking about six o'clock, please? And I may need to enforce a subpoena—"

"We'll consider it when the dominie returns," Van Klost decided for them all.

Hard on the heels of the dominie's departure up the trail to Red Hook came a herald from the governor galloping down the Kings Highway from Flatlands. This self-important worthy, eager to share the provincial council's edicts in view of the emergency, was outraged when Pa, the only Selectman who could be found, took an instant dislike to him and obstreperously refused to have the alarm sounded so his proclamation could be read aloud. "You just tack it up on the front of the kerk, matey," Pa said, "and we'll see that everyone learns about it." There were protests. "I'll send my son out with you to show you where to put it."

I wolfed down my remaining two spoonfuls of porridge and led the grumbling fellow over to the kerk, an edifice quite impossible to miss in New Utrecht. He threw out a few disparaging remarks about my progenitor, which I permitted to pass without objection. "What actually happened in Brooklyn last night?" I asked him.

"Oh terrible, terrible," he avowed. "Two whites injured, two blacks killed—awful."

"We heard there were two whites and five slaves dead."

"You did? Well.... One boy's arm was broken, and a man lost his sight in one eye, that's bad enough. And there were three blacks who belong to the province that the army's surgeon had to patch up. Lots of bloodied noses, of course."

"Has it all calmed down yet?"

"What, the town? This was last night at dusk, and it was all over in fifteen minutes."

I held the proclamation against the wall of the kerk as he tacked it on. "How come the governor's ordering a general curfew across the province, then? That's free blacks, as well as slaves? No blacks in jail are to be released for another fortnight, whether their sentence is up or not? Their owners won't be happy about that! Good lord, *anyone* detained in violation of curfew is to be placed in military service?"

"I'm just the herald, lad," he reluctantly admitted. "How do I get to Gravesend from here?"

*   *   *

Very curious, that button. Notwithstanding the latest developments, I was eager to find out more about it. But that meant examining the painfully timid crippled boy Sander. Worse, having been reminded about forms by the dominie, I was now wondering whether any statements made by the slaves would be accepted by a court.

The more I thought about it, however, the firmer my resolution became. I had to talk to the boy, and I had to do it away from the interfering presence of his mistress and her daughter—preferably without arousing their suspicion. Furthermore, for the same reason I'd concocted a paper deposition last night, I wanted today a witness beside myself.

But whom? Not another slave, clearly; and both seniles and juveniles were to be avoided—as were habitual inebriates, for that matter. Van Klost, Bertie, and Harmanus were toiling in their fields, while Mother had absented herself to offer consultation to her expectant client north of town. That left one.

Despite her prim appearance and unquestionable piety, my sister-in-law, Anneke ter Oonck Dordrecht, unlike her husband, has always been found to be easily likeable by others. As opposed to many of our Calvinist background, though very strict in her personal observance, she is never judgmental of others, a trait that is such a relief by contrast, many imagine her to be natively gregarious, which she is not. However, she is also constitutionally incapable of false witness and when I explained my problem and asked her to invent an excuse for borrowing Sander for half an hour, she was horrified.

"You must need an extra pair of hands for something!" I begged.

"Well, but nothing for which I'd ever honestly need to borrow a slave, Thomas." She thought for a second. "I mean, I suppose I could use him to ball up this hank of wool, but it's nothing that couldn't wait until Berendina gets home from school, you see."

The impasse was finally resolved when it occurred to me that *I* could prevaricate about what *she* needed. Though Anneke was still uneasy with that, she did concede. It then took upwards of twenty minutes of being charming and mendacious to Vrouw Van Klost—You'd think no one had ever borrowed a neighbor's slave!—before I finally led the anxious boy to the second floor sitting room in our house. Anneke concluded nursing the baby just as we arrived, and made gentle small talk with the boy while I fetched the wool and a jug of sweet cider.

Sander, having limped up the stairs and beheld for the first time a pleasant room whose outside windows he'd looked at for years, had been growing calmer until I sat down to join them. Then he nearly spilled his cider. Anneke took control, however, and showed him how to hold the hank while she pulled it into usable balls. I watched this quietly, sipping my own cider, for several minutes, until I estimated there was no further point in waiting. "I was wondering, Sander—you know I've been made the deputy schout—if you could tell me what condition the stocks were in, the morning that you washed them down."

Anneke did manage to *look* as if she perceived nothing bizarre in this peculiar question. Assuming an innocent visage does not, I suppose, constitute a violation of the commandment. Sander nonetheless trembled for a few seconds. Anneke tugged lightly on the strand, which made him concentrate more on the repetitive process—and perhaps less on his fright.

"I mean, were there a lot of stones about? Pieces of charcoal?"

"Some," he whispered.

"I suppose there was a great deal of blood on the wood?"

Sander shuddered with the recollection. "Yes."

"Did it take you a lot of time to scrub it off?"

"Yes. Mostly dry."

Ha! I hadn't thought of that. Of course it would be—if it had been there for hours. "Was there anything unusual around the stocks, anything you might not expect?"

Sander looked panicked for a second, then caught himself. "Pumpkin seeds!"

Again he had offered an observation I should have thought to request of him, corroborating my assumption regarding Mr. Stanley's innocence. No one will imagine that a man bent on murder would first wipe his victim's face with the slimy innards of a squash!

"Pumpkin seeds?" Anneke couldn't resist interjecting. "How odd."

"Were there many?"

I looked back to the slave boy. "Many. Handful," he said.

"Uh huh." I endeavored to keep myself perfectly still. "Sander, was there anything else out of place there?"

He looked nervous and furtive again, and swallowed hard before replying—to the walls. "That's where I find pretty button."

I knew it! Yes! It was all I could do to keep from jumping. "Oh? The one Vrouw Van Klost gave to Anneke yesterday?" Anneke realized the implication of this too; I could tell from her shocked, widened eyes.

"Yes."

"You found it by the stocks, not out front in the road?"

"Yes. I think somebody throw at bad man!"

"Of course, of course."

"All messy. Sticky."

"Had it fallen in the blood?"

"All covered. I wash."

"Uh huh." For another ten minutes, until the chore was completed, we struggled to make bland small talk. Then my sister-in-law, having guessed that I wanted to continue with the boy alone, announced that she would leave us to put the baby to bed. "Have a little more cider, lad," I said, pouring him some more whether he wanted it or not. I poured more for myself, trying to make the wretched boy slightly less ill at ease. Vainly. He looked perfectly terrified, as if he imagined me leveling the musket—which he *had* seen me carrying just hours before—directly at him. "That was a frightening encounter this morning, wasn't it?" I said.

Sitting in the straight-back chair, staring out the window, Sander trembled from head to foot and made no reply.

"Nobody seemed ever to like Wim at all. None of the Dutch, and none of the slaves that I could see?" No reaction. "Except perhaps, his woman. I suppose that was his woman who screamed?" No reaction. "The one Lotje was fighting? What is her name?"

After a minute, Sander collected the courage to say, "Dael."

"Oh yes, Dael. She belongs to the Westerhofs, doesn't she?" Another minute passed before he inclined his head very slightly. This was hard-going. I wasn't concerned to inquire who had killed Wim—I felt morally certain I knew that. What I wanted to know was why he'd been slain. "Did Zwarte Jan ever quarrel with Wim?"

Sander seemed moved by the simple mention of Zwarte Jan; I surmised Jan might have been unusually patient with him, as he normally was with others. But he replied, "Wim mean!"

"Ah. Yes yes. Well, Wim always seemed mean to me too. Never friendly." Despite an apparent surfeit of emotion, there was no reply. "Was he never friendly to you?"

He vigorously shook his head. "Wim mean. Him brag!"

"*Uh huh*, he was mean and a braggart. No surprise there, no." I paused. "What did he feel he could brag about?"

Sander was breathing heavily and twitching in the chair. "Him *brag* he set fire!"

The fire! I'd almost forgotten it. I'd only been guessing Wim had challenged Hans for hegemony in the quarter. "The Oosterhouts' barn? He came right out and bragged about it?"

"Mean."

"What else?"

"Him want a revolt! Him mad."

"This all came out when, Sander?"

"We hear about Brooklyn...."

"Just this morning? And Hans said that was crazy?"

"Wim crazy. He say Jesus speak him last night! Say King George protect us." It was all so stupefying, I couldn't talk. "Say we can't wait. They take Jan, they take Bette, they take Nonna boy. When we fight, he say."

"And Hans?"

"Hans say he stupid, he get all us in trouble, get all us more grief. He hit Wim, they fight, they fight...."

And that was where we had come in.

"I go now? Vrouw want me?"

"Thank you, Sander."

"No tell Hans?"

I shrugged. Most slaveholders would be glad that Hans had taken care of an arsonist and would-be factionalist. And the other slaves should be thankful that Hans had forestalled the massacre that would inevitably have been the result of a firebrand's gaining a following. There was no way out of this business that was clean or decent, I thought grimly.

Sander tired of waiting for a more affirmative response from me, and charged down the stairs. I doubt any slave has ever answered the call of Constantija Van Klost as fast as Sander did.

*   *   *

I spent the next several hours marshalling my recollections and making notes.

Dominie Van Voort returned shortly before two o'clock, having had excellent luck with his transport and none at all with his mission. He was angrier than even his fulminations against the Romanists would have suggested possible, and furiously repeated his complaints to everyone he encountered. "The man wouldn't even receive me, Thomas! He flatly refused to see me! No matter how urgently I pressed our case, I couldn't get beyond some assistant's assistant, a sniveling milquetoast of a clerk no doubt posted here by Whitehall as a purgatory, who insisted that His Lordship—always 'His Lordship,' mind you—was too terribly busy to be bothered with the fact that one of the wealthiest counties in the province was shortly to go up in the flames of a slave rebellion!"

"Good heavens! Do have a seat, Dominie, and I'll fetch you an ale."

"A gin, if you please, Thomas. And I'd been kept waiting nearly an hour, standing outside the building in the sun, just to see the wretched clerk! Not even a bench, anywhere on the parade ground!"

"There. Did he offer any excuse for this outrage?"

"Oh, that was the worst of it. It was all something to do with the war. The governor was preoccupied with the army's strategy and logistics and financing, and therefore hadn't even a moment to devote to his foremost duty of keeping the peace at home!"

"But—"

"I gave the fool a piece of my mind, I can tell you! It's all very well that we should fight off a coven of papists and savages hundreds of miles away, I said, but what avails it to our security if we are all to be murdered in our beds by the very bondservants whom we confront every day?"

"Certainly a point to be reckoned with."

"Do you realize there are probably three times as many Africans on this continent as there are French? And they are right here in our midst, not lurking about in buckskins among the ice floes of the St. Lawrence!"

"Indeed."

"Then this Anglican popinjay had the effrontery to accuse me of being overwrought! 'No need to shout like you're in a revival tent, Reverend,' he says! As if one could ever associate the predominant—if not official—true religion of New York with those appalling imposters who presume that God descends upon them at their will!"

"Terrible."

"Then he capped all these insults by turning on *me* and asking how *I* could be so petty and unpatriotic as to trouble His Lordship with minutiae at a time when the fate of the empire itself was hanging in the balance! Minutiae! The British *empire* so dangerously out of balance that a mere company, not even a whole regiment out of the thousands of redcoats we are feeding, can't be spared to protect Kings County!"

My father walked in, and the vehement harangue recommenced from the beginning. I broke in to announce that I'd seek out the other Selectmen, and fled. I took the horse and cart and quickly retrieved Loytinck, ter Oonck, and Van Klost.

By quarter past two, all were back in the tavern, and the dominie, having recited his litany five times over, was at last exhausted. But the others—even ter Oonck who'd had misgivings about the errand—were truly shocked by the dismissal their dominie had received. It was Pa who brought their meeting to order. "So, what do we do now?"

"Voskuil and his son are on watch tonight," Van Klost announced hollowly.

"Good," Van Voort said. There was a long pause. Apparently the Selectmen were bereft of ideas.

As I was about to speak up, I realized that naming Sander would put the boy in jeopardy, so I invented a story to cover it. "Gentlemen, if I may, while you were recessed, I took the opportunity to revisit the quarter, and—"

"I certainly hope you carried your musket!" my militia captain exclaimed.

I revised the fable to state what I'd truthfully done the day before. "Actually, I'm afraid I didn't, Meneer Van Klost."

They all assured me I'd been extremely foolish. To get on with it, I eventually feigned contrition as well. This could develop into a very bad habit! "But what I learned there…. Nobody would say who killed Wim—"

"Balt and Hans," Loytinck asserted flatly.

"You think so?" Van Klost asked, wide-eyed. Loytinck simply rolled his eyes and shook his head.

"Yes … well, nobody would say it, but I did find out *why* he'd been killed."

"Yes?" ter Oonck said. "And why was that, lad?"

"We've always sensed Wim was a particularly rough character. Never got along with the other slaves, much less with us."

"Stanley always had trouble with him," Loytinck affirmed, "although once he was persuaded to work, he'd produce more than most."

"Aye. Well, it seems Wim was plain crazy. Claimed he had visions. He believed that Jesus wanted him to lead the blacks of the county to demand freedom from the King, whom he imagined would support the venture." Pa and Van Klost were agape with disbelief, but news reports from around the continent indicated such mad fantasies were not unprecedented. "When he heard of last night's riot in Brooklyn, Wim told the others of this vision, and he was so confident of swaying them that he openly bragged that he'd been the one who set fire to Oosterhout's barn."

"*Wim* set the fire?" Pa exclaimed.

"Aye. But by himself. He never came to help put it out, you'll recall." The Selectmen checked each other's faces to confirm that no one's informal roll call had marked Wim's presence. "And apparently the other slaves were so furious that he'd brought them all under suspicion, his bragging led to an argument which turned violent, and the upshot was that Wim was killed whether they had guns and knives or not."

"They think—*you* think—that Wim had no following at all, then?" Van Voort asked.

"He was deeply disliked. Vrijdag told me weeks ago that he himself put that scar on Wim's forehead last summer, when Wim had harassed both Roosje and Bette."

"I knew something was wrong," Van Klost muttered.

"Wim told me he'd stumbled while sharpening the plow blade," Loytinck said. "Should've known better than to believe that!"

"Well who cut Zwarte Jan down from the tree?" Pa asked.

"That I don't know—but it's not difficult to guess, is it? Jan had three grown sons, a daughter, his common-law wife, grandchildren. And they all loved him and—"

"Hans probably picked out the burial site while Jan was still in Brooklyn," ter Oonck said. "We've never found it, have we?"

"No," Van Klost admitted.

They mulled all this over for half a minute. "But who was Jan's accomplice in the murder of Bates?" the dominie asked.

"*That's* the very question about which we must all satisfy ourselves, Dominie," ter Oonck asserted before I had the opportunity. "That's the root of all our problems, and until we are satisfied about that, the entire county will not rest in comfort." I couldn't have said it better, and was glad that he had spoken up. "If our deputy schout wishes to put his understanding of events before the community, I think it would be a good idea for us all to entertain him."

The others looked rather dubious of ter Oonck's expression of confidence in me; it was fortunate that I'd thought my assumptions through again, or I might have wilted under the pressure of their critical regard. "It *would* be a good thing to clear this up—once and for all, if possible," Van Voort said slowly. "Six o'clock, then?"

"Is that all right with you, Sergeant Dordrecht?" Van Klost asked, making an obvious attempt to magnify my stature in his own mind.

"Yes sir," I replied, "although I'd like a word with you privately regarding one individual who I believe may be reluctant to come voluntarily."

"We'll see about that!" Van Klost said. We arranged that the official rationale for the convocation was that the Selectmen wished to discuss the crisis with the generality of townsfolk, in the manner favored in Suffolk County and in New England. Given that no reference to Bates' murder would therefore be necessary, I confidently hoped the man I planned to accuse would blithely present himself into the trap.

Loytinck, ter Oonck, and Van Voort left, each giving me hard looks that suggested they were not entirely happy to be settling any part of their own reputations into my untested lap. I stood and returned their gaze as forthrightly as I could manage. Pa slipped quietly out the back, but I was in too resolute a mood to allow another disappointment in him to show.

*   *   *

Van Klost and I agreed on the assignment of four of the sturdier militiamen—Ijsbrandts, Royan, Grijpstra, and Bertie—to procure Mrs. Bates, the witness from whom I anticipated reluctance. They'd also be asked to stand at the ready during the proceedings. Van Klost requested me to notify the several households not yet informed, and I immediately determined to bribe my niece and nephew to attend to all the neighbors on the west side of town, saving myself half the job.

I ventured back to the kitchen to start making these arrangements, and met my mother, with whom I hoped to make yet another. She'd been eavesdropping, for which I could hardly blame her. "You've climbed pretty far out on a limb, young Mr. Dordrecht!" she said, her eyebrows arched. "Are you sure you can climb back before—"

"With your help, Ma!" I asserted, grasping her hand.

"Aha. Flatterer! Very well, what can I do?" I explained that it was imperative to the case that Geertruid once again be brought to New Utrecht. "She was here yesterday?"

"*Uh* … yes. I'll explain sometime, but she's needed tonight. May be summoned to Brooklyn eventually, too. Perhaps Berend should come to see her home."

"*Um hmm.* Very well.... We'll have a lot of people in?"

"Half the town, likely."

"I shall rouse the rest of the family to marshal food and drink."

She made me smile. "Oh aye! No harm in turning a small profit out of this calamity."

An hour or so later, having personally notified the Zuykenaar, Schuppert, Royan, Gripstra, and Traube households, I approached Loytinck's stable in search of Mr. Stanley, himself both a free person of the town and a witness whose testimony I was concerned to secure. I came around the back from Traube's, and was surprised to see Mr. Scoffield mounting his horse to depart, just as I turned the corner of the barn. He'd told Mother yesterday that he owed more time to his prospects in Flatbush. I fell back out of his line of sight.

"I beg you to reconsider, Miss Katelaar," I heard him say. "Promise me you will?"

Marijke Katelaar did make some response, but I couldn't hear it. Scoffield trotted off with a great smile on his face, riding back toward the tavern. The front door of the house banged shut.

Desperately curious, but reluctant to appear intrusive, I moved to the door of the stable and peered inside. "Mr. Stanley?" I called. Though there was no invitation, I walked inside, thinking to pass through and look for him at the back of the house. However, I became distracted by the chestnut filly, the very beast that had been born the night Bates was killed, now already eating solid food and grown at ease with humans. She was a gentle, pleasing, handsome creature, and I lost a moment admiring and petting her. Finally recollecting my duty, I turned—

"Ah!" Both of us squawked and literally jumped.

"Thou hast startled me, Mr. Dordrecht!"

"Aye," I said, attempting to laugh away my nerves, "and, *uh,* thou surely didst the same to me, Mr. Stanley!"

Flushed and panting, he seemed to have gotten the worst of it. "I beg pardon then. What may I do for thee, Mr. Dordrecht?"

"Well," I said, recovering myself, "I came to notify you that the Selectmen encourage all citizens to come to a meeting at six o'clock at *The Arms.* Regarding the recent troubles."

"I shall be there, of course, if they so desire."

"And also, as their deputy schout, I may be called upon to report, and ... I may need to refer to the statements you made to me on Monday."

"Indeed?" He looked at me quizzically, nervously. "Well, as I say, thou may depend on my presence."

"Thank you very much, sir, and a good…. I *am* sorry to have alarmed you, Mr. Stanley. I fear I was confounded for having accidentally spied on—"

"Ah!" Stanley's moon-face took on the hue of a tomato. He wheeled about, bowed his head, clasped his hands, and appeared to be urgently reciting a prayer.

"I beg your pardon, sir, I only wished to inquire about what I accidentally overheard, and—"

"My shame, Mr. Dordrecht, stems from the fact that I too overheard some things, but I fear it was not accidental on my part, heaven forgive me!"

The gentleman surely suffers from his exacting sense of propriety! But any deal that Scoffield might have been trying to wheedle out of Juffrouw Katelaar in her grandfather's absence was of too great interest to allow him to suppress it for embarrassment. I pressed him. "Mr. Scoffield appeared to have made your mistress an offer, Mr. Stanley, which she appeared to have refused, but which he was begging her to reconsider. Do you—"

"The arrogant *swine!*" Stanley abruptly exploded, his face flushing crimson once more as he shook with emotion. "Ah, forgive me yet again, Mr. Dordrecht, I…. It's none of my place to eavesdrop on my employers or to have opinions on their affairs, none at all."

He had to be calmed down. "How came you to overhear them, Mr. Stanley?"

Stanley looked ready to weep. "I was just refreshing myself with water in the kitchen, Mr. Dordrecht, when I heard a knock at the front door. I would have answered it myself, save I heard Miss Katelaar, whom I'd not known was at home, rising to answer it."

"It was Scoffield? This was how long ago?"

Again he had to overcome a rush of mortification. "It must have been … near half an hour ago, Mr. Dordrecht. Yes, the clock chimed three-quarters just after he arrived."

"*Uh huh.*"

"And I fear I…. It's not my concern, of course, but when the man is suddenly *here* whenever Mr. Loytinck is *out*, it's…." His anger appeared to choke him.

"It's very curious, surely."

"Yes. He brought her home after she called on thy mother on Monday afternoon, then spent hours with her yesterday … and this was his *second* call today!"

"Good heavens! Was he urging her to remonstrate with Mr. Loytinck in some fashion?"

"Mr. Dordrecht, I—"

"Surely he couldn't be suggesting she attempt to have her grandfather declared incompetent to run his own business?"

"Oh heavens, no!"

"Was he proposing to purchase a parcel of Mr. Loytinck's landholdings?"

"Mr. Dordrecht, thou art placing me in an impossible position, sir! I am already remiss in having secreted myself during their interview, I cannot in decency indulge in public gossip. I beg thee to desist!"

He was of course perfectly justified, and for an interval I debated acceding. But Scoffield's business ventures in the county clearly must have had *something* to do with Justus Bates. "Mr. Stanley, I appreciate your sensibility, and I sympathize. But I urge you—speaking not as a chance passer-by but as the town's deputy schout investigating a murder—to tell me more of this conversation."

"Mr. Dordrecht, I cannot!"

"It's murder that I'm inquiring about, Mr. Stanley. Please—"

"Surely thou daren't think *she*—"

"No no, I know that to be impossible from your own previous testimony. But whatever exchange Mr. Scoffield was trying to arrange with Miss Katelaar might shed some light on his ... personal motivations." Stanley regarded me, horrified, with sudden realization of my drift. "And I promise you, I'll do what I can to avoid mentioning the source of any information that may be used."

"It's not that, Mr. Dordrecht," he said simply. "This is between me and God." I sighed, stumped by the solidity of a faith that, in Stanley's case at least, I respected without sharing. However was he to be convinced? A minute passed. "Murder, thou sayest?"

"I do say that, Mr. Stanley. Odd though it may seem, what Mr. Scoffield offered Miss Katelaar may bear on just that."

He took a deep breath. "What Mr. Scoffield proposed to her was *marriage,* Mr. Dordrecht!"

CHAPTER 18

So staggered was I, on leaving Mr. Stanley, that I was half-way home before I recalled I'd not notified Halsema and Edwards of the meeting. Had to go back.

Forty-eight hours after his introduction to Juffrouw Katelaar, Mr. Scoffield had proposed *marriage?* To her, directly, not even in the presence of her grandsire? It stifled all respiration. Knowing what congress had recently transpired between him and Yvette Bates, one could hardly believe he was suddenly smitten to the point of unreason by Marijke Katelaar. What then might have prompted his declaration?

He hungered to inherit Teunis Loytinck's substantial landholdings, obviously. But would the other-worldly Juffrouw Katelaar perceive that? Would her grandfather suffer an apoplexy on learning of it?

Anneke and Berendina were busy scrubbing the tables as I walked in. "Has Mr. Scoffield returned?" I asked mildly.

"Aye. He's napping, I believe," Anneke said. "I told him we were expecting the whole town at six, and he seemed to be delighted."

"Really?"

"It would give him an opportunity to transact further business, he said."

I had to pinch myself hard to forestall over-confidence.

There was an enormous amount of preparation to be effected, and I was drafted into helping. Mother returned with Geertruid and Berend, and they too were commandeered. Pa appeared and Ma took him efficiently in hand to smarten his appearance. The others seemed to find the atmosphere positively festive. I might've too, almost. Long before six, townsfolk streamed into the tavern and commenced ordering food and drink. It was of course not strictly in accordance with the law that we should be serving spirits in advance of a public meeting, but the meeting was extraordinary in the first place, so we anticipated no repercussion from it.

The church bell tolled six strokes. The Selectmen entered from the highway and Pa joined them as they stood in front of our serving bar. Harmanus rushed in at the last moment, having been reluctant as always to leave his fields an instant earlier than necessary. There were nearly sixty men and women stuffed into a room that was normally crowded by thirty. As the room filled, the children and dogs had been thrust out to play in the yard. We'd thought to open all doors and windows wide, but though it was blessedly cool for the day preceding Midsummer's, the physical atmosphere quickly became stifling. Believing that the purpose of the gathering was to deal with the unruly slaves, few were losing any time announcing their strident personal opinions on the subject.

The deafening noise level abruptly dropped as Dominie Van Voort stepped forward to pronounce a benediction. Everyone stood and the men doffed their hats. The dominie pleaded with the Almighty to grant wisdom—he used the word three times in as many minutes— to the citizens of New Utrecht in their hour of peril, and stressed that it was clear that their mortal salvation would be dependent in this instance on that wisdom alone, unaided by any other temporal power. Everyone had by now heard of the dominie's affront, and they were sobered by the gravity with which he seemed to regard their prospect.

A very nervous Van Klost next stepped forward to issue greetings and thanks for attending, to announce the watch schedule for the next three nights ... and to become suddenly flustered over explaining the true purpose of the current gathering. Although I knew how I planned to proceed, I'd neglected to consider how the meeting should be brought to order. Amid growing impatience—the unquestioning respect the dominie enjoyed did not extend to the militia captain—he begged Meneer ter Oonck to explain what was afoot.

Gosselick ter Oonck, who did enjoy public confidence, came directly to the point. "Just a fortnight ago, one Justus Bates, a servant indentured to Mr. Robert Scoffield, whose presence and business we have enjoyed in New Utrecht for three weeks past, confessed, as you know, to having attacked and defiled young Bette, slave to Meneer Karel Schuppert, who died on Monday of wounds that Bates inflicted as he took unholy advantage of her. For this crime we, the Selectmen of New Utrecht, sentenced Bates to twenty-four hours in the stocks, a sentence that began at noon on Friday the 8th of the instant month. At some point in the night, however, Bates was murdered, and that second crime—for which Meneer Van Klost's slave Zwarte Jan has already been tried, condemned, and executed—has set off a series of calamities that has brought us to the sorry pass where the entire province is now living in terror of a slave revolt. Soon after Zwarte Jan had been hanged, however, some of us began to suspect that, at the least, he must have had an accomplice in murdering Bates. Having an accomplice to murder still at large was a sufficiently alarming prospect that we enjoined the schout, Rykert Dordrecht, to undertake an investigation. Owing to the pressures of his business"—hearing a couple derisive snorts, ter Oonck increased his pace—"Rykert Dordrecht appointed his son, Sergeant Thomas Dordrecht, as his deputy. Young Mr. Dordrecht has just now indicated that his report might be best presented in public, where all those who have seen or heard facts relevant to the case—as opposed to having merely speculated thereon—may come forward. And as that is our true purpose in this gathering, I shall now turn the meeting over to him, with the prayer that the wisdom Dominie Van Voort has invoked for us all be visited upon him especially."

Amid much rustling and murmuring, I stood and faced our neighbors with a thumping heart, and offered my absolutely sincere gratitude to Meneer ter Oonck. I bade everyone a good evening. "Speak out, boy!" a man hollered from the back—and this unnerving remonstrance somehow girded me into taking fuller possession of myself.

I straightened my back and looked directly outward. "It was I who discovered that Justus Bates had been killed. The discovery occurred just before sun-up on Saturday morning—minutes after four o'clock. I had risen early and gone out to the common to converse with my father, the schout, who was guarding the prisoner overnight. It happened that I found him asleep—which is really not unexpected given the circumstances." Noting raised eyebrows, I too hastened onward. "Even in the half-light, it was obvious on close inspection that the prisoner's throat had been cut. Within a minute of our discovering this horror, we heard a commotion in the trees nearby, and chased its source until it turned and faced us. It was old Zwarte Jan, known to everyone in New Utrecht. Jan waved his hunting knife, avowed that he had slain Bates, and fell on his knees begging God for forgiveness. With the assistance of Meneeren Boudewyn and Lukas Voskuil, the schout and I arrested and incarcerated him.

"Now it was a great shock to perceive Zwarte Jan, who'd always been regarded as the gentlest of slaves, as a perpetrator of extreme violence. However, seeing him at that instant, not a hundred yards from the stocks, I for one was completely convinced he'd done exactly as he said. His roar—'I kill'—and his plea for divine forgiveness were entirely compelling. And of course we knew that the girl Bates had attacked was Jan's granddaughter. On the strength of

Jan's confession, he was tried and convicted in Brooklyn town, and hanged here last Thursday."

"And *why*, I'd like to know," bellowed a red-faced man standing and shaking his fist at the Selectmen, "has no one ever been punished for cutting him down?" Many of the attendees rumbled supportively.

"Gentlemen, gentlemen, one matter at a time, pray!" Van Voort entreated. "We may return to the question later, but for now let us permit Sergeant Dordrecht to complete his, *uh*, report."

"But I really want to hear—"

"Proceed, Thomas!" the dominie ordered, glaring at the objector.

"It was some time after the execution that certain contradictions in our understanding of the sequence of events surrounding Bates' murder began to present themselves. First of all, although Bates' body and the stocks themselves were covered in gore, Zwarte Jan's shirt and breeches—he was wearing the same garments when he was hanged—were free of blood. More importantly, the force and passion of Jan's outburst had led us to assume that his crime had been committed scant minutes before his apprehension—that he had cut Bates' throat only seconds before my own arrival, in short, which perhaps had been what frightened him away from the scene. May I ask Meneer Voskuil, was this your impression as well?"

Boudewyn Voskuil stood, slightly disconcerted, and announced that his first assumption had been that he was helping to interrupt a crime in progress.

"Exactly, thank you, Meneer. This apprehension was so strong, it overpowered the simple evidence of my senses, for I had needed to touch Bates' corpse that morning … and it had already been cold. Further, when Meneer Van Klost, Bertie Hampers, my brother, and I returned to remove the corpse immediately after securing Jan here in our cellar, we found it stiffened—an effect that, as is generally known, is found only after some hours have passed since death. Could Jan's passion have been sustained for hours? Or been renewed just then, at dawn? Not impossible, of course, but improbable.

"So Bates had actually met his death hours before I arrived on the common. My father and I had had a private conversation for several minutes, both of us thinking the prisoner was merely asleep. This revised timing made it important to reconstruct everything that had transpired on the common that evening, to learn when this crime had taken place. And the first project, obviously, was to trace Zwarte Jan's movements. The schout had not seen Jan at all since sundown, nor had anyone else. So I asked in the slave quarter." There were sighs of disapproval. "And none of the slaves had seen Jan since sundown—save his woman, of course." I ignored a dozen shaking heads.

"I knew that Zwarte Anne's testimony would be inadmissible, but I hoped she might lead me to truths that could be submitted for jury review. Anne, however, merely said that Jan was home abed as usual at sundown, and only arose at the first hint of dawn. Of course, any wife, not just a slave's, might be suspected of attempting to protect her spouse from suspicion. Except that I questioned her only two days ago, long after Jan was already executed. But I asked how she'd known Jan had not left her side all night, and received a surprising reply—because she'd stayed awake with a friend. Who was he? I asked—and received an even more surprising reply."

"Oh no," Harmanus moaned, guessing.

"It was not a fellow slave but my own grandmother, Emke Dordrecht, whom many here remember as an asset of this community before she succumbed to senility some five years back. Grootmoeder, it appeared, had left the house alone late that night, and joined her, *uh*, friend, the slave Anne, to watch the full moon." Harmanus buried his face in his hands. Everyone took alarmed glances at Grootmoeder, who was knitting in her chair by the fireplace, barely aware of the enormous crowd surrounding her. "Grootmoeder, everyone has observed, is now incapable of responding to all but the most rudimentary statements and questions, rather like a young child. But we in her family have found that one of us, my elder sister Geertruid Dordrecht Kloppen of Flatbush, is still able to communicate with her, and so at my urgent request she rushed over yesterday for just that purpose. I am going to summarize the relevant evidence—or observations, if you will—and ask Vrouw Kloppen if she has any emendations.

"Grootmoeder rose before midnight that night, gathered her knitting gear and, feeling her way out of the house with the fortuitous assistance of candlelight from our tenant's room, made her way by moonlight through the common to the slave quarter. Knowing the hut shared by Anne and Jan, she entered it, saw both, and wakened Anne to join her in observing the transit of the moon." Now Van Voort was shaking his head in dismay. "The two remained awake for over three hours until the moon set, less than an hour before dawn. That day was actually two days after this month's full; it had rained on both the previous nights. At that time, Anne roused Zwarte Jan, who escorted Grootmoeder back here to *The Arms*. On their return, as they passed through the common, Grootmoeder discovered her son to be asleep. She asked Jan to take the blanket, which had fallen onto the ground, and put it over him. Jan put it over his *head*, and Grootmoeder was perfectly satisfied. Have I left anything out, *Zus?*"

"I don't believe so, Thomas."

"Can you tell us, *um*, Vrouw Kloppen, if you felt any reason to doubt the complete truthfulness of Grootmoeder's statements?"

Geertruid burst out laughing. "Good heavens, Thomas!"

"Please, *Zus!*"

"Of course not."

I scanned the room and saw little evidence of skepticism regarding this tale. Grootmoeder—and Geertruid—were well enough known to all that the ostensibly preposterous story was deemed credible. "Well then," I resumed, "if we accept my grandmother's statements, which confirm those of Zwarte Anne, then it follows that Zwarte Jan could not possibly have delivered the blow that killed Justus Bates." This deduction occasioned considerable comment despite its obviousness. "Furthermore, it's fairly absurd to think that Jan might have been acting in league with an accomplice, yet slept right through the event." Again I had to pause while this assertion was digested. "And the implication of that is that, whether Zwarte Jan was tried and condemned for that crime or no, some unrelated person murdered Justus Bates."

This brought about a minor uproar. "Order! Order please!" Van Voort called.

"I have a speculation I'd like to offer you," I continued, "about what Zwarte Jan actually did in the half-hour or so before we confronted him. I've no proof, but it's obviously immaterial to his fate ... and this is what seems most reasonable to me. Jan and Grootmoeder returned through the common around three-thirty in the morning. It was as dark as it got that night, and my guess is that Jan saw both the schout and the prisoner apparently sound asleep, and conceived a personal revenge against the man who'd raped and disfigured his granddaughter and left her for dead. When Grootmoeder had asked him to replace the blanket, he'd set it over my father's head *deliberately*. He took Grootmoeder to her door, then walked back to the common. There was still no one around, the blanket was still completely covering the schout. Had anyone or anything startled Jan as he crept up on Bates, I venture he might've shied away, but nothing did. He pulled back the prisoner's unresisting head and drew his hunting knife across the throat of a corpse—never once realizing, in his excess of passion, that it *was* a corpse. Then he hid among the trees beside the common, undecided and unwilling to return to his home and face his guilt, only to betray himself within minutes as Pa and I presently discovered Bates' fate.

"As we removed the body an hour later, I noticed there was more than one gash across the neck. Hans, the gravedigger—who happens to be Jan's son, though that would have had no bearing on his statements when I spoke with him—asserted that there were two strokes, and that they were different in character. One stroke was deep and bloody and appeared to be caused by a thin, sharp knife. The other was shallow, drew little blood, and appeared to be caused by a thick, roughened knife. Perhaps," I said, producing Jan's hunting knife and thinking myself very dramatic, "one like this one, the one Jan surrendered to us that morning." I passed it to the Selectmen. "You'll note there's just a little trace of what might be blood on it. It's been right here in the stable, not washed or used. My guess is that Jan's stroke drew little blood because the corpse had already lost all its blood."

"You're saying he killed a dead man!" Oosterhout yelled, so convinced he'd uttered a witticism that he followed with great laughter. A few others joined in.

I waited it out. "Yes, that's what I think happened. But the real point is, Jan couldn't possibly have been the true agent of Bates' death. Somebody else had to have killed him. It has been suggested that Vrijdag, a slave who now belongs to us, the Dordrecht family, might have been responsible. He had been ordered to stand guard with the schout through the evening. Vrijdag did join the schout at dusk as he relieved my brother Harmanus, who'd watched while our father partook of supper. Meneer Westerhof stopped for a conversation, and later the Bilderbeeks waved as they took an evening stroll. All, I've confirmed, observed Vrijdag at his master's side. However, my father did not notice him after he last saw the Bilderbeeks, nor did either of the two later witnesses. Although Vrijdag certainly had some cause to be offended by Bates, the most plausible explanation is the one he asserts: that after a long interval of perfect calm on a bright night, with the schout and the prisoner both asleep, he saw no reason not to go back to his woman and his children. For what it's worth, Vrijdag's woman Roosje confirms this."

"It's not worth anything, lad," Meneer Smilda complained. "Get on with it!"

There was no gainsaying this virtually universal attitude, so I shouldered on. "When my grandmother first ventured over to the slave quarter, I forgot to mention, she of course passed through the common. I estimate that to have been just before midnight. We elicited her observations at that time—and she had not seen Vrijdag, but she stated positively that both the schout and Bates were snoring." I looked hopefully at my sister.

"Oh yes, that's so," she confirmed, smiling.

"We have more precise timing for the next event, thanks to the hall clock maintained in the Loytinck household. On that evening, Juffrouw Katelaar and Eben Stanley, Meneer Loytinck's foreman, were attending the foaling of a mare. The delivery coming later than expected, Mr. Stanley requested a moment's reprieve shortly after twelve-fifteen. Though he'd been deeply injured by Bates, he'd eschewed tormenting him with everyone else during the daytime. Yet in the quiet of the night, he could not resist." Stanley, sitting rigidly in the midst of the hearty farmers, hung his head to avoid their gaze, which was not so much disapproving as curious. "Around twelve-twenty, he woke the sleeping prisoner and vented his rage by smearing his face with the pith of a rotten pumpkin. The schout—"

In view of Stanley's excruciating sensitivity, I'd intended this statement to be earnestly dramatic…. "With *what?*" screamed a man next to the window.

"He dumped a pumpkin's innards all over him!" roared another, as the room began to shake with mirth.

"Remind me to try that next time *you're* in the stocks, Matthijs!" bellowed a third. It did not take much to amuse the burghers of New Utrecht. Stanley doubled over forward on the bench, probably interpreting the ponderous thumps on his back as a chastisement.

"Order! Come to order please, gentlemen!" called the dominie.

"The schout," I resumed, "was roused by the prisoner's commotion— cursing and spitting—in time to see Mr. Stanley disappearing behind the kerk. Mr. Stanley states that he wished to atone for what he regarded as a terrible sin, by praying on the sacred ground of the graveyard."

"Oh naughty, naughty!" teased Oosterhout, who doubtless had more to atone for than did Stanley.

"Thou be-est the penitent pumpkin-pusher!" whooped Edwards, touching off another round of communal hilarity. The moon-faced Stanley, I reflected with some chagrin for my hand in it, would undoubtedly be known as *Mr. Pumpkin* for the rest of his tenure in Kings County.

*   *   *

I nodded a pre-arranged signal to Ijsbrandts, then resumed. "Mr. Stanley states that he remained in prayer for about ten minutes, then recollected his duty to Juffrouw Katelaar and started back to Loytinck's, passing in front of the kerk. We shall return momentarily to the startling things you then saw, but first, sir, can we quickly confirm a few facts? You saw no one at all, to that point, save Bates and the schout?"

"That is so, Mr. Dordrecht," Stanley said hoarsely.

"Specifically, you never saw the slave, Vrijdag?"

"No, I did not."

"And Bates was alive as you left the common?"

"Assuredly."

"If I may, Juffrouw Katelaar…." The big lady started, modestly. "Can you confirm, as you did to me two days ago, that Eben Stanley returned to your stable before the clock struck the three-quarter; and that you both remained there until the filly was born around three o'clock that morning?"

"Aye sir, I can," she said gravely, her head erect.

"Thank you. Now then, returning to the moment when Mr. Stanley left the graveyard, at about twelve-thirty-five, he was very startled—"

"Watch where you put your hands, you!" screeched a woman's voice from the back of our house. "You ain't paid for.... What the hell?" Yvette Bates halted, suddenly confronting the huge assembly. For a second, she was as taken in shock as they, but a clamor of commentary, disparagement, laughter, and whistles presently engulfed the room. Mrs. Bates recovered herself enough to scan around, and I saw her gaze alight on Mr. Scoffield. "Robin!" she breathed—as he uncomfortably attempted to ignore her presence.

And I could have *kicked* myself! How many times had I strummed the chords while Adelie Chapman sang, *"For bonny sweet Robin is all my joy?"* Ophelia's *True Love* song itself. What a foolish lad I am. Talking to birds, indeed! Happily, the tumult covered my confusion. Seeing no place to move, or even sit, Yvette Bates and her guards stood nervously next to the bar, where they'd entered the room. The Selectmen huddled more tightly to the side, avoiding them.

"As you approached the front of the kerk, Mr. Stanley, you told me you were amazed to see somebody in the moonlight. Who was that?"

Stanley was glad for any question that did not involve pumpkins. "It was that woman, Mr. Dordrecht," he said, pointing at the newcomer.

Mrs. Bates looked frantically to Scoffield for assurance. He looked up at the ceiling beams. "You *lie*, you stinking mouse turd!" she shrieked at the little Anabaptist. "You slander my honest name!"

No doubt unused to being called a liar, Stanley turned so white I feared he'd faint. The rest of the assembly, however, greeted the accusation with the derision it deserved.

"It was this woman we all thought had left Kings County, Mr. Stanley asserts. Mrs. Bates, do you still deny that you were here in New Utrecht in the middle of the night your husband was in the stocks?"

"I do! He lies! No decent lady would be—"

"Mr. Stanley, exactly *where* was she standing?"

"At the edge of the road, sir. Between this house and the maple tree in front of your neighbor's." He pointed at the tree, visible through the window.

"*Uh huh.* This is not a great distance, and it was a bright night?"

"Yes." Meneer Ligtenbarg stepped out the front door onto the stoop, obviously verifying the line of sight for himself.

"How did you recognize Mrs. Bates?"

"I wasn't there! I wasn't anywhere near!"

"By her gown, Mr. Dordrecht. She was wearing then what she's wearing now."

"You mean," Edwards roared, "that she was *not* wearing then what she's *not* wearing now, *eh,* Stanley?" Another guffaw was roundly enjoyed by all—all the *groundlings,* as my theatrical acquaintances would put it, that is.

"Mrs. Bates, if you were not in New Utrecht, where do you contend you were? We had understood that you were returning to Pennsylvania."

She looked about uncertainly. Scoffield again avoided her. "I was in my abode, near Denyse's Ferry."

"Aha. Perhaps that was where you were found this afternoon. Meneer Ijsbrandts, where did you locate Mrs. Bates?"

Ijsbrandts, fifteen years my senior but completely unready for public attention, looked abashed for seconds before mastering himself. "Like you said, she was on the *Anthea Rudge.*"

"And did appearances suggest that she'd been living on the wreck for some time?"

"That's right."

Few among the assembly had any doubt of the implication of her residence on a wrecked boat in sight of the ferry dock, and they all troubled to spell them out for the less sophisticated. Lacking a gavel, the dominie slapped his palm on the bar as he again called for order.

"Mr. Stanley, when I first interviewed you, you asserted you had heard Mrs. Bates utter a curious phrase—"

"He's lying!" she yelled.

"You heard a phrase that perplexed both of us. Would you repeat it now, please?"

"But I must have mis-heard. It made no sense," Stanley protested.

"I beg you, sir, please state exactly what you believed you heard."

"Oh very well. As I told thee, Mr. Dordrecht, I thought it was, 'Well, hello there, my robin.'"

Two seconds of general mystification were broken when Ijsbrandts pointed at Scoffield and blurted out, "Well, that's what she called *him!* Just now, when we brought her in. I seen it!"

Those most fluent in English ways took it upon themselves to explain that, while a robin was indeed a *roodborstje, Robin* was a pet name for lads—particularly those with the given name of Robert.

Scoffield grinned and shook his head vigorously, attempting to laugh it off. I caught the eyes of Bertie and Grijpstra, the two men Van Klost had posted next to him, and mouthed the great Netherlandish motto, *Waakzaamheid!*—Watchfulness!—in their direction. Mrs. Bates stamped her foot, and shrilled, "I never said anything of the sort on that night. I couldn't have, because I was *not here!*"

Scoffield resumed his arrogant posture, but then modified it to avoid appearing too triumphant before the assembly. They had obviously conspired to deny their encounter on the night Bates had been slain.

I faced the Selectmen. "Mrs. Bates, I contend, is obstinately perjuring herself, and—"

"Perjury is a serious violation of—" Van Voort began.

"The hell I am, boy!" she squalled, costing herself most of whatever sympathy she had left.

She'd appalled the dominie so completely, seconds passed before he again cried for order. I decided I would have to use the desperate measure I'd conceived to dislodge the wanton's pathetic loyalty to her fickle Robin.

"This impasse forces me to make public some shocking information that's come my way, which normally I'd prefer not to disclose. I ... see no way around it." I hesitated again, debating myself one last time. "No. Juffrouw Katelaar?"

Nervous murmurs were heard through the room, as everyone wondered aloud what on earth Loytinck's granddaughter could have to do with this seamy situation. Quite pale, the woman looked up. "Yes?"

As a hush came over the room, I decided I'd now no alternative but to spit it out. "Have you ever received a proposal of marriage from Mr. Robert Scoffield?"

When the presumptive heiress of the largest estate in town is met with so little as an unexpected glance ... it's *electrifying* gossip for the entire population. Here, pandemonium broke out. Everybody voiced an opinion, no matter how devoid of factual basis. Quite a few looked at me with an indignation bordering on fury. Juffrouw Katelaar reddened with outrage, tightened her shawl about her neck, and impatiently awaited calm. Mr. Stanley cringed and tried to look smaller than he was. Loytinck appeared deeply shocked, and in fact clutched his chest—to the point that ter Oonck and Van Voort called for brandy and endeavored to support him. My mother, I was baffled to note, looked extraordinarily distressed. Scoffield showed the first signs of nervousness, and appeared to be calculating the distance between himself and the open window. Grijpstra, however, was keeping a sharp eye on him, undistracted by the public chaos. Yvette Bates was standing stock still, her face drained of color and expression.

The recovering Loytinck and his neighbor Halsema looked ready to give me an irate piece of their minds, but Juffrouw Katelaar stood up and spoke first. "Mr. Dordrecht, how *dare* you!" she stormed. "How dare you raise such a private question in a public meeting of the town? This is an outrage, sir, it's indecent!"

Although taken aback by the force of her ire, I did note, with relief, that her eyes were flashing at Scoffield with equal fury. Of course! She had no idea that Stanley and I had even been inside her house this afternoon, and her necessary assumption—which I felt no call to disabuse—was that if I'd come to know of the proposal, it must have been through the would-be bridegroom. And as I'd somewhat shamefully expected, a question of that sort, like a slander, cannot simply be protested into non-existence, no matter how unfair. At least I could cover the public embarrassment with public necessity. "I do apologize, ma'am, I most humbly apologize. But I assure you, I ask you to state the issue only out of a desire to bring our town's torment to a speedy closure."

"What on *earth* does that have to do with—"

"Stand down, boy!" her grandfather finally shouted. "You're way beyond your mandate!" Several others echoed him, to the point where I almost wavered. Almost. But presently the clamor subsided, and I held my ground in what I hope was a pose of respectful anticipation.

"I don't see why this is anyone's business...." Juffrouw Katelaar once more attempted.

Intolerably, however, everyone's eyes were upon her. They all wanted to *know.*

She drew a great breath, then shook it out. "Yes. This very afternoon."

Among the dozens who exclaimed aloud was Yvette Bates. At first deeply stunned, she appeared to be slowly gulping air and recouping her stores of shrewish energy.

But Juffrouw Katelaar was not yet free to sit down. Though I could not ask it—having imposed enough already—there was one more question she *had* to answer. "I refused him, of course," she said, putting everyone out of their suspense. She sat down looking deeply galled, frowning and crossing her arms over her chest. Though she looked desperately lonely to me at that instant, she rose higher in my esteem by keeping her head high. Meanwhile, relief was palpable across the room. Even those who'd counted themselves Scoffield's friends had found such a proposal outrageous. My mother shared a smile with Vrouw Nijenhuis, again bewildering me—though I'd no time to consider it. Loytinck took a sip of his cordial and seemed to breathe more easily.

"You *filthy* gutter rat!" Mrs. Bates abruptly shrieked at Scoffield. "You proposed to that stuck-up battle-axe after all I've done for you? You got down on your damn knees and—"

"Watch your tongue, woman!" Van Voort demanded.

"*Hold* your tongue, wench!" Van Klost demanded, signaling Ijsbrandts and Royan to grasp her arms. "Get her out of town, lads, she's an offense to—"

"Nay, nay, Meneer Van Klost!" I objected. "If you please, we still need Mrs. Bates as a—"

"I *ain't* Mrs. Bates! I never *was* goddam Mrs. Bates! It was all his idea to—"

"By what name shall we call you, then, madam?" I inquired, trying to restore civility.

She turned on me. "*You* may call me Princess Augusta Frederika!" she announced, insolently holding out her hand for obeisance. "And *you* may kiss my ... buttocks!"

I confess she disarmed me for a few seconds. But the room immediately split into two noisy factions, the intolerably outraged and the irrepressibly amused. The entire Dordrecht family—rather to my astonishment—was among the latter.

"*Uh*, Madam," I said, having regained my composure as they quieted down, "I've seen a portrait of the crown prince's sister, and it's ... it's not you. We shall perhaps continue to call you Mrs. Bates."

"Oh bloody hell."

"Yes. Well, can we at last return to the question with which we began? Was it not you, madam, whom Mr. Stanley saw right outside here, after midnight on the night Justus Bates was murdered?"

Once more, despite everything, she looked over at Scoffield; once more he examined the ceiling. She shook her head. "Oh yeah, it was me."

"Why had you come to New Utrecht in the middle of the night?"

"Well, you wouldn't let me in, in the daytime, now would you?" she bawled. "He hadn't given me nothing to live on, that's what. I come here, I tap his window. He don't answer, so I peeks in and I can see just enough. He ain't there, but he's been there. I checks in the privy, to see if he's—"

"Was he there, Mrs. Bates? It's all we need to know."

"No. So I'm stuck! I go out through your side gate and look about the highway. Moon's high above, I can see both ways up and down the road. And all a sudden, there he is!"

"Your 'Robin?'"

"Yeah."

"Was there anything—"

"Gentlemen!" Scoffield blared at the Selectmen. "I've been very patient, but this *charade* has gone on long enough! I have nothing to do with this harlot, I've not set eyes on her since I escorted her to Denyse's Ferry at your instance, and I will not allow my reputation to be besmirched by her!

You must evict the baggage and instruct your deputy sheriff to confine this extremely irregular procedure to more acceptable lines of inquiry!"

The Selectmen, startled, moved to confer among themselves.

"Gentlemen!" I countered, forcing my voice lower in the hope I'd sound more mature than my actual years. "I have evidence beside that of Mrs. Bates, that points inevitably to the conclusion that Robert Scoffield murdered his own manservant Justus Bates while he sat helplessly disabled in the stocks! And I suggest this is as good a time as any for you to arrest him in the name of the king!"

*   *   *

The entire assembly seemed jumbled, though I did notice Van Klost nodding at Scoffield's guards to second my warning to them. Briefly disconcerted, Scoffield drew himself up and shouted, "That's absolutely absurd, boy! Why on earth would I ever do in my own menial?"

This quite logical question submerged everyone into silence. "Why would he, Thomas?" my father asked softly.

"Gentlemen"—I addressed myself to the Selectmen—"I confess I cannot fathom the motive. Why, other than as retribution for the mortification he'd caused, Mr. Scoffield should slaughter Justus Bates, I don't know. I only know that all the evidence suggests that it *was* Robert Scoffield who killed the man."

"Arrant nonsense!" Scoffield bellowed. "I demand that this be brought to an immediate close!"

The Selectmen conferred again. The moment seemed interminable, but was probably no more than twenty seconds. "Proceed, Sergeant Dordrecht!" Van Voort said. Scoffield protested vociferously until the dominie commanded him into silence.

"Mrs. Bates, can you tell us the substance of your congress with Mr. Scoffield on that meeting? He appeared surprised to see you, I take it?"

"Yeah."

"What did he say?"

"He says, 'What the hell are you doing here?' I tells him I need money for some food at the very least."

"His response?"

"Says I should never have come. Says he was planning to visit me the next afternoon—as if I ain't heard that before!"

"Yes?"

"Then he's pushing me back toward *The Arms,* here, the back entrance, all the while saying to be quiet. Says he'll give me some coins if I'll just go back to the ferry."

"Did he bring you inside the house?"

"No! I thought he *would*. Thought he'd like to have a little snog, long as I was here. Normal-like, he can't keep his paws off me, you know, but that night he holds his hands behind him all the time, and—"

"I beg your pardon? Did he never take your arm or shake your hand?"

The woman halted, stumped, and tried to recall. "No, no, he never done none of that. Walks funny, with his hands behind him."

"Clasped behind his back? Curious. Did you—"

"I started to ask him, but he snaps at me to be quiet."

"I see. Did he in fact give you any money?"

"He goes tippy-toe into his room. I thought he's going to check his purse and bring me some coins, but he just throws them out the window and slams it down. I picks them out of the path and walks all the way back."

"*Uh huh*. Have you seen him on any occasion since that night, Mrs. Bates?"

"Oh yeah. He come over every other day or so."

Deciding to hold the sailors' statement for later, I thanked the woman and asked her to remain. The assembled townsfolk shuffled and fidgeted on their benches.

"Next I wish to show why Mr. Scoffield, whom we've held in some measure of esteem here, first came under suspicion. It was because of certain lies he told, falsehoods all the more curious for their apparent inconsequence. For example, when I first inquired whether he'd heard anything that night that could lead us to Bates' attacker, he told me quite emphatically that he'd slept through the night without interruption. Yet Grootmoeder, as she left the house just before midnight, had been able to find her knitting needles thanks to the candlelight from his room.

"And another matter: the morning before Bates was put in the stocks, Mr. Scoffield disrupted our household by announcing he intended to chastise his servant himself. As all the family left the house, I saw him take his horsewhip down to our cellar. There were then over a dozen loud snaps of the whip, each followed by pitiable shrieks from Justus Bates. As we are all aware, such a beating would leave welts, at least, on the back, that would last far longer than a day. It was only as an afterthought that I asked Hans the gravedigger about them. He told me the skin on Bates' back was clear."

Over the general agitation, Meneer Voskuil said, "You're suggesting they conspired to play-act this whipping?"

"Aye sir. Bates bore marks of the indignities he'd suffered in the stocks, but none of a whipping."

"Well, why—"

"Now wait, lad," Smilda objected. "Hans is a slave, and you can't trust anything that a slave says about anything!"

"Sir, I understand that his testimony may be inadmissible in court, but I can imagine no reason at all why we here should doubt Hans in this particular, as the answer produces neither profit nor problem to anyone among the slaves, whatever it may be!"

Matters ran out of my hands for a couple minutes as our neighbors contested the question. I bitterly observed that one awful consequence of the ownership of slaves was that their masters would never trust them—or *vice versa* for that matter—for honest responses to any question more significant than the product of two times two. I was squeezed to admit that while I credited Hans' statement, I had not directly seen Bates' back. But it then occurred to me that I'd seen the shirt *on* his back—lacking bloodstains. I set this out, but they were uneager to give it much consideration.

"Thirdly, we have Mr. Scoffield's assertion that he escorted Mrs. Bates to Denyse's Ferry and never saw her again. This is directly contradicted by Mrs. Bates, and—"

Scoffield shook his fist. "You're going to take a whore's word over—"

"Who're you calling a whore, Robin?" she howled.

"Order!" the dominie demanded.

"Now there's another matter, one into which I've not previously enquired but want to do so now." I addressed my startled father. "Schout, as the inn's proprietor, it became your duty to inform Mr. Scoffield of his servant's death when he appeared for breakfast that morning. You took him back to the alcove for privacy. How did he react to this news?"

Pa overcame a brief fit of nerves, and replied that Scoffield had reacted as one might have expected. He thought a second more, and added, "He did seem confused when I said it was Zwarte Jan we'd taken on the scene. 'That old slave next door?' he said. I said it was so. 'But where was the young one, your fellow?' he asks, but then he says, 'No matter, no matter,' and we came back into this room."

As I made a sudden connection in my own mind, I berated myself for not having pursued this inquiry earlier. But time was pressing. "We also have a very plausible candidate object for the murder *weapon*, ladies and gentlemen. It's one of the tavern's very own dinner knives—although I can no longer tell you which one. Every one of you who has eaten a meal here has used one of the set. We own fifteen in total. Like all knives used for cutting beefsteak, they are long and thin and kept sharpened." Mother took it upon herself to produce one from the drawer, which she handed to the dominie to compare with Jan's knife. This inspired me to elicit the facts by means of a quick dialog with her, the most important observations being the timing of the knife's disappearance and recovery; that it had been Vrijdag who'd called attention to the loss; that Scoffield had been present; and that it had been found in the old well in a filthy condition—the filth most likely including blood. "Now, a curious question. Vrouw Dordrecht," I awkwardly addressed my mother, "regarding the old well on the common.... It looks exactly like any other well, does it not?"

"Yes."

"And yet every resident of New Utrecht, free or slave, knows perfectly well that it's dry by early spring, isn't that so?"

"True."

"But every *visitor*, looking at it, would suspect nothing of the kind?"

"That's also true."

"If a local person were in the common, then, and wished urgently to dispose of an object such as this knife where it would never be found, would they think of that well?"

"Not if they hoped for any certainty in the matter."

"If a visitor to the town wanted to rid himself of the knife?"

"Ah! He would imagine the well to be ideal!"

A hubbub of commentary followed this exchange, during which Meneer Bilderbeek, ever the stickler for propriety, urged that the Selectmen should post a warning on the well, lest unwary travelers—

"Can we manage to concentrate on the business at hand, please!" ter Oonck authoritatively interrupted him. "Is there more, Sergeant Dordrecht?"

"Aye, sir, there are two more observations."

"Proceed."

"Firstly, I ... must offer an apology, mainly to my family, but also to my militia captain." All, save Harmanus, looked perfectly mystified. "For the past five nights, I have secreted two renegade sailors in the hayloft over our stable—"

"*That's* where all that bread went!" Mother exclaimed. "I was blaming your poor nephews, Thomas!"

Suppressing my flush of guilt, I endeavored expeditiously to explain how and why I'd aided the men in such questionable circumstances. I could practically watch the local opinion of Rykert's youngest boy deflating in front of my eyes. "Yesterday afternoon," I persevered, "notice came that their ship had moored in Sheepshead Bay and, in accordance with our plan, I led the two men there last night."

"There was a universal curfew last night!" Van Klost objected.

"I was aware of it, sir. I do apologize."

"You'll be cited for this, Sergeant Dordrecht!"

"Oh do let him get on with it, Van Klost!" my father said. I was rather touched.

"The instant we were out of earshot, Nicholls, the elder sailor, burst out with a relation of what they'd overheard in the stable the night before."

"There was men in that stable?" Yvette Bates suddenly exclaimed. "Oh Jesus, now you're—"

"Be *quiet*, you stupid cow!" Scoffield snarled—before realizing the outburst made it hard to credit that he had "nothing to do" with the woman.

"About midnight, the night before last, the sailors were awakened by the horses whinnying below them. They became aware that a person was pacing about, and that *she* was attempting to calm the beasts. Though they could see nothing, particularly as no candle was ever lit, they then recognized the voice of Mr. Scoffield as he joined the woman. They'd heard him often talking with my nephew. The first thing he said was 'What the devil is it this time, Yvette?' Actually, one thought the name was Eva, the other thought it was Annette; I leave it to you to—"

"Don't be daft, of course it—"

"*No!*"

"Of course it was me," she finished, defying him.

"Her response, as they remembered it, was on the order of 'I came to warn you. That boy is poking around. Somebody says he saw me that night.' This could only be a reference to the interview that I conducted with Mrs. Bates aboard the *Anthea Rudge* some hours before on Monday afternoon." Both Mrs. Bates and Mr. Scoffield seemed immobilized. "Scoffield's reaction, according to the sailors, was to berate her for waking him for something inconsequential. He repeatedly told her simply to deny she was there." Scoffield jerked about as if making ready to object, but thought better of it. "There were then some considerable moments of ... conversation the sailors were unable to make out distinctly, after—"

"Oh Christ!" Mrs. Bates muttered.

"Spare us your blasphemy, woman!" Van Voort shouted, red-faced.

"Oh Christ!" she repeated witlessly.

"After which," I continued, "occurred the most material exchange they overheard, which I committed to paper once we'd arrived at Sheepshead Bay and met their future employer. I'll ask Dominie Van Voort to read it ... with apologies for my penmanship—we had very little time."

Van Voort took the proffered sheet and made a face as he perused it. I could tell he greatly objected to its form, but presently he decided circumstances overcame the objection. Finally sensing the impatience of his congregation, he read it without comment.

DEPOSITION OF SHADRACH NICHOLLS
& JACK NICHOLLS, MARINERS

Gravesend, New York, twelve-fifteen a.m., June 20, 1759.

In the middle of yesterday night, sleeping in the hayloft
of the Dordrechts' stable, we were awakened by the
voice of a woman on the floor below. She was joined
by a man whose voice we recognized as the tenant.
We thought he called her 'Eva' or 'Annette.'

They were together over an hour and spoke only in
English. Amid much conversation the woman said,
'So you did for Bates? I heard he'd been strangled. You
sliced his throat?' The man made no denial. His reply
was, 'One can knacker one's broken-down horse. I don't
see why I can't knacker that useless fool if I want.'

The soft clack of Grootmoeder's needles was suddenly audible. The
dominie looked at me pensively. "That's it?" I nodded at the paper in his hand,
indicating that I desired him to convey the entirety. "The marks of Shadrach
Nicholls, able seaman," he resumed, "and of Jack Nicholls, able seaman,
are appended below these paragraphs, and are attested by the signature of
Captain Zechariah Jameson, master of the schooner *Hasty* of Newport, Rhode
Island."

With the uncertain air of a man too staggered to speak, the dominie
passed the sheet on to Van Klost and sat down. I had feared a babel of aberrant
comment, but the assembly pensively allowed the statement to sink in.

Even those most extreme in their personal distaste for their bondsmen
knew that both law and religion forbade the perfect equivocation of man and
beast that had been asserted.

Both Mrs. Bates and Mr. Scoffield seemed to be wishing themselves
elsewhere. Finally the townsfolk began to fidget, and I spoke up lest we
sacrifice our focus. "There is one last item of evidence, gentlemen. Yesterday
evening, I chanced upon my sister-in-law, Vrouw Anneke Dordrecht, repairing
our boarder's coat—the same that he is wearing at present. She was sewing a
button to his right cuff that she'd noticed had been missing for over a week.
I was curious enough to inquire and learn that she'd gotten the button from
Vrouw Van Klost, who'd found her slave lad Sander playing with it, and
assumed he'd just then found it out front in the road. This morning, I made
an excuse to interview the slave lad, recalling that it had been he who'd been
assigned by his master to clean the stocks immediately following our removal

of Justus Bates' corpse. After some inquiry, Vrouw Dordrecht and I learned that Sander had retrieved the button then and there, picking it out of the blood-soaked mud next to the stocks." Anneke, all eyes uncomfortably on her, finally overcame her modesty and nodded.

"This is complete and utter nonsense!" Scoffield shouted aggressively. "I demand an immediate cessation of this star-chamber!"

"As I examined the button last night," I continued, ignoring him, "I also noted incompletely washed out bloodstains on the lining of the coat itself, which you also might wish to examine." I nodded to the Selectmen as meaningfully as I could.

Van Klost took only a second to respond. "Let's have it!" he demanded. He pointed at Bertie and Grijpstra, who instantly shoved Scoffield back against the wall and began forcing the coat off him.

"Well don't tear it, you damn fools!" Scoffield roared.

As the coat was handed over, Scoffield did make a lunge for the window, but Bertie and Grijpstra were too fast for him, and he was hauled back inside.

The Selectmen looked over the coat and turned the sleeve inside out. "You are now under arrest, Mr. Scoffield," Van Klost said.

CHAPTER 19

⊰⋊⋉⊱

To my dismay and consternation, Van Klost—perhaps preoccupied with securing Scoffield—abruptly declared the meeting adjourned. Instantly all was chaos. Half of the townsfolk, resisting any craving for further details, fled the stifling room; others stayed to order drinks or finish their meals. Juffrouw Katelaar, clearly distressed, was quickly escorted away by her grandfather and Mr. Stanley. Van Klost nodded significantly to the men flanking Mrs. Bates, then tagged both my father and myself to cross the thronged room to accost the prisoner. "You'll suffer for this, Van Klost!" Scoffield blustered. "I'll make this town pay for this!"

"We shall see, Mr. Scoffield," Van Klost replied evenly. "In the meantime, gentlemen, we must incarcerate him overnight. I shall escort him personally to Brooklyn in the morning." Automatically, we all began shoving Scoffield to the cellar door, and on down the stairs.

A much-alarmed Vrijdag looked up as we reached the floor. "Oh lord," Pa said, "I'd forgotten he was here." To tell the horrible truth, in the flurry of events, so had I. "What do we do now?"

The problem was that there was only one chain and one manacle attaching to the foundation. For five seconds, this seemed an insuperable quandary. "Wait," I said, shaking myself out of it. "There's no reason to detain Vrijdag now that we all know who killed Bates. He shouldn't be in danger. Let's loose him, and then we can shackle Scoffield."

"What about the governor's proclamation?" Grijpstra objected. "Said we weren't to let any blacks go for a fortnight!"

"Well, Vrijdag wasn't put here as a punishment," I countered—ignoring the slave's stony scowl. "We locked him up to keep the likes of Oosterhout from attacking him."

"Oh right."

"Yeah, undo him," Pa said.

"Whatever you say," Grijpstra allowed dubiously.

Vrijdag was released and Scoffield indignantly shouted that it was an outrage that he should be restrained in a place vacated by a slave. Van Klost was about to consider that when Pa said, "Oh shut it, man, I spent three days here myself!"

The instant Scoffield's handcuff was locked, we turned to leave, ignoring his vociferous protests. Vrijdag stoically followed us back upstairs.

"Hey!" Smilda yelled, seeing us again in the tavern room. "You're letting him *go?*"

Van Klost turned to Pa. "Your problem! I've got to deal with the harlot."

"What's that to you, Smilda?" Pa demanded belligerently.

Smilda, to whom we'd sold more spirits than we should, colored and thrust himself within inches of my father's face.

"Meneer Smilda," I said, working between them and taking him by the elbow, "Vrijdag is, *uh*, urgently needed by my brother in the fields. And he was only detained for his own protection. And it was all so unnecessary in the first place, don't you see?" Smilda clearly did not see. "Because there's been no insurrection, Meneer Smilda. No conspiracy, no threat at all."

"There was the barn!"

"Aye, but that was just the one opportunist ... and the slaves themselves have settled him for good."

"Then why is the province all in arms, *eh?* Answer me that, since you're so sharp."

"Because one thing has led to another, sir, and at each step of the way, the worst possible interpretation has been put on events."

"But—"

"It's been so diabolical, one might almost think someone intended it to work out this way!"

"Rot!"

"At any rate, Vrijdag here—" Except he'd gone, which briefly rattled me; fled to Roosje and fresh air, no doubt. "Vrijdag had nothing to do with any of this. He should be left alone!"

"You think he's learned his lesson, then? He's a *good* slave, *eh?*"

This had been the town's received opinion of Vrijdag for years. Why did it suddenly strike me as repulsive? "This whole affair was Bates' and Scoffield's doing, Meneer Smilda. We'll only hurt ourselves the more if we abuse our slaves as a result." He seemed somewhat mollified. I turned to leave him.

"*Your* slave," he grumbled to my back.

Van Klost was just sitting down with Harmanus, Bertie, and the dominie. Anneke set tankards of ale on the table, and the militia captain nodded to me to join them. "I've had your father and Ijsbrandts escort that strumpet back to the ferry," he announced, "and I instructed her to remain available in the county for dear Robin's trial in Brooklyn."

"You *instructed* her?" Harmanus guffawed. "What'd she say to that?"

Bertie smiled as Van Klost and Van Voort blushed. "Said she'd always be available ... at quite reasonable rates!"

"She is ... some piece of work," Harmanus marveled.

"Thomas—*er*, I'm sorry, Sergeant Dordrecht," Van Klost began, "have you pieced together what actually happened that night?"

"It seems the entire town was parading through the common all night long!" Bertie exclaimed.

"I think so, gentlemen," I said, "although much is perforce a conjecture."

They seemed disappointed. "Let's hear it, nevertheless," Van Klost said.

A tankard finally arrived for me, and I took a very deep pull on it. "Well, first, I think Scoffield purloined the knife himself, while we were here at supper. He has a fine knife of his own. I think he didn't want to risk it, and—"

"He was pre-meditating this crime, you believe?" Van Voort asked. "Was he anticipating it that morning, when he counterfeited a chastisement of the indenturee?"

"He was surely pre-meditating it by suppertime, Dominie," I asserted. "When he first conceived it, I don't know." I took another drink. It was surely wonderful to be sitting down! "But I think he intended to throw suspicion on Vrijdag. Why he should, other than to keep it away from himself.... Unfathomable! He was evidently befuddled that Jan had been arrested."

"I remember Scoffield kept refilling Uncle Rykert's mug," Bertie observed.

"He did?"

"At least twice that I saw. No doubt he could then feel confident of his falling asleep."

"Aye. At any rate, Pa relieved Harmanus—who'd relieved Hendrik—at dusk, nine o'clock. Vrijdag was already out there.... That was Scoffield's idea too!"

"So it was," my brother confirmed.

"Presently Westerhof stopped by for a pipe, and then the Bilderbeeks took their evening constitutional. But by ten o'clock all was quiet, and both Pa and Bates fell asleep." I lost my train of thought for a second, wondering whether I should relate how the enraged Vrijdag had wrestled with his conscience ...

and deciding against it. "After another hour of uninterrupted peace, I find it completely plausible that Vrijdag simply left and went home."

"I suppose," Van Klost observed. "But had Jan not confessed, he'd have been the first I'd have suspected as the culprit."

"Meanwhile, it was getting well into the night. Scoffield decided the time was ripe for his plan and lit his candle. Then he heard Grootmoeder stumble in the hall, and quickly snuffed it out again. Grootmoeder—Lord only knows how long this has been going on!—wanted to be with Anne before the moon reached its zenith. I estimate she passed through the common just before midnight. She said Bates 'snored funny!'" They all chuckled and looked in her direction. She was still there, knitting obliviously; she had probably progressed several inches since Van Voort's benediction.

"Meanwhile, Mrs. Bates and Stanley and Scoffield were independently converging on the common. Stanley arrived first, effected his private revenge on Bates—"

"The pumpkin man!" Bertie rioted. We all smiled.

"And then he suffered his fit of remorse, and walked around behind the kerk to the graveyard. Pa woke up for a second, but so far from leaping to Bates' defense, he fell right back asleep without even noticing whether Vrijdag was still beside him or not."

"Oh heaven, whatever are we going to do with Pa?" Harmanus moaned. No one offered any suggestion.

"Scoffield probably waited for a goodly stretch before he realized Grootmoeder would not be returning to her room. Eventually he decided to brave it, and got himself over to the common, where he found the schout asleep. Perhaps he waited for a passing cloud to cover him, but my guess is that he dispatched Bates pretty quickly."

"Why didn't Bates call out?" Van Klost wondered.

"Why would he? If he was awake, he'd just see the same man who'd faked his beating that morning, he'd have no idea that slaughter was on his mind." We all shivered. "I doubt Scoffield noticed his missing button, but he knew he'd gotten blood all over his hands and the knife. With the peace of the area still undisturbed, he crept around behind Pa to the well, and dropped the knife into it. Then he moved back, probably staying under the trees ... and was completely astonished to run into his paramour on the highway. As she said, she'd come up to the house, probably within minutes of his having left it, and wandered out to the road, unable to decide her next move. Stanley saw her as he left the graveyard—but he missed Scoffield, who'd kept to the shadows. Scoffield herded Mrs. Bates back to the house, and threw her some money, all the while concealing his soiled hands from her view. She never had a chance—or never *thought*—to ask what he was doing up and about in the middle of the night. Then he washed his person and his coat in the chamber pot, poured the water out the window, and went to sleep. He was snoring away as I left the house just before dawn."

"Damnable! Truly!" the dominie said. It sounded infinitely more serious, coming from him.

We all took great swallows. "I fear the town will not look kindly upon your father's role in this matter," Van Klost observed primly, "which has been neglectful in the—"

Harmanus was grinding his teeth with the same resentment I felt. "Had *the town* not seen fit to select as its schout a man well known to have a problem holding his liquor," I said heatedly, "the town might have spared itself much of the mischief that's befallen it!"

The militia captain gulped. "That's true," Van Voort said glumly.

But then Mother and Lisa and Anneke came in with supper, and cheer returned. Would normal life begin again at last?

*   *   *

Normal life! A comforting idea, I clung to it. The sooner my life returned to normal, the sooner I could get ahead with something altogether new and different!

Meneer Van Klost, Pa, and four militiamen transported Robert Scoffield to Brooklyn the next morning. I might've found it gruesomely amusing to be present as they explained to the Justice that they were arraigning a second man accused of murdering the indenturee Justus Bates, but was content to be spared. At any rate, Scoffield was detained on Van Klost's presentments, and a trial was set for July 2—ten days' preparation being afforded in view of the increased gravity of the matter. This increased gravity apparently lay in the fact that it was a free and substantial citizen who stood accused.

It being a Thursday, however—a *normal* Thursday—I made a shopping trip into the city. A cracking thunderstorm had ushered in slightly cooler, drier weather overnight, and it was a glorious pleasure to paddle the canoe through the Buttermilk Channel and across the East River. In addition to restocking the tavern after the previous day's unexpected business, Meneer Van Klost had worriedly asked me to investigate whether the contracts that he and other farmers had signed with Robert Scoffield would still be honored if the latter were convicted of murder. "It hit me like a thunderbolt in the middle of the night!" he exclaimed. Pa belatedly added his own concern.

Mr. Martin, our regular grocer, was much relieved to hear me say that we felt we had finally neutralized the party responsible for the irritation between New Utrecht's slaves and masters. "Such things are not good for anyone, anyone at all, lad!" he admonished—and I heartily agreed. I troubled him for the favor of perusing Van Klost's contract with Scoffield, and he suggested I should speak to someone more in the financial line than himself, "although even if the contract were to be deemed invalid, I can't imagine anything would prevent him from selling his produce at the market rate as usual."

After consigning my purchases to be delivered to Jacob's care at Old Slip, I decided to look up Mr. Glasby, whom I'd not seen in six weeks, in the hope that he could enlighten me regarding the validity of Scoffield's contracts. I walked up Broadway to Mr. Colegrove's house and place of business—only to be told quite brusquely by a new clerk that Glasby was no longer associated with the firm! He'd no idea where I might locate him, he informed me as he nearly slammed the door in my face.

Biting back my indignation, I walked smartly east toward Mr. Fischl's, where I hoped again to resume my erratic musical education.

"Thomas, over here!" my cousin Charles called. He was sprawled on a bench outside the tavern across from my destination and had, I realized with less annoyance than before, been waiting for me. I also realized I was even becoming able to tolerate *the wig*.

"Good day, cousin!"

"Sit down, lad. I intend to purchase your dinner again." My pride slighted, I recoiled a step or two. "Oh don't be ridiculous, boy, I need to hear everything that's happened in New Utrecht since last I saw you." He pulled out a stool and bawled to the waiter to fetch an ale. "The worst is over on the south shore, I collect?"

Mollified, I sat. During the course of a long, hearty, and tasty but overpriced—for him—meal, I related all that had transpired.

Cooper sat back and looked at me curiously. "You did well, Thomas, very well indeed."

"Sir?" He confused me, as usual. Was this a compliment? No one else had praised my career as deputy schout.

No explanation was forthcoming, however. "I fear I rather doubt that Scoffield will hang as he deserves," he said.

A blow across the face would've hit me with less force. "I ... You ... can't mean that, Charles," I spluttered. "He—"

"He will find his partisans among the powers-that-be in this province, Thomas. Our propertied aristocracy will hasten to the succor of one of their minions!"

"What on earth are you talking about, cousin? Surely the law cannot be bent so far!"

"Thomas, my lad—"

I bristled and pushed away from the table, but he took no notice.

"You mustn't be naïve, they—"

How could he accuse *me* of naivety, the pretentious twit? I who am barely a year from my majority!

"They have their ways of managing their subversions without causing public distress."

It was absurd, preposterous! I looked at my cousin, who seemed gripped by some high passion, with alarm ... and finally disregard. "Well. I simply can't agree with you, Charles. The evidence is overwhelming." He looked back at me with unswayed condescension. Very irritating ... but of course he was family ... and he'd just bought my meal. "What does puzzle me," I said, striving to change the subject, "is *why* Scoffield decided to murder the man."

Cooper graciously allowed the subject to be changed. "It is a peculiarity. No matter how great an encumbrance the fellow was, it still seems beyond all reckoning to destroy one's own servant."

"Exactly. Although Scoffield is impetuous."

"And it appears he's extraordinarily arrogant!"

"How so? I admit I long found him bold and high-spirited—"

"Simply bringing those two into New Utrecht was an act of supreme arrogance, Thomas. The man felt he could get away with anything." It was so; I nodded. "And you tell me he proposed marriage to the poor Katelaar woman? My god!"

"You think his simple arrogance alone could account for his actions?"

"I don't know, Thomas. There is also considerable calculation in the man. But certainly the feeling—one can't say the *belief* in Scoffield's case— the feeling that one is above the moral law ... can lead to extraordinary criminality."

"But you think there's more to it?"

"There's always more to it." We both sighed and downed the last of our drinks. "Well, I thank you for your information, Thomas, and—"

"Thank *you* for the meal," I mumbled, still smarting from his reference to my juvenile status.

"—and I congratulate you for bringing the scoundrel to account, which apparently none of your elders was quite able to manage!" Now I was struck dumb. "With New Utrecht pacified once more, we have only the rest of the province to worry about!"

"I beg your pardon?"

"There was another ruction in Brooklyn last night, worse than the last. You haven't heard? And surely you've noticed the near-total absence of blacks on the streets here today?" I hadn't ... but now I did. "Locked down, old lad!"

It was very dispiriting. "When does it all end?"

My cousin shrugged. "Not until the weather cools down, I fear."

*　　　*　　　*

My lesson with Mr. Fischl was a debacle. As I arrived, his son was whining, "Why do *I* have to do it, Papa? Why can't—"

"I told you," Fischl replied crossly, "we're not sending her out today, and that's final!"

My instructor then severely berated my performance and exclaimed that Handel must be cringing in his coffin. "You have to practice regularly, Herr Dordrecht, if you've any aspirations to musicianship at all!" He later apologized for being so sharp with me, explaining that he'd been upset by a letter from his father informing him that his younger brother had been killed at that battle near Frankfurt two months ago. I offered my condolences and assured him I took no offense.

On returning home, entering the house from the back, I noted that the south guest room had been scoured and aired as thoroughly as its opposite had been some days back. After stowing our purchases I was startled to realize I could enjoy over an hour at leisure—a commodity that had been in short supply over the past weeks. I rushed to my attic room to practice my guitar ... only to get involved in the opening chapters of *Candide*, the most notorious and eagerly sought new book in Europe, reliably said to have been authored by the *philosophe* Voltaire. Another patron of the Society Library had surrendered to me only after realizing the sole copy was in French. Presently, however, the drowsy heat of the afternoon distracted me from the hero's fumbling efforts to direct his life ... to my own.

Though it occasionally discountenanced me to admit it, there was no denying that I was still attempting to postpone the inevitable decision of a direction to my life. I don't *want* to choose, I want to do everything! I want to become a great player on the guitar! And on the harpsichord too! And I want to master languages, and trigonometry and electricity and commerce and astronomy! I want to make lots of money and be a man respected not only in our province, but in the whole British Empire and beyond! I want to play my part in the inevitable progress of our global Enlightenment!

One might think the fragility that I'd observed in life over the past few weeks—the past year—would have stiffened a resolve to concentrate my purposes. Not only had I seen Mother Nature to be capricious in snatching life away, other men were often shockingly cavalier in depriving their fellows of it—a fact that deeply outraged me whenever and wherever I observed it. And just since I'd returned from the North both disease and accident had called attention to my own mortality.... And yet I still rebelled against the choice.

Of course I *do* mean to apply myself productively, and we can't all be polymaths on the order of Dr. Franklin, and I know my name's not Van Rensselaer, but—

"Uncle Thomas!" a high-pitched voice yelled from below. "Grandmother's calling for you!"

But … not today.

Normal life had, to some degree, returned to New Utrecht, but so had normal death. At Saturday morning's militia muster, Van Klost declared the curfews at an end and cancelled further overnight vigils. We all nodded with dull relief. The decision slightly mollified the awful news that had also gone round that Meneer Karel Schuppert, the blacksmith, who'd contracted a pleurisy on Wednesday—explaining his absence from the town gathering— had worsened rapidly and expired in the night. Although neither he nor his wife had been born in New Utrecht, they'd lived here as long as I could remember, and were well-respected though never among the leading citizens. Everyone seemed as saddened as I felt, no matter that his decline had presaged this demise months back.

But among the men who stopped for a quaff after the muster I also detected a perturbed worry over the future of the smithy. "There are two smiths in Flatbush," Meneer Bilderbeek was saying, "and both are constantly at work. But they've both fathered daughters and neither can find apprentices to assist them."

"Tyson in Gravesend is older than Schuppert was," Halsema observed. "He does fine work, but his son nearly burnt his right arm through five years back, and—"

"The German fellow in Flatlands, Hausner, has three boys, but they're young yet and he has plenty of work right where he is," Voskuil added with a sigh.

"There's *no one* who could take over here?" Oosterhout, the newest arrival, asked.

"Schuppert could never find an apprentice either," Bilderbeek explained. "He made do with that slave that Loytinck nearly beat to death, but Dordrecht has him now and of course he needs him in his fields."

As if it had been staged, the four in unison drew on their pipes, took long swallows of their beers, and set their tankards back down. "The widow?" Oosterhout inquired.

"My wife says Machtel has long since decided her future," Voskuil stated. "She'll send the two girls to their other uncle and she herself will move to her sister's in Bushwick. She means to sell the properties here."

"Properties? More than one?"

"She thinks—and I don't see why not—that the forge is far enough from the houses that it and the turf around it could be sold separately."

"*Uh huh*. Funeral?" Halsema inquired.

As none of them responded, I spoke up. "Six o'clock. I heard the dominie telling Van Klost."

"Ah," he grunted, standing. "Best I pay respects before going to the fields, then."

He needn't have hurried, for field work was precluded when the skies opened up and it poured rain all through the afternoon, the funeral, the interment, and the Sabbath.

*   *   *

As I drove the horse and cart to Red Hook Monday morning, carefully skirting great puddles and muddy ruts, I was still unsure how to proceed with the special commission of parsing Scoffield's contracts. I knew no one in the financial line other than Glasby, and how could I find him in a city of near twenty thousand? Van Klost and Pa had been joined by Harmanus and my mother in their dissatisfaction with vague assurances on the matter.

I was well down my list at Mr. Martin's when a lilting voice called out, "Why, Mr. Dordrecht!"

"Why, Miss Chapman!" I said, delighted. "How very lovely to see you."

And indeed she looked lovelier than ever, and it was more than the fact that it had been five weeks since I'd last seen her. She was wearing a handsome burgundy taffeta town dress, which was startling enough, as I'd only seen her in costumes or in working garbs since we'd been introduced. And her chestnut hair had been swept back and elegantly secured in the current fashion. She seemed quite radiant—and simply couldn't be as old as my sister alleged!

"Have you seen this day's *Examiner*?"

"No ma'am. I mean to pick it up at Fischl's later."

"Well! There's a dispatch from Philadelphia, Thomas, relating that a certain grand impresario by the name of Gershom Ingraham, and his wife, *Collette*"—we both arched our eyebrows in amusement—"having put forth a performance of *The Tempest* in a condemned stable a week ago Thursday, have unexpectedly debarked for South Carolina, leaving behind a goodly number of distressed creditors."

"No!"

"What a pair of rogues, Thomas!" We burst out laughing. "But tell me, how does the sign look? Has it drawn new customers for you?" I reluctantly confessed that a full month after she'd completed it, the advertisement was yet to be properly mounted. She looked disappointed. "Well, I have heard about the terrible troubles you've had in New Utrecht, but I hadn't imagined they'd have interfered with simply hanging a tavern sign!"

I felt compelled to justify my inaction on that score by beginning to relate my activities as a deputy schout.

"Wait! I am interested, Thomas, truly. But I just stopped in here to buy a mite of cheese and a peach to take over to the Battery. I've been cooped up for two days by this endless rain, and I'm longing for a stroll. Won't you join me?"

How could I not? Avoiding Martin's look of benign amusement, I very hastily completed my purchases and soon found myself basking in the envy of the shore idlers, none of whom had a woman half so attractive on his arm. Given the beautiful day and the splendid company, I made no haste with my story ... but eventually I had to relate how I'd completely forgotten the use of "Robin" as a nickname despite our many rehearsals together.

"And what was this man's name again?"

"Rob*ert*—Robert Scoffield. Robert's not a common name among the Dutch, and—"

She'd turned pale and gripped my forearm. "*Scoffield,* you say?"

"Aye. You ... know of him?"

Her confusion brought a halt to all storytelling. But what I'd sensed as dismay quickly turned to anger—deep anger. "The man presumed to woo me, Thomas. Last fall. I fear I was for some time taken in by his smart and refined appearance—notwithstanding his repulsive manservant, whom he kept at a great distance, and—"

She halted, twisting her handkerchief and looking askance upriver at the distant Palisades of New Jersey. "You knew of Justus Bates as well?" I asked in confusion.

The happiness we had enjoyed together just sixty seconds before had flown. "I really don't wish to speak of either of them, Mr. Dordrecht." She turned away from me and began to gather her things.

Stunned and perturbed, I sat with my mouth open—until a presentiment struck me forcibly as an irrefutable insight. "Scoffield was the villain whom you fended off with a knife!" I asserted.

She turned to me, perfectly dumbfounded. "How on earth did you know that?" she breathed. "I've never told a soul! Surely *he* didn't tell you?"

"I learned of the weapons you procured for my mother and sister, Adelie, and I wormed it out of Lisa that you'd once been forced to stab a man in the leg in your own defense. And then only a week ago, Scoffield appeared half-dressed before my brother and me when the town alarum was sounded at dawn, and I saw a livid gash on his upper left thigh...."

Adelie Chapman nodded somberly, but again turned away. "Can you …
forgive me, Thomas, for bringing weapons to your womenfolk?"

"Forgive! Adelie, I'm *glad* they have some means to protect themselves. It
terrifies me that Mother travels alone at night."

"Ah."

"I thank you for it!"

She sighed heavily and her shoulders slumped with relief. I was so forward
as to put my arm about them and she abruptly burst into tears. "It was
the most ghastly moment of my entire life, Thomas!" she said eventually,
recovering her strength as she spoke. "I was completely unharmed in my
person, but it was a fortnight before I recovered the least humor, the least
sense of security.… Having Ingraham cheat me out of the seven bob he owed
me was nothing in comparison."

"I only saw the wound for a couple seconds," I said, "but I think there
must've been at least two dozen stitches to it!"

She grinned at the macabre observation. "Not four dozen?" Trinity's bells
struck noon. She shook her lovely head and stood.

"You don't want to hear the rest of the saga, Adelie?"

"Ah, thank you, Thomas, but—some other time. I actually have urgent—
and quite pleasant—business to be attended."

She again took my arm as we turned back toward the center of town.
"May I ask you—if it's not too distressing—"

"Nay nay, it was but a temporary shock. I'm quite restored, my dear."

My heart fluttered, but I quickly cautioned myself not to make too much
of her address. "I've no doubt that Scoffield murdered Bates, Adelie, but I
can't sum up a motive why he should have done so. No matter that Bates was
a mortification—"

"Was he even any good as a manservant? Did you see?"

"He seemed at least acceptable in that respect. Took care of the horse and
cart. And his master's dress."

We walked another fifteen paces, thinking. "I really can't help you,
Thomas. I had a sense of the man's ruthlessness from the first. I just never
imagined it might be visited upon myself."

"Ah. And—"

"I think Scoffield sensed my antipathy for Bates right away, and thereafter
managed that he was never around. I doubt I set eyes on him more than
twice." We reached the Bowling Green, above Fort George. "How is your
guitar-playing coming, Thomas? We must perform together again sometime
soon!"

Smitten and eager to avoid mentioning my teacher's recent rebuke, I
burbled incoherently about Handel as she looked around in preparation to

bid me farewell. "Ah, I beg your pardon, Adelie, but there's one other thing you might help me with. You recall Mr. Glasby?"

She flushed and smiled broadly and looked away for a second. "Indeed. Of course."

"It seems he's no longer employed by Mr. Colegrove. I've lost track of him."

"Ah. I just happen to know he's now retained by a Mr. Leavering, a factor from Philadelphia who's lately opened a trading establishment here. It's on the eastern side of Peck's Market."

"Aha!" I rejoiced, very glad of the information. "Excellent! Perhaps there's a sign?"

"Yes!" she said. "A far more modest sign than either Colegrove's or *The Arms*, but indeed, there's a sign."

What was I thinking, to be hoping for a kiss at mid-day on a public square? She shook my hand and gaily waved me farewell.

*   *   *

"My dear Dordrecht, how are you!"

"I'm well, sir, and I trust you—" There was great confusion in the bustling offices of Castell, Leavering & Sproul, Shippers—purposive, busy men intent upon their commerce.

Glasby himself seemed greatly distracted. "Never better, my lad! But you'll have to forgive me, I can't stop to chat now. We have two ships in today, one right after the other. But we must get together! I should like to introduce you to my new employer, a fine man and—"

A stevedore demanded to know where to put the rum, given that all the room on the second floor was taken. "Just outside on the street, then, for the time-being," Glasby replied immediately. "We'll have to get the lumber to the roof and the rum inside before nightfall." The stevedore knuckled his forehead and left, and Glasby exhaled, apparently near to panting. "Better rain on the lumber than the rum, eh?"

"Perhaps if I came around at midday on Thursday, Mr. Glasby, we might—"

"Thursday! Excellent! Things are not always so frantic here, truly! Where did I put that manifest?" He snatched a piece of paper off a windowsill. "Ah!"

"Mr. Glasby, I'm really sorry to trouble you, but can you possibly spare just two minutes to scan this contract? There are several like it in New Utrecht, and—"

"Of course, of course, not *that* busy," he said, taking the proffered sheet as well. He quickly read it through, and shrugged. "Looks plausible enough. What's worrying you about it?"

"The agent who wrote it up is under arrest for murder."

"Good heavens!" he said, recoiling. "I'll bet therein lies a tale—for Thursday. But it shouldn't affect the contract if the company is legitimate. I trust your friend verified that independently before he signed?" I made a dubious face. "Well, I've never heard of these folks, but my first suggestion would be simply to go there and *ask!*"

I gaped, thunderstruck. Why hadn't *I* thought of that?

"It's only eight blocks further up."

I spent the whole eight blocks hopelessly attempting to justify myself, inventing reasons why it might be thought prudent to be shy—even in broad daylight—of any company that had employed for a moment a criminal such as Scoffield.

The property of the Trans-Hudson Produce Co. at 7 Catherine Street was a large, ordinary two-story warehouse a few doors up from the shore. I must surely have passed it many times without taking note of it. The only thing surprising was who opened the door: Joachim, the German fellow who'd answered to me when I'd managed the warehouse on Front Street last winter. I was so completely at a loss, it was he who had to speak first. "Herr Dordrecht! It is good!"

"Joachim? Well.... Yes, it is good to see you too!" I said. We stood for a few seconds staring at each other, grinning. "What are you doing *here?*" I asked.

He sighed heavily. He looked more disheveled and more hopeless than ever. "I move barrels, I load carts, I lock door, I never see sky."

"No no, what I meant was, why aren't you at one of Mr.—"

"Get back to the stockroom, damn you!" bellowed an approaching male voice. Joachim visibly trembled as a large, heavy man a decade my senior appeared. He shoved his fist against Joachim's shoulder, almost knocking him over. "I told you to answer the door, not...." Noticing me, the man's demeanor instantly changed, though he did chase the retreating Joachim with a scowl. "Begging your pardon, sir—Big dolt's so useless!—how can I help you?"

I couldn't suppress my annoyance. "Perhaps if you tried reasoning with the fellow, you might—"

"*Aw,* ain't no reasoning with the likes of him. He don't even speak the language—though I hear he's had plenty opportunity to learn. That one's a disaster. Told my boss to sell him and get me a new one. But what may we do for you, please?"

I shook off my confoundment and produced the contract. "Are you the manager here?" He nodded. Odd that he neglected to introduce himself—almost invariably the first thing a businessman does. "I'd like to inquire about this agreement, if you please."

He pulled it just slightly roughly from my hands, but had far more trouble than Glasby in reading it. "Ah. Well, this is one of ours, Mr., *uh*, Van Klost, and it—"

I started to protest that I was not Van Klost, but decided to let it go.

"Seems to be in order. Is something the matter?"

"Perhaps you're unaware, sir, that the agent who arranged and signed this contract, Robert Scoffield, is under indictment for murder in Kings County?"

The man almost chuckled. "Oh yeah, because he did for his dogsbody, right? Heard about that. Well, you needn't worry. One way or another, we'll be expecting to see your crop here come November." He scanned the sheet again and handed it back. "Thirty pence and a farthing? Be sure of it, sir, the chief will be only too happy!"

"Might I inquire your principal's name, sir?"

"*Uh*, I was told to assure our suppliers and customers that they may rest content with the name of the Trans-Hudson Produce Company, Mr. Van Klost."

What? The effrontery was staggering. "And your own name, sir?"

"Smith. If you'll excuse me, Mr. Van Klost, I must check on that fool in the stockroom."

"But—"

"A good day to you!" And again I had a door shut in my face!

The afternoon becoming hot, I stopped at a tavern on Wall Street as I returned to collect my boat. Two brokers were also at the bar, and I made bold to request the current price of wheat. "Wheat? Touched thirty-seven this morning," said the one.

"Down to thirty-six and a half just now," said the other.

"It varies a great deal?" I asked. Both nearly laughed as they nodded. "But is it *averaging* more than is customary?"

"Oh yes, the range is much higher this year."

"By far!"

"And yet, I've heard the farmers are anticipating a fine crop!" I said.

"Ah, so have we—and a good thing too!"

"Higher call for it than ever, lad," the second man explained. "You can't feed an army on pine needles!"

"More's the pity!" snickered his associate, and they turned back to their drinks as I thanked them.

*   *   *

Once my purchases were stowed, back home, I was immediately pressed into assisting preparations for supper. This was necessary, Anneke explained, because Mother had unexpectedly received and accepted an invitation to tea from Vrouw Nijenhuis.

"*Tea?*" I exclaimed. "Since when does Vrouw Nijenhuis serve tea? Since when does Mother—"

My sister-in-law shrugged. "She said she simply had to go, because they needed to discuss replacing the altar cloth with the dominie and Juffrouw Katelaar."

"What's wrong with the altar cloth?"

Lisa impatiently put two empty buckets in my hands. "First priority's a trip to the well, Thomas."

As I returned, struggling as always to keep the buckets swinging from the yoke on my shoulders and slopping over, I noticed Miss Chapman's artfully painted sign leaning against the outside wall, and it occurred to me that it was now urgent to complete the final step of its installation before the local forge might be more or less permanently shut down. It took some doing to persuade my brother to spare the slave for this project, though he'd known it would have to be done eventually.

At seven on Tuesday morning, therefore, Vrijdag and I presented ourselves at Vrouw Schuppert's door to beg her permission to fire up the hearth and execute the supports for the tavern sign.

The widow looked harried and uncertain at first, then resolved on it. "I'll only charge you for the materials if you'll have him finish the four jobs Karel left waiting. They're only little jobs, but he was insisting I should take them to Flatlands if he proved unable to complete them."

I took a glance at Vrijdag; his expression was impassive. "All right," I agreed.

She gestured at the slave. "He'll need help, you know. Have you got a boy to pump the bellows?"

This hadn't occurred to me, and it would take precious hours to negotiate. "I'll be here with him," I said, surprising both. "Just for a day," I added defensively.

"Do we light the fire first?" I asked Vrijdag as we entered the gloomy smithy.

He propped the door open, which relieved the air and the darkness. "No. First clear ash." Ignoring me, he proceeded to do just that. I scanned the tools and the stock in order to keep from feeling useless; then I noticed a second wheelbarrow, and volunteered to run the clinker to the tip while he shoveled.

Presently he lit the fire and showed me how to work the bellows. "Do we have enough raw stock?" I asked, suddenly struck by the worry.

"Plenty blank. That all wrought iron," he said, nodding at the pile leaning against the opposite wall. "Schuppert pay thirty pound. Said good deal."

We began on the outstanding orders the smith had left unfinished as illness had overtaken him, which were simpler matters than the inn sign. At first too overwhelmed to do much more than gawk, I presently began demanding an education in the process. For his part, Vrijdag was at first somewhat taciturn, but waxed enthusiastic as work continued. Before noon we had regained the slightly brittle informality we'd shared on the roof. It was as impressive to observe his measurements and calculations and sketches as the actual heating and pounding and quenching; I'd always taken finished ironwork for granted. At one point in the afternoon he held up with his tongs a component piece we'd been hammering for twenty minutes. "Good!" he exclaimed before dousing it in the slack tub.

"Bet you'd like to just keep doing this forever!" I breezed—and instantly regretted.

Vrijdag had to turn away from me for a spell. "What *I* like!" he muttered bitterly.

I quickly changed the subject. Vrouw Schuppert came in a few minutes later, bearing a pitcher of cider ... and one mug. I made no move to drink, though I was parched from the heat. As she left, I accompanied her outside and endeavored to make small talk by way of expressing thanks. "How are your plans coming along, Mevrouw?"

"Another few days, Meneer Dordrecht. The girls will be off to Flatlands on Friday, and my brother-in-law will pick me up on Saturday." She sighed heavily.

"It must be very hard, ma'am."

"Indeed, young sir," she bristled, pushing aside any pitying from me. "But I am most relieved to have those jobs done. My husband made me promise, you see. And Meneer Van Klost assures me that there will be no problem separating the forge property from the deed of the house, so at least I'll be able to sell the latter in some timely manner."

"Surely the smithy must be very valuable, ma'am?"

"One would think so, but I don't suppose I'll get much for it. There's no one around who can run it. I've asked Hausner; he said he'd consider the tools and the stock, but not the building itself. But without tools, the building's just an inconvenient storage shack." One of her step-daughters called and she excused herself.

Vrijdag was either concentrating on his job as I re-entered the forge ... or deliberately avoiding having to recognize my presence. I filled the mug and gratefully drank it down. He couldn't help being aware of that! Then I refilled it and passed it to him. For a few seconds the slave's pride fought his common sense, but the latter finally won out. I refilled the mug a third time, drank it down; refilled it a fourth time, passed it to him. Presently the mood in the sweltering, clangorous enclosure began to lift. "Schuppert offer forge to Hausner last summer," he volunteered. "Ask hundred twenty. Hausner no want."

"I'd have thought this smithy worth a great deal more than that."

"Hausner have big shop, Flatlands. Been there. Two hearths."

"Schuppert took you along to see it?"

"To load, unload," Vrijdag corrected, neutrally. "But I do see." He held up the piece he'd been hammering, turned it over a few times, clucked approvingly and tossed it into the pile of completed sections. "Now we do first rivet."

We finished the work about seven o'clock, but Vrijdag made a great fuss of damping the fire, cleaning the tools, and straightening the shop before locking up. After paying our respects to the widow, the two of us carted the heavy, awkward sign-holder over to the house where, having checked it against the front wall, we deposited it outside the stable. "You scrape, thorough," Vrijdag instructed. "Three coats black paint. I help you hang Friday, if brother agree."

"Oh Thomas, that's really very good!" my mother suddenly called. "It'll serve splendidly. Congratulations!"

I shuffled uncomfortably. "Actually, it was Vrij—"

"But don't you dare set foot in the house before you wash up!"

Vrijdag didn't seem to notice any awkwardness, having spotted his woman waiting for him in the next yard. "I'll talk to Harmanus about Friday."

"*Uh huh.*"

"I'm ... very pleased with the job, Vrijdag. And ... it was an interesting day for me."

"Ah."

I swallowed, not knowing how to say what needed to be said. "*Uh* ... thank you."

He looked a trifle startled, a mite pleased, all with little overt show. He nodded slightly and dashed over to Roosje.

*   *   *

An inchoate idea of how to solve some problems of disparate individuals, the Dordrecht family, and the town of New Utrecht all at once was presently occupying me. But before I had the opportunity to discuss it with Mother—the one person who might help translate any such notion into pounds and pence—she and Lisa were finally summoned by the frantic husband of their country-side client. Thus I was further stuck with minding the tavern until they returned Wednesday evening, exhausted from a difficult but successful childbirth.

Therefore it was Mr. Glasby and his new employer, Mr. Benjamin Leavering, to whom I first broached my notion. Mr. Leavering is a hugely obese fellow of some three-score years, whose rather gross features and unstylish dress make one quite overwhelmed to discover a genial nature and an extremely keen intelligence.

"You want to buy the smithy," Glasby parsed aloud, "set the slave Vrijdag to work it four days a week—leaving two for your brother—and take over Joachim's indenture so he can assist on the farm full-time?"

"Yes, that's it!" I said, breathless from having spilt it all out in a rush. "We could learn to produce lightning rods, I was thinking!"

Both men smiled as they raised their eyebrows noncommittally. "Well, it seems reasonable enough to want to do that, Dordrecht, but does your family have all this money to spare?"

"Sir?"

"The capital, lad," Mr. Leavering said. "Indeed you may be looking at worthwhile ventures and at competent fellows to run them, but it's going to cost you well over a hundred fifty pounds to get started. And this must be repaid from profits before your family will show the least return."

"How much did you pay for the slave?" Glasby inquired, breaking the ensuing silence.

"You've some notion of the value of the smithy?" Leavering demanded gently. "Of what it costs and returns annually?" I was flattered that both men were willing to entertain my enthusiasm. They seemed to be computing the figures in terms of value over time. "And you're thinking of using the indenturee to cover the farm work from which the slave will be excused?"

"I'm not surprised to learn that Joachim's been sold," Glasby observed. "He never had any stomach for what was needed of him."

"They have him doing exactly the same labors now," I said.

Glasby shook his head dismissively. "You could at least find out what they paid for him, if you check the city records."

"Records?"

"Oh yes. Like deeds, all indenturee and slave transfers are supposed to be recorded."

"And taxed," Leavering groaned. I dimly recalled that Pa and Loytinck had signed some piece of paper to formalize Vrijdag's purchase. "You may have a viable concept somewhere, young sir, and I think such enterprise is always laudable in the young, but the details," he sighed emphatically, "need further thought."

"Yes sir," I admitted reluctantly.

Mr. Leavering then requested an expeditious review of the "late unpleasantness in Kings County," as he was urgently required at his counter. I rather think he stayed longer to hear it than he'd intended. "A sad business," he summarized, finally rising. "Shocking how small problems quickly snowball into enormous ones. Good luck with your endeavors, my boy! Glasby, I'll see you shortly. Don't rush!" He hastened away and I had to control my amusement at his buffoonish gait.

"I've actually known him some years," Glasby observed. "Colegrove had many dealings with him while he was in Philadelphia. Seems ordinary and solid enough, but he'll frequently disarm you with vehement and quite unconventional opinions."

I was too preoccupied with my current problems to feign any interest in Mr. Leavering's character, or Glasby's peculiar assessment of it. "Why have you left Mr. Colegrove, may I ask, sir?"

"Ah...." Glasby flushed, and I regretted the question. "I'm not prepared to discuss that, Mr. Dordrecht. One should beware of speaking ill—"

"I do beg your pardon, sir, I shouldn't have been prying." Glasby wordlessly gestured that he wished to say no more, and I awkwardly searched for a new topic. "You don't suppose Mr. Leavering would be interested in investing in a smithy in New Utrecht? He surely has the capital?"

Glasby smiled indulgently. "Perhaps so, but you don't amass capital by investing in every last project that crosses your desk, my friend!" I trust I looked as abashed as I felt. "You'd do better to seek out someone locally, I think—someone with funds available for investment who knows how greatly his own business needs a ready smith, for example."

"Meneer Loytinck!" I exclaimed instantly.

"There. You're closer to the mark, at least. Keep at it." A church bell tolled the quarter-hour. "Ah, now I must run. 'Time is money!' Dr. Franklin says. But ... you'll be shopping again on Monday?"

"Yes."

"Then you must join us—*uh*, be my guest, that is—for dinner at noon, at the *Province Arms*."

"Good heavens!" It was reputed the finest establishment of the city.

"I have a surprise!"

"I thank you, sir," I said, flabbergasted, "but Scoffield's trial will be on Monday morning, over in Brooklyn."

"Ah me. Well, do hurry along as soon as it's over. I particularly wish you to be in attendance."

"I'll do my best, of course," I said, bemused as we parted.

Mr. Fischl was less emphatic than before, but my inattention to his suggestions and failure to have practiced obviously distresses him. I simply *must* do better!

It was two-thirty when I remorsefully left his shop. The realization that I had time to locate and visit the provincial records office, however, brought me out of my slack mood. It was in the basement of the city's chief government building at Wall and Broad Streets. A clerk dutifully accompanied me to the section I needed in a stiflingly musty room where the sales records of slaves and indenturees were kept month by month. I found nothing in the files of this May or June, and so tried to guess when Colegrove had purchased Joachim. A dim recollection of a conversation from last winter suggested August of 1757—and there it was: Joachim Bauern's indenture had been sold by the captain of a ship out of Bremen for fifty-five pounds. The indenture was to persist until August 12, 1764, when—presuming he was free of debt—he was to be released with two new sets of clothes and shoes, plus twenty acres of land in the province. This last provision, the clerk explained, was why prices fell so sharply in the last years of a servant's tenure. A sudden curiosity gripped me regarding the terms of Justus Bates' indenture, and I inquired whether servants imported into the colony, rather than purchased here, were registered.

They were, but in another section. After starting with July 1758, I found the declaration in the September file. Scoffield had produced a paper from Barbados showing that Bates was indentured to him … until September 26, 1759. "There's nothing here about the provision for a released indentured servant," I observed to the clerk.

"Seldom is, in a contract imported from elsewhere," he said. "But if resident in New York, the owner would be subject to our regulations on it."

"And those are?"

"Same as the other one."

"Very expensive!"

"Need to save ahead. Presumably they've been getting more than their money's worth all along!"

Curious. Another question struck me. "Are businesses registered here?"

"Upstairs, yes." He was good enough to take me to the room. "New York County?" I nodded. "They're arranged alphabetically. What—"

"Trans-Hudson Produce Company, of Catherine Street."

"Oh I recognize that one. Brand new. Just bought their property in March, I think."

He quickly found the folder and produced the paper, a "Registration to Conduct Business in His Majesty's Province of New York." It listed six partners—the name DeLancey prominently stood out—and was attested by "Aaron Colegrove, Treasurer." Disbelieving my eyes, I read it twice.

The reason I'd found no record of Joachim's transfer to Trans-Hudson was that he'd never been sold! I thanked the helpful clerk, left the building, and walked down toward the slip in something of a daze. If Scoffield was an agent of Trans-Hudson, and Colegrove was its chief financial officer, then Scoffield was an agent of Aaron Colegrove. And Glasby had deliberately been kept in ignorance of it! He'd been perfectly unaware of Trans-Hudson, and was as perplexed as I at the thought that Joachim was toiling anywhere but in Colegrove's known establishments.

But Colegrove had always been an enigma. I looked back more dispassionately on my own firing. I had, after all, earned exemplary notice there until the one instance of admittedly lamentable public behavior—oh, and the less said about my undetected scenic painting in his storehouse, the better—and yet he'd dismissed me without warning. Although masters of apprentices and junior clerks are renowned for their sharp punctiliousness, I'd still never heard of a lad being let off without a single warning. It seemed entirely excess—

It hit me with such force, I had to stop and lean against a hitching post. *Aaron Colegrove had repeatedly expressed the most intense and peculiar fascination with the tiny hamlet of New Utrecht!* With the crops my brother raised, the size of Meneer Loytinck's properties, the character of its militia captain! And three months later, his agent Robert Scoffield had appeared in our midst in search of crops and lands.

I myself might've been the unwitting leavening to all the mayhem that Scoffield had created!

As I stowed the goods I'd bought from Martin into the canoe, I was pondering the notion that Loytinck might invest in my scheme to preserve the smithy ... and recalled that Loytinck was endeavoring to do precisely the opposite, to convert all his holdings to cash.

These thoughts were enough to depress anyone's spirits. I rebelled against their hold on mine and resolutely enjoyed my paddle back to Red Hook, then hurried directly home to apply the third coat of paint before supper.

*   *   *

Though often intermixed, the most frequent mealtime arrangement at *The Arms of Orange* is that paying guests are served, first, at one of our long tables, while the enormous Dordrecht clan sits together at the other. As supper drew to a close Mother was sitting, as usual, at one end, and I was between her and Lisa, opposite Harmanus and Anneke. The latter spoke up during a lull in conversation: "My father spoke very highly of your efforts at the meeting, Thomas," she announced.

"He *did?*" all the rest of us replied in unison. The Selectman is not given to effusiveness, and his regard is highly valued.

"He said you were well-organized and that you had convinced him."

Zounds! Lisa grinned and stroked my shoulder. Mother looked inordinately proud. My brother looked as awestruck as if a donkey had been elected to membership in the human race. It seemed a good moment to broach some new topics. I begged another hour of Vrijdag's time to attach the sign finally to the house, and got no objection. As the others left the table to clear away or be scuttled to bed, I attempted to explain my convoluted notions to Mother and Harmanus....

"First of all, I've located an indentured servant we could get, cheap, for five years."

"But we already have a slave, Thomas," Harmanus instantly objected.

"Hear me out, please! He's a big, strong German lad about twenty-five, named Joachim; he has five years to go, and he hates being cooped up in the city."

"I can understand that!"

In reverse, so could I! "Probably could buy the contract for fifty pounds." They were shaking their heads. "You'd love him, Harmanus," I teased. "He doesn't speak Dutch *or* English, and he longs for farm work!"

"Religion?"

Uh oh. "I ... never asked. Lutheran?" He made a face, and I skipped ahead. "Now, the *town* has a problem, in that its smith has died, and its forge is going begging, and—"

"What's that to do with us?"

"The only person in town who could conceivably operate that forge is our slave."

"Who is only a slave and whom we can't spare anyway, if we hope to—"

"This is my idea. We need an investor, first, because we can't afford to buy the forge, even though I think it could be had for only a hundred pounds."

"That's perfectly true," Mother asserted with finality. Then she said, "You think it'd be only a hundred?"

I nodded. "So we persuade an investor to buy the forge, and then we rent Vrijdag to him—"

"I *need* Vrijdag!"

"—for, say, two hundred days a year, roughly four days a week. Then we arrange for him to spend one hundred days, to be chosen by prior arrangement, in the fields with you. The investor takes the profit of the forge, and we use the rent to buy Joachim."

Harmanus' eyes were very nearly crossed. "This would require very careful figuring, Thomas," Mother said, "but the first problem is, where's the investor?"

"Yes. I was hoping you both could help with that. I think one could be found, because if the town loses that forge it will be a problem for everyone. Every lost horseshoe, every chipped plow—you'd have to trek to Flatlands?" Harmanus groaned. "Perhaps a company can be configured that—"

"You're imagining that people will accept a slave as their blacksmith!"

"Why shouldn't they accept a black blacksmith, *eh?*"

"Oh now you're bandying words again, Thomas. Be serious!"

"He worked with Schuppert for over two years, Harmanus, they saw him there then. And there's that free black in Flatbush, who's accepted as a tanner. And ... we can work out the details. If objection is made to giving cash to a slave, Vrijdag could write out a chit, and we could register and ledger it here, you see."

"It would take a deal of getting used to." Harmanus looked exhausted.

"The first man I thought of as an investor was Teunis Loytinck, of course; but he's taken our advice, it seems, and is striving to accumulate cash to leave to his heiress, so we'll—" My mother was smiling most oddly, but she shook her head when we looked inquiringly at her. She can be completely inscrutable at times, I swear! "We'll have to seek out other arrangements."

"You were dividing Vrijdag's days before, Thomas," Mother said. "I counted three hundred."

"A few too many, actually, Mother, because with fifty-two Sundays and four or five holidays, that'd leave only eight days for Vrijdag himself."

"For himself!" Harmanus exploded. "He's a slave! What does he need with days for himself?"

"We need to give him something, brother, if he is to man the town's forge essentially on his own...."

Harmanus sighed, baffled. "I don't suppose you've asked *him?*"

"Oh no," I confessed quickly. "I haven't got that much nerve. But I.... He seems to like the work."

"I've heard," Mother observed, "that slaves can sometimes save enough money to—"

"I don't *like* being a slaveholder, I must say," Harmanus announced unexpectedly. "Van Klost and Loytinck seem to feel it gives them standing, but.... Dear heaven, children are quite enough responsibility for me!"

Mother patted his hand. "I've heard," she resumed, "that slaves can sometimes buy their own freedom. You know, after saving for twenty years or something?"

"The freedman in Flatbush did just that, I understand."

Harmanus snorted. "A lot can happen in twenty years, Thomas."

"Well, not to put too fine a point on it," Mother interjected, "a forty-one year old slave is worth much less than a twenty-one year old, so it wouldn't take the same two hundred thirty pounds."

"Right," Harmanus said crossly, "so it'll only take him seventeen years, perhaps. But a lot can change in seventeen years."

"Oh *phoo*, Harmanus! I doubt we'll still be blessed with George the Second, and I surely hope this awful war will be over and done with, but other than that, what could possibly happen between now and, *um,* seventeen seventy-six?"

And on that note of absurdity, discussion was tabled for the evening.

CHAPTER 20

Meneer Van Klost had assured me, ever since he'd returned from delivering Scoffield to custody, that his prosecution would be attended by the best the province had to offer. But as yet no one had come to New Utrecht to depose any of its citizens, and certainly my notes on the events of the night of June 8th had not been requested, much less subpoenaed. Anticipating that they would be, I'd troubled to copy them out in my best hand. After Vrijdag and I finally succeeded in mounting the sign on Friday morning, I pressed Van Klost on the subject. Alarmed, he elected to send young Voskuil, who'd just broken his arm and couldn't assist his family in the fields, to Brooklyn.

After he'd returned, I was again assured that everything was all right.

Following militia muster on Saturday, I had taken myself to my nook in the graveyard, eager to conclude the absorbing and enthralling escapades of Candide and his lady Cunegonde, when Petrus was sent to fetch me back to the house. I returned to find Mr. Wicklow, the constable from Brooklyn, waiting. "Oh hey!" he said. "Where's Ryk? You serve whiskey here, don't you?"

"Of course, Mr. Wicklow. Prices are posted over there by the window."

"Aw," he whined, disappointed.

"And I'll do my best to locate my father for you. May I ask what this is in reference—"

Pa ambled in. "Hey Joe!" He roared.

"Ryk! How the hell are you?"

They downed two shots apiece before Wicklow stated his business. "Justice sent me to pick up your notes on the Scoffield case, Ryk."

"What notes?"

"All them notes about who done what to—"

"He means *my* notes," I interjected, furious.

"Oh yeah," Pa agreed insouciantly. "My boy Tom," he re-introduced. "Nailed that bastard's nether parts to the floor. You should've seen him!"

"Who, Scoffield? Seems all right to me! We've been havin' a good time since he—"

"Go fetch those notes, Tom!"

I threw the apron down on the counter and stomped upstairs, as furious at being presented to this unwholesome crony by my nickname as anything else. When I returned, resolved to keep my temper, Wicklow was saying, "...gotta collect this wench Yvette. She's livin' in some boat?"

"Yeah, set her back there myself. But Tom can...." He blanched at my scowl. "Thomas can tell you the way."

"All right. Well, maybe *Thomas* can get me one for the road. I'm thinkin' I might buy me some of this gal's favors before I *escort* her to Brooklyn, so I'll hoist one to screw up my courage—my *Dutch* courage, you get it?"

The two men screamed with laughter for nearly a minute. After he'd downed yet a third whiskey, I gave him the directions and he was blessedly departed from sight.

But he was back ninety minutes later, demanding yet another tipple. "She ain't there, boy!" he bellowed. "You sure you gave me the right boat?"

"I believe there's only one wreck on the shoreline, Mr. Wicklow?"

He spotted something on the floor, and bent to pick up ... my notes. "Must've dropped these before," he grunted, stuffing them indifferently into his waistcoat. "Where's Ryk?"

"Hard at work in the fields, Mr. Wicklow. That'll be sixpence, in total, please."

"*Sixpence!* I only have four."

"We'll take that, then. Good day to you."

As soon as he was gone, I saddled the horse and rode to Denyse's Ferry. It was overcast and blustery, and the waves lapping the stern of the wreck made it creak. Perhaps Wicklow had simply flinched at boarding it? I got soaked to the knees as I crossed onto it but, sure enough, there was no trace of Yvette Bates on the *Anthea Rudge*. Fortunately I spied the fishwife who'd directed me before. Three days ago, she explained, a fine gentleman of middle years in a dark green suit with a fawn waistcoat had sought the harlot out. Rather than make use of her, she sniffed, he'd immediately escorted her to the ferry. Then the two of them had gone across to Richmond County, and neither had been seen since.

Must be halfway across New Jersey by now, I thought, sighing as I thanked her.

In kerk the next day, I was uncharacteristically fervent in prayer, my last hope of justice for my hometown.

*   *   *

At eleven-thirty Monday morning, I stood in glaring sunlight outside the tavern, half again as large as *The Arms of Orange*, that served as the seat of Kings County, immobilized in a state akin to shock.

Robert Scoffield had been acquitted.

Even now he was standing a free man not fifty feet away, being pounded on the back by Wicklow and his solicitor—a prepossessing fellow in a dark green suit and a fawn waistcoat. Nearer to me, Floris Van Klost was snarling, "Well, rely on this, if that man ever sets foot in New Utrecht again, he'll face some rough music!"

"The same in Flatbush!" LeChaudel asserted angrily, his ire rather amusing the passing townsmen, for whom riot-minded courtroom mobs were dependable entertainment.

Other voices joined in as emphatically, however, including that of the Scotsman from Bushwick who'd served as jury foreman and attempted to pronounce the verdict "Not proven." The Justice had condescendingly insisted that his was an English court, and therefore only two verdicts—Guilty or Not guilty—were acceptable.

"Come along, Thomas," my cousin Charles Cooper said, pulling me away. "You've shopping to do, I collect? If we don't hurry, we'll have to cross with that fiend in the same boat!"

"But—"

"They've sounded the *bell,* lad!" The ferry's warning was audible for hundreds of yards. He dragged me for a few paces, with the sudden forcefulness of which he was occasionally capable, before I continued, however blindly, of my own volition. The ferryman was about to cast off as we arrived, panting, on the quay. We found seating behind the livestock corral—loaded with pigs today—apart from the other passengers.

"Charles, how could they?" I shouted over the din of panicked oinkers. "The man is guilty as sin! Surely—"

"Yes yes, cousin, and anyone with sense can *smell* it, as easily as one can smell these pink brutes!"

The reason we had room to ourselves was that we'd sat on the downwind side. "But then—"

"Thomas, I hate to tell you, but according to the rules of British justice, you have *not* proven your case. It would not have served even if it had been you doing the prosecuting, rather than Wicklow and that jackass the court appointed."

"But Charles, that's absurd. Everyone in New Utrecht was convinced, not just Van Klost and Pa, but ter Oonck and Van Voort and Loytinck and Voskuil. And LeChaudel—he's no great friend of mine!"

"It doesn't signify, lad. You convinced your neighbors because your neighbors know every person and every place in your story. When that buffoon simply *read* your notes, they—"

"They were *only* notes, Charles! Surely anyone with half a brain would've called forth people to testify. They didn't even call Stanley, much less me. The only man they called—"

"Was Voskuil, from whom they cleverly extracted exactly the same testimony that convicted Zwarte Jan three weeks ago. We should be thankful they didn't put Uncle Rykert on the stand—I fear he'd have been quite an embarrassment."

I groaned, and briefly felt queasy. I've never been seasick on a ferry. Could it be the midday sun? Disgust with my father? The court? Myself? The pigs?

"As Gerrison said—"

"Who?"

"The defense solicitor."

"Him!"

"Yes. As he said, the jury was being asked to compare the word of the respectable-looking Scoffield against those of 'a boy, a daft old woman, two renegade sailors, their smuggler captain, a vanished whore, and at least three slaves!'" I stared at him. "I wrote it down. Superb rhetoric! Extremely vicious."

I despaired of ever understanding Charles Cooper. "But the burghers at home saw no objection!" I protested. "And I can assure you, they've no special love for their slaves!"

"But they *know* the particular bondsmen, Thomas, and they can at least trust them when they sense there's no reason to lie. They *know* your sister and our grandmother. I'm amazed Geertruid got anything coherent out of the old bat, incidentally—that's impressive! As for the sailors and their captain, the further you get from the shore, the less sympathy you'll find for deserters and smugglers, so you're truly asking a great deal from the jurors here, not to mention the legal system."

It sounded logical enough, but I was too disturbed to be satisfied. "That solicitor! He spirited the Bates woman away to Staten Island. I went there after Wicklow failed to find her, and was told—"

"A terrible disappointment to us all, cousin, her not appearing! A third of the room cleared out directly the announcement was made!"

Exasperating man! "Gerrison tampered with the evidence, Charles! Surely there's something illegal in that?"

Cooper snorted. "Way too much trouble, too much expense to prove, Thomas. Scoffield got the best in the city. I do wonder he was able to afford it!" Something in his sarcastic tone assured me Cooper had a theory. "Darius Gerrison's a stalwart of the DeLancey faction, you know. And surely you've seen him before, in—"

"I don't believe so."

"In the offices of your former employer?"

"Colegrove?"

"One of Gerrison's regular clients, lad."

"I haven't told you, Charles, I discovered that Scoffield was an *agent* of Colegrove."

He stared at me intently. "You *know* this? How do you know this?"

"I followed up the contracts Scoffield wrote in New Utrecht. Went to the firm's warehouse. I was thrown to find Joachim, the indenturee who'd worked with me last winter, but I got short shrift from the managing clerk. So I visited the public records in City Hall and there it all was. Two DeLanceys were among the six partners, and Aaron Colegrove is the Treasurer."

"The name of it?"

"Oh. Trans-Hudson Produce Company."

Cooper's face slowly tightened into a fierce, rather frightening smile. "*Yes!* We've got them! You're a genius, Thomas!"

Oh for heaven's sake. "How's that, again?"

"I've had advice since last autumn that I could never trace, that an entity known as 'THPC' had made a very sweet arrangement with the army, completely outside the commissary's normal channels, to provide food and fodder at roughly a forty percent premium over last year's going rate."

"That's ... robbery!"

"Exactly. Exactly."

"Do you have any hope of proving this 'according to the rules of British justice,' Charles?"

He smiled mysteriously. "Probably as much as you had of convicting Scoffield. *But* ... there may be other means."

"Get your hand inside there, sir!" screamed the ferryman.

I jerked my arm off the gunwale and three seconds later the boat slammed against the pilings, setting off cacophonous protest from the corral. Unnerved by this near-call with major injury, I gazed stupidly at my cousin. He shrugged, made his silly hand-twirling gesture, and exclaimed, "Somehow we all do muddle through, Thomas!"

*　　　*　　　*

"Are you heading down to Martin's?"

Where was I going? "Yes.... No! Oh my lord, no. I'm going over to Broadway!"

"Ah. Me also. I'll walk with you."

We set off up the slope, pressing through throngs of businessmen, agents, artisans, laborers, and slaves ... and horses, dogs, pigs, chickens, and rats. A typical summer day in the city—except that it was less hot than might be expected. "What do you think will happen to Scoffield, Charles? Do you expect that he'll face any consequences at all for having caused all this trouble?"

"Well, he undoubtedly heard Van Klost bellowing as well as we did, Thomas. If he values his skin, Kings County is shot of him. I'll be quite surprised if he doesn't quit the province altogether, frankly."

"Why would he do that?"

Cooper again smiled enigmatically as we negotiated a busy intersection. "Shocking, the slanders that do appear in the public journals, Thomas! The Council really ought to shut them all down!"

There was no answering him when he was taken by these moods. We picked our way around two rigs that had gotten entangled as they passed each other on the sadly misnamed Maiden Lane; the respective drivers were cursing each other in the language unsuitable to any member of the fair sex. "I did find something to explain why Scoffield would want to be rid of Bates," I volunteered.

"Eh? And what's that?"

"His indenture was due to run out in September. Scoffield would've had to set Bates up with clothes and property."

"*Hmm.* Plausible. Certainly an incentive."

He was unsatisfied. I was about to inquire why ... when the bells of Trinity—and New Dutch—and the German Reformed Church—all began to clamor at once, despite having tolled twelve-fifteen not five minutes before. "What on earth?" Instantly curious, I moved to join the throng crowding toward New Dutch. "Let's go—"

Cooper grabbed my sleeve. "Nay, come along. I know what it is."

I allowed him to pull me aside under the shade of a tree as a tidal wave of men and women of all ranks and descriptions hastened excitedly down Nassau Street for the news. "*You* know what this purports?" I demanded impatiently.

"Of course, it's been obvious for weeks, but—"

Would I have to clobber him? "*What?*"

"... but I did learn the details last night." I stood, fuming, wondering how many seconds I could hold out before I'd resort to blows. "Amherst has taken Ticonderoga, of course!" I nearly swooned. Cooper steadied me by the elbow. "Oh. Sorry, Thomas!"

Ticonderoga! In British hands at last! Ticonderoga, the critical fort at the nub of Lake Champlain that had stopped the British moving north and would now stop the French moving south. Ticonderoga, where I with sixteen thousand others had fought in vain last summer. Where we'd been routed despite our superior numbers. Where hundreds of men from England, Scotland, and all the lands of America had perished through blind folly, including a dozen well-known to me. Including my best friend of the time. Very nearly including myself.... "When?"

"Last Wednesday. I'm sorry, I forgot that you—"

"Nay Charles, I'm all right. Were his losses ... very high?"

Cooper snorted, again risking a fist across his chops. "Not a one, Thomas. Zero!"

Was he heartless enough to jest in such matters? "I ... rejoice, Charles, but—"

"That's something they won't be boasting of at the church doors, Thomas. There were no losses because the French blew the fort to kingdom come three days in advance, and retreated in good order to the next fortification north."

"Crown Point?" I said dully.

"Aye, that's the one."

"Ah." So the object that had cost at least seven hundred lives last year had cost not a one this year. Surely I was glad of Amherst's victory and yet.... Dear heaven, how repugnant it all was! For a moment I stood watching in disconnection as a festive holiday atmosphere grew, and one inanely grinning face after another passed us by.

"Are you unwell, cousin? If not, I—"

"No no. Let's be on." But we could find no more to say and it was nearly impossible to hear one another anyway. And presently we were in front of the *Province Arms*. "This is me."

"Here? You have an engagement *here?*"

A flash of irritation touched me before I recalled how much else there was to worry about in the world. "Aye." With my hand pushing the door open, I made to wave farewell.

"But this is where I—"

"Dordrecht!" Glasby bellowed happily. "Ah Mr. Cooper! Welcome, welcome! You've heard the brave news, of course? We'll have more for you presently. Get yourselves a tipple. We've taken the whole house this afternoon. At last we can begin!" He was off into his flock of guests.

"Glasby?" I heard Cooper say. For once, he sounded more mystified than myself.

But I too was confused. I'd more or less imagined Glasby had a small coterie of businessmen he wished me to meet, but here were over three dozen people swirling about—and near half of them were ladies! I was just about to remark this to Cooper, who was still hovering behind me—though he'd managed to acquire a drink for himself but not me—when a man hollered, "Why there's our young friend Dordrecht!"

It took two seconds to recognize him. "Simon?" The carpenter? What in blazes was he doing here?

"Aye. And you remember the lovely Katherine, I'm sure?" Katherine? My word, one of the costume seamstresses was hanging on Simon's arm.

"Yes yes, of course," I averred, thinking I'd been away from the city far too long as Simon nimbly snatched a mug of ale off a waiter's tray and thrust it into my eager hands.

"Have you heard the brave—"

Ringing a bell for order, a beaming John Glasby was standing against one wall in the middle of the narrow rectangular room. "My friends, my dear friends," he began, "I greet you and hope you'll avail yourselves of all the *Province Arms* has by way of food and drink—" Enthusiastically grateful applause interrupted him for some seconds. "As some of you may have guessed, in the sad absence of parents, the extremely happy announcement I have to make must be made by none other than myself!"

There were huzzahs all around. I wondered that he could be truly so besotted with his new employment that—

"A lady, a beautiful, wonderful lady, has consented to make me the happiest of men! On the third Sunday of this coming September!"

There was wild cheering as I strained to see through him to the person on his right, undoubtedly the lucky bride-to-be.

"With great pride and pleasure, I therefore present to you the future Mrs. John Glasby, the lovely—"

"Oh my god!" Cooper moaned.

"Miss Adelie Chapman!"

The tumult that reigned inside the *Province Arms* exceeded even the glee outside it, save perhaps for two stupefied grandsons of Cornelis and Emke Dordrecht, who had trouble managing polite smiles. As everyone was now standing, two stools were available against a wall. Cooper took one. I slumped onto another. We both took morose pulls on our tankards. "You knew about this?" he accused.

"No, not at all," I hollered through the racket.

"What does she see in that clod of a businessman?"

"Glasby's an extremely intelligent and decent sort, Charles!" I protested dutifully—though feebly. "And what exactly is bothering *you?* I never thought—"

"She's the only woman I've ever been able to tolerate for more than ten minutes at a stretch!"

Undoubtedly a reciprocated sentiment, too! Good lord, the preposterous fop with the ridiculous wig was fancying himself *her* bridegroom! One had to laugh.

"And what's *your* interest here, boy?" he snarled. "Surely you weren't imagining...." His lip curled. "Oh my god, you were! But you're just a sprog, Tommy, a mewling infant!" My hands closed into fists. "Whatever made you think a sophisticated woman like that would ever—"

I stood up, slammed my tankard down, and mastered my temper just in time to stop myself from pummeling him. "And which one of us went to Ticonderoga last year, Charles?" I challenged blindly.

"And which one of us had the sense *not to*, Thomas?" he shot directly back.

The retort was so outrageous, so treasonous, so impossibly shocking ... I simply had to turn my back on him and bite my lip.

Miss Chapman was introducing various relations and notables of the party, each of whom was dutifully applauded. "And of course," she gaily continued, "we particularly want you all to know the young friend to whom we'll remain forever grateful for first introducing us ... Mr. Thomas Dordrecht!"

I had introduced them? "Take a bow, lad!" Glasby bellowed as I struggled to smile at the clapping throng.

"I'll *never* forgive you!" Cooper whispered bitterly into the back of my ear.

*   *   *

And yet an hour later, holding a plate heaped with food, I sat down next to the corpulent Mr. Leavering only to discover that Charles Cooper—with whom he was apparently already acquainted—was settled on his other side. Though tempted, I could hardly depart Mr. Leavering's company for more congenial tablemates.

"You have to hand it to Glasby for audacity, you know," Mr. Leavering was saying admiringly—though with his voice somewhat lowered. "In Philadelphia I doubt any man of his standing and ambition would dare attach himself to a woman who'd sung in public, a woman who'd ever been on *the stage!*"

Cooper and I both cleared our throats with great difficulty. "We New Yorkers are famous—or perhaps infamous—for our toleration, Mr. Leavering," Cooper said.

"Not that *anyone* could doubt Miss Chapman's honor!" I whispered with some asperity.

If Leavering noted the tension, he elected to ignore it. "Oh I beg your pardon! Are you two gentlemen acquainted?"

"We are," Cooper sighed, "first cousins, Mr. Leavering."

Mr. Leavering looked back and forth, and decided to change the subject. "Indeed. Now then, Mr. Dordrecht, you must complete your story of the great slave rebellion of Kings—"

"The great *non*-rebellion!" Cooper interjected.

"Of Kings County," Leavering finished.

Despite constant interruption and correction by my cousin, I brought Mr. Leavering, who appeared to find the subject deeply curious, up to the moment.

"The judge admitted none of the testimony you'd accumulated?" he said at length.

"He balled up the deposition Thomas had thought to take from the sailors and tossed it at the prosecutor!"

"Before it had even been read!"

"Over the objections of the man from Flatbush—"

"LeChaudel."

"Who asserted personal acquaintance with the captain, *uh*—"

"Jameson."

"Jameson!" Leavering exclaimed. "Of Newport? I know Zecharias Jameson, he's perfectly … honest, though I suppose not entirely respectable as the world has it."

"Your meaning, sir?" Cooper demanded.

"What is called smuggling, my lads, is no more or less than commerce across the borders of nations that is disapproved by persons of power!"

"But surely—"

"Let him *finish*, Thomas!"

"And though these persons of power will produce myriads of public rationales and righteous justifications for interdiction, if you scratch them hard enough, you'll find"—both of us leant in toward him—"that there are invariably brazen pecuniary motives at stake."

"Yes!" Cooper angrily and emphatically agreed.

I was shocked at them both. "Surely you exaggerate, good sir!"

Cooper silently and sarcastically parodied my statement, but Leavering merely said, "I fear not, Mr. Dordrecht."

"But many products are prohibited as war measures, sir!"

"Oh!" Leavering exclaimed in disgust. "That! Can't discuss the war today, Mr. Dordrecht. Today is a happy day!"

"Ah, because Ticonderoga is taken, Mr. Leavering?"

"Because John and Adelie are to be wed, my boy!" For once Cooper's enthusiasm for Leavering's point of view was decidedly muted. "By the way, I think it was quite decent of you to shelter those sailors."

"I … did not know what else to do, sir. My brother was most disapproving when he found out."

"He should not be. The means the crown employs to man its navy are quite outrageous, quite akin to enslavement, and one cannot blame men from fleeing such injustice at their first opportunity!"

"The chief objection to the case," Cooper said, returning to the subject, "was that so much of the evidence was based on the statements of slaves."

"Well, of course," Leavering said plainly. "Given the premises on which this province is founded, that would have been the eventual decision anyway."

"But *why*, Mr. Leavering?" I wailed. "Why should the testimony of slaves be categorically disallowed? We believed them in New Utrecht. Why—"

"Surely you don't wish to return to the Roman system, Mr. Dordrecht?"

I'd forgotten my reading of Montesquieu. The ancient Romans allowed slaves to testify in court—but only after they'd been tortured first. Absurd and barbaric. "No, no sir," I moaned.

"The reason you can't permit slaves to testify is simple, Mr. Dordrecht," he said. "Nothing to do with trust. If they were to testify, they'd have to swear an oath on the Bible. The reason we respect that in white men is that we know that Christians treat that as deadly serious. If you let a slave take such an oath, you're admitting he's a Christian. And at the peril of his soul, no Christian may enslave another, so…."

"You have a circle of reasoning?" my cousin said.

"Exactly, my boy, a circle that is also a self-imposed prison. Thanks to it, we would rather free a murderer to commit future mayhem than admit that our slaves may ever be relied upon to tell the truth."

Was it the heat and smoke of the party that were making me gasp? "But this circle, Mr. Leavering…. Is there no escape, for any of us?"

Leavering sighed and shook his head. "I see none, young sir, none at all."

"It *has* been the way of the world, since time immemorial," Cooper observed morosely.

"I *can* tell you my own resolution," Leavering said, brightening slightly, "and that is to have nought to do with it directly, personally. Neither to own slaves nor to deal in them, that is. A pathetic choice, perhaps, but all I can manage."

We absorbed this notion thoughtfully for a second, but were presently interrupted by a thoroughly intoxicated guest who was the twentieth to inquire whether we'd heard *the brave news*. Cooper somehow managed to accommodate him in a comfortable chair—facing into the corner. "It still amazes me," he said, returning rather pleased with himself, "that one crime in New Utrecht can so paralyze a town, a county, a whole province."

"It was worked so diabolically, you'd positively think it was intentional," I concurred, relieved at his lightened mood.

"Well, gentlemen," Leavering said thoughtfully, "have you not considered that it might have *been* intentional?"

My cousin and I both froze. "How so, Mr. Leavering?" Cooper asked.

"Lads, lads! Why did Colegrove send Scoffield to Kings County in the first place? To buy crops and property at the best rates so he could satisfy his private arrangement with the military. He neither knew nor cared what Scoffield's methods might be, and he surely didn't care that Scoffield brought a footpad and a harlot along with him."

"Colegrove should be hanged!" Cooper exclaimed.

"Oh," Leavering demurred, "that's a bit strong, Mr. Cooper. But to continue. Did Scoffield truly care when his man raped the slave girl? No. All he cared about was whether Bates' presence would hinder his pursuit of his goals, which were not, I understand, proceeding very successfully at the time, despite some early triumphs." I nodded. "So as Bates was placed in the stocks, Scoffield coolly calculated the benefit of murdering Bates against the risk to himself. He was confident your bondsman would be blamed for it. So not only would he be rid of a hindrance, he would spare himself the impending expense of Bates' redemption." Leavering halted for a swallow of his punch. *"And* he would throw the village of New Utrecht into a perfect turmoil, which would inevitably soften property values and make the farmers far more eager to secure a certain compensation for their crops."

As it sunk in … it began to make sense. "He deliberately tried to implicate Vrijdag, did he not?" Cooper offered suddenly. "And when poor old Jan claimed responsibility, he was disappointed. But unruffled. And then a week later, he tried to implicate Vrijdag *again!* All to keep the pot boiling!"

"And to shake the confidence of the community," Leavering agreed, "which he incontestably did, at very tragic cost."

"But why then attempt to ingratiate himself with Juffrouw Katelaar?"

"Obviously to lay claim to Loytinck's properties for himself," Cooper said impatiently.

"Aye, and perhaps betraying Colegrove in the process," Leavering added.

"But he did it after having so completely upset the value of those properties, you see! Why—"

"Ah, if I may offer a lesson of age, young sirs?" Leavering said. Cooper and I both merely blushed, and he went right on. "There really *is* no honor among thieves, gentlemen. Scoffield hoped to win over the Katelaar woman, and knew that the ups and downs of this year will pass, but their fundamental value should only rise. And as arrogance is apparently his byword, he truly thought he might get away with it. He had, to that point, gotten away with murder!"

"Still has!" Cooper growled.

"Do you think," I asked after a swallow, "that Mr. Colegrove intended all this? That he *meant* to visit mayhem on Kings County? That he—"

"Really should be hanged!"

"Nay nay, Mr. Cooper, Colegrove may have encouraged some sharp practice in New Utrecht, but he's no worse in principle than half our species, so I do think hanging's a tad much."

"Will you continue to deal with him, sir?" I asked after a pause, curious.

Leavering frowned, considering. "Possibly ... but on a ready-money basis!"

"Or until he's convicted of fraud!" Cooper added hopefully.

Our interlocutor, already waxing merry, swallowed yet another draft of the punch, then hunkered down confidentially. "Perhaps I shouldn't be telling you this," he said quietly, "but I do believe our friend Glasby may have noticed that accounts were not properly adding up in Mr. Colegrove's books, and—"

"You think he smelt a rat?" Cooper encouraged.

"I'll say no more! I've respected Glasby for some time, and long ago offered him a position. But his acceptance was unexpected and most abrupt."

"I *see!*" Cooper exulted—to my sudden alarm. Poor Leavering had no idea that *Sejanus* was sitting right next to him!

The businessman observed him nervously. "Ah!" he said, pushing his great bulk away from the table. "Well, lads, I fear Mrs. Leavering will be most annoyed if I do not make my way home directly!"

"Is there no way we can break out of *this* circle, Mr. Leavering?" I begged, ignoring this. "It seems to be ... another vicious cycle of chicanery and corruption."

"Easier, perhaps, lad," he said, rising. "At least in theory."

"How's that, sir?"

He downed the last of his punch. "Don't start wars, my boy!"

Forty minutes later, having finally made some belated effort at politeness to the rest of the party, I expressed all the gratitude and felicitation I could muster to my hosts. After the jubilant Glasby had hammered my back for half a minute, Miss Chapman shook my hand, as always, and guilelessly expressed the hope that *we* should often be seeing *you* in the future—charming and confounding me, as always, in the same sentence.

Presently I found myself in the fresh air outside the *Province Arms* ... with my cousin once more at my heels. The afternoon was still hot, the crowds were still rejoicing, and I still had all the shopping to do. But Cooper was looking inordinately smug. A trifle tipsily, I grabbed him by his shirtfront. "Charles! You do realize that if you spill any of the confidences just overheard, the consequences to Mr. Leavering, to me, and to Miss Chapman's intended could be quite severe!"

"Oh my oh my!" he exclaimed blearily. "Aren't we the big tough soldier now!" Irritated, I released the shirt, but stood my ground for a reply. "Oh do relax, Tom-*ass*"—he liked that, and I fear I might be subjected to it again— "I'd be just as likely to give *myself* away, now wouldn't I? Never fear, lad, the scent will be very deftly thrown far, far away!"

His confidence was unimpaired, no matter what the state of his speech. I had to laugh. "Do give my dutiful regards to your mother, Charles!"

"Of course, dear boy. And mine ... to your *father!*"

I effected the family shopping at Martin's in record time, and was once more aboard the Brooklyn ferry an hour later. It was loaded with dressed pig carcasses. Surely not the same porkers? No matter, I bought a hind-quarter. The morrow might well be declared a provincial feast day.

*   *   *

An hour or so later, quite tired and feeling overwhelmed by the wildly swinging events of my day, I was approaching the crossroads of our town when, passing the Loytinck house, I saw Dominie Van Voort stepping down from its porch. Automatically I halted to offer him a lift. "Hallo Thomas!" he cried, stepping briskly up onto the seat beside me. "Have you heard the—"

"Oh *of course* I've heard the brave news, Dominie!" I snapped.

"Not that!"

"I've heard the brave news a thousand times!" He looked quite shocked, which recalled me to my manners. "Oh I beg your pardon, sir, I do beg your pardon! I—"

His professional interest took precedence over whatever affront he felt. "Something's amiss, lad?"

"I apologize again, Dominie, but…. Of all today's events, I'm still left in some despair that Robert Scoffield has eluded justice."

"Ah."

"You had heard that … *un*-brave news?"

"Oh yes. Hours ago. Mr. Stanley informed me."

"I just can't reconcile myself to it. I mean, we all felt sure—we all *feel* sure of the man's guilt, don't we?"

"No question about it, I fear, Thomas, but…. Some things are beyond us, lad. Some things are truly in the hands of God."

"Well, pardon the blasphemy, Dominie, but I do wish God would organize things a little better!"

"Oh Thomas! You're most exasperating, but we'll set that down—this time!—to your tender years!"

I drove on in silence for another minute, unsure that my tender years had much to do with anything. But it'd be unfair to blame the dominie for failing to unravel my spiritual quandaries. "You're most accommodating this afternoon, sir!"

"Well, one might expect so on such a day!"

The weather was fine. "Sir?"

"The *other* brave news, Thomas?"

"Sir?"

"You truly haven't heard?"

"No!" I pulled the horse to a halt in front of his house opposite the kerk. Zwarte Anne was standing in front of it holding a basket of the dominie's laundry.

"The banns have just been published, lad!"

"The banns, sir?"

"Juffrouw Katelaar is to be married!"

My mouth dropped. "Juffrouw Katelaar! My, *uh*, my heavens! I mean, that's wonderful! But—but—to whom?"

"You don't know?"

"I…. I…."

Beaming, he punched me in the shoulder. "Why to *me*, of course, you silly twit!" I've never seen the man laugh so hard. He even looked over to the slave woman, pointed at me, and said, "Did you see his face! Oh my goodness!"

"What? When? How?"

"Oh! Well, it's been on my mind for the longest time—and I think on Juffrouw Katelaar's as well—but I only last week got up the nerve to speak up to Meneer Loytinck, notwithstanding our long acquaintance. Such a formidable fellow, my grandfather-in-law-to-be!"

"Indeed, Dominie?"

"But *he* wasn't hard to convince at all. Nay, he immediately expressed his consent—his delight, in fact! But, oh dear oh dear, the ladies of the congregation were not at all sure such a union would be appropriate. Marijke's age, and her attendance record, and her contributions, and her failure ever to serve on a women's auxiliary were all examined in exhaustive detail," he sighed. "It was your mother and Vrouw Nijenhuis, particularly, who required the most thorough and patient argumentation on the subject!"

"My mother?" *My mother!* As he babbled on about the planned nuptials, the vista of difficulties that would be resolved by this auspicious, unexpected union opened out before my eyes. The end of his embarrassing attentions to Lisa. A suitable marriage for Juffrouw Katelaar that would allow her to continue to manage her farms. The properties—including the slaves—of Teunis Loytinck to remain intact in New Utrecht. Even the prospect that Loytinck might now be willing to entertain a proposal for investment in the town's smithy!

And by some master stratagem of indirection, my mother had convinced the man it was all his idea! I shook my head, laughing with the relief of it. I offered my hand, which he vigorously shook before bounding out of the cart like a schoolboy. Zwarte Anne looked on impassively. I caught my breath with a sudden, painful thought.

"Something wrong, lad?"

"Oh no. No, Dominie. It's just…. I just thought how fortunate it might have been if this engagement had happened to be consummated some months back. Scoffield was really eager to acquire Loytinck's farms, you know, and … all of the grief…."

"Which grief is that?" he asked impatiently.

"The grief he caused—Bette, Jan, the barn, Nonna's boy, the riots—"

"Ah."

"—might have been spared."

"Aha, I see. Well it can't be helped, Thomas. And as I say, my friend, it's not given to us to understand the intent of providence."

"I suppose not, sir."

"Nor to question it." He waited for a few seconds in the hope of an acknowledgment from me. Giving up at last, he said, "We'll be visiting tomorrow. I hope to see you then!" He dashed up into the house, clearly expecting the slave to follow.

"Of course, sir. A very good evening to you!"

Zwarte Anne remained rooted to the spot, gazing vacantly up at me … almost as if searching straight through me to the skies beyond. For a few seconds, I felt an honest, electric, human connection with the old slave woman—if only that of genuine anger and despair. But her far-away stare might as easily be one of fierce rebuke—and I smarted from it and rebelled against it. Why am *I* being reproached, I protested mutely, I who have restored Zwarte Jan's good name? I who have driven away the evil man who caused his death? I who have defended Vrijdag and saved him from separation from his woman and children? Why....

She continued to stare at me silently.

I could not meet her eyes.

ABOUT THE AUTHOR

Photo by Margery Westin

Jonathan Carriel possesses a B.A. and M.A. in History from New York University. He lives in New York City, and has spent decades supporting computer networks in each of its boroughs. *Great Mischief* is his second novel, continuing the projected series of Thomas Dordrecht mystery and adventure stories that began with *Die Fasting*. Each novel will take place in the context of a specific historical year in the turbulent second half of the eighteenth century—the decades of the industrial, American, and French revolutions.

He invites his readers to visit ***JonathanCarriel.com,*** where they will find material to pique their curiosity about the era, in addition to material expanding upon these fictions.